STAR TURN

ff

NIGEL WILLIAMS

Star Turn

faber and faber
LONDON · BOSTON

First published in 1985
by Faber and Faber Limited
3 Queen Square London WC1N 3AU

Printed in Great Britain by
Redwood Burn Limited
Trowbridge, Wiltshire
All rights reserved

British Library Cataloguing in Publication Data

Williams, Nigel
Star Turn
I. Title
823'.914[F]   PR6073.I4327
ISBN   0–571–13296–0

To my mother.
And in memory of my father.

PART ONE

9.30 a.m., 13 February 1945

I am what I remember. Nothing else.

Always assuming, of course, that I can remember what it is I am. My memory is appalling. I forget birthdays, names, debts. . . . I'm very bad on debts. Especially debts I owe. I can be alarmingly precise about money that is owed to me. I have total recall of the compliments paid to me in 1929. There were not many of them.

But, on the whole, even as regards that most crucial of subjects (to me at any rate) my life, I am aware that my imagination supplements my memory to an unhealthy extent. Which is why, to some ungenerous-minded people, I might seem a little less than reliable when talking about the past. And yet I wish to do so. I come to you open-handed, nothing up my sleeve, with no pretence of the objectivity or dispassion claimed by some historians. Neither am I possessed of some system of ideas that claims to transcend such objectivity. I'm an ordinary sort of chap. Shifty, yes. Unreliable, yes. But with the honesty to own up to such faults.

Yesterday, for example, I became convinced, at about ten in the morning, that I had had my appendix out. I was sitting at my desk in the office and, as I reached for another piece of paper, I had a sudden vision of a small, red, swollen thing next to me in a glass jar. I saw the glass jar first. Then I saw the glass jar was on a table, that the table was topped with white plastic and that, above the table, was a nurse's face. She was wearing a blue uniform and a white apron, and she was tucking in the sheets around me.

"There we are!" she was saying.

I appeared to be wearing a pair of white bedsocks.

Well, I thought, at least I've had my appendix out. At least that's taken care of.

Then, towards lunchtime, as I tried to remember other things about the loss of my appendix, I found that there was nothing surrounding those two or three images. Nothing at all. At this point I began to worry. Might not this appendectomy be, so to speak, hysterical? The product of some deep-seated neurosis? And might not the relationship of the neurosis to the appendix have a very straightforward significance? Sweating, I reflected that I was probably equipped with a real corker of an appendix, fat, hairy, crusted with slime, or whatever it is that encrusts appendices, ticking away the days, hours and minutes to the moment of eruption. The more I concentrated on this possibility the more real it became to me. I jabbed at my left side. Was my appendix on my left side? Unable to remember even this simple medical fact I jabbed wildly at my right lower stomach. It hurt. Was this simply because I was jabbing at it? Was this pain real or imaginary?

I foresaw hysterical crises of the appendix, in which doctor after doctor would be convinced by my symptoms, open me up and grope through my gut with a rubber glove only to find a gaping hole. I saw prominent surgeons ripping off their masks in cold, professional fury as they whispered to their juniors: "I could have sworn he had an appendix."

I am, you see, confident of my ability to convince others. When my memory has a confident voice, she can convince anyone of anything. The day before yesterday, for example (you can see how sure of my dates I am), I was at a party. Yes, even towards what *must* be the end of a long, grey, painful war, we lucky civilians have parties. Sometimes, in the early days of the black-out, I used to imagine, behind those shrouded windows, thousands of illicit evenings. Like bootleggers in Prohibition, were the guilty non-combatants prolonging the illusions of the last decade, with only the dull thud of the bombs to act as conscience?

Now our parties seem to express the guilty hope (or fear) that there will be a future. Once it was that the planes were going to come over, followed by mile upon mile of drifting gas. After that – desolation. Tessa, I remember, as far back as '37, kept a full bottle of aspirin by the bed "for when the Germans come". Now we gather together to ask ourselves anxiously: "Well. When it's all over. *What*?"

Like young children coming to terms with death we have had to learn to accept that this war, too, like the earlier one, will have its peace. And perhaps that peace, in due time, its war.

At this party I found myself in a corner with half a bottle of unspeakable Spanish burgundy and a man I shall call Harris. Harris, it transpired, had written a book.

"I've read it," I said. "It's called *The Playground*."

Harris smiled politely.

"Well," he said, "actually it's called *The Basement*. But I'm glad you've read it."

"Listen," I said, in a bantering tone, "it's called *The Playground*. I'm sure of it."

A steely look came into Harris's eye.

"So am I," he said. "I'm sure it's called *The Basement*. And I wrote it."

I was not to be defeated.

"Surely," I said, in my jus' plain folks, East End voice, "surely. You wrote it. But – ", I grinned matily, "I read it."

His lips opened and closed like a shubunkin's. I think I felt that as I had paid him the compliment of reading his bloody awful book he might, at very least, give me some latitude in the question of the title. Either that, or I was so embarrassed at being caught out in a lapse of memory over something as important as the man's creative work that I immediately censored my own mistake. After all, this creature had probably spent the best years of his life slaving over *The Playground* or *The Basement* and to have some anonymous fool at a party get the title wrong might well have destroyed his self-confidence for the rest of his life. The very least I could do was to use my considerable skills as a propagandist to convince him that, although he could not remember the title of his own book, at least ordinary people out there cared about it. He wanted to communicate, did he not? To that extent he and I are in the same business.

Or are we? "Artists" traditionally have a contempt for my kind of work. They agonize over the difficulties of remembering, describing, interpreting.... I remember reading somewhere that Cézanne wrote or said, "It is very hard to make apples round." Here at the Ministry of Information we can make apples square if that is how you like them. We can make them bright purple and rectangular, eighty feet in length, if that will help The War Effort. With typical British hypocrisy we call ourselves "The Ministry of Information". Whereas we all know that what we are in fact supplying is that dangerous Continental delicacy – propaganda.

Perhaps, like all propagandists, I have a soft streak and this manuscript is merely a gesture towards the notional honesty of art. It is true that, as I go back over my life, I am exquisitely aware of the dangers of recollection. Somehow or other I have to describe millions of moments such as the one at the party, or rather to decide which ones to recollect and which ones to suppress. The faults inherent in my attempt to summon up the colour of a dress, the taste of a glass of beer, spread like a stain across an old canvas until, in my picture of the past, old friends are unrecognizable, old causes impossible to decipher.

When I started to think of writing this book it was to be Isaac's story. The faithful record of his life – by A Friend. I even consciously attempted to excise myself from the story, as writers of fiction are traditionally supposed to do. But that, I decided, was the worst kind of lie. A bloodless one. Since we are condemned to tell untruths by the act of description, at least let our untruths be daring, dangerous, unpredictable.

"When you write about it," my wife said, looking at me rather oddly, "you must write about *it* and forget I, I, I, I."

"What's *it*, though?" I said. "*It* might be I for all I know."

I'll tell you about my wife later.

"Good writers", she said, carrying a plate of soup out towards the scullery, "efface themselves."

I am almost sure that our kitchen is of the very latest design. And I am pretty positive that I followed the woman who bears my name out into its well-lit spaces, and leaned on the jamb of the door as she scraped vigorously away at a couple of dinner plates.

"Oh," I said, "people can just *disappear*, can they? Just like that."

She put down one of the dinner plates.

"I believe", she said, "in good prose style."

And began to scrub away at the sideboard, in a self-effacing fashion.

I know all about "good prose style". And about the writers who affect it. Writers who efface themselves in order to shine. Writers who are dying to see reviews of their books in every newspaper with words like UNOBTRUSIVELY BRILLIANT written over them in letters eight feet high. I'm not unobtrusive. I'm obscure, irrelevant, unknown, despised, but not unobtrusive. After all, as I often tell people at parties, I am working class. I have had a hard life. Considering what I have been through I have done amazingly well. No –

I may be only a boring little clerk at the Ministry of Disinformation ha ha ha but I have *seen* things.

The people at parties look at me as I say this, clearly doubting that I have done well. Doubting whether someone as anonymous-looking as me can possibly have seen things except as a result of alcohol, or defective pairs of glasses. Doubting, too, that I am working class. After all I no longer speak with a working-class accent or get dirt under my fingernails or do anything even vaguely horny-handed. And yet I remember my childhood well enough to state categorically that my father wore a flat hat and a muffler and was frequently heard to say things like "mate" and "Gorblimey". If he was alive today I expect he would look at himself in the mirror, catch the grey face, the hands clasped round the pint and the fag drooping from one corner of the defeated mouth and say, "Oh *no, no!*"

There I go again. Attributing my thoughts, my feelings, to my father's image. My uncertainty about what he felt, or would feel if he were alive today, when all working-class people are alleged to be heroes (perhaps because they are being killed in extremely large numbers) extends to what I felt about him, and then to what he and I said when we were alone together. From there my uncertainty proceeds to that flat, high above the Shadwell basin, the look of the wallpaper, the smell of my mother's cooking, until doubt infects all my memory.

I sometimes think I dreamed Isaac. Even Isaac, the most important person in my life.

A Russian Orthodox priest said to me the other day (these are the kind of people I mix with): "Just because a man dreams of a sweetheart does not mean that he will not find the sweetheart of his dreams."

I thought at the time that this was a profound and moving thing to say. I think I was responding to his robes, his beard and his eyes, bright as beads, deep as artesian wells. What the old faker was really saying was "If you want what you get you'll get what you want" – which is exactly the sort of rubbish you might expect from a representative of a Church that has kept millions of peasants enslaved for thousands of years.

I'm not anonymous-looking actually. I'm six feet two, with a mass of tangled black hair and a face like a white crow. People usually say

I need "feeding up". I nod politely when they say this, recalling the drab little meals my mother served me. Then the ghost of my mother rises up between me and the people who say this (they are usually women) and the backs of my eyes become stiff with unshed tears. I move away, smiling, towards the drinks table.

Was Isaac what I wanted? Did I get him?

I don't think so. I think he was a separate individual like my father. It is only my love for him that wants to make him part of myself, to mix him in with my dreams and memories. In writing about him, I reinvent him, finally getting the Isaac I wanted. I must have started this manuscript twenty times. Sometimes I think of it as a novel, sometimes as autobiography – whatever form I choose for it, it always deals with the same subject matter and, so far at any rate, it always defeats me.

To start with, I remember, I tried changing his name. I called him "Misha". I showed the manuscript – well twenty pages of it anyway – to Alan. Alan said, rather petulantly, "Misha. What kind of name is that – 'Misha'?"

"It's a Jewish name, Alan," I said, "and this chap was a Jew."

Alan looked at me curiously. Alan is Jewish, and for some reason the fact often surfaces in conversation between us.

"It's a wet, soppy name," said Alan. "Little Jewish boys in the East End aren't called Misha – they're called – "

"What are they called?"

"Isaac."

Just because you have dreamed a thing you assume it does not exist! What a bleak world you inhabit, my friend. Isaac was my friend's name. He rose up before me as Alan spoke, like one of those crystals that flower in water.

Alan is my boss so I accepted his suggestion. Sometimes, anyway, it may be tactically necessary for propaganda to tell the truth. There are occasions when nothing else will do. Fortunately they are usually concerned with unimportant details like names or dates. I remember saying to Winston Churchill once: "Effective communication is a question of what you leave out. The great writers of history – by which I mean historians rather than great writers who belong to history – have been so because of their capacity to ignore reality rather than their skill at interpreting it. Take Cézanne," I said, as Churchill edged away from me in the direction of the door. "He didn't *see* the Mont Saint-Victoire, he only saw part of it. But so powerful and narrow is the human vision that those parts of the damn mountain have become the whole. Go and see it. Go and see the damn mountain."

This conversation took place, by the way, in 1940. But Churchill did not comment on the difficulties of taking a holiday in Provence at that particular time, or indeed on my attempt to convert Cézanne into an historian for the purpose of illustrating my thesis. He chewed on his cigar – or the piece of wood he had made to look like a cigar – and said in that wheezing voice of his: "Beaverbrook even manages to ignore *me*. I think you had better go and see him."

Which is how I ended up in Alan's office.

But that's another story. Alan and I are another story.

Picasso once said to me, when I had the good luck to meet the well-known Spanish painter in Brighton in 1937, "I once could only see the colour red."

I goggled at him, wondering whether he had bought a flat opposite a GPO terminus.

"For a whole year."

But now I think I know what he meant.

And so, in telling Isaac's story I will try to see only us two. Which ignores the people we met – celebrated – or reduces them to the status of tourists or Martians. Even Tessa, when I think of Zak and me in this way, becomes a faint outline, a few remarks, an extension of the shadows that belonged to the two of us. I'm a skilled propagandist. I can make one German plane downed over the Channel sound like the end of the line for the Reich, but because of this artistic scruple of mine, because of this absurd and impractical desire to remember correctly, I am determined not to write propaganda for myself. I am going to rise above what I have become, transform myself into a truth teller. And now this country needs one – complacent, marginal little kingdom that it is.

The fires of the Blitz are long gone. Everything now is as grey as the newsreels that bellow out our victories remorselessly. And, while the voices reduce all the war – the landings in France, North Africa, the Atlantic convoys – to the same local, cosy Englishness, the island itself seems to shrink, to wither under the weight of its own complacency, and the long years of loyal silence, of shoulders to the wheel, give us the tools and let us finish the job. . . . AS THE

FORCES IN FRANCE SWEEP ON TO VICTORY A WAVE FROM ONE OF THE
MEN WHO IS HELPING TO SHOW THE GERMANS JUST WHAT WE CAN DO
WHEN THE CHIPS ARE DOWN.

All around the Peabody is a stew of broken bricks, of open spaces, boarded-up shops and abandoned playgrounds. The people who once seemed to wear the smiles of the propaganda posters are as grey and careworn as they could be. When, oh when will it end? I want some red meat and a bottle of decent wine. I want chocolates, champagne and American cigarettes. But, instead, my only leisure is to serve myself the past. For I am one of those for whom history stopped in 1940. One of those who went into our finest hour, too numb and confused by what had gone before to understand or be a part of it. Not yet fifty, I am old, as old as the century.

I think I'm going to hate this book.

*　*　*

It all started a long time ago. In a room in the East End of London on a hot summer's morning. I may deny prescience, dreams, all yearnings of a spiritual nature, but in my heart I know it. *That day felt special before it began. That was the day you met him.*

Remember?

Of course I do. Didn't I say it? I'm the memory man.

I heard my Dad get up, tiptoe through to the kitchen, and start the long search for his boots. He could never remember where he'd left them the night before. A chair creaked, the curtains rustled, I heard him mutter to himself, and then – "Aaah." Like the air going out of a tyre. He'd found them.

I heard the grunts and whispers as he laced them up, then the muffled giant steps as he headed for the door, a pantomime of quietness. He was a big man, my Dad, and determined not to wake us. He closed the door with the solicitude of someone bandaging a wound, but as soon as it clicked shut I heard my Mum turn over in bed next door. We were both awake. Always.

I stared at my window and the disappearing dark, trying to picture my old man threading his way through the streets that led from our flats to the docks. I tried to imagine the rest of them – in jackets, mufflers, caps, all on the march to the huge dock gates, like beings on a doomed planet, drawn by a supernatural voice to their idol and master. Grown-up work was like some savage god to me. It took my father every morning and gave him back to me when it had drained everything from him, even the kindness from those big, grey eyes.

"You there, Amos?"

"Yeh."

Where did she think I was? Did she imagine I'd climbed down the drainpipe in the middle of the night? Or perhaps she suspected me of changing shape during the hours of darkness. Perhaps she had some vision of me hanging upside down from the ceiling by my toes, transformed into a bat-like animal, and wished to give me the chance to change back into human form. I don't know what accounted for the nervous distance with which my mother treated me. Thinking about it now I suspect she was scared of everyone on principle and saw no reason to exempt me.

I lay like that, staring at the window, hearing the distant noises of the Thames, and the rumble of a wagon from Marchant Row. Then I heard her swing her feet out and on to the floorboards, and try out the first cough of the day.

"Amos – you all right?"

No – I died in the night, Mum.

"I'm all right."

"I'll make the tea."

Flip flop flip flop *creak* shuffle shuffle *creak* shuffle shuffle rattle – Aaah! She'd found the kettle.

It was light now – printed hard through the thin curtains. As usual she'd laid my clothes out in a line at the end of the bed – a sort of idiot's do-it-yourself dressing-up kit. I looked at the trousers, the shirt and the shoes. They looked as if they were lying in wait for someone. I put on one sock and a pair of underpants, went to the window and looked down. From our flats you could see right the way across the river. We were on the south side of the Peabody estate, six floors up, and, in summer, I'd spend hours at my windowsill, looking down at the houses cramped together below us, and the huge, silver arc of the river beyond them. This morning I was on a ship pulling away from harbour – the whole estate was rolling and swaying, as –

"A–mos!"

"Coming, Mum." *It's re–eady!*

"It's re–eady!"

"Coming, Mum."

"It" was breakfast. Bread and jam. I quite like jam, but in my mother's hands it acquired a relentless quality. "Well ... there's a nice bit of fish," she'd say to my Dad in the evenings, "or the cheese is all right or" (and here her voice would acquire a wheedling, seductive quality) "there's always ... *jam*...."

I dressed and went through to the kitchen. As usual, avoiding her eyes, I concentrated on the bread and jam and she concentrated on me concentrating on the bread and jam. You had to eat everything on the plate but you had some discretion as to how you ate it, and a piece of bread and jam offered a surprising amount of scope. I started each corner separately and ate my way into the middle by degrees. I gnawed at the crust savagely, keeping my eye on the mushy centre of the bread in case it tried anything.

"Woch you doin'?"

"Just eating." *I'm a rat, Mum. I'm a giant rat. Is that OK?*

"I dunno...."

When I'd finished being a rat I got down from the table and went back to being Amos Barking. This was quite boring so I added a squint. I squinted behind my Mum's back for several minutes, but she was chewing her piece of bread and didn't appear to notice. I added a sort of pitch-and-toss roll to my repertoire and walked around our kitchen, rolling and pitching and tossing and squinting. Finally she said: "Woss up with you?"

"I'm a pirate," I said.

"Oh," she said. And went back to chewing her bread. Eventually she said: "You'll be late."

We never had any clocks in our house. My Dad always said your body told you when to get up. His body certainly told him when to go to sleep – nine o'clock every night in his chair. My body never told me anything like that. It refused to supply me with the most elementary information – whether I was hungry or thirsty or tired or sick. The one tune my body beat out in those days was YOU ARE TOO TALL AMOS BARKING YOU ARE TOO TALL AND TOO PECULIAR.

I was late though. I could tell that as I clattered down the open stairway of the flats and into the street that led up towards the Whitechapel Road. There was something about the general lack of urgency of the passers-by that suggested I had entered the magic hours after ten o'clock when grown-ups sauntered through the sunshine, running time, *their* time, through their fingers like prospectors with new gold. I lowered my head and buzzed up the street like a wasp. Bzzz – past the open doorway of the baker's, smelling of heat and yeast. Bzzz – across Lorimer Street, cluttered with horses, cartwheels and the shouts of the men unloading at the pub on the corner, and bzzz bzzz bzzz into Pack's Passage, where the two-storey houses faced each other with almost shocking intimacy across a yard or two of rough dirt road. I suppose Pack's Passage was a slum – certainly my mother always spoke of the people there with a sort of horrified quietness, but to me it was always a romantic place, and the black interiors of the houses and the smeared faces of its children, always up, always curious, seemed to promise something. I zigzagged up past a woman leaning at her open front door. Her face flashed whitely past me; her arms folded together seriously, she had the air of someone who plans to do quite a lot of talking and leaning in the hours ahead. She passed me like some racecourse marker, moving at unwholesome speed out of my field of vision. I was front runner, now, in the Derby, Golden Boy or Extravagance or Fields of Clover come on Amos you can make it boy go on you're going to –

I felt my head cannon into something soft. There was a squawk, a sound as of a suitcase falling downstairs and, when I looked up, there was a small fat man, lying on the road in front of me.

I knew straight away that he was an Ikey Mo. But not a hard line Ikey Mo (you'd never have seen one of those in Pack's Passage). On the whole they kept to their streets and we kept to ours. Anyway he didn't have a beard or a broad-brimmed hat or look as if he was on his way to or from a curious combination of prison and church. He was wearing normal clothes – a dark, shabby suit, a white shirt and tie, and looked, inasmuch as he looked like any grown-up I knew, like the man who came to collect the rent every Friday. He rubbed the bald top of his head in a puzzled, thoughtful way, muttering to himself in a language I did not understand.

"Sorry," I said.

"I should worry," he said, "it's just my head that's all. Who needs a head these days? A head is a luxury. An extravagance. Don't you agree?"

I couldn't think how to answer this question. I wasn't even sure whether it required one or whether it was the sort of puzzle grown-ups liked to set in order to have the satisfaction of solving it for themselves. I shrugged my shoulders in what I hoped was a grown-up way and the fat man looked up at me, suspiciously.

"You could be any Jew," he said suddenly, indicating the ripples cast by my gesture with what looked like a certain pride. "Don't I know you?"

For some reason I felt rather pleased at the idea of being a Jew. It seemed rather a mysterious and interesting thing to be. I continued to shrug, this time adding what I hoped was a Jewish flavour to the shrug.

"Don't overdo it," said the fat man.

Pack's Passage ran into Wharf Street, a featureless thoroughfare that led from our part of Wapping up towards the Whitechapel Road. On Wharf Street, twenty or thirty yards away, unbounded by houses, the sun had been set free, and bounced back from the metalled surface of the road in blocks of solid gold. From the Passage it was like looking into a theatre and, as my eyes travelled from the fat man's censure towards the light, I saw the black, backlit shape of a boy, about my age, walking steadily in our direction. On his head he wore a skull cap, his clothes seemed to be a smarter, smaller version of his father's (I knew at once that this was the fat man's son) and round his neck was a gigantic satchel.

As he came into the shadow I saw his face. His complexion was dark, his hair black and curled and his nose, which looked as if it had been beaten out of copper, was full of whorls and crevices. It was also, for a boy of his age, of remarkable weight and size. But what really struck me about the boy was his eyes. They didn't look the way boys' eyes were supposed to look – small and squinty – they were big and brown and thoughtful. Girls' eyes he had. For a brief moment he cast them down in what I thought was a soppy way, and yet, when they came up again, they were cool and level, aimed not at his father but at me. They seemed to be judging me in some way.

"Isaac," said the fat man, "we are late."

"I don't want to go", said the boy, "to that stupid school."

He had a clear, precise voice, and his prim manner did not seem to go with clothes or parent. As if to confirm this impression, he pulled the skull cap off his head and ground it into a small ball. The fat man looked up at him.

"So?" he said. "There's something wrong with the school?"

The small boy called Isaac looked down at his father as coldly as he had looked at me.

"It's full of Jews, that school," he said.

"So?" said the fat man. "So?"

"They're so ugly," said the boy called Isaac

The fat man seemed to think this was extremely funny.

"What does the boy want?" he said. "What do you want? *Pretty* Jews? You want pretty Jews? He wants the moon."

He turned to me and tapped his head expressively.

"He wants the moon, this boy," he said. Then he rattled off something to the boy in a language I didn't understand. The boy did not take his eyes off the fat man's face as he spoke, that same calm, aristocratic gaze. When his father had finished, the boy said: "I do not speak that language, I'm afraid. Or at least I choose not to in this my adopted country."

"That's not a language," said his father. "That's Yiddish I'm talking to you. Who said anything about a language?"

"I did," hissed the boy with sudden fury, darting a look at me, "and I would be most grateful, father, if you contrived not to let me down in the presence of my chums."

He flashed me a brilliant smile.

"Fearfully sorry, Bagshot," he said, and stalked past us, his satchel banging against his legs as he did so.

As he went on down the street the boy gestured to himself, as if he was the hero in some play, while his father, rubbing his bald head even more furiously, continued to play comic relief. Finally he struggled up to his feet and, gazing up at the sky, said: "Wants to be a Christian!" Adding, *sotto voce*, "I blame his uncle." And then he shambled off down the street after the boy. Their act, which at first I had thought might be for my benefit, was now a private affair. I gazed after the two of them, open-mouthed, feeling I had missed something. As they disappeared into a group at the end of the passage, the fat man turned and said: "Me – I'm only trying to make a living." And was gone.

I was a Jew for the next four hours. When I finally got to school and was taken to Mr Lewens for eight strokes of the cane, I shrugged to myself in the way the little fat man had done. As the whippy bamboo cut into my trousers, I whispered to myself –

"Schlitzer". I thought that this was a Jewish-sounding word. And as I trailed back down the high, dark corridor I tried to picture myself in a skull cap such as the boy had worn. What would it be like to actually *be* one of those dark, serious-looking people I had glimpsed on the corner of the Whitechapel Road?

When the boy called Isaac came to our school about a week later, at first I did not recognize him. He was no longer wearing the skull cap, but he had the same sorrowful brown eyes and his nose was as high wrought as ever. But his manner transformed his appearance, eradicating all traces of the thoughtful or the hesitant. He marched into the classroom and looked up at the teacher with what I can only describe as a businesslike air.

It was another sunny day and the light from the two barred windows lay around Miss Thomas's desk. Isaac stepped into the light and put one foot on the raised wooden platform that separated her from the pupils. Isaac's satchel banged against his legs as, putting one hand on his hip, he said, in a sporty, confidential tone: "My name is Shadbolt, Miss Thomas. I shall be with the class this term."

"Oh," said Miss Thomas. "Oh."

"Did the Head inform you, Ma'am?" said Isaac.

Miss Thomas seemed about to burst into tears. "I think he did," she said eventually. "I think he did."

Isaac smiled at her encouragingly and extended one hairy hand in her direction. Miss Thomas received it with the tips of her fingers and shook it lightly, at which Zak turned and marched smartly back into the row of desks. When he reached a vacant one he turned to her and, with military precision, said: "Is here satisfactory, Ma'am?"

'Yes," gasped Miss Thomas, "yes. I suppose...."

But the new boy was already rummaging through his satchel, pulling out new chalks and inks, geometrical instruments and many other things that the pupils of St Saviour's Elementary School saw only infrequently, usually in the hands of other people. When he had arranged himself in his desk, he sat up and stared across at her with an expression that seemed to say "Teach me. Teach me." Miss Thomas did not attempt to teach anybody for a full half-minute and, when she did, could only manage a few garbled sentences from a book called *A Child's Example of History*. All the way through the lesson she did not take her eyes off the neat, composed child in the third desk from the back.

In the playground at first break, the O'Malley twins went over to the new boy.

"Wocher doinere yerIkeymocunt?" said one of them.

"I beg your pardon?" said Zak.

'InchyergonnerchryayidschoolyercheekyIkeycunt?" said the other O'Malley, who was always reckoned slightly tougher than his brother.

"Tom Shadbolt," said Zak, "at your service, gentlemen." And he bowed shortly to them. There was something about his clear, contemptuous treble that checked them. Eventually the first one said: "CarmoffovitIkeywe knownanIkey when weseenoneincher?"

"I have chums who are Hebrews," said Isaac, clearly and slowly, "and some are not bad sorts."

Repartee was not the O'Malleys' strong suit. Besides which, as the new boy said this, there was no trace of the girlish moue, the downcast shrug, or the apologetic, inward look I had noticed in his father. His eyes dared them to continue the inquisition and the O'Malleys, like rhinoceroses puzzled by some man-made vehicle, sniffed and retreated a step. At which point the bell was sounded and we trooped into the dark school for another session with Miss Thomas. Miss Thomas taught us everything except Scripture. For some reason they didn't trust her with Scripture.

You judged the passing of time in the classroom by the patch of light around Miss Thomas's desk. As the afternoon wore on, it grew longer, paler and, finally, was swamped by the shadows. Then, from further within the building another purposeful shake of the bell and an elaborate charade of calm from Teacher.

"Good afternoon then, class."

"GOOD AFTERNOON, MISS THOMAS."

I was always the last to leave. Not because I had things to say to the teacher, but because my mind was still dazed with wonder at the facts and lists she had produced during the course of the day. I was simply that kind of child.

"Hurry along now, dreamer. . . ." she'd say. And I would reply, listless, still dreaming: "Yes, Miss Thomas."

That afternoon the boy called Isaac was only just ahead of me. He took two or three minutes to replace chalks, inks and ruler in the satchel and, when he'd finished, looked up at me, still affecting that borrowed, aristocratic fierceness: "Some of the men here", he said, "are not the best sort."

I didn't reply to this. As I watched him his shoulders suddenly dropped and an immense weariness came upon him. He began to tug at his forelock, nervously. In a voice that sounded like his own, he said: "Am I going bald?"

"I don't think so," I said.

"Eight is young to go bald," said Isaac, "but. . . ." He shrugged, as if to say "these things can happen". Then he slung the satchel round his neck and padded out into the dark corridor, through the side gate, across the playground and out through the door in the wall that separated us from the Whitechapel Road. That door was, to me, a barrier as magical as the platform that separated us from Miss Thomas or the stern façade of Mr Lewens's office. The carts and wagons were hardly audible from the playground – once out into the world the noises of the market, the traders and passers-by and all the carnival of the summer afternoon lifted you away from the rules and terrors of St Saviour's and up towards the impossible privileges of the grown-up world.

The small, fat man was waiting for him at the door. He made a great performance of doing up all Isaac's buttons, although the afternoon was still seductive, almost tropical. Zak stood very still as his father did this, looking like some gentleman with his valet. His father winked at me. "How did he do?" he said. "How did young Shadbolt do?"

I did not answer.

The fat man put his finger to his lips. "I'm a convert already," he said. "For him. Anything."

Isaac stared off into the distance. When he spoke to his father it was as to an equal. "I do not see why," he said, "a Jew should not have the benefit of a Christian education."

"There's no such thing as education," said his father. "There's no such thing as a Jew either if it comes to that." He winked at me broadly as he said this, and then banged at his forehead with the heel of his palm. "A genius," he said. "The boy's a genius!"

And the two went off together down the Whitechapel Road. As they went Isaac continued to tug at his forelock. It was as if he suspected his own hair had been stolen in the night and replaced with a wig. I followed them, about thirty yards behind, as they moved off through the afternoon crowds. They turned off the Whitechapel Road well before Wharf Street, cutting through a narrow alley that was unknown to me. There were no people in the street here, just abandoned shops – and there was a dank, abandoned smell, as if the summer had never reached the place. In the middle of the cracked paving stones, weeds had surfaced. A cat watched us, suspiciously, from the roof of an outbuilding.

Left, left, right and right again. Finally we were in a cul-de-sac of about eight houses – two of these were empty, the windows broken. At the far end of the cul-de-sac was a sign jutting out of the wall, on which was written, in shakily painted lettering – RABINOWITZ AND TURNER: NEW AND SECONDHAND BOOKS.

The fat man turned and saw me looking up at the sign. "In fact," he said, "there aren't a lot of new ones. If there are any new ones they become secondhand quite quickly."

"How do they do that?" I asked.

"He reads them," said the boy flatly.

"Who's Turner?" I said.

"Who's Turner?" said the fat man with another of his eloquent shrugs. "Indeed, who's Turner?"

The two of them went towards the shop hand in hand, rather formally and carefully, as if they expected a large reptile to be lying in wait for them somewhere near the entrance. I followed them, somewhat hesitantly. Just as they went in, the boy called Zak turned to me and said: "Are you following us, Amos Barking?"

This seemed an unnecessary question. Indeed, his father looked at me over his son's head as if to apologize for the genius's awkward way of putting things.

"Of course I'm not," I said.

Isaac pursed his lips suspiciously. "That's all right then," he said.

The two of them went into the shop. There was the clang of a bell as the door shut behind them and then the little cul-de-sac was quiet again. I stole up to the edge of the windowfront and peered in. All I could see, piled as high as the roof, were books. Books books books books. Books with green covers, books with red covers, books with no covers at all, spineless books, gaudy books, posh books, annuals, magazines, encyclopaedias, novels, plays, sheet music, all heaped together carelessly like earth in a field.

I thought about the books as I trudged home towards the Peabody Estate in the late afternoon sun. I thought about how many of them there were and how many and how amazing must be the facts and stories hidden within them.

I was quite Jewish that evening at tea – which was cheese and a thick slice of bread. I don't think my mother noticed, but my Dad said, looking over his left shoulder, surprised, as usual, to find me in the room at all: "Woss up wiv you?"

"I'm Jewish," I said.

"Oh," said my Dad wisely, then went heavily to his chair and sat, hands folded over his stomach, staring at the empty wall. There was one picture in our flat – of the baby Jesus and his mother – but it was kept in the front room where there was little danger of anybody seeing it.

I was always in bed by eight in those days. If they let me play out in the yard, which they did sometimes in the summer, it usually ended in a fight. Not because I was aggressive – I wasn't – but because halfway through the game I would forget about the bat or the ball or the chase and stare off over towards the river, my attention distracted by the sound of a passing ship or a group of sparrows squabbling in the dust by the wall.

"WOSSERMARRERWIVYERBARKIN'?"

I'd bark back at them, sometimes even try and look threatening in order to cover my embarrassment (the thing I most dreaded was that others might discover the secret world in which I lived for most of the time) and then it was off up the long stone stairs to my clean, empty room and the noise of Mum's voice through the wall, soft, patient, everlasting.

I was especially early for school the next morning, but when I got into the playground, there, alone in the middle of the yard, was Isaac, satchel by his side, squatting like a tailor over a thick, black book. I went over to him and looked across his shoulder. The book was open at the first page and it read: JACK AND THE GOLDEN GUINEA. Beneath this, the words: "The following tale of boy life, from the time of leaving home for school until early manhood, is taken from the pages of the *Boy's Own Paper*. One special recommendation of the story is the life-like fidelity with which its various characters, their temptations, failures and triumphs, are portrayed. These boys, at least, are no mere pasteboard figures, but healthy, flesh and blood lads of precisely the kind that, for good or ill, one meets every day in school or college."

Isaac looked up at me but did not seem to see me.

"Tom Shadbolt", he said, "has wagered half a crown a side that he will run a mile in four forty – and if that reckless swaggerer Scutchens is not hard put upon to match his wager I will be most fearfully surprised."

"Oh," I said. It was all I could think of to say. Isaac cupped his chin in his hands and snaked down into his book once more. I envied his trance, which seemed to shut out the tall brick walls, the children streaming into the playground through the narrow door, their voices rattling like coins in the summer morning. I looked from his face to the cliff-like sides of the school rearing up above us and thought, "Why isn't my father a bookseller?"

We didn't speak much before Miss Mack came out to ring the bell – the signal for us to line up in front of the huge doors labelled INFANTS or UPPER SCHOOL. But I stood close to Isaac in the queue, aware that the distance between us was at least of some interest to him. Usually when I stood next to people they were not even aware that I had done so.

When we swept into Miss Thomas's class I edged in on the outside and, as we scrambled for our desks, I tried once more to engage the new boy's attention. But once in the classroom he addressed himself, as he had done on the first day, to the task of unloading his briefcase, waiting for Miss Thomas to glide in, hands halfway to her neck in a posture that now recalls to me outraged virginity, her profile shimmering above us like some statue symbolizing Truth, Beauty, Hope and many other things in short supply at St Saviour's Elementary School, Whitechapel.

It was curious. As I looked sideways at Isaac's profile he already seemed far less Jewish than he had the day before. Perhaps his name *wasn't* Rabinowitz after all.

"And now," said Miss Thomas, without looking in the new boy's direction, "now . . . Nature."

There was a warm sigh in the classroom. We knew all about Nature. Nature was when you looked at two or three furry twigs in a jar. Miss Thomas glided off towards the cupboard at the back, while Louisa May and Myrtle Dunlop (her favourites) ducked out of their desks like accomplices in a vaguely risqué church service. She was at the cupboard door when, from the main door, came a thin man with a scrubby beard. He looked, I thought, a little like the dogs that hung round the dustbins on our estate, and his eyes were as big as the wolf's in the fairy story. He did not, as most adult visitors to our class tended to do, address whispered remarks to Miss Thomas over our heads, but instead stopped just to the left of the blackboard and stared at us. Then he held out his arms. This made him look a bit like Jesus in the picture on the wall of Mr Lewens's office.

He wasn't carrying furry twigs. He was carrying a huge pile of bluebells. We'd seen pictures of bluebells.

When Miss Thomas saw him, she did not, as she did when Mr Peters came in to borrow chalk, gather us behind her or ask him his business in an outraged, maternal tone. Instead she made a noise like a drain emptying, and followed this by allowing the glass jar to drop to the floor, where it smashed, dramatically. The thin man did not speak but continued to stare at her. Eventually Miss Thomas said, in a shocked, sepulchral voice: "You have brought the bluebells, Lawrence."

"Yes," he said, "I have brought you bluebells." Then he threw back his head (I had often read of people doing this but I think this was the only occasion in my life when I actually saw the action being performed) and laughed. "Ha", he said, "ha ha ha."

The class shifted uneasily in their seats. At the back I could hear Louisa May and Myrtle Dunlop whispering as they swept up the remnants of the glass jar. I kept my eyes, however, on the man with the scrubby beard, who was now staring rather rudely at the front row of the class.

"You're studying Nature?" he said to a boy called Martin Poop.

"Yeth," said Martin Poop.

The man seemed to be about to say something but before he had a chance to speak, Miss Thomas had swept up to the blackboard and begun to write, in large shaky letters, MR LAWRENCE. As she wrote she said, in an even shakier voice: "This is Mr Lawrence, class."

"Hullo, Mr Lawrence!" we said.

I wondered whether he might be an Inspector. I had heard about Inspectors. They went round checking up on teachers. Sometimes, I had heard, they told the teachers off. Certainly Miss Thomas seemed in some way frightened of the little man. When she had finished writing she turned and held out her hands to him. Her voice was now low and thrilling. I hunched forward in my desk, anxious not to miss a moment of this.

"Lawrence – " began Miss Thomas.

But the thin man ignored her. Suddenly he hurled his armful of bluebells to the floor and pointed down at them dramatically. "Look", he said, "at the living incandescence of them."

I decided he was not an Inspector. Miss Thomas, who was behaving in a more peculiar fashion with each moment that the stranger was in the room, started to pace around in the area near the blackboard, wringing her hands and murmuring to herself. Meanwhile the thin man stooped to the flowers, picked up one and held it up for us to see. I looked round at the rest of the class. None of them, not even the O'Malleys, were giggling. They were staring ahead as if the ground had opened up in front of them.

The only person who was not struck still with shock was Isaac. He was leaning back in his desk clenching and unclenching his fists and glaring at the thin man as if he knew and feared him, for some incalculable, adult reason. When the thin man spoke it was to Isaac he addressed himself. "Oh, we all know about the bluebell," he said. "Not a bad little fellow, the bluebell, is he? He's just a flower after all. Won't hurt us, will he? Oh no. Poor, poor little bluebell."

I looked at the bluebells on the dusty wooden floor of the classroom. I felt quite sorry for them.

Isaac and the thin man now appeared to be having a private conversation, above the heads of the rest of us. Zak was making a curious little noise at the back of his throat. The man with the beard – it was a dull, gingery colour – did not take his eyes from the new boy's face. As he spoke he waved his arms in the air and made skipping motions on the classroom floor, as if he was dancing on an oven in his bare feet. He was looking straight at Isaac. The noise in the back of Isaac's throat stopped.

"But he isn't *English*, is he?" said the little man. "Oh no. Not in the quivering, little bluebell heart of him he isn't, is he? He's altogether not our sort of chap, with his quivering little bud-like flowerness is this bluebell of ours, is he? He's not quite our sort, don't you find? So let's tear the womanish little bluebell flowerheart of him, shall we?"

31

The man picked up an armful of flowers and began to rip them apart and hurl them around the room.

I looked away. Not that there was much else to look at. The pictures of the Kings and Queens of England. Those two barred windows. The big, frightening blackboard. And, of course, the faces of the other children, their smocks, their pinafores – all as expressionless as a row of newly polished shoes. It must have been quite hard for the people in charge of St Saviour's Elementary School to make the inside even more depressing than the outside – but somehow or other they had managed it.

I stole a glance at the new boy. He was staring at the little man as if his life depended on it.

"Shall we," the man was saying, "shall we say 'no' to our bluebell then? Shall we jump up and down on his immense and hateful meekness? Shall we damned well – "

"Lawrence!" called Miss Thomas sharply.

Adam Sales had giggled when the man said "damned". But he stopped giggling as Miss Thomas swept towards her visitor, her arms stretched once more in his direction. She didn't look as if she was going to hit anyone on the back of the knuckles with a ruler, but you could never tell with Miss Thomas. She was one of those unpredictable teachers. The O'Malley twins swore they had seen her with a fancy man in Whitechapel market.

The little man was screwing the cap of his boot into a bluebell. When he'd made absolutely sure that this particular bluebell wasn't going to leap up at his throat like a cornered rat, he ground it into the wooden boards with his heel.

"I thought", said Miss Thomas, seizing him by the elbow, "that we were to teach them Nature?"

The little man seized her by the arms and, shaking her, began to laugh wildly.

I looked around the class again. I don't think any of us had seen grown-ups behaving like this before. Not even at home. This, the row after row of rapt, spherical faces seemed to say, is better than Punch and Judy.

They appeared to have forgotten completely that we were there.

"Isn't this Nature then, Florrie?" the little man was saying. "Isn't this prison we are in Nature? Isn't the struggle of living things not to be broken apart Nature? Isn't the struggle of the Man with his Sex nature and the Woman with *her* Sex nature, oh Florrie, isn't that the Nature of all of us? To be torn apart on the This question and the That question as if we were no more than a suffering bluebell?"

At this point Miss Thomas burst into tears. "I understood", she said to the little man, "that you were to come to Cricklewood."

The little man was kicking around the bluebells as if they were autumn leaves on a pavement. From the end classroom I could hear Miss Farr banging the school piano. It sounded like a hymn. Everything sounded like a hymn at St Saviour's Elementary School.

We all stared at Miss Thomas as she broke away from her visitor. Florrie, I thought to myself. Well well well *Florrie*. In keeping with her strange new name, she whipped round and glared at the class as if she was seeing them for the first time since the stranger had walked into the room.

"Continue with your work, children," she hissed, and most of us bent our heads over our desks. The man with the beard – his clothes were as mangy as the hair that fringed his mouth – backed away from her. He looked suddenly furtive, like a fox surprised by a henhouse. There was, too, something beaten about him, a look I had seen on my father's face once when he'd been turned away from work at the dock gates. Miss Thomas rounded on her visitor. "Yes, all Nature is Power to you, Lawrence, is it not?" she went on. "The Sex Nature and the Man Nature and the Woman Nature. These all hide your search which is for the deep, cold destructive Power Nature, which you seek."

The man laughed. It was a curious laugh. He put one hand on his hip and, when he spoke again, I noticed something odd about the way he spoke. The "a"s and the "o"s seemed to have been stretched out of shape and the consonants kept colliding with each other. "A man cann't speak to one a' thy kind," he said, "wi'out tha repeats a man's message back t'im. A man wud be faer tozzled t'see thy wud in's mouth, woman."

That is roughly what he said anyway.

Miss Thomas appeared to understand this. Most of the class were, to borrow the stranger's phrase, "faer tozzled" by this time, but it was to us that Miss Thomas now appealed. She tended to do this at odd moments in the day, addressing large and unanswerable questions to us, along the lines of "Was Mary Queen of Scots a bad woman?" or "Is not the autumn more beautiful in its way than the springtime?" This time she raised her hands above her head and positively shouted at us: "Well, class. Does power currupt? Is it betraying the soul to act in the world and for the world? Does all mankind seek power? And if mankind does, should not we seek power in our way – to act for good?"

The class gazed at her impassively. I don't think any of us were in the habit of answering Miss Thomas's rhetorical questions. There was also the fear that, if one did say something, and the thin man disagreed with it, he might throw a bluebell or a desk at one's head. He was glowering at her and us, alternately, taking short, caged strides around the pile of flowers on the floor.

Suddenly Isaac got to his feet. In a clear voice he said: "Some of us are born to be in charge of other fellows and if we can make sure that fairness and good order prevail, in the house and on the field, there will be little to complain of as far as the School is concerned. None of us likes to hear the shirkers and the moaners, for I think we know there is a job of work to be done, Ma'am."

Miss Thomas clutched at her desk. She looked as if someone had just kicked her hard in the stomach. The rest of the class swivelled their heads in the direction of the new boy's desk, but Isaac, oblivious of all attention, simply bowed stiffly at the teacher and took up his seat again. The thin man was the only one to react to this interruption. His mouth started to quiver in a jagged line, he raised one finger and pointed it at Zak, like an Old Testament prophet selecting a member of the court for damnation. Then he began to jump up and down and howl, like a mongrel left alone in the house.

"I know your sort," he screamed, "oh I knew your sort as soon as I walked into this room. But a child and already the damn mark's on you clear as day. One can see you're *that* kind of fellow right enough, though God knows where you managed to learn such stuff. Power of power that's your game, sonny, isn't it? That's what interests *you* right enough. The awful little death power that gives you control of living things as if men were nothing more than a row of black beetles. Ugh! I don't want your little boy's Power. Florrie – you've got a little sham in your class. A little faker has come among you and wants to learn the ways of the wicked world so that he can sham away with his twisted little Sex power and order this and that and – "

I had the feeling that something of tremendous importance was

34

being said, although I could not for the life of me think what it might be. The new boy had folded his arms and was staring back at the stranger, quite calmly. Suddenly I was frightened of him, of his still-ness, the immaculate nature of his performance. It occurred to me that that longing look bestowed on him by his father might be more complicated than devotion. Was he too a little frightened of this curious child?

Sometimes when I think of that afternoon in the classroom, I think it happened much later, when Zak had been at the school for quite a while. Sometimes I worry that it might have been much later that the two of us first came across Lawrence, on one of those walks we took, south of the river, on our own, just before the war. But now the image in my mind is of Zak glaring at the man, his arms folded, and of Lawrence's mouth suddenly dropping open, his feet scuffling back among the bluebells and, finally, of the huge door of the classroom opening to reveal Mr Lewens, standing in the dark corridor outside.

"Lawrence," said Mr Lewens, "I had understood from Croydon that you had given an undertaking not to enter these premises."

Miss Thomas started to quiver. "As Mr Lawrence is a personal friend – " she began. But Mr Lewens motioned her to be silent. He was a big man with protuberant eyes. He stepped into the room, his big, brown shoes squeaking ominously. Mr Lewens always radiated disapproval but on this occasion his displeasure was such that I was frightened he might, as he sometimes did, grab one of us and beat us there and then, in front of the others. But he was not interested, for once, in any misdeed we might have committed. He went to Miss Thomas and very nearly snarled: "I will speak to you later, Miss Thomas. It is not only this affair. But I have had a com-plaint from the parents of Guido Fanfani."

Miss Thomas moaned to herself and put one delicate hand up to her mouth. The little man spoke again: "Ay," he said, "here's another one out for Power and the Power – "

But Mr Lewens cut him short. "Pray do not talk to me of Power, sir," he said. "I am entrusted with Power by the governors to run this school on orderly and Christian lines and to guard against persons who have brought disgrace to the teaching profession. Make no mistake, sir, we have heard of the disgraceful affair that went on with the rabbit. I – "

"Strut," said the thin man with the beard, "strut all you may. Strut out your days if that is what you choose. Is that your choice, sir? I fear it isn't mine. It won't sort with me at all, this Power of yours, for it is shameful to so pervert the minds of the innocent. Look here, sir." Here he gestured back at Isaac. "There's one in your image already. All tied up and ready for market. I won't have it, sir. I will not. And so I bid you good day."

With which he marched out of the room. Mr Lewens went across to Miss Thomas who was facing away from us, staring at the wall. He placed his head close to her neck and whispered: "I must ask you, Miss Thomas, to return to the staff room and collect your things. Until this affair is clarified it will, of course, be impossible for you to continue with your teaching duties."

Miss Thomas widened her nostrils. "My Reputation – " she began, and then stopped, as if she didn't really want to discuss her Reputation. Mr Lewens looked at her stonily and indicated the classroom door. Without a backward glance at 5C, Miss Thomas paced over to it. She said only one more thing before she left: "Lawrence is a genius."

Mr Lewens did not respond to this at all.

When she had gone he closed the door carefully behind her and picked his way, through the shattered bluebells, into the middle of the floor.

"Did that person say anything to you?" he said.

Isaac replied without looking at him. "Nothing of importance, sir," he said. "We could see at once that he was the worst type of scoundrel."

"Yes," said Mr Lewens slowly, examining Isaac's face for traces of a smile, "quite so, Shadbolt."

Then he went heavily over to Miss Thomas's desk and looked at the rest of us. "You will forget anything you have heard this morning," he said.

The class, their heads still lowered, murmured their assent, while Isaac, his hands flat on the desk, stared boldly back into the headmaster's eyes. Mr Lewens flicked over the register, slowly, like a man looking for some item of evidence. Then he said, in a menacing tone: "Very well. Multiplication."

It is a fact that Zak always wanted to be English. He *was* English, as I kept telling him, but that wasn't enough for him. He wanted to be English English. Roast Beef and Yorkshire Pudding and Rugby and Beer and God knows what else. When I started to read Lawrence, at the shop, at the beginning of the war, Zak asked me once what "sort of stuff" it might be and, when I told him, dismissed it with some curt phrase or other. "Gertcha" most likely, for by then he was affecting his street-boy manner, a style that sat on him much less easily than the exquisite manners of Tom Shadbolt.

People become their names, don't you think? People called Walpurgisnacht acquire a stoop, cadaverous cheeks and hands as cold as the grave, while people called things like Weg-Prossor or Porteous-Smythe tend to have a knack for hailing taxis or bullying waiters. And such things are not merely the result of heredity. They can be learnt. Whatever name it was that Zak had given himself – I'm pretty sure it was Shadbolt – he acted up to it with such passion that I soon found it impossible to think of him being called Rabinowitz. I remember saying to Alan once (his second name is Brown), "Is your real name something like Braunstein?" We had been talking, as so often, of being Jewish, of what it meant and of how someone like me could never understand it. He looked at me oddly as I said this and his reply was in the form of a question: "What do you mean my *real* name?"

"The name you were born with, I suppose."

I was born with the name Barking and have never had any good reason for changing it. No one had tried to kill me or drive me out of town or refused to allow me into the golf club because my name is Barking (although they sometimes become a little reserved when I tell them my first name is Amos. "Oh," they say, "like in the Bible." They express no interest whatsoever in my surname. It goes with my personality, as white, common and faceless as the East End street where I was born.

I never discovered whether Zak's father had changed his name to Shadbolt when they arrived in this country. For all I knew he had bought the shop along with the sign and their family name in Russia (if that was where they were from) might have been Lyuchevsky or Snorbowitz. The fact of the matter was that who precisely Zak was or where he was from was something he liked to alter to suit the needs of the moment. But the name I associate with the early days of our friendship, the days that were as unclouded as the weather back there in 19—— or whenever it was, was Shadbolt. He became even

more well and truly Shadbolted when I began to read the boys'
stories he loved so much. I played his games with an enthusiasm
that sometimes dismayed him, referring to his father as "your
pater" and occasionally asking him to "my place in the country".

Zak used fantasy for tactical purposes, to give him time to think,
to surprise those who might be hostile to him; for me it was, and to
some extent still is, a way of life. "Tophole", I said to him once, "to
have servants. Don't you agree?" And he smiled tolerantly, accept-
ing that I was an odd creature, lived in my own world, tended to . . .
well, to lie sometimes.

I didn't say to him, as I would now, that it is others' lives that
provide a framework for my own. That I am not alone in the deceit
racket. That every single person in this city lives and dies by it. That
it was simply that Isaac's lies had the knack of successfully posing as
the real. For a time anyway. I didn't say any of these things because
I adored him. Just to be allowed to walk back to the shop with him
during that first summer was an inestimable privilege. I have
always been at the mercy of my acquaintances, and soon I could not
wait for the next evening, when we would be standing talking in the
cul-de-sac.

"Take Africa," he would say. "Africa. . . ."

And I would see swamps, Negro porters, jungles, great, dry
plains across which herds of cattle moved against the setting sun. It
was as if my imagination had needed his certainty to flower, as if the
story I had been telling myself all these years suddenly turned out to
have a meaning and a purpose.

Night after night we stood outside the bookshop, talking until the
dusk turned violet and the small fat man banged wildly on the glass,
shouting: "Oi, genius!" With a wink and a nod to me. He seemed to
need me as some kind of accessory. Perhaps, as his son didn't want
to be a Jew, he had to decide to adopt me as a kind of honorary Jew,
and the kind of nods and gestures we exchanged through the
windows of RABINOWITZ AND TURNER: NEW AND SECONDHAND BOOKS
were probably as wild a parody of the world from which Zak had
come as my talk of "halves" and "fags" and "studies" was an
unconscious mockery of the standards of the land Isaac so much
wanted as his own.

For most of that summer nobody bothered us. To my mother, I
said: "I've got a friend."

"Oh," she said, "nice for you." And looked at me sideways. I don't think she was altogether convinced that it was good for me to have a friend. My Dad had never had any friends, had he?

"Woss 'is name?"

I thought about this for some moments, then said: "Shadbolt."

"Oh," said Mother, *funny* name."

That more or less closed the conversation. There never seemed to be any question, in those days, of asking him back. Not that I was keen for my family to meet him. I wanted to keep this exotic creature, with his weird, adult vocabulary, his air of mystery and his odd, impressive calm in the face of aggression, to myself.

At first I think people were frightened of Zak. If it hadn't been for the O'Malley twins perhaps my only memory of Zak would have been those long talks outside the shop or the occasional blessed half an hour when his father would ask me in and feed me sweet, sticky cakes that weren't like any I had ever eaten.

Although there was a rumour that one O'Malley was tougher than the other, it was almost impossible to tell one twin from the other. They were fat children who looked about forty-five years of age. About their only social grace was their persistent impersonation of each other – a completely pointless exercise, since, as well as looking exactly like each other, they had the same opinions, shared the same stock of knowledge, said the same things, wore the same clothes and were, to all intents and purposes, the same person.

Their specialities included a thing called the "Thumper", in which one of them sat on your chest and the other pulled your hair, and the "Ear Torture", which was worse than it sounds. O'Malley P. and O'Malley M. sat at the back of the class in a big wooden desk close to the wall and, in the weeks after Zak arrived, spent a great deal of time lobbing bits of paper, soaked in spit, towards the back of his head. Zak never once turned round or allowed this to affect his concentration in any way. I think this unnerved the O'Malleys, who thought of the world as constructed on feudal lines, with them as liege lords. In their universe an Ikey Mo was an Ikey Mo, and Zak's bland usurpation of his improbable name struck at the heart of their world's system, brought them constantly to the point where they felt it necessary to punish him and, at the last minute, checked them.

'Shadfuckinsteindonchermeanyercunt,'' muttered O'Malley P.

(or was it M.?) as we returned to our corner of the playground to compare notes about the grouse season or the relative merits of soccer and rugger. We didn't live exclusively in the imaginary worlds conjured up by books like *Black Evans* or *The Team's Honour*. We shared a taste for metaphysical speculation, more common among small boys than is usually supposed. Sometimes we would construct minutely detailed projections of our future lives. In these games, Zak was always a general, a leader, sometimes a monarch, and I granted myself the privilege of being wise. Somehow or other I was going to know everything. The actual business of sitting down to learn it seemed to me utterly tedious, but I loved to think of myself at a desk not unlike Miss Thomas's, bestowing kindness and instruction on a group of pupils, who always looked a little like me.

The O'Malleys never offered Zak violence. Not until the business of the graffiti. I think they felt that if they offered him violence he might refuse it.

I was responsible for the graffiti. On the walls of the lavatory, on some of the desks, on the far side of the playground, I had, at various times during the summer term, written THE O'MALLEY TWINS SMELL. This, as it happened, was perfectly true, but there was no doubt, as far as the twins were concerned, that it fell under the heading of classified information. They spent a great deal of time trying to find out the culprit. Their technique of detection being to beat the smaller members of the class, while shouting at them: "Yoodunnitdinchercuntehdincherehehdincher?"

Strangely enough they had not tried this on Isaac and, I think because I was associated with the new boy, I, too, had been spared the privilege of an interview of this nature. I was unable to stop doing it. Like a spy tapping out a message home, deep inside enemy territory, I continued to make my simple affirmation of the truth, THE O'MALLEY TWINS SMELL. So frightened was I by what I was doing that I did not even mention it to Isaac.

One afternoon in July I completed my masterpiece. Alone in the playground after school (I had allowed Zak to go ahead with his father), I wrote, on the wall of the school in paint stolen from some builders who were working two streets away, THE O'MALLEY TWINS SMELL REALLY AWFUL.

I wrote this message in the way gazelles are supposed to make love, with one eye constantly over my shoulder for teachers, pupils or the twins themselves. They seemed to me to have a divine ability to sniff out rebellion. Even in bed I never felt entirely safe from the O'Malley twins. As soon as I had finished I ran for the door in the wall and tumbled out into the dusty glare of the Whitechapel Road.

As I went out O'Malley P. (I knew it was O'Malley P. because Mr Lewens had stencilled the relevant initial on each of their foreheads) pushed past me in the doorway. O'Malley P. was no great intellect, and often had difficulty deciphering the most simple declarative sentences, but this one, I felt, would not take long for him to grasp. Nor would he take more than a minute or so to realize that I had been carrying a brush and a pot of paint, or that the paint, like the wall slogan, was bright green.

I ran.

I ran until my legs were matchsticks, manipulated by someone else, and my breath was raw, sulphurous and in very short supply. When I stopped and turned round, O'Malley P. was thundering down the Whitechapel Road after me. He was followed closely by O'Malley M. Where he had come from I never discovered. Maybe he materialized on the spot if ever his twin was distressed. Neither of the O'Malleys was a beauty; their faces always looked to me as if they had been put on with a plasterer's trowel, but on this occasion the unrelieved nastiness of their expression (they shared one between them) was enough to set my matchstick legs off again on the giddy passage towards Wharf Street and home.

Something made me turn off before Wharf Street, down the alley that led towards Isaac's place. I sobbed and heaved my way past the derelict houses and into the cul-de-sac. They were standing, the two of them, arguing some point. Caught like that Isaac looked most un-Shadboltian. He was tugging at his forelock again and, when he turned towards me, the eyes had the anxious look of someone in a prison photograph. As soon as I saw him I slowed to a walk. He frowned. Zak always like to have warning of visitors. I wondered, I don't know why, whether they had been speaking English.

I could feel my back prickle, as I slowed even more, trying to look casual. Isaac and his father seemed to offer some kind of sanctuary. I looked up at Mr Rabinowitz, who, in his turn, had lost all hint of Shadboltness. The prickles in my back got worse. Had they turned the corner yet?

"Good evening, Barking," said Zak, rather stiffly.

41

Isaac's act started off his father on the eye-rolling and forehead-bashing routine; my relief at seeing the two of them was mingled with the sorrow and resentment I always felt at being excluded from their world, at the fact that we needed these elaborate games and rituals in order to meet at all.

"Hullo, Shadbolt!" I said.

"Are you in a fix?" said Zak.

"Er – "

And then, abruptly, the O'Malley twins fell into the open end of the alley, their flesh shaking the ground. As soon as they saw Zak's father they stopped and slowed to a walk. The three of us went on towards the shop. *Please ask me in*. I prayed. *Please*. It was a rare treat to be asked inside. *Please*.

Isaac's father looked down at us when we came to the front door.

"You boys all right?"

"Of course, Father," said Zak.

I let him go in without another word.

Like gunfighters walking down the main street of a Western town the twins wobbled and leered their way towards the two of us. Isaac did not attempt to follow his father. Instead he looked up the street at the O'Malleys. I saw his shoulders stiffen. He braced his legs.

"Shadbolt – " I began, nodding towards the shop and the welcoming piles of books.

Zak lifted his arm. "Please don't trouble yourself, Barking," he said. "These fellows are quite incorrigible. I have a mind to pluck them out by the roots." I don't think that was what he said at all. I think by that time we were quite natural with each other. What he probably said was, "It'll be all right" or "Don't worry, Amos" but his attitude – which is what I recall most clearly about the afternoon – went with words like that. His chin was up, he stood very still and the twins, as so often in his presence, halted, looked suspicious and took on that look of animals foiled by some machine unfamiliar to them.

To be honest with you I can't precisely recall what accident it was that brought the little Jewish boy to my so-called Christian school. Maybe he was part of some quota, I don't know. I've heard of things like that. All I do know for certain is that his face, as the twins came up to us, had the simplicity and directness of those pictures in the books we read together; and I would like to think of him saying something along the lines of: "If your pride and ill manners do not go unpunished then the other fellows will certainly suffer. I counsel you to leave this lad alone unless you wish to be thrashed by someone who will have no scruples about such a course of activity." Judging from the expression on the twins' faces, he might as well have said something like that. Whatever it was he said to them, O'Malley P. and O'Malley M. forgot all about me as soon as he said it. One of them said: "Gicherarseahterevere." And the other said: "Want a fight?" They could speak quite well when they wanted to.

"Name your time and place," said Isaac.

"After school Tuesday," said O'Malley P., "up by the common. Which of us do you want to get done by?"

"I'll take on both of you," said Zak, very quietly.

At this moment his father's face appeared at the window and he tapped twice on the glass. The O'Malleys, with the kind of sneer usually employed by gaolers and murderers in the plays of Shakespeare, retreated back up the alley. I wiped my forehead.

"Come in, Amos," said Zak, "please."

"Thanks," I said, "oh thanks a lot."

I can still smell that bookshop now, the sour dust, the sweet decaying smell of paper, and the dust, itemized in the shafts of sunlight, across main streets lined by works of mathematics and philosophy, boulevards bounded by popular novels and narrow lanes, dark with towering buildings of books in languages I did not understand. A world. I think it was that afternoon, as we hurried in from the O'Malleys, that the book smell got into my blood. I sniffed at it like an animal as Mr Rabinowitz bowed and smiled among his stock like a waiter welcoming a favourite gourmet client.

"You a reader?" he said.

"Oh yes," I said, "I'm a reader."

It sounded a good thing to me.

Rabinowitz Senior, who still looked less like a bookseller than an unsuccessful travelling salesman, went to the wall of books at the far end of the room. Isaac looked at me, pouted slightly and raised one of his two bushy eyebrows. When his father came back he was carrying a slim, grey volume.

"You're how old?" he said. "Eight?"

"Nearly nine," I said.

"You should read this," he said, pushing the book at me.

I tried to behave as a reader might when confronted by a book. Presumably readers, when near such things, got hold of them roughly and shoved their noses into them like pigs at the trough, hardly able to wait. With a wild, reader-like stare I yanked open the book and read:

> After these preliminary remarks we come now closer to our proper subject, the philosophy of the beauty of art, and since we are undertaking to comprehend its Science, we must begin with its Concept. Only when we have established this Concept, can we lay down the dimensions, and therefore the plan of the whole of this science. If not undertaken in a purely exterior manner, as it is in a non-philosophical work, it must –

Must what? Must wear trousers? Must sing and shout? Must –

I could not understand this sentence. I could not understand the *words* in the sentence let alone the sentence. I closed the book with reverence and sneaked a look at the spine – "Heggle."

Rabinowitz Senior laughed uproariously. "Haygel," he said.

I wondered whether this was some kind of Jewish toast.

Oh now I know all about Hegel. I know just what's wrong with Hegel. I'm an expert on him – the way I'm an expert on the German Air Force and the Spirit of Britain and all sorts of things I've never seen or even come near seeing at first hand. Sometimes I think I knew as much about Hegel then as I do now. When he was a password into a strange boy's home I sometimes think that I understood him better.

"Aesthetics," said Rabinowitz Senior, "that's the thing." His eyes glinted sadly. "You're the type," he said, "you're just the type. This one. . . ." He jerked a thumb towards his son. "This one's a doer."

"Oh," I said politely.

Thinking back now I can see that Zak's father was more than a little crazy. An atheist, a philosopher . . . . I suppose the Jewish community near us had rules as inflexible and stupid as the community that failed to afford it a decent welcome. Maybe it was his father that had made Isaac the one Jew in a class of gentiles; and Zak's act was no more than the brave words of a child confronted by an impossible duty. His father wanted him to be a rebel, an outsider. . . .

I noticed that Zak was studying the floor as his father talked. Despite a growing feeling of disloyalty I nodded as he talked himself off into a world of his own choosing. "To describe the world," he said, "that's the thing. To record. You know?" He pointed at his son's head. "Genius," he said, "genius. The genius wants to be up and doing. Big genius. My son the genius. I tell him stay where you are. I tell him wait for *them* to make the move – " He spread his hands, white palms upwards. "Safer." He crossed to another shelf and began to pull books out of it, throwing the unwanted ones over his left shoulder. He seemed to be looking for some specific work, but clearly the chances of finding anything in this shop were minimal.

I am almost sure now – as I concentrate on that image of him pulling dusty volumes out from the shelf, that Papa Rabinowitz – or whatever they called him – had driven his son to our school, as a kind of revenge. Their discussions were so intense, their views of the world so different, even when Zak was eight. Isaac, unlike me, felt that his future was a subject over which he had some control, and yet that measure of self-determination was precisely the thing that generated his rage against what appeared to be his destiny.

"Action," his father was saying, "the boy wants action. The boy wants to make guess what? The boy wants to make history. Always has. Tiny baby plays with soldiers, yes? Bigger baby walks around telling other babies what to do. A tyrant in the making, I can tell you. Wants to make history. I tell you – there's no such thing as history. Just a mad succession of names and dates and places, all of them lies."

Books were flying past his shoulder like midges rising in a swarm on a summer evening.

"Spencer," he snarled. "Macaulay," he yawned elaborately. "Marx," he howled. "Step into history. Roll up roll up roll up. Pay your money and take your choice. Step into history. Who wants to step into history? There's nothing for you in history but lies and lies and lies and more lies. . . . Yes – " He stopped and turned to me. "But to record it, yes?" he said. "To tell the truth!"

"I try to tell the truth, sir," I said.

"Yes," said Mr Rabinowitz, "yes indeed." And he sighed.

Well I do *try*. It's impossible to tell the truth since no one can agree what the truth is. It's possible to state the obvious, that's another matter, but the truth is simply a convenient fiction that we use to measure our conduct. Perhaps this manuscript is a homage, not to

Zak, but to his father, and my realization that everything I have recalled, the dialogue, the weather, the smells, sounds and tastes of the East End all those years ago *is not as it was*, is a tribute, not to the real people who stimulate these words scribbled on Ministry of Information paper, but to the very tricksiness of art.

"At least", said Mr Rabinowitz, "we have the cheek to make the attempt. You and me, eh? Writers, eh?"

I caught sight of Isaac, who was watching his father with that impassive expertise children practise upon their parents.

"Daddy", said Zak, "is writing a book."

"A novel," said his father, "but who reads novels? They want something they can believe in these days. Like the Crimean War. Unbelievable that. Don't you think? If you put it in a book they wouldn't believe it, yes?" He stopped and gave me that shrewd look of his. "You want my boy to look after you?" he said suddenly. "I tell you this. It's him that needs the looking after."

From the door at the back came a gaunt, good-looking woman of about forty. She looked at me and then at Isaac and inclined her cheek into her outstretched palm with great deliberateness and sorrow. Suddenly I felt very tired. I said something about my parents worrying and went towards the door. I did not like the idea of having to look after anyone.

I left the room, as usual, without grace. All the way back home I thought about what Isaac's father had said. The phrase I kept coming back to was this one: "He's a doer." Well, I thought, he would need to be a doer if he was going up against the O'Malley twins. Otherwise he was liable to get extremely done.

* * *

When I met Miss Thomas at a party near Fleet Street, sometime around 1936, I asked her, when I had got over the blue hair, the high giggle and the obvious drunkenness, whether she remembered St Saviour's School.

"It wasn't called St Saviour's," she said. "That was just what we used to call it. St Saviour's was up the road. We were Hammond."

I should have known, from this point in the conversation, that I wasn't going to get much sense out of her. But, anxious as always for pictures of my past, I pressed on with the inquisition.

"You remember me and Shadbolt?" I said.

She looked at me oddly. "Shadbolt?"

"A little Jewish kid – " I began and, all of a sudden, her face shone with pleasurable recollection.

"Little Rabinowitz," she said. "I'm *so* glad we got him."

"My name", I said, "is Barking. Amos Barking. . . ."

She'd never heard of Amos Barking. But it must have been the same Miss Thomas, even though drink had obviously done terrible things to her memory, because she went on and on about Zak. "He was so *bright*," she said, "so *intense*, such a *character*. Has he done well? Is he something important? I always felt he would be something important."

I decided to be satirical at her expense. She wasn't really paying much attention to me anyway, but ogling an enormous journalist called Porter over in the far corner of the room.

"I wonder", I said, with heavy irony, "how a boy called *Rabinowitz* got into a church school. After all it's not often you get a Jewish pupil at a school called *St Saviour's*. . . ."

Miss Thomas shrieked with laughter. "Silly boy," she said. "We were Hammond. You couldn't keep the Jews out of Hammond." She lowered her voice and peered around the room, heavy with cigarette smoke, and added: "You can't keep them out of anywhere, can you? I think Herr Hitler has a point, you know. They're *everywhere*."

I gave her up after that and spent the rest of the evening getting drunk on metallic red wine. Somehow or other, at the end of the evening, Porter, Miss Thomas and I were the only ones left. She was hanging on to Porter's arm, her hair disarrayed about her face and, as the three of us went down to the cold November street, she slipped and fell forward. I caught her and whispered in her ear: "Tell me. Tell me, Miss Thomas. What about the school? What happened exactly to you at the school? Did they give you the sack? Were you a Modern Woman once, Miss Thomas, who read all the Modern books and corrupted the young? I want to remember. I look back and I can't remember. I can't even connect you, you see, with that creature who stood in front of us at St Saviour's. Tell me what happened."

She held her profile up. Suddenly I recognized my old teacher in a tilt of the chin. Vanity, at least, is a constant factor. She looked almost girlish for a moment, as if about to embark on a flood of reminiscence. Then I made the mistake of asking another question: "Was Mr Lewens a bit sweet on you, Miss Thomas? I can't remember, you see. Was he sweet on you or something?"

I seem now, as I sit alone in the space of another endless official day, a three-sheet newspaper on my desk, crammed with carefully selected, week-old news, below me a city continuing its six-year charade of normality, as foreign to myself then as I was to my childhood memories. I am chasing a shadow chasing a shadow, gripping a stranger by the arm, who turns to another stranger (who turns out to be me) and screams with pure hatred in her eyes: "I remember you now. Barking. Stork of a boy. Odd. We all thought you were odd. You were a liar then I remember. Nasty, deceitful little thing you were. Why you palled up with little Rabinowitz I shall never know. He was a nice child. He was going to be something special, I always knew it. Did he become something special?"

"He became dead," I said, "you stupid, sentimental, lying, drunken, old bitch."

She continued to scream after me as I walked off down the road, but nothing she said made any sense. I should never have talked to her. One shouldn't treat one's past as a comparative exercise. It is a holy secret and should be guarded as such. I only set down the incident now because I am so determined to be honest. It would be easy for me to do what historians and politicians do – take this account and that account, and balance them, produce a sort of bland confection that will offend no one and satisfy no one. But I am determined to proceed from *precise recollection*. And the fact of the matter is that my horror at that old crone's denunciation is as fresh and vivid and sharp as the image of the thin man with the beard.

And how, precisely, shall I remember and honour Zak, whose book this is? What quality can I summon up to make him live again for me? For you? I do recall (I think) that one of the things Miss Thomas remembered about him was what she called "his toughness". She didn't specify whether she was referring to a moral or physical quality when she used this word. In her sodden brain the two were probably identical. When she used the word, I recall, that hot July evening at the end of the summer term materialized around me and I was with Isaac, making our way up towards the common.

The common was where we had all the fights, or rather where

they had all the fights. It wasn't a common at all but a patch of waste ground between Leman Street and the river. If there was a fight on, then kids would come from all round – the Beit Yeladim (I think that was the name), Rockley Road Elementary and, if it was a big fight, the apprentices from the Institute in Malory Road.

This, I could see when we were within fifty yards of it, was going to be a big fight. A trickle of non-paying spectators was already visible on the path by the brewery.

"Shadbolt," I said, "you don't have to do this."

"Barking," he said, "you don't have to do this either."

"Do what?" I said.

He grinned. I thought that he looked rather magnificent.

"Hold my coat," he said.

Then, spoiling the effect, he tugged violently at his forelock as we went on down towards the common. I sneaked a glance at him as he strode on beside me in the clinging dusk. He did have broad shoulders and his hands, thick, supple, slightly yellow-skinned, were like a man's hands. I wondered whether there was a special Jewish technique of fighting...kosher wrestling...Orthodox boxing. I had a sudden happy image of two fat boys flying through the air, Zak looking up at them, rubbing his hands.

Halfway down Leman Street you turned off into a short road, lined with warehouses. Nothing ever seemed to come in or out of these tall, forbidding, box-like structures, and between them the path was cobbled and littered with abandoned boxes, great rusted iron chains, the detritus of some industrial orgy that had had to be hastily abandoned. Between the warehouses ran a battered line of railings, and from here you could see across to the lights of the river. When we reached the gap that led on to the waste ground I could smell the river, smelling as rotten and aged as it does now, the great, brown artery of London. Down here there were clouds of midges that swarmed at your hands and face.

We stopped by the gap and looked across the dark mud and grass. There were forty or fifty spectators strewn across it. Some of them had climbed up on to one of the derelict wooden sheds on the river side of the common. I looked at their faces, white studs in the gloom, and listened to their shouts and whistles. I felt as if we were about to step on to a stage. Somewhere out of sight a barge hooted mournfully, like an animal calling its mate, and the beginnings of a breeze stirred Zak's hair. I noticed that he wasn't looking out into the field. He was gazing up the street towards the gas lamp, about twenty yards further along. I followed the direction of his gaze.

Under the lamp was a tall, pale man, with straw-coloured hair. He was wearing a dark overcoat and, as we watched, cracked his knuckles nervously. What I noticed, even at this distance, was his eyes. Pale, pale blue, almost the colour of light reflected in water, they conveyed, even more than the jerky dissonance of his gestures, an impression of only just subdued terror. Next to him was a short man in a flat hat. This man did not look at all nervous. Perhaps it was his level stare that was causing his companion's lack of sang-froid – for, as the pale man talked on, in an unfamiliar, sibilant language, flat hat was examining him with the reserve of a judge in an ice-skating competition.

"Oh *no*," muttered Isaac, "Slobedev."

"Who's Slobedev?" I said.

But Zak did not wait to answer. He ducked his head and prepared to slide under the railings and towards the waiting crowd. Before he could make his escape, however, the man with the straw hair was advancing on us, his face garnished with a smile that only increased his resemblance to a domestic animal on the threshold of a slaughterhouse. He grabbed Zak by the hand. "Vell, vell, vell," he said, "basically, vell basically, here is Slobedev, I think."

"Hullo Slobedev," said Zak. He turned to me. "Mr Slobedev comes to the shop a great deal," he said. "He is a friend of Daddy's."

"Vell basically," said Slobedev, his eyes hunting the street for potential assassins, "basically, vell basically, Slobedev and Daddy vell argue, yes?"

"Yes," said Isaac.

All this time the man in the flat hat was looking between Zak and the pale man, steadily and coolly.

"Slobedev", said Slobedev, "is Bolshevik. Yes?"

"Yes," said Isaac, wearily.

"Slobedev", went on Slobedev, laughing in a somewhat unconvincing manner, "is fully paid-up member of Bolshevik clique I think basically, yes? Is vell basically, vell basically, is international revolutionary activist I think basically, yes?"

Flat hat put his hand on Slobedev's arm and rattled some more of the strange language off at him. As flat hat spoke, Slobedev laughed even more wildly. He sounded like a man trying to enjoy the fact that someone had put treacle in his shoes, or made him an apple-pie bed. "Ilyitch says", he said, "that more suitable for me basically vell more suitable for me would be the name Arsehole, yes."

Flat hat talked some more and Slobedev translated. He seemed happy to do this.

"He says", he went on, "that I am not member of Bolshevik Party. He says – this is difficult word to translate but vell basically he says I am a sort of twerp, yes? I am a foolish man who is following him all way from Simbirsk vich is vell basically in Russia, yes? He says that I could not be member of Bolshevik Party if I tried how is your father, Isaac?"

"He's very well," said Isaac.

"You are out for vell basically a walk yes?"

Isaac looked across at the common. I could see the O'Malleys now. They were surrounded by a group of their friends and had started to chant:

> What oh what is Ikey's game
> When he says Shadbolt is his name?

Zak's mouth curved slightly in contempt. "I'm going to give a couple of louts a beating," he said, quietly.

Then he looked away from the two men and towards the group on the grass. He looked like an athlete poised for the start of the race. Flat hat started to talk again, this time addressing his remarks directly to Zak. There was a cruel urgency about his speech which made me long to understand it, but Isaac showed no sign of interest in the stranger's address. He continued to look out into the darkening field. Beyond the O'Malleys were a group of Jewish kids, none of whom I recognized – they were shouting their own slogans.

"What's he saying?" I asked the pale man.

"Ilyitch says," said Slobedev, "vell it is difficult to translate this but vell basically he is saying that worker fights worker while the landlord reaps the profit posing as guardian of petty bourgeois morality. This vell this is basically vot Ilyitch says at the moment basically."

Zak turned back to the two men. "Talk talk talk," he said. "That's all you and the people who come to Daddy's shop do. Talk. You

51

never do anything, do you? Of course you don't." He switched his gaze from Slobedev to flat hat. "They were going to hit him," he said, indicating me. "They think nothing of that. That's wrong, isn't it? Are you another of those people who won't fight back? My Daddy won't fight back. When people were rude to him in the shop, when they called him all sorts of beastly, stupid names, when they said 'Jew' at him as if it was a sort of insult, he wouldn't fight back. I'm not that sort of person. I'm not going to be that sort of person, do you understand? What's right is right. And now I would be glad if you would leave me to get on with it."

Slobedev looked from Zak to flat hat during this speech. He seemed wary of the job of translating it, but to my surprise flat hat appeared to have understood perfectly well what was being said. His button black eyes glowed with the malicious glee of the debater and he raised a stubby forefinger in Zak's direction. I got a good look at the forefinger. It seemed to have been constructed specially for the purpose of making debating points. Squat, muscular, pregnant with unshed energy, it was the kind of forefinger that expected, and probably got, obedience from every quarter.

"*Right*," he said through gritted teeth, in English more harshly accented but no less fluent than Slobedev's. "*Right*. Morality? What, pray is this, your morality? Is it something messieurs the bourgeoisie have devised to swindle you? Please ask yourself, my friend, for whom you are conducting this 'fight' of yours."

The forefinger travelled away from Zak as flat hat spoke and, as I watched it, the dark blue evening, the lights on the river and the shouts of the spectators seemed to disappear, or rather to be transformed into bolder, brighter colours, like the pictures in a story book. I had the feeling I could remember when Mr Rabinowitz had pulled out that mysterious-looking book – the conviction that, out there, safely in the hands of adulthood, was some magic key that would unlock the mysteries of the world.

The forefinger, however, exerted no such charm over Isaac.

"For me and him," said Zak, "and right is right. However much you talk. If you can't see that you're stupid."

Isaac's opposition to flat hat is somewhat ironical in view of his later career. But one has usually abandoned the over-simple view of the world held at the age of eight by the time one has reached the age of twenty, even if, later on, the views of eight-year-olds may acquire as much charm and coherence as those of any other age group.

I followed my friend as he pushed his way through the gap in the railings and made his way forward over the thick, uncared-for grass. I heard flat hat's voice echoing behind us as we walked, mocking our progress.

"By all means fight each other," he was saying, "and when you have done their work for them here, messieurs the international capitalists will arrange a larger show for you, in the shape of a squabble over markets, a war no less, gentlemen, in which you will find yourselves, in all probability, dying, for this selfsame petty-bourgeois 'right' of yours, eh?"

Isaac gritted his teeth. He was the very acme of Shadboltness as he said: "I wish my father wouldn't have these types around the shop. They fill one's head with such a rotten sort of talk, one can't see one's way forward for their awful preaching."

I couldn't laugh, as I was supposed to, and not only because the world of the man in the flat hat had had the disturbing effect of a spell or curse in a foreign language, or that I could now see the group of boys by the wooden buildings more clearly. It was that Zak had gone beyond Shadbolt. His square shoulders and lifted eyes suggested characters with impossibly hyphenated names – Farquhar-Torresen-Smythe or Nugent-le-Perrivale (Snr) who, in Yap's House at St Osaph's in *Playing the Game* by Kent Carr, had thrown five slackers and bullies down the steep stairs leading to his study. I trotted in behind him as we came into the circle round the O'Malleys and the crowd grew greedily silent.

"Stillfancyadoinoveryercuntthendoyer?" said one of the O'Malleys.

It was now too dark to read the coding on their respective foreheads.

"Take my coat, Barking," said Isaac, handing me his shabby black jacket. He stepped out in front of the two of them. Hissing, like some huge snake, the crowd wound in round the three of them, as Zak placed two leathery brown fists up in front of his face. My God, I thought, he's been practising. Flexing his knees, the new boy placed them in an on-guard position, and the O'Malleys backed away, puzzled by this attitude, unsure, momentarily, of what to do next.

There was now no sound from the spectators. Still looking like something out of a sporting print, Isaac pawed his way forward and jabbed at one of the twins. The two of them backed once more.

The rules of conduct of any fight were fairly simple as far as the O'Malleys were concerned. Their opponent was supposed to languish for a period of time, looking apprehensive, after which one or both of them would throw him to the ground and sit on him for two or three minutes. Zak was not playing to these rules and this disconcerted them.

"Wocherfinkyerplayinachyerschoopidcunt?" said one of them.

"*This*," said Isaac, and darting forward, rapped one of them on the chest with his fist. Before either of them had a chance to react, Zak had skipped back, his fists clenched out in front of him like some heraldic emblem. Other parts of his body were doing things I had, up to that moment, only read about in the works of Kent Carr and Loukes Wainwright. His chin was jutting and his eyes were quite definitely flashing.

"Go on, Shadbolt," I shouted, "you can paste them. Go on, Shadbolt, you really can."

I got some odd looks from the crowd around me for this remark, but I thought I detected a suspicion of panic on one of the twin's faces. Zak started to skip forward and then to dart away nimbly with shouts of "Ha!" or "Ha there!"

All of this, I thought, was pretty good. If I had a doubt it was that it didn't seem to be leading anywhere. What needed to happen now was for Shadbolt to swoop forward and deliver a sharp blow to each twin's chin. He did seem to have the advantage, for the O'Malleys, bemused by his manœuvres, were not, at the moment anyway, prepared to attack. But after several skips and sorties and more than a few shouts of "Ha!" and "Ha there!", the twins began, very slowly, to lumber towards him. I ground my nails into my palms and waited for Zak's first blow. He was watching the two of them with almost amused concentration. Closer. Closer. Closer. At the last moment he struck – a leap forward at the front twin and a violent blow up at the chin. His fist connected and I heard the O'Malley grunt with pain but, before he had a chance to retreat, the second twin grabbed his wrist and had dragged him into range. As he was pulled forward, Zak lost balance and, as he fell forward on to the grass, both O'Malleys fell on him, like a couple of millstones. I heard a cracking noise and a muffled shout from Isaac.

"ZA-AK!"

I would like to say that I ran into the circle and pulled the two of them off but that is not what happened. I stood there miserably as the two O'Malleys worked their huge bodies on top of him and kicked, punched and swore at him.

"OwyerlikethatthenIkeyehowjerlikeitcunt?"

I can remember his screams as if the fight had happened yesterday. I can still hear the dull, vegetable thud as fists after fists drove into his stomach, and see his legs thresh wildly as the O'Malleys held down his shoulders and slapped at his head, which bucked insanely, like a target in a shooting gallery. I can remember the crowd, too, although this happened nearly forty years ago, pressing in on the group of bodies, swallowing the conflict with the slow sigh that so often accompanies a foregone conclusion.

"WossermarrerwivyerIkeycunteh?" they shouted at my friend, as he twisted under their blows.

"LEAVE HIM ALONE!"

They paid no attention to my cries. They stopped in their own good time. They didn't even bother to look at me as they climbed off him. Hitting me would be something of an anticlimax. As the two of them went back up to the far end of the field, followed by a crowd that now seemed to be composed largely of their friends, I went alone to Isaac, who was lying face downwards in the grass. I draped his coat over his shoulders. The grass was rank and unwelcome and there were now no lights on the river. It didn't feel as if we were in the city at all. I put my hand on his arm, tentatively.

"Isaac – " I said.

"Where were you?" said Zak.

"I was here," I said.

"Oh," he said, "I didn't see you."

"I was here," I said, "all the time."

He lay with his face down for some time. Then he began to sob. I looked over at the disappearing crowd. The two men to whom we had spoken earlier were still over by the gas lamp. Flat hat was shouting something but I could not, at this distance, hear what it was. Zak was clawing at the earth as if it might afford him some

55

comfort. "They'll get theirs," he said, "if there's any fairness they'll get theirs."

"Yes," I said.

Then he started to cry again, thorough, choking sobs. I patted his shoulder hopelessly. I didn't know what to do when people were crying. Funnily enough my awkward gesture seemed to help him.

"Get *off*," he said in a voice that was more like his own. After that he got to his feet and struggled into his jacket. He was bleeding from the mouth, quite heavily.

"I'm sorry," I said, "it's all my fault."

"No, it isn't," said Zak. "It's nobody's fault. Nobody's fault." He seemed to shrink as he said this and a great adult sadness bowed his shoulders. His right hand, as if under a power of its own, sidled up towards his scalp and began to tug at his forelock. His eyes went away from mine and his frank glance was exchanged for a wry perusal of the ground. It could have been his father talking when he said: "What can you do? What's possible?"

He almost shuffled across the field and, when we reached the gap in the railings, greeted Slobedev's motherly cries of concern with the patience of a horse being bridled. "I'm all right," he said, in a flat voice. He seemed too tired to go any further. Slobedev's companion said something to him which provoked a brief, but violent, discussion, at the end of which Isaac said, very quietly: "Can we go past you, please?"

Flat hat seemed angry about something. As we pushed past them and went on over towards the brewery I saw that forefinger of his climbing to attention. It seemed to hang over our path like a sign as behind us he spoke again in the unfamiliar language.

"Look vell basically", Slobedev was saying, "this upsets Ilyitch to see vell basically vorker against vorker he is wondering how we ever unite and combine vell yes basically he says your England is two nations and – "

The two voices, one as hard as a corncrake's, the other weak, full of apology, faded behind us. Isaac wiped away a smear of blood from the corner of his mouth and we went on in silence towards the great, silent warehouses.

"What's a Bolshevik?" I said.

"A sort of Russian," said Isaac.

"Oh," I said.

We walked on into the dark.

"Not a very good sort I don't think," he added. Then he turned to me and patted me on the shoulder. I think that evening was the last time we played the Shadbolt game, but there was some of the *élan* of that legendary character in Zak's voice as he tried to jolt me out of my grief and confusion.

"What's the matter?"

"He was frightening, that man," I said, "with the hat. He was really scary."

"Don't worry, Barking," said Isaac. "The Bolsheviks won't come to anything. My Dad said so."

* * *

Alan has just come into the office and told me that last night we lost eight aircraft.

"How many targets did we hit?" I said.

"Haven't a clue," he said.

Well this was a state of affairs that we could not possibly allow to continue. We are, after all, the Ministry of Information. We're supposed to know how many of our targets we hit. So we sat down and made something up.

Official figures must, after all, be credible. This is Alan's view anyway. Not for us the "thousands of enemy slain" clichés of the Nazis. We, says Alan, should be masters of the tasteful, well-judged, English lie – the British version. Like a lot of immigrants – like Isaac – Alan takes great pride in being what he calls a "Britisher". When I want to annoy him, which I do quite often, I tell him, his attitude to being British is very German. No one but a German, I tell him, would be so *thorough* about it.

"Fifty?" I said.

"They'll never believe that," said Alan. "Say ten. Or eight."

"And how many did we lose then?"

"Five," said Alan. "Five sounds about right."

I'm very against this pretence of objectivity. I told him we would do as well to give war news in the manner of a child's bedtime story – "Last night some bad Germans came over but we chased them away." He smiled tolerantly at the office cynic and told me to get on with it.

There's something odd about him today. He's got news for me. He's found out something about me – about who I am and where I come from. I've been vetted. I didn't like the way he looked at me at all.

Still – I am supposed to be the wordsmith. I got out the typewriter and wrote the first sentence of the press release: "Last night our Bomber Command planes returned from large-scale raids on fifty German cities." I hadn't checked which cities so it seemed safer to leave their identity obscure. The more I looked at this sentence, however, the more blatantly fictional it appeared. I started to imagine groups of amateur plane-spotters in towns all over England pooling their resources and agreeing that the Ministry's figures, even allowing for the doctoring of information traditionally practised in wartime, were an insult to anyone with any intelligence whatsoever. "We acknowledge", I could hear some MP roar, "that discretion must be used in making public figures supplied by the Air Ministry, but it seems to us that someone at the M.I. is attempting to guy the very – "

I began to sweat. I took the piece of paper out of the typewriter and took out my book again. Here at least, I persuade myself, I can tell the truth, even when it seems most unbelievable.

I've lied too much in my life. I lie to the people here and I am afraid they know it. I've erased my origins so carefully that no one would possibly guess where I come from. I sometimes believe that I never did lie awake in that clean flat in the Peabody Buildings. I sometimes believe, as I tell them here at the Ministry, that I did go to a minor public school and, as I look at my reflection in the mirror in the hall, a tall, pallid creature, with a face too full of right-angles, I sometimes think my name actually *is* Henry Swansea.

I chose the name Swansea after I started in journalism. I thought that a Welsh seaside town was what I needed to bring me up in the world.

"Swansea?" Isaac used to snort. "You can't call yourself Swansea. Swansea's a place, not a person."

"It's a person now," I said.

And so it is.

Mind you, I still jerk with surprise when Alan puts his head round the door and says, in that abstracted way of his: "Er ... Henry. ..."

Uh? I think, peering round for someone of that name. And then I stop.

I'm Henry. It's my name.

There are incidental pleasures to be gained from working under a false name. For instance, when I showed the manuscript of this book to Alan, he said: "I can see you don't want to use your real name. But *Amos Barking*? No no. It doesn't convince. It sounds like a Wesleyan preacher."

No, I thought, it doesn't convince. It didn't convince me. Even when it was my name. That was why I changed it. Something in my expression must have unnerved him for he went on to say: "Is it. . . ?"

"What?"

"I mean is it . . . well . . . autobiographical?"

"Of course it is," I said. "It's all perfectly true."

He laughed then, reassured to be back with the office cynic, the office joker. Never believe anything old Henry says. You can rely on him to make a tall story up about the least thing. Alan thinks I'm writing an autobiographical novel whereas in fact I am writing a novelized autobiography.

I didn't – because it lies outside the scope of my office persona – show him the bit about my feelings for Isaac. Alan and I never discuss our feelings for each other – perhaps because he has a European delicacy about what he takes to be my English reserve. I want to say to him sometimes, "I haven't got any English reserve. Inside I want to shout and scream and sing." But then it occurs to me that such a display might embarrass him.

I did let him see the bit about me waking up in the morning and, as he thinks I was brought up in Devon, he said: "You've really got into the skin of the character."

Hardly surprising, I felt like saying.

Sometimes I find myself wishing that I hadn't met the people I have met. It would in many ways make it easier to write about my early life if I hadn't blundered into so many extraordinary encounters, crossed paths with history so many, many times.

Alan, for example, would be incredulous, or irritated, about the scope of my acquaintanceship. Alan has Serious Views about the subject of history and those who are said to make it. In his world, history is too important to take account of people like me. He thinks he knows what history is, that is, he has the insolence to assume he knows what might or might not have happened to me and, by the same token, to know when I am telling the truth about it. Like all people with Serious Views, Alan is very easily taken in by the most unlikely and ridiculous stories and, conversely, pours ridicule on the sort of tale I find most credible. I imagine his ridicule to be more than usually passionate and violent in respect of something that had actually happened to me.

"Listen," he says sometimes, when we go for a drink over the road. "Listen. Hitler is taking the Jews of Europe by bus and by train and he is having them slaughtered. By the million he is having them slaughtered. Men women children the *lot*. You understand."

Alan's face goes dark with passion as he says this, reminding me once more of Isaac. I ask him for evidence. He tells me about a man he met who met a man who met a man. The usual "reliable sources". Some agency in Switzerland. I think of all the reliable sources I have known. I think of Zak in the early twenties, his face blanched with the passion that now animates Alan, and I say, primly: "I'm sorry, Alan. I just don't believe it's *that* bad. Throughout history dictators have eaten children and burned babies. Especially when the dictators are on the other side. Don't tell me about atrocity stories. I was a journalist."

"The trouble with you, Henry," says Alan, "is that you can't tell the difference between fact and fiction. That's the trouble with all of this hopeless country. They've been lied to so long they think everything is a lie. This happens to be true. He is slaughtering them."

I'm not in favour of the war. Alan knows this. I think it's corrupted language, destroyed the respect for truth, all the things that I have betrayed that are yet the things I still believe to be most important. I see my job here as a chore. Alan sees his as a vocation. I've lived through one war already. That was enough.

I hate the official forms. I hate the shortages. I hate the lying and the secrecy. The secrecy is so all-pervasive and self- and official censorship so widespread that often one does not know whether one is lying or telling the truth or – more often – attempting something halfway between the two, a version for the good of the nation. Our "figures" about raids for example do not appear in any newspaper in any but the most generalized form. Our information – or, at the moment, our guesswork – is refined by someone else higher up the line and eventually, like sewage, emerges into the great bland sea of Wartime Information.

"What do you feel?" he asks me. "What do you care about?"

I don't tell him the truth. That I have long ago given up feeling things. I know it is important to conceal what you have in your heart, even if what you have is blank despair, nothingness. And so I tell him another small lie. What is another lie among so many?

He wants something out of me today. What is it?

I still can't bear to get out the release about last night's raids. I'm sitting here with the papers I have scrawled on in front of me, going back twenty years or more. Headlines, privately observed faces, landscapes whiz past the eye of memory until images become concertinaed into each other, like cars in a road accident. Sometimes Isaac is wearing Alan's blue ministry suit, my mother appears to be shouting a speech into a microphone, and I wear several faces... my father's first... then someone I knew in the first war (Rea?), and finally the expressions of famous men... Stalin, Mussolini, Haig....

The surface of my friendship with Isaac was untroubled by anything until the beginning of the First War. One of the many things I hold against that unusually pointless quarrel is that it was the source of our first disagreement. But in the beginning there were none of the usual jealousies of childhood between us. I never wanted his friends nor he mine because neither of us had any friends. Nobody wanted us. After the fight with the O'Malleys, we were, I suspect, something to be laughed at but also, to some degree, something to be feared. We were like members of some strange sect, whose absurd vulnerability might yet be the cause of a revenge exerted by their underrated deity.

Our deity was each other. That's how I saw it anyway.

Some things stand out. Isaac round at my flat, sitting very straight in his chair, my mother hovering over him with the teapot, devastated by the thought that at last her son had managed to bring home not merely a friend, but a friend who looked like a real gentleman ("'e doesn't look anything like your normal run of Jew.") Me round at Zak's father's shop, sitting in the late autumn sun by the window, reading as if my life depended on it, while in the room at the back Isaac and his mother whispered sorrowfully together. The day Mr Rabinowitz took the two of us in a tram up to Vicky Park, the day

61

my father tried, unsuccessfully, to get us to go fishing with him. . . . It is all blurred together.

When I look back and try to fix an exact date for this or that occasion, I cannot do it. Sometimes I think I hear someone say "Agadir" – but whether I am recalling word and incident from some forgotten history book or whether I do have an authentic record buried somewhere within me of what was happening outside the narrow limits of immediate experience, I could not say. Sometimes I get a clear picture of my dad in his open, grey, flannel shirt, thumping the table and talking about the Taff Vale case, but I know such things are wishes rather than memories. It is useful for a socialist – even a disillusioned one – to have had radical parentage – but my dad was never a very strong union man.

How old was I when war broke out? Fourteen?

I couldn't say. My parents were unusually imprecise about dates (I have inherited *something* from them) and could frequently be heard, when discussing my age, delivering themselves of such comments as: "'e's nine. 'e must be nine. 'e was born after Ronald Taylor got his down at number five gate which was three years before. . . ." Etc., etc. I think I was probably twelve when, one spring afternoon, Isaac's Dad said to me: "You got a job to go to?"

And I said: "No."

And he said: "Could do with a hand here."

It was a fine April day and they had opened the door at the back of the shop, which gave out on to a small yard. Here, amid stones and moss, upturned pails and old cases of rotting books, was a clump of daffodils. Next to the daffodils I could see Isaac, who also had no job to go to, bent double over a large iron bar. On the ground in front of him was an open copy of a booklet I knew to be entitled *A Simple Path to Manliness and Physical Strength* by someone called Professor Stephen Forbes Harrison. It had been sent to him from Wolverhampton earlier in the week.

"The genius won't be much use," said his father. He said this, though, with a kind of pride, as if the business of ordering, classifying and trying to sell books was well beneath the dignity of someone like Zak. Someone who was – in Miss Thomas's phrase – clearly going to "do things".

"I'd love to, Mr Rabinowitz," I said.

"Good," said the old man, switching his eyes back to me, "that's very good."

One of my chief responsibilities was to try and stop Rabinowitz Senior from buying every book that was brought into the place. He would turn the pages of *Fifty Ways of Tackling the Servant Problem* or *Lesser Known Techniques of Early Viking Calligraphy*, mutter to himself, "Ye–es . . . ye–es." He was one of those men who was always just about to "get around" to reading the 1876 Baedeker Guide to Florence, a treatise on the mechanics of light by Snor-refuss, as well as a children's book that had done quite well four years ago. He had, Zak told me, to be physically restrained from reading by his wife.

The two of us entered the shop that summer, two weeks after leaving school. I was to work "out front" and Zak was to do something mysterious called "learning the business". What that meant was that I spent most of my days with Isaac's father while he seemed to spend most of his days on the streets, that I grew even paler while Zak grew even browner.

The subject that held most fascination for Mr Rabinowitz, in spite of his constant abuse of its practitioners, was history. Or, rather, History – for history was always History to Mr Rabinowitz and sometimes even HISTORY. He enjoyed even its most ludicrous manifestation, *A Child's Catechism of History*, including such gems as

Q: What caused the downfall of the Roman Empire?
A: The laxity and greed of the Emperors.
Q: How was this eventually checked?
A: By the invasion of the barbaric hordes.

He also loved books with titles like *A Typical Day in the Life of a Norman Peasant*, especially if they had pictures of the said peasants in them. For more complex, seriously regarded works he had a more troubled regard. Sometimes these authors (of whom I had never heard) would rouse him to such a pitch of fury that he would hurl the volumes across the room and, when he wasn't looking, I would thumb through them, eager to discover the secrets of a work that could excite such passion.

"Such a *scheisskopf*," he would yell at a half-open copy of Macaulay's *History of England*, "such a *scheisskopf* you are. You can't see it, can you, *dumbkopf*? You can't see the wood for the trees in front of your face. Progress?" (Here his voice rose to a scream.) "Progress? The only progress is in your head Mr Oh so Clever Macaulay and nowhere else. History is the tale of stupid and cruel practical jokes, don't you think? It is a steamroller and our only job is to get out of the way, don't you think, you stupid little *scheisskopf*?"

Once he hurled a copy of Hegel across the shop. Usually he was quite well behaved with Hegel but as soon as I saw this one was called *The Philosophy of History* I understood, and got on with some vigorous dusting (it was very unwise to disturb Zak's father during one of these rages).

"The Idea becomes clothed in Reality? Does it? Yes? Nice for it. Listen, you *schleppwurst* – " (Mr Rabinowitz's insults were of a sort of composite Yiddish devised by himself that bore little relation to the language but afforded him immense amusement.) "My Idea of your Idea of Reality capital R is that you wouldn't know the difference between reality and a circumcised *schlitzfurter*."

Like a lot of people obsessed with History, he failed to notice when it was happening around him. The day the First World War broke out (a revealing phrase that – in my experience, wars do not "break out" but sidle, crablike, to the front of one's consciousness), it was I, not a newspaper, that broke the news to my employer. He was standing on top of a ladder at the back of the shop, balancing a pile of books in his hand, when I rushed in from the street and shouted: "Where's Isaac? Where's Isaac?"

He looked down at me. Nobody ever knew where Isaac went during the day. He went sometimes to a gym up near our old school, where he said he was learning to become a boxer, but I don't think he ever did more than lean against the wall and watch them train. His father looked sad at the mention of his son.

"It's war, Mr Rabinowitz," I said, "it's war."

"War?" he said. "Which war?"

I gawped up at him. I didn't know of course, at that stage, that it was the Great War or the First World War. It was, as far as I was concerned, just an ordinary, common-or-garden, run-of-the-mill war. I thought it sounded rather fun.

"With Germans," I said. "We're at war. With Germany."

Mr Rabinowitz looked at me thoughtfully. "Who's 'we'?" he said.

"Us," I said. "You and me. Britain."

He nodded slowly. "Ah," he said, "Britain."

"Yes," I said. "Us. Britain."

It was at that moment that Isaac walked into the shop. Over his shoulder he carried what looked like a kitbag, on a short length of rope, and he swung it as he came in. He let the door bang against one of the bookcases and made no attempt to close it. The August evening breathed through the book smell – in the alley beyond I could hear the shouts of children playing. There was an insolence about Zak, and a natural swagger to the summer day outside, that made his father, and me, hesitate, doubt our right to continue the conversation.

Isaac held up the kitbag on its string with one hand and punched it, hard, with the other. "Talking abaht the war?" he said.

Since leaving school Isaac had aspired to be one of the boys. Not to be with them, you understand, just to be one of them. He seemed, as usual, to be perfecting the act for his own benefit. But this was the first time I realized how perfectly he had got it – the hands on the hips, the head slightly to one side, the ready-for-trouble movements of the shoulders. All of a sudden I did not recognize my friend.

I don't know precisely how old Zak was either when war broke out, but I know that was when his adolescence began. His father knew it too. Up there on the ladder his face went white as paper and his eyes clouded with the shadow of impending death. "Isaac," he began, "that voice ... you...." But Zak wasn't listening to him. He was dancing his way out towards the backyard, the punchbag held out in front of him, jabbing and thrusting at it, moving his feet to left and right as he went. With a *one* and a *two* and a – "Should see some action now, eh?" he said.

"ISAAC!"

Zak stopped and opened his eyes innocently. "Yeah?"

"*Yes*. And where have you been?"

"Gym."

"Your friend I pay, Isaac, but even though I pay him, I – "

"You what?"

He looked across at me as he opened the door to the yard.

"I thought he was your friend, father. Talks more to you than he does to me."

"Zak – " I began.

But he slammed the door.

His father went across to it and yanked it open. I muttered something about leaving. No one paid me any attention. Out in the yard, Zak was tying the kitbag up to a hook on the wall, in order to make an improvised punchbag, and his father was shouting at him. In Yiddish. Isaac, as usual, if he understood a word of what was being said, gave no sign of it. Then, with his father still shouting at him, he started to hit the punchbag very hard. By now he had quite well-developed shoulders (maybe we were older than I had thought we were, I don't know) and, as he punched at the bag he darted back and forward as if trying to catch it unawares. His father stopped shouting and looked at his son, with infinite sadness.

"And where do you go, please? You never tell me. You – "

"War," said Zak. "There's a war on."

He was devoting all his attention and energy to the kitbag. He had (whatever he got up to at the gym) a boxer's passion for the clinch. His father spoke to him again – this time in English.

"You know what happens in wars? People get killed, that's what. For no reason. They just want to get killed, that's all. War for the colonies. War to stop the Russian bear. Don't talk to me because I've heard all about it. I know what lies they tell you. I know they get you to go for the best possible reasons. Your nation, God knows what. Wars are nothing. All wars. All history."

Zak turned from the kitbag.

"Everything's a waste of time as far as you're concerned," he said. "You're so clever you don't believe in anything, do you? You can do it all on your own. You don't want to belong to anything. Not to this country or that country, nor to any Jew or any Christian or any – "

"Isaac – "

I was embarrassed by the intimacy of this conversation. Quietly I began to walk towards the open door and the cool of the alley beyond it. I was almost there when Zak rounded on me.

"And you – " he said, the voice slipping into his favoured manner of the moment, "woch you think yore doin'? Eh? 'oo are you with, eh? Brigade a' f—in' Guards, is it?"

"STOP THAT LANGUAGE!"

"WELL STOP TRYING TO MAKE HIM YOURS! STOP TRYING TO MAKE

66

I froze at the door as I heard Zak's voice catch.

"Stop crowding me so f—ing much, Daddy, can't you?"

When I looked back the old man was the colour of oatmeal. In his right hand was one of his beloved books. He looked down at it stupidly, as if it might offer him some advice, some line that would stop him being an old, sad, cranky man who loved his son too much. When I looked down I saw that I had a book in my hand too. Jesus, I had read so much in my time there. That was my education. But Zak was looking at me now with that impetuous cruelty I came to know so well later on. "I'm going out, Amos. Coming?"

"Look – " I began feebly.

"Are you coming? And don't bother ter bring that *bloody* book. I've had enough of books. He pushed past his father and on out into the cul-de-sac. When he was safely outside, he stood, quite still, his back to me, waiting for me to make my move. The old man went to the kitbag and fingered it, running his hands over the canvas lovingly, like a blind man examining a human face for clues to character. The sun shone, warm and gold, on his neck. He bowed his head like a man going for execution.

"I'm sorry, Mr Rabinowitz," I stuttered, "I'm. . . ."

He turned and looked at me but he didn't see me. I let the book fall to the floor and went out into the alley. That was the last time I saw Zak's father for nearly five years.

War was my adolescence too. My life has been bounded by wars. I sometimes think they are the unique and only subject of this book. They've perverted my youth and soured my middle age, made it impossible for me to see anything straight.

For the fact of the matter is, I enjoyed those early years. I liked it when the recruiting bands came down into the East End. I stood and cheered (though not as loudly as Zak) when the Wapping Bantams marched past. A whole regiment of people under five feet six. Christ, they thought of things a lot sicker than that – the Pals Battalions over at Poplar. Let's all go and get killed together. Every night of that late summer, Isaac and I were out on the street, carried along by the mass of people that seemed to drift from one meeting to another.

"You got a job to go to?" was the constant question from my

father (I hadn't been back to the bookshop since that scene with Zak and his father). And yet the thought of anything steady or permanent, even though I had no plans to get into uniform of any kind, seemed impossible to entertain. I can't remember how I lived then, except people always seemed to be slapping me on the back and giving me half a crown and telling me I was a jolly good fellow.

Zak would have gone straight away – whatever age he was then – if it hadn't been for his mother. His mother, apparently, worried. I'd never seen her do anything else. The two of us haunted outdoor rallies, gnawed at sandwiches while listening to men in khaki and, sometimes, such was the camaraderie generated by that contemptible exercise, found ourselves playing football with the boys on my street. The war, for a brief moment, absorbed us, made us part of the city and, as I recall it now, flags and the smell of sweat, brass bands in the autumn sunshine, I feel a dull anger at the contemporary version – the Our Boys Can Take It rubbish we churn out by the yard here in a faceless room high above the city.

As usual, of course, Zak and I were left behind by it all. If we hadn't been I suppose I would have been part of those early regiments of rookies wiped out in weeks on the battlefields of France. *Kindermord*, the Germans called it – for none of those bright, chirpy little groups, the 51st Battalion of Tobacconists, the 21st Bootblacks (those aren't the right names but they used any classification to generate togetherness), survived. Most of them didn't know which way up to hold a rifle.

Somehow it was winter and summer and winter again, and war didn't seem quite such an attractive proposition. We got a job in the market, I remember. I missed the shop and the walls of books. I think I was on the point of returning to Zak's father and asking for my job back when, in the second spring after the thing started, one chilly, March afternoon, Zak said: "There's a meeting today."

"Oh yeah?"

"Soldiers. Remember?"

"I remember."

I felt no sense of danger. I thought I was well past all of that. War, like love, likes to seduce the unsuspecting.

The meeting was over by Tower Hill. The Tower, as usual, squatted above us prettily, as if aware that it had been overtaken by events, and, just below the ragged turf bordering the monument, was a low trailer, jammed up against the wall. The trailer was decorated with Union Jacks and festooned with sandbags – presumably for artistic rather than military purposes.

On the trailer was a man with a thin, pointed head. To try and give the head a touch of authenticity and, perhaps, to reduce its resemblance to an inverted parsnip, he had grown a moustache. But the moustache had little enthusiasm for life – it straggled apologetically across his upper lip like a plant starved of water. To increase the absurdity of his appearance the man had decided to wear a large khaki hat and a uniform stiff with improbable-looking medals. Next to him was a woman in a black hat, who was reading from a scrappy piece of paper. There weren't more than twenty people listening. They shifted uneasily in the March wind, unable to keep their eyes on the group on the trailer. Crowd, as well as speakers, had a depressed, shopworn air.

"Let's give it a miss," I said.

"No no," said Zak, "might be a laugh in it."

In those days he had modified his East End voice in a way that seemed to symbolize his delicate negotiations between home and the wilder streets that surrounded it. There was still a swagger, a cockiness, in the way he spoke, but it was more carefully applied. It had something of the elaborate calm of the gangster; my own attempts at toughness were never much more than the chimes of assent expected from a sidekick. He pushed his way to the front of the crowd.

"One of the things", the woman was saying, "that is often forgotten is that fighting men need support. For heroes to brave shot and shell, heroes must eat, must be well shod and cared for."

She had a plaintive, upper-class voice. She sounded like a vicar's wife appealing for men to man the tombola. Her hands, chapped with the wind, gripped the paper harder as she continued.

"On my left," she said, "someone who has come all the way from Devizes to speak to you. General Parrish of the Royal Victual and Ordinance Unit."

I looked at the thin man. It seemed impossible to believe that he was a general, or, if he *was* a general, that he did the kind of things generals were supposed to do, such as ordering men to their deaths, spurring his horse on to battle, etc. He beamed when she referred to him, his Adam's apple jerking up and down like a yo-yo.

"General Parrish", said the woman, "has to have a vast amount of food at his fingertips. He needs to know the precise number of hot dinners the British Expeditionary Force will require over a six-month period. His men are hand picked, experts in their field. And believe you me this aspect of the war effort is not being ignored. Thousands of men are going to be required to help others fight. It is not fanciful, in a modern fighting force, to speak of a whole battalion devoted to washing up."

Zak was standing on tiptoe, his face alive with delight. I nudged him as General Parrish beamed once more. What I couldn't understand was whether this was a recruiting drive or some primitive form of supplying the public with information. Or perhaps these were not soldiers at all, but members of a local lunatic asylum?

"Who knows?" went on the woman, confirming my suspicions. "Soon we may see an even more grand design in the field of ordinance – the Royal Regiment of Greengrocers. It is, I concede, a fantastical thought, but for those of us deeply involved in this work and aware of the vital need to maintain supply, these are not laughing matters."

Over to my right a lone spotty youth burst into unspontaneous applause.

Perhaps, I thought, the woman on the platform was his mum.

"In battle," she was saying, uncharismatically, "the task of feeding the men and clothing them is a tough and manly occupation, not a job for the feeble or the sick. Often this work is done under great danger and stress and though the peeling and preparation of vegetables might seem a dull and thankless task, believe you me, when shot and shell are bursting overhead the denuding of a carrot or the topping and tailing of a sprout can be a hair-raising affair."

She halted suddenly. Either there were no more words on her piece of paper or else she had been forcibly struck by the absurdity of what she was saying. Next to me I saw Zak had started to clap his hands in what looked like satirical approval. I shifted nervously.

"Ye–eah," he was saying, "ye–aah. . . ."

The woman on the platform was looking at him oddly, as if unable to decode his intentions. The man next to her cleared his throat nervously. The woman leaned forward over the trailer. "Yes," she said with sudden violence, "applaud. Applaud anything that moves. Applaud and throw your hats in the air. It is war, is it not? Throw your hats in the air."

The spotty youth, in an unconvinced manner, took off his hat and threw it rather limply into the air. It landed about ten feet from him. He did not seem to have the energy to go and pick it up. But others round him, slightly roused by the alteration in the woman's tone, were beginning to applaud. She began to speak again, while beside her the man in General's uniform did a fast serve up and down his gullet with his Adam's apple.

"It is war," she was saying, "war to the last vegetable. Even the innocent vegetable has not escaped. In France – "

The man beside her produced a large picture of cauliflowers. Beneath it were the words LEGUMES A VICTOIRE.

" – it is grow grow grow. Grow that we may destroy. Look at you all. Throw your hats in the air. Applaud anything that moves. Applaud a uniform, no matter how absurd the call, you must answer it. Is not this the dance of History?"

From behind the trailer came three women dressed in long black robes. Behind them was a man carrying a scythe and an hour-glass. The women produced, from beneath their garments, three identical dolls which they held aloft, like some Greek chorus. They began to sing, in reedy voices:

> Behold the innocents.
> Behold the slaughter of the babes.

Things on the rest of the platform were looking up too. "General Parrish" had removed his uniform to reveal a fine pair of hairy legs and a shirt on which was emblazoned the words STOP THIS SENSE-LESS WAR, while the original speaker was hurling card after card at the audience: "You will swallow any lies. You will swallow what you have been given. Learn to distinguish. Learn the truth. Oh, my country, if I told you to kill your children for King and Country would you do it? Oh my children oh my children!"

"Hurray!" shouted Zak. "Ye–eah!"

Yet more middle-aged ladies were appearing carrying vegetables – there was obviously a vegetable theme intended – broccoli, carrots and potatoes, all of which they held aloft, joining the song sung by the first three women.

> *Living things*
> *Ye may respect them.*
> *Life not death*
> *We implore ye!*

The reaction from the crowd was far more appreciative than it had been for the earlier part of this performance. If it was intended as some satirical anti-war cabaret it certainly failed in its intention, for the mood of the audience was now enthusiastically warlike. Paying no attention whatsoever to the words being spoken up on the trailer, young men were throwing their hats into the air and shouting things like "Down with the Hun!" and "Attack!" It was possible that they were under the delusion that the group was about to give away the vegetables they were carrying, for they began to surge towards the speakers, calling and whistling.

Successful peace movements need to be conducted with military efficiency. As the mood of this one became clearer ("General Parrish" was now pointing to the slogan on his chest and howling STOP THE KILLING MAD YOUNG MEN OH STOP THE KILLING!), the crowd became divided among itself. There were those who found, after all, they agreed wholeheartedly with them and there were those – by far the largest number – who felt that it was time free vegetables were distributed and grew incensed when the women on the stage continued to hold them above their heads, wailing things like:

> *Behold*
> *Behold*
> *Life in its purest form. . . .*

Finally there was Zak and myself. Zak was simply part of the crowd. He dived into the mass of people, his eyes shining, like an actor before the grand performance, buoyed up by the noise and movement, uncaring of what, if anything, it might signify, prepared to follow the sudden storm of action to wherever it might lead. "Ye–eah!" he was shouting. "Ye–eah!"

And I, like a fool, followed him.

From the other side of the Tower, came the police. They arrived at the high point of the spectacle when, from beneath the pile of sandbags – which were, I now saw, not sandbags at all but things got up to look like sandbags, came a group of middle-aged men, most of whom seemed to be wearing German army uniforms. They had been made up, with considerable skill, to resemble seriously wounded men, and their faces, livid white, smeared with what looked terribly like blood, set the angry crowd back, as they leaped from the trailer singing something like "We for nothing die . . . ." As the police reached the struggling crowd, the Germans set off down towards the City, followed by the ladies in black gowns, Old Father Time and a short fat man, whom I must have missed on the platform, who was dressed as a sprout.

"Ye–eaah . . . ." Zak was shouting. "Yea–aah. . . ."

He started after them. He didn't care what he was following. Down towards Tower Bridge and then across to the west on the north side of the Embankment. Down through the thin spring rain, along the grey highway that leads back into the City. The policemen were coming from the north, from up towards Aldgate. They had uniformly red faces and, even more than their pursuers, reminded me of some comic troupe, extras from a circus. They were at a diagonal to the main pursuit, running in groups of three or four, as the bizarre convoy threaded its way through the cabs, cars and carts and off towards the cobbled hill that leads down to Southwark Bridge.

Old Father Time was in trouble. He had gashed his right foot and was limping on one of the arms of the women in black dresses. The rain was falling more heavily now and the party ahead of us were slipping and sliding on the wet cobblestones. The sprout was in difficulties. He lay on his back like a tortoise, groaning, as three fat policemen seized him. Just as pursuers and pursued were about to merge in one crazy watercolour, as the police hurled themselves into the thin line of fleeing pacifists and the crowd, or what was left of it, embraced the conflict according to its various persuasions, from a road over to the right, from the north, the City side, I heard the sound of drums and trumpets.

"What the. . . ?" Zak was saying.

Before either of us could restrain ourselves we were in the middle of the fighting.

I remember Zak jabbing and dancing, a fat policeman just out of range thwacking at me with a truncheon, and then the noise of the drums and the trumpets was unbearably close and a group of soldiers had arrived in the pantomime. Except that they weren't part of the pantomime. They set about them seriously, as if they were looking for some specific troublemaker and were cutting their way through human undergrowth to arrive at the guilty party. One by one, onlookers, members of the charade we had just witnessed and even one or two policemen (ruined by a comic-opera face or a moustache outside the bounds of probability) were attacked and dragged towards two huge trucks, parked on the near side of the Tower.

"Run for it!" I shouted to Isaac.

But he was too busy and too excited to run. He was ducking and weaving and shouting and laughing, and the last thing I remember – before the butt of one of the soldier's rifles caught me on the side of the head and sent me sliding down to the cold, rainy pavement – was his face, alive with excitement, his eyes packed with a miser's glee and his voice, as harsh and wild as that man who had frightened me down by the common. . . .

"YE–EEEAAAAHHHHH!!"

And once again –

"YE–EEEAAAAHHH!"

* * *

When I woke up I was lying on a stone floor in a room about ten feet by ten. The only other thing in the room apart from Isaac, who was not awake, was a large wicker basket. The basket was almost as large as the room. On the side I could read the words DOVER: WAR DEPARTMENT. THIS WAY UP.

I went to the heavy door and tried the handle. It was, as I had expected, locked. Down on the floor Zak stirred and groaned. There was no clue in the room as to where we were except, for some reason, I decided we were underground. The walls smelt as if they had been washed recently with soap, but the cleanliness of the place was of the sinister kind that seems to be trying to conceal something.

"What happened?" asked Isaac.

"We joined the army," I said.

"Ha ha ha."

There was one window, in the top right-hand corner of the wall facing the door, and from it I thought I could hear shouts, the crash of boots on gravel and a distant, spindled drumming, like rain on an iron roof. Then, from the other side of the door, came the noise of something rattling and an upper-class voice, surprisingly clear and close, saying: "Are you the basket detail?"

I looked at Zak. A number of keys ground their way into a number of antique locks and, very slowly, the door began to open. Some animal urge made me cross back to where Zak lay and hide myself down behind the basket, as the door creaked its way open. I lay there next to him, waiting for a voice to call: "You two! Out from behind there! Move it!"

But no voice came. Instead the pleasantly modulated voice I had heard earlier said: "Well, basket detail. That's the basket. Now come and sign the paperwork and we'll have the blasted thing out of here, shall we?"

No mention of prisoners. If it were in army hands, it was quite clear that the bit of the army that knew about us hadn't told the bit of the army that knew about the basket about us. And, I expect, vice versa. Nobody in armies tells anyone else anything if they can possibly help it. As the footsteps retreated down the corridor, Zak squeezed my arm.

"Try the lid."

"You what?"

"Try the lid."

"You try it."

He jerked to his feet and put the tips of the fingers of his right hand up to the wicker frame. As he pushed, the lid of the basket opened easily and he peered down into it.

"Christ," he said, "pants."

I thought at first this was some kind of private oath of his but, when I struggled to my feet and joined him, I saw that in the basket was a pile of beautifully monogrammed underwear, white and neat as new snow. They were the kind of pants that reach from waist to ankles, and were equipped with more buttons and slits and flanges than seemed possible or necessary on merely human underwear. The vests, though of soft material, were as elaborate as corsets, and the ensemble was overlaid with several sheets of tissue paper.

"Pants," he said again. "Amazing. Pants."

One of Zak's most charming characteristics was his ability to become fired with enthusiasm for the most mundane objects, views or opinions. This enthusiasm, developed in adolescence purely as a social manner, became with the passing of time a genuinely felt part of his personality, and it was with real passion that he said again:

"*Do* look at those pants."

"I don't see", I said grimly, "that pants are of much use to us in our present situation."

By way of answer he lifted one leg over the side of the basket.

"What are you – "

"I've never been to Dover," he said, grinning fiercely.

At that moment I heard the sound of boots on the stone floor outside. The two of us climbed into the basket together, falling into each other and the new wool as we scrabbled for the lid; I remember holding myself as still as I could in an attempt to stop the paper crackling.

It was not as dark as I had expected it to be in the basket – Zak's heavily accented face was clearly visible, barred with light and charged with the grin that had not been off his face since the beginning of the meeting. He had a wolfish look about him.

"Basket detail," I heard the pleasant voice say, "carry on."

We swayed upwards.

"What's in this?" I heard a voice say.

"Search me," said another voice.

Through the wicker it was possible to distinguish shapes and colours, but in a blurred, impressionistic manner. The early part of our journey was all grey – moving from plastic to solid to fluid like some fermenting experiment. It was cold and then stifling hot, deathly quiet and then suddenly there were horses' hooves, the sounds of wheels and, much later, the laboured breathing of a train. I don't know for how long we lay there among the undergarments, but I do remember that at some stage in this dreamlike progression I heard a man say: "Where's this for then?" And another man answer: "France."

That was when I tried to get out. The lid was buckled down fast and, though I pushed it as hard as I could, it would not move.

"Help!" I called, reedily.

"They can't hear you," said Zak.

And he was right.

After that I recall the rattle of coaches, periods of sleep, wakefulness, and then the sound of seagulls, ropes being hauled and the cold sea wind on empty water. I remember Zak holding forth in his manner of those days, about the war. Scorn was his forte. He had moved from patriotism to its opposite in a matter of months: "It's a joke, all a *joke*, Amos, a huge *joke*." And yet his cynicism was only a style, to be picked up and discarded when he should be no longer amused by it. It was belied by the endless appetite suggested by his smile, his gestures. He thrust one cheek, scrawled across which was the suggestion of a beard, past me and, in his Long John Silver voice, hissed: "Stay with me for the duration and we'll all be rich men."

I don't know what Zak believed in those days. I don't think either of us actually thought about anything for long enough to be able to believe in it. We were trying on larger ideas than we had as children, but wearing them as children do; bright colours and violent noises seduced us. We could have been anything – then. But it was always Zak who took the risks, who went so close to the dangerous heat that abstraction can generate for adolescents that, at any moment, it seemed, *something* – love or nihilism or physical bravery – seemed bound to consume him.

"All war is wrong because – "

"No no no, war is justified if – "

I can't recall who said what. But I do remember waking out of our longest sleep with a crash. The basket seemed to have been dropped from a height on to a stone floor. I could hear voices and the now familiar, clipped, percussive sound of military boots crossing this way and that in a manner designed to convey urgency and authority.

Then someone rapped on the lid and a voice said: "These are for the C.-in-C. New batch."

More of the boots. Then another voice: "Woss in it, sir? Narf 'eavy."

"Underpants, Corporal," said the first voice. The voice yawned. "Field Marshal Haig", it went on, "is particularly concerned about the state of his underwear."

There was shocked silence after this remark. The unseen corporal cleared his throat rather nervously, clearly unsure as to how to take this news.

"Yore 'avin' me on, sir."

"There are, Corporal, about eighty pairs of interlocking vests and pants in that basket and Field Marshal Haig can expect to get through those in a *week*."

"Yes, sir," said the corporal tonelessly.

I started to get a mental picture of the owner of the first voice. I saw him as tall and blond and languid. He might even be wearing a monocle.

"The Field Marshal, Corporal, changes his pants three or four times a *day*, often leaving General Staff meetings to do so. He has said, Corporal, on many occasions, that in an ideal world he would like most of the General Staff to do the same."

I looked at the underpants. I looked at Zak. They were not as clean now as they had been at the start of the journey. Although there was a mocking tone about the languid voice, it was impossible to read its owner's intentions. It sounded almost menacing now, as if accusing the corporal of failing to live up to the high standards of personal hygiene set by the Commander in Chief of the forces in the west.

"I believe his mother was particularly keen on his being clean 'down there' and often writes to him quite lengthy letters demanding to know whether he has an adequate supply of 'you know whats'."

"Yes, sir," said the corporal.

There was a long, tense pause. No sound from the room at all.

"If", said the languid voice finally, "the C.-in-C. were not to have completely fresh pants I am sure that the damage to the Allied war effort would be incalculable. Incalculable."

"Yes, sir."

"Without completely fresh pants, Corporal, he might be unable to concentrate."

The corporal coughed. "I'm the same, sir," he said.

The languid voice barked out a laugh.

"I never know, Captain Rea," said the corporal, "whether to take you seriously."

"You must take me seriously," said the languid voice. "I'm a war hero. I'm missing a leg, therefore everything I say must be listened to. At least for the duration of the conflict. When we get back to Blighty, Corporal, every Tom, Dick and Harry will be walking around with one leg. The really smart thing will be either to have none at all or just the usual two. Us types with our Distinguished

Conduct Medals and our one legs will be unable to get a decent seat in any restaurant. Children will probably come up to us and offer, instead of white feathers, lemons for having been damned stupid enough to get into this show."

The corporal coughed again.

"Are you sleeping, sir?" he said.

"Not a lot," said the languid voice, "not a lot."

"What do I do now, sir?" said the corporal.

There was the sound of someone scuffling to his feet.

"Why, Corporal," said the languid voice, "you guard the pants. You stand guard over the pants and make sure no beastly Hun tries fo snaffle them. Of course you do. That's what you're here for."

"Sir."

"Carry on."

The boots retreated across the floor. Isaac was crouched up to the wicker, one eye fixed to a narrow gap between basket and lid.

"Can you see anything?" I mouthed at him.

"No," he mouthed back.

My heart ticked away wildly. If these were Douglas Haig's underpants (and I had some idea of the importance of the man), then we were not going to be very popular when discovered among them. Perhaps we were committing treason. If they weren't, and the unseen Captain Rea was merely amusing himself at the corporal's expense – then why had someone been set to guard them? Perhaps the underpants were just a cover? Perhaps they concealed some secret weapon? Perhaps "underpants" was a kind of code. Anything was possible.

I moved my right elbow. Moving set off a series of needle-sharp aches across my back and a dull pulse along the surface of my skin on all my upper body. But I didn't, for once, notice the awkwardness of my position. For my right hand had made contact with the lid of the basket and the lid had, quite unmistakably, moved.

"Isaac," I mouthed, "the *lid*. . . ."

He looked at me, puzzled, then following my upward glance tested his fingers against the surface of the basket. The lid rose some two inches and jerked to a halt. Both of us levered up our heads painfully and looked out.

We appeared to be in a kitchen. There was a huge, wooden table to our right, covered in hams and loaves of bread and, in the centre, three or four bottles of wine. From somewhere came the enticing, salty smell of soup. Against the far wall, underneath a row of sauce-pans, sat what must be the corporal – a shabby-looking man of about forty, decorated with webbing and pouches. His rifle was on his knees and he was staring at the flagged floor with the sort of misty passion that suggested he was probably very drunk or very hungry. As we watched, from the door behind came a man in a tall, white hat, carrying a ladle.

"'ey," he said, "warn some zoop, Termy?"

"Termy" looked up, blinking.

"Parleyvoo," he said, not unamiably.

"Zoop," said the man, making scooping motions with the ladle.

The corporal grinned. "I'll say," he said. And shambled out after the man in the chef's hat.

Almost as soon as he was gone, Isaac raised the lid up and allowed it to fall back on the far side of the basket. I put my hand on his arm. "Come on," he said, and flipped out on to the floor, as if he had not been lying in the foetal position for the last twenty-four hours. Once out, he crouched, looking this way and that like a sprinter unsure of the direction his race was due to take. His sallow face had lost the fluidity of extreme youth – that nose, once as fancy as a piece of statuary, was now a proboscis, twitching in search of unseen signals that might promise danger, and those eyes, once girlish, passive, now shifted and changed in the grip of an unseen calculation. It was he, more than anything else, that made me believe that we were actually experiencing what was in front of our eyes, that all of this was not a hallucination induced by a blow to the side of the head from a rifle butt.

I vaulted over the side of the basket and followed him out into the corridor.

My feet fell into the thickly piled carpet. Ahead, as far as I could see, was a straight, narrow passageway, lined with mirrors, Every ten or fifteen yards was an occasional table, its legs bowed out, plumply, from the wall. At the end of my field of vision was a huge french window, through which I could see sun, trees and the distant spire of a church. Zak was running ahead of me. Then, motioning back to me, he slowed to a walk. I did the same. Around the corner came a young man in smart khaki, waving a piece of paper. If he was surprised to see two scruffy youths in civilian clothes he did not show it. He ran past us, the carpet shrouding the panicked speed of his feet.

When we got to the french window, we turned right into another expanse of corridor. There was something frightening about all this space and the two of us stopped and hugged the wall, listening for the noise of voices. There was no sound whatsoever.

Simply to escape the glare of all that emptiness I tried the ornate, gold handle of the first door I came to. It opened easily. The room I found myself in was about thirty yards long. In the middle was a table of about half that length and, at the now familiar, monotonous intervals along the walls were a series of gigantic oil portraits of men in wigs, on horses, thrones, battlefields, cliffs . . . puffy, long-dead faces in the fancy dress of the past, avoiding the spectator's eye with a disdain peculiar to royalty.

Incongruously, on the table, piled as high as the banquet that should have decorated it, was a mound of uniforms – caps, trousers, boots and overcoats – and, on the quilted chairs were cardboard boxes, overflowing with military equipment – guns, belts, important-looking folders. Isaac followed me in and we closed the door behind us.

"Well," he said, "I always wanted to be in the army."

"You think we should – "

"Of course," he said, indicating the pile of rough khaki cloth.

"Can't you be shot for pretending to be a soldier?" I said.

"Don't be stupid," said Zak. "It's when you pretend not to be a soldier they shoot you. What are they all doing anyway? Pretending to be soldiers."

"I – "

I felt that if we apologized nicely for the trouble we had caused they might send us back. I have always had a fatal weakness for casting myself on people's mercy. As Zak struggled into a pair of ludicrously baggy trousers and a peaked hat several sizes too big for him, he explained to me that there was only one thing to do with mistakes. Pretend they hadn't happened. "You've got to carry on," he said. "Just do it and do it and do it. And if you've got the nerve you'll get away with it. All you need is the nerve and you can get away with anything. Otherwise you'll end up like my old man."

I've never believed it possible to get away with anything. I some-times feel the only safe thing to do with life, as soon as one is able, is to report to the nearest hospital; and ask them to look after you until you die. It was terror, not bravura, that made me follow Isaac's example and kit myself out in another outsize selection of khaki clothing.

"Won't they see we don't look like soldiers?" I said plaintively. "These are far too big."

"I bet none of their uniforms fit," said Isaac. "What *does* a soldier look like?"

Opposite one of the paintings (of a man in a breastplate, his left leg thrust forward like a dancing master) was a full-length mirror. Isaac saluted himself in it. Then he gave himself the thumbs-up sign. He did, I had to admit, look very like a soldier. I went over and tried out the same routine. I thought I looked like a member of the back row of the chorus in some patriotic musical. But then, I reflected, I never looked much like a schoolboy, or a son, or an apprentice bookseller, or any of the rather pathetic things I had actually been, so it would have been too much to expect for me to step easily into the role of fighting man.

Fighting. They did that of course. I gulped and followed Zak out into the corridor.

The uniform seemed to have given him confidence. He walked on, down the corridor, up some stairs, across two or three landings cluttered with furniture, across a gigantic hall and, finally, along a sort of internal balcony. The balcony overlooked a hall that had once, clearly, had the style of the room where he had found our clothes, but was now so crowded with men in uniform, of every conceivable variety, clustered in groups round blackboards and wall charts, scurrying off towards the huge doors at the far end of the hall waving pieces of paper, calling to each other like bookies at a racecourse, that it looked more like the Stock Market than anything else. At the far end of the hall was a long, polished table, behind which a group of very important people were sitting. You could tell they were important, partly because they were sitting down, and partly because they whispered to each other occasionally and laughed in the kind of way that suggested that no ordinary person would ever have got the joke. A heavy hand fell on my shoulder.

I turned and looked up and saw a Frenchman. I knew he was a Frenchman immediately, largely because of his moustache. English moustaches at that time didn't quite have the staying power of French ones, and this man's forged up into his cheeks and off over the upper part of face, ears, eyes and hairline, like one of those unstoppable American rivers they'd told us about at school. There were other things that told me he wasn't English. He kept grinning at nothing in particular, the way foreigners do; the way he moved his hands was a lot too public for my taste, and when he spoke the first thing he said was "''aig."

My first thought was that he was arresting us and that this was an agreed wartime formula for such a procedure. But then I saw that he was gesturing towards an imperturbable-looking man in the centre of the table at the end of the hall. The imperturbable man wore a moustache that seemed designed to express his essential Englishness. It was a model of understatement, and went perfectly with the man's still, quizzical profile and his immense reserve of manner.

"''aig," said the Frenchman again and, clasping his hands together, improvised a cheering gesture.

Oh my God – and we've spoilt his underpants. The three of us peered over the balcony, as through the mass of people came the young man who had passed us in the corridor outside the kitchen. Haig nodded graciously at him as he approached and handed over his piece of paper. Perhaps it was a cable from London, INTRUDERS SUSPECTED IN UNDERPANTS: SEARCH CASTLE. If it was, Haig gave no sign of it. He slit it open with a silver knife on the table in front of him and rose to his feet. Immediately he did so the hall fell silent.

"Gentlemen," he said, "the wire has been cut at Amboisey-les-Trois-Chauffons."

This went down very well with the audience. There was even a small ripple of applause from some of the men at the back which Haig silenced with a wave.

"At Chambonnay and Carliers the Fourth and the Fifth are moving forward to their agreed positions under cover of darkness. To the north everything is proceeding as was agreed at the General Staff meeting to the salient north-north-west of Poivreux."

One of the men next to him whispered discreetly in his ear. Haig smiled.

"I'm sorry, gentlemen," he said, "*Pervreux.*"

There was a soft rustle of laughter in the hall at this sally. Perhaps because of the business of the underpants I was unable to give the credence to the man's words that they seemed to demand. He seemed to be reading from some prepared script and, perhaps because of the drabness of his delivery, I was unable to make the imaginative leap clearly required by his speech and conjure up thousands of stealthy, disciplined men crawling forward under cover of darkness.

"At Gaspart and Les Trois Rochers," went on Haig (he sounded now like the chairman of a company reading the annual report) "the wire has never been so well cut and the Twelfth and the Fifteenth are making their way in a half-circle to a position south-south-west of Danson where they will be able to support the French advance on Dulac. They will be supported in this flanking movement by the Eighth Brigade and the combined remnants of the Thirteenth and the Twenty-second, who fought so well at Moissiers, will group together to make an additional prong."

The man next to him whispered again and this time Haig broke into a grin. It was a pleasant, outdoor sort of grin, suggesting a manly confidence that warmed the hall.

"I'm sorry, gentlemen," he said, "I should have north-north-east of Danson."

This got an even bigger laugh than his first gag. The underpants, however, were now looming so large in my consciousness that I was beginning to doubt, not the reality of their importance to the impressive figure at the table, but the relation to reality of the man's speech. Supposing he was just making all this up – suppose he had decided to tell the assembled soldiers anything.... Suppose he was in the grip of a nervous breakdown because of what might or might not have happened to his underpants. I realized that I was dizzy with tiredness and not fully able to catch what Haig was saying, that I was rearranging his words, even as he spoke them, into new patterns.

"I have been told", I heard him say, "that the offensive planned for tomorrow is an impossible dream. I have been warned of every type of risk that may befall us in this enterprise. But when I ask the ordinary man in the line – when I see him and ask him what does he want – I'll tell you what he wants, he wants – "

"He wants bang bang bang," shouted somebody.

I looked round and saw that it was Zak who had spoken. He was leaning forward over the rail of the balcony, face cocked with amusement. Was he even more dizzy and hysterical than I was? This was clearly the signal for us to be marched off to some military gaol. I gripped the rail and watched Haig's eyes travel up the hall until they fell on Zak. The silence in the hall was now almost too painful to bear.

"Quite," said Haig, "exactly so, soldier."

There were murmurs in the hall of "Quite" and "Well said, that man" and I noticed several heads turn up towards us. I distinctly heard one man, quite close to us, whisper, "That's Dummerton – the Field Marshal's batman."

With impressive slowness the Field Marshal walked over to a huge map of France and jabbed his finger at Bordeaux. "Tomorrow night," he said, "we shall be here."

From time to time I saw Haig glance uneasily up at the balcony, as if unable to trust the evidence of his eyes. So caught up was Zak in the moment, the perkiness of his uniform, the air of complex deliberation in the hall below, that I, too, doubted my senses and wondered whether it was life in London that had been a dream. Had Isaac been here since it started? Sometimes mocking, sometimes joining in? He had in spirit anyway – his unrelenting search for adventure in the streets near us had at last borne fruit.

Haig paced back along the length of the table. He was very good at pacing. I wasn't so sure about his map-reading though. He wheeled round at the head of the table and charged back to the map. This time he jabbed a forefinger at Stuttgart. "This", he said, "can be ours tomorrow. With God's help."

There was a reverent murmur from the crowd. They liked the idea of Stuttgart. As Haig was going back down the table again, an orderly in a white coat crept up to him. The orderly muttered something. Whatever it was, it was not to Haig's liking, for he rounded on him, his face bursting into violent bloom. "WHAT DID YOU SAY, SIR?"

The orderly found himself alone on the stage. He looked helplessly back at the crowd in the hall.

"Er...."

"WHAT DID YOU SAY?"

"I said ... er...."

The orderly simpered.

"I said ... dinner was served."

85

The audience did not quite know how to take this remark. There was much turning of heads and discreet mumbling. I got the impression they could have been about to cheer, or to swarm round the table and tear the unfortunate man limb from limb.

"DINNER?" screamed Haig. "WHAT DO I WANT WITH DINNER WHEN BRAVE MEN ARE ABOUT TO DIE?"

Search me, I thought. What do you want with dinner when brave men are about to die? Mustard? Redcurrant jelly? I looked across at Zak who was now hung over the balcony, mouth open, relishing the spectacle. Above Haig was a huge picture window and, as he smacked the table with his fist, a crowd of pigeons broke cover and winged across the sun-filled rectangle of glass, off up to the calm trees I could see in the distance. The image of peace became confounded with my confusion about the underpants and my puzzlement at the scene we were watching. Dizzy again with tiredness, I scratched my wrist hard.

"WHEN I THINK OF PLATES OF GRAVY," went on Haig, "FULL OF GRAVY AND BEEF AND CABBAGE WITH A THIN WHITE SCUM ON THEM. WHEN I THINK OF HALF-FILLED WINE GLASSES AND MOUNDS OF UNEATEN BREADCRUMBS, I THINK OF NO MAN'S LAND, GENTLEMEN, AND THE WIDE EXPANSE OF MUD AND BODIES! I THINK OF THE FRONT, GENTLEMEN, WHEN I THINK ABOUT MY DINNER!"

I now realize that looking at his dinner was about as close as Field Marshal Douglas Haig ever got to the front, but at the time his words had the eerie power of a ritual prayer on me. Carried away by tiredness and lack of food I found myself leaning with Zak, out over the hall.

"TOMORROW'S ATTACK, GENTLEMEN, WILL BE WITHOUT DOUBT DECISIVE IN THIS SECTOR OF THE WAR AND I ASK YOU NOT TO CONSIDER ANYTHING BUT THE OBJECTIVE IN VIEW! IN THIS WAY WE WILL ACHIEVE WHAT WE SO DESPERATELY NEED!"

There were cheers and ragged applause from the hall, in which Isaac and I joined enthusiastically. When they died away Zak was still shouting, in what seemed to me a plainly satirical manner, whirling his cap above his head and yelling: "BANG! BANG BANG BANG!"

His voice fell into the quiet and once more Haig's eyes travelled up to meet his. Zak's mouth was open in a slack grin, his tongue hanging out like a dog's. Now, I thought, we are for it. Now they are about to find out about us. There was a curious sense of release about this thought. An image of my mother and father came to me, sitting in our quiet kitchen, and the narrow streets, the dark warehouses and the big, brown river clamoured for my attention, blotting out the ludicrous formality of what was before me.

"BANG!" said Zak again. "BANG. BANG. BANG."

Haig smiled. "Yes, soldier," he said. "Yes." Then he rounded on the whole audience. "There is the man who will do it," he yelled. "There is the man who will brave shot and shell and walk into enemy lines where no one else follows. There is Tommy Atkins."

I thought for one ghastly moment that Zak was about to tell him that his name wasn't Atkins but Rabinowitz. He did not. He gazed down, slack-jawed, at the Field Marshal. Haig stepped round the table and, with the professional showmanship of the career general, said: "Don't I know you, soldier?"

Zak grinned loosely. "Yessir," he said.

"You're with the Twenty-first," said Haig.

"That's right, sir," said Zak.

I learned later that Haig was always doing this. In order to humour him, one corporal attached to his staff had owned up to being in everything from the Bengal Lancers to the Enniskillen Fusiliers. He had a quite appalling memory for faces as well as for the disposition of his troops.

"The Twenty-first", he was saying, "have been in the line for month after month. They have suffered as no other unit has suffered. They have been in constant peril of their lives. They are tired. Soldier – "

Zak grinned at him encouragingly.

"Soldier. Take a rest. Attach yourself to Captain Rea. And concern yourself with dinner for a change."

Tumultuous applause greeted this last remark. Heads were lifted up in our direction and, from the floor, a short, plump man started towards the stairs that led up to the balcony. The top table rose to their feet and, pushing their chairs aside, moved towards the doors at the back of the hall. Everyone seemed in a very good mood. I looked up to see if the Frenchman was still there but he had gone.

"What is this?" I said to Zak.

"It's a lunatic asylum," he said.

When the short, plump man appeared, I realized from the

moment he opened his mouth that it was he who had spoken at such length in the kitchen on the subject of Haig's underpants. It was only when he came level with us that I saw he was missing one leg, from the knee down.

"How do you like the C.-in-C.?" he said.

"Isn't he a one, sir?" said Zak.

Captain Rea grinned bleakly. "He's insane," he said. "He is stark, raving mad. Come on. I'll show you your quarters."

* * *

Captain Rea was a specialist in deadpan humour. He made even greater demands on my credibility – in those first few months in France – than did the evidence of my own eyes.

"Where are we?" I asked him that first evening.

"We are", he said, "in the château of Montreuil – the GHQ of Douglas Haig. Which is why, on each corner, of each corridor, you can see a map with MONTREUIL written in letters six inches high, next to this castle. And next to that you may observe an arrow pointing to it, opposite which are the words YOU ARE HERE."

Although he lacked one leg below the knee, Captain Rea never used a stick. He had perfected a kind of slow-motion hop, which gave him the air of a flamingo or stork. In fact, when you had been with him for a day or so, it was very difficult to believe that he had actually suffered the loss of part of a leg. Zak and I came to the conclusion that he had it tucked up his trouser leg and that one day he would ruffle it out, flex it, and give us that slow smile that transformed his pudgy face into something as sunny and alive as the park outside the château.

"How did you get your wound?" Zak asked him once.

"I tripped over a large-scale map of the Marne," was Rea's reply.

I think he was from Devon, but his voice, fluting and exquisite, conjured up the closes of cathedrals, cricket lawns and brave young things in white jerseys. He had a job in what was called Staff Liaison, and shared a small and cheerful room with a young man called Smythe, above a kitchen yard at the back of the château. Zak and I slept just off their office in two lumpy cots and at night we could hear the sound of horses backing restlessly in their stables. In the morning the doves and pigeons woke us and on slow after-noons – of which there were many – we lay on our cots and listened to the bright threshing of the wind in the elms just beyond our kitchen yard. We could have been on holiday in spring in England.

"How did you wind up here?" Rea said to us after a while.

We tried telling him we were from the Twenty-first but he told us there was no such thing as the Twenty-first. When Zak told him he was called Rabinowitz and he had stowed away involuntarily in a linen basket, Rea nodded.

"That sounds about right", he said, "for this show. That sounds about right."

"And how did you get into the army?" I said.

"I was abandoned by my mother", said Rea, "on the doorstep of the Royal Brigade of Bumsuckers."

"No such regiment," said Smythe.

"Don't you believe it, Chopper," said Rea.

Rea and Smythe had been at school together at a place called Rugby and – when they weren't trying to hit empty wine bottles with stale pieces of bread – they spent most of their time doing impressions of a master there whose name was Smudger. The only time they looked at all military was when the bell over the door of their office rattled (it was connected to a dubious-looking piece of string), at which Smythe would say: "His Nibs." And the two of them would leap to their feet and begin a complicated game of scissors, paper and stone, to see who was to answer the call.

"What do you *do*?" I asked Rea once.

"I don't *do* anything," was his reply. "I'm just *here*. The function of a soldier in wartime is to be there."

Rea's other favourite sport was what he called the suicide hop. He would conceal himself behind a mound of piled-up tables and chairs and Smythe would stand at the opposite end of the room; after a while Smythe would shout "OVER THE TOP!" and Rea would hop, at high speed, over the obstacles towards his friend, who descended upon him with squeals of simulated rage. The game always ended with the two of them rolling around on the floor shouting "YOU'RE DEAD YOU'RE DEAD YOU'RE DEAD!"

Rea and Zak did not get on. Some time in the first month, Rea said: "Are you a Jewish chappy?"

And Zak said: "Yes, I am. Want to make something of it?"

"No, old boy," said Rea, "I wouldn't."

The other problem between them was that Isaac liked to affect an iconoclastic style. I knew it. It was only a style – like his Shadbolt voice or his "Kid" Zak voice – but it irritated Rea beyond belief.

"War," Zak would say, "what a *joke. . . .*"

To which Rea would reply: "On the contrary, old boy. Extremely serious business."

"How do you work that out?"

"War is never ridiculous enough as I see it. The whole problem with war is that people take it seriously enough to say things like 'It's a joke.' As yet – it seems to me, old boy – the joke hasn't gone far enough. What we want isn't young men – or women for that matter. We don't want bantam regiments or miners' platoons. We want really teeny tiny minuscule little regiments. We want to involve the nursery in all of this, don't you think? We want front-line infantry composed of children under five. We want teeny tiny hospitals to sew up their teeny tiny tummies when teeny tiny shells rip them to bits and we want teeny tiny generals to – "

"How did you get your wound?" said Zak.

"I was set upon by a crowd of pacifists in Piccadilly," said Rea.

There was one day of the week when Rea and Smythe were not in evidence. Every Tuesday they would disappear very early in the morning, leaving Zak and me to roam about the château alone. It was always, for some reason, deserted on Tuesdays. The two of us went into vast ballrooms, hung with sheets, the pictures turned to the wall, and, as summer came on, wandered unmolested through the nearby villages. In the fields near the castle, peasants hacked at hedges and, in the middle of the blue sky, larks stayed where they were, like faults in an old master. Our parents receded and our lives became bounded by the narrow bedroom and the Staff Liaison office.

One afternoon, Zak said to Rea: "Where do you go on Tuesdays?"

Rea smiled and put away his pack of cards.

"The front, old boy," he said. "Bang bang bang."

"What . . . happens there?" said Zak.

We were in the saddle room – there were no saddles there, although it smelt of leather, but it looked over a gabled courtyard, where they stabled horses. Rea hopped over to Zak and put his arm on my friend's shoulder. Zak shook it off. Rea smiled again and motioned him over to the window. I followed, looked down and saw three huge, brown stallions, being wheeled and backed, like clumsy vehicles, out towards the path that led to the grounds. They were being led by elderly men in green baize aprons, who treated them with reverent fondness, as if they were antiques. As the hind-quarters of the last shuffled off towards the green, dappled light beyond the yard, Rea said: "Douglas Haig gets on one of those you see and rides up there. Every Tuesday morning."

"Where is *there* precisely?" said Isaac sullenly.

"Charollais Wood."

At this moment Smythe came in. He was wearing a white boater, no shirt, and a pair of long grey shorts. Smythe was a fatter version of Rea and the outfit did not help his appearance.

"Chin chin chinaman," he said.

"Jumbo," said Rea.

Smythe went out again, apparently satisfied by this response.

"*Where* is Charollais Wood?"

"Charollais Wood", said Rea, "is about the only place on the line that Douglas Haig can get up to and back from on a Tuesday morning. And as Tuesday morning is the only period on his schedule when he is not in meetings, drawing arrows on maps and sending thousands of men to their deaths, Charollais Wood is where he goes."

During this speech Smythe had re-entered the room carrying a large piece of cheese. He watched Zak with some amusement as my friend stared moodily down at the courtyard.

"What's there?" said Zak.

Both of them seemed to find this very amusing. Rea hopped over to a disused chair in the corner of the room and fell into it, his pudgy face swept upwards in glee. "What's *there*?" said Rea. "I say, what's *there*, Smythie? What's at Charollais Wood, eh? What's there?"

Smythe struck an attitude. Then he inserted his forefinger into his cheek and made a popping sound. After he had done this he flexed his knees and mimed a man riding a horse. He made it seem rather lavatorial, but that was probably the effect of the white flesh hanging over the top of his shorts.

"Bang bang bang," he said. "That's what's there."

"Oh," said Zak, and sniffed.

"What a joke, eh?" said Smythe to him.

"Yeah," snarled Zak.

I was over by the window. One of the men had brought back two horses. The larger one was standing by the far wall, while the man in the green baize apron attended to the other. He looked as if he was trying to brush its teeth. There was the kind of tense pause that often fell on us after Zak had said something.

"You can come if you like," said Smythe, "and see for yourself."

"Certainly," said Isaac boldly.

"Smythie – " said Rea.

But Smythe had begun to sing a favourite song of his, the title of which was, if I remember correctly, "Roland Orlando the Lowland Land Roller". Rea yawned – something he always did when he was irritated.

"You wouldn't like it," he said to Zak.

"Would we go on horses?" I said.

"Don't be stupid," said Zak. "We'll go in a cart. With the plebs."

"Correct," said Smythe.

And he eyed Zak narrowly. By this time he actively disliked my friend. I had heard him once refer to Isaac as "the Jewboy" – a description that seemed to cause Rea some slight physical pain, as if someone had used a vulgar word in front of a lady.

"On Tuesday week, eh?" said Rea.

Zak nodded shortly and went out of the room. When he had gone Smythe sucked in his lips and made a currant-bun face after him. Rea yawned again. Then Smythe went out. After he had gone, Rea said: "Your friend sees himself as a bit of a wild man. Don't you think?"

"I suppose so," I said.

"And what about you?" he said.

"I don't know," I said.

"You're a couple of children," said Rea.

He hauled himself up and hopped over to the window. We stood there looking down at the horse standing patiently as the man in the apron scoured its hooves with what looked like a scrubbing brush. It was calm and quiet. I tried to imagine Charollais Wood and failed.

"I like him well enough," said Rea, "but do you know what?"

"What?"

"I'm frightened for him."

"Why are you frightened for him?"

"I find violence very frightening," said Rea, "violence of thought or opinion as well as the physical kind. I've always thought opinions should be expressed in whispers." He sighed. "And yet look at me," he said. "I never thought I would feel as violently about anything as I do about Douglas Haig."

"How did you lose your leg?" I said to him.

Rea turned his pudgy face to mine.

"A bound volume of Lord Kitchener's memoirs fell on it," he said.

The man in the yard had finished cleaning the horse and was leading it inside. Rea hopped back to his chair and sat there glumly. I caught a glimpse of myself in the mirror on the far wall – as gaunt and peculiar as ever, but my uniform no longer the mockery it had seemed when I first put it on. I grinned at myself and gave the thumbs-up sign.

"I think your friend is . . . remarkable." said Rea.

"Why?" I said. I felt vaguely flattered by these confidences.

"I don't know exactly . . . yet." said Rea. Then he said: "But don't stick too close to him, young man."

"No?"

"No." Rea began to massage his stump thoughtfully. "He'll poison you," he said.

I couldn't get him to explain what he meant by that. I'm not sure that I understand it even now. But, even in recollection, it has the dark solemnity of a prophecy and I picture myself at the window, white-faced, suddenly fixed by fear.

The morning we went up to Charollais Wood, there was sun on the yard, very early. There was sun, too, on the green behind the château, where lines of horses, wagons and vans were arrayed in carnival splendour. Zak and I were put into a two-wheeled cart which was loaded with wicker baskets and driven by a very old man wearing what looked like a pair of blue pyjamas. The horse looked even older than him. Rea and Smythe were further down the line, looking very formal and anxious. Beyond them I could see a fungus growth of khaki uniforms. The people around us seemed to be, for the most part, French civilians – they were craning their heads forward like people trying to catch a glimpse of royalty and, from behind the line of the château wall, came the nearest thing to it in this part of the world.

On his horse, Haig seemed a more credible figure. He sat bolt upright, turning his profile this way and that, as if to catch the light, and then trotted to the head of the column. He presented, on this occasion, a far less operatic face to the crowds of soldiers and hangers-on and, paradoxically, I found it harder to believe that on his order all of us would be more or less obliged to march, run or crawl in whatever direction he dictated. When he reached the head of the column he turned and looked back at it appraisingly. Then he raised his right hand in a curt salute and the thing jolted to life, like one of those jointed wooden snakes that are given to children.

The line creaked its way out in a circle away from the château. From up ahead I saw Rea riding back towards us. So serious was his face that I thought at first that he had some announcement to make, but as he drew level with our cart all he said was: "Enjoying the party?"

"Why", said Zak, "do we need all these people?"

Rea yawned. "Lunch, old boy," he said.

As the column wound over to the left and on to the metalled road we could see Haig more clearly. He was well out ahead of the leaders, bobbing up and down on the giant buttocks of his horse like a cork in water. He looked neither to left nor right. A constant stream of young men, on slightly smaller horses, rode up to him, whispered something in his ear and galloped off back down the line, but Haig did not acknowledge their attentions in any way. He might have been some mechanical toy, put there to encourage the others.

The sun grew hotter.

"Where's the wood then?" said Zak.

"I think *wood* is putting it a little strong," said Rea.

I looked at Zak.

"There are only about twelve trees left standing on the whole of the Western Front," he added.

Isaac had turned his head away from the conversation, as if to indicate his contempt for it. I could tell, though, from his attitude, that he was listening hard to what was being said. When Rea spoke again, it was to the back of Isaac's head that he addressed his remarks.

"You see there are about six trees at Charollais-le-Haut-Boisson. Hence the 'wood'. They're completely twisted by mortar fire of course, but they are standing. Just."

Zak turned half round. The wagon swayed and rolled like a ship and he gripped wildly at the sides, wrecking his pose of nonchalance.

"Are we going to capture the trees?" he said.

Isaac was trying to conceal his interest in much the same way as Haig had somehow mastered his vanity at the head of the column. But the attempt only seemed to make his excitement more tangible. He rubbed at his forehead. Rea looked down at him, almost kindly, and said: "Tree, boy. Tree."

Tree? We were going to capture a tree, were we? Well, at least that sounded a lot less arduous than a whole wood. From further down the line I saw Smythe break ranks, wheel round and come galloping back towards us. In full-dress uniform he appeared newly made – the plump lines of his face had hardened and, when he reined in next to us, I felt I was looking into a stranger's eyes. He confirmed this impression by ignoring Zak and me and speaking to Rea in a curiously formal voice.

"The C.-in-C. feels", he said, "that if we can get one of our people up the tree. . . ."

Rea yawned.

"What?"

"From the observational point of view," said Smythe, "it would be something of a coup. Don't you think, Captain Rea?"

And, tugging sharply at his horse's reins, he was off down the line. As we jolted onwards (the metal road had given way to a rough dirt-track), I said to Rea: "What will they see from the top of this tree?"

"God knows," said Rea. "Berlin, I expect."

The subject obviously did not amuse him. He pushed his hat back on his head and I noticed beads of sweat starting under his hairline. The animal smell of the horses, the swaying of the cart and the fierce sun were making me feel dizzy. I looked ahead to see if I could see trees or some shape that resembled what I imagined the front to look like. All I saw was fields. How did I imagine it would look, anyway? My expectations have become jumbled with what I saw, and what I saw recorded afterwards, so that sometimes I pictured us

95

bucking through wastes of mud, craters, pools and sludge-ridden tracks littered with bodies. Sometimes it is in sepia I see it all, sometimes in brilliant, primary colours. . . . There is no consistency to the images I can recall. The only thing that seems real and true is the mounting sense of fear and horror I felt as we trekked on in the sunshine and, some way ahead, heard the dull thud of guns.

"Why – " began Zak.

"Why?" said Rea. "Don't ask why. Please don't ask why. Don't keep asking for reasons. Stop polishing up that intelligent expression of yours and realize there isn't a reason for any of this. Not a good one, anyway. It is best to assume that it is not happening. That it is the result of too much cheese at dinner. If you look closely at it you will find that that is what it is most like. Don't expect it to be like life, unless you want to lose faith in life itself. And for God's sweet sake wipe that look off your face. Stop, please, looking like someone who wants to understand because I cannot bear it."

As he rode back off down the line Zak shouted after him: "Where did you get that wound?"

"It was bitten off by the mistress of a French general," came back the reply.

And, as he slid his horse in next to Smythe's, I saw his head rock back in the widest yawn I have ever seen.

I still have no clear picture of the landscape around Charollais Wood. I would like to be able to say that we rounded a bend in the road and saw it, stretched out like some giant Victorian canvas, like an artist's impression of hell. I would like to conjure up broken gun-carriages, men with bandaged eyes, shattered lean-tos, an acned, lunar landscape that gave no hope of life ever again. I would like to say I saw the First World War, I suppose.

What I saw was an entirely different thing.

I know there was a rise and I know there was mud on the rise. I know there was grass, too, but I am almost positive there was more mud than grass. I am convinced there were no birds or flowers or animals there or any people. There were no fences or hedges or gates or roads, or anything to enclose and order the landscape before us. Beyond the first rise, the ground swelled and diminuendoed away in the summer sun to a point about three or four hundred yards away. There, on the edge of the horizon, it might have been possible to see barbed wire, or at least some smudge that someone told me was barbed wire. And near the barbed wire might have been, I suppose, sandbags and shelters and more barbed wire. And beyond *that* barbed wire, right at the ultimate point of my field of vision, it is conceivable that there was mud – a stiff sea of faceless brown.

Did I see the enemy? Can I paint them in?

Yes, I am sure that beyond *our* wire was *their* wire. I am sure I did see that. And while we're at it perhaps I saw the tips of their rifles, heard, even at that distance, the guttural sound of their voices; after all, this was the front. You can't have a front without an enemy, can you? As I often remind Alan – if we didn't have Hitler we'd have to invent some other bogyman. The man is merely a tribute to the sickness of the age's imagination.

Let me be definite. On the first rise before us, as the column halted, were a row of guns. The guns were dull grey. I saw now that there were people here, but the people were only here to look after the guns. They were wearing circular helmets and they ran up to and away from the snouts of the artillery, like waiters at a crowded table. They would jam shells into the mouths of the gun barrels, spring back, salute and then run off for more shells, ducking their way backward and forward in a palsied rhythm, set by the jerking of the machines. The guns themselves seemed in pain; they threw themselves back against the sandbags that surrounded them like patients in a fever.

"What's this?" I said to Isaac.

"Artillery," someone else replied.

The column now began to halt, or rather the front section halted, the section behind them fanning out to the right and left. As if at some prearranged signal men in blue uniforms, who looked like hospital attendants rather than soldiers, were running up to each wagon, pulling off tarpaulins and throwing what looked like packets of bedlinen on to the ragged grass. They laid them out, like paper clues, in a line away from the wagons and towards the guns. Smythe rode up to our wagon, whose driver was hurling wicker baskets to the ground.

"Geta tableclorth", said Smythe, "and make yourself useful."

"Yah," said Zak, "suttinly."

And, saluting satirically, he jumped over the side of the wagon. I followed him. An elderly woman who seemed to have crawled out from under one of the tarpaulins was unloading food from the baskets. I have never seen so much food. Pies, jellies, loaves of bread, bottles of wine, all as perfect as the plaster-of-Paris food from a doll's house, were spreading out on to the white cloths, like a rash. I seized a tablecloth, relieved to discover that, insomuch as we had any military status at all, we appeared to be members of the Catering Corps. They didn't shoot members of the Catering Corps. Did they?

The course we took, as we laid the cloths on the ground, brought us nearer and nearer to the guns. I did not mind this as much as I thought I would. Although they were the only conspicuously violent thing about the scene before us, they were pointing towards the enemy. The shells seemed to be landing, for the most part, in the brown expanse between the two lines. Occasionally, from the other side, almost obscured by the midday sun, would come a puff and a distant flash, a ghostly parody of the colossal display of our own weapons.

I was about to start back for the wagon when I looked up and saw, atop a giant brown horse, the man Rea always referred to as Douglas Haig. Haig was shouting against the noise of the guns. At first I could not see who or what he was shouting at but then, on the far side of his mount, I saw a young officer, his face blackened by smoke and his eyes dark with strain. He seemed more frightened of Haig's horse than anything else and, each time the creature stirred, the young man flinched, as if he expected it to strike him.

"Where is it?" Haig was saying.

"Where's what, sir?" the officer replied.

"The wood," said Haig, rather testily.

"Doesn't appear to be there, sir," said the officer.

Haig screwed himself round in his saddle and looked across at the undulating stretch of ground before us. Then he leaned back towards the officer. "Why?" he said acidly.

"Well, sir," said the officer, "we've been shelling this area for two days."

Haig leaned down into the youth's face. I would have put the lad at about Zak's age or mine.

"Listen," said Haig, slowly and menacingly, "I want that wood back in position on the double. It is a tactical objective of some importance."

"Sorry, sir?" said the young officer.

"Lieutenant," went on Haig, "at the moment the wood is not there. Unless the wood is there we cannot put anyone up the trees that comprise the wood. So get out there on the double and get the wood back in position. Sharpish."

The guns were jerking in a frenzy. I was not sure that I had heard the last part of this conversation correctly and, to judge from the expression on the young officer's face, neither was he. He was shaking himself in rhythm to the meaningless ejaculation of the artillery. His eyes were on something a long way from this conversation and, when he came back to it, he looked like a child waiting to be told a story. But his commander did not speak again and the youth, seeming to answer what was not said rather than what had actually been spoken, whispered: "Very good, sir."

At this the Commander-in-Chief reined in his horse and rode towards an incline about twenty yards behind us. He lifted his head proudly into the morning air and waited for his orders to be obeyed. I heard a cough behind us. It was Rea.

"I don't believe it," Zak said.

"You keep saying that," said Rea sharply. "It is getting monotonous."

The enemy gunners were growing more ambitious. One shell landed between us and our own lines, diving aimlessly into the earth, throwing up a cloud of stones and dirt. No one paid it any attention. In front of us, the young officer was supervising what looked like an elementary carpentry lesson. A group of men were nailing bits of wood together, with the same automatic frenzy that others displayed on loading the artillery. There did not seem to be much system to their work and, when completed, what they had made resembled stunted crosses rather than trees. Haig did not register any emotion other than his usual intense, slightly dangerous, dignity. He was looking out towards the German lines as if about to wipe them out with the power of thought.

Large numbers of people in uniform, who did not appear to have any function whatsoever, were squatting down on the ground and opening bottles of wine. Pies were being split open and pieces of chicken bitten apart by well-fed, moustachioed faces. Zak and I found ourselves at a tablecloth with Rea, Smythe and a man called Toto Hodge. I remember nothing about him apart from the fact that he had a high, squeaky voice.

"What *is* going on?" said Zak.

"GHQ are always like this," said Toto Hodge.

"The Jewboy", said Smythe, grease trickling down his chin, "wants to know what it all means."

Rea yawned. "Soon be over," he said.

The German shells were falling closer and closer. There did not seem to be any pattern or system to the way they were falling – some were hundreds of yards to the left, others comparatively near to where we were eating, but our companions paid them no more attention than the bedraggled, pale-faced group working on the pieces of wood over by the guns.

"Mad squarehead gunners," said Rea, "trying to put the wind up us."

"What is *happening?*" said Zak again, urgently, looking from Rea and Smythe over to Haig and then back towards the landscape that separated us from the Germans.

"It's an intelligence test," muttered Rea.

The enemy barrage now seemed to be concentrated on the patch of ground between us and our own lines. I could see little purpose in their blasting a few hundred acres of barren French soil and, since there now seemed some design to the way in which the shells were falling, I said to Rea: "Why are they shelling that bit?"

"They're attacking Charollais Wood of course, old boy," he said.

"I thought we were attacking Charollais Wood," I said. "I thought it was supposed to be the other side of *our* lines."

"Look," said Rea, seizing a piece of bread, "no one knows where Charollais Wood is or was or shall be any more. Charollais Wood is a movable bloody feast, OK?"

And he indicated the group of men by the guns. They had moved forward from the rise and were flopped down on their bellies preparing to crawl out into the ground ahead of us, clutching their pieces of wood. I should think there were forty or fifty of them all together. Haig leaned forward in his saddle like a man watching a bowls match. All of the group round us averted their eyes from the food and looked up. As they did so the enemy barrage stopped abruptly, transforming the scene back into the pastoral. Even the depredations of the explosives now seemed a logical feature of the landscape.

The silence lengthened. Then, moving in groups of three and four, the men began to crawl out into the empty stretch of ground, clutching the piece of wood to them. They looked like moths clinging to the side of a wall, so infinitely patient, almost undetectable, were their movements forward. After they had gone beyond the first slope, you would have thought there was nothing out there moving. Our group, apart from Zak, had their eyes fixed on the last position of the men carrying the wood. Zak was squeezing his hands together and murmuring, rather theatrically, "Jesus God...."

It seemed an age before, in the far distance, halfway between our artillery and our lines, a line of ragged props wobbled upwards from the earth. Still there was no fire from either side. If any of this was visible to the Germans, if they suspected that the line of homemade wooden trees was some secret weapon, they had not yet evolved a military response to it. The men stood there in the blue and gold day, black shadows against the sun.

I looked round at Haig. He was studying a huge field map. He looked puzzled.

"What", I heard him say, "is the exact position of the wood?"

The man on the horse next to him peered over his shoulder. "It should", he said, "be fifteen degrees west-south-west of the salient at Ondoise-les-Marbres."

Haig sucked his moustache thoughtfully and looked out towards the "wood".

"Well, it isn't," he said. "It isn't anything *like* fifteen degrees west-south-west of the Ondoise salient."

"It should be, sir," said the man next to him.

"Yes," said Haig, "it should be."

I heard Rea muttering behind me. "If it isn't, the map must be wrong. And if the map's wrong you never know where it'll end. We could be in the bloody Transvaal or halfway up the Bloemfontein Road. We could be in the Arctic. A man has to have some standards...."

Haig stopped chewing his moustache. "Tell them to move it to that position", he said eventually, "on the double."

"Sir," said the man.

Eventually a runner departed for the wood. Now that the guns had stopped, it seemed impossible that they would ever start again.

The figure made its way down to the group of men and, in a few minutes, the line, this time making no attempt at concealment, staggered nearer to the beginnings of our lines. Now almost out of vision, the men were no longer as prominent. All we could see was the line of shapes and it seemed quite natural when Smythe said: "Christ – the bloody wood's cutting it a bit fine, don't you think?"

There was general agreement that the wood was moving out from our lines and into no man's land, but as people seemed unable to agree precisely where our lines ended, it was hard to understand why they all seemed so certain about the position of the trees. From this distance (had they been further camouflaged on the way?) they looked even more like trees, apart from their habit of shuffling from side to side like a formation-dance team. I looked back at Haig, but he was bent over the map, his shoulders hunched. He seemed to have lost interest in Charollais Wood.

Rea had opened a bottle of white wine and everyone had started to get drunk. Exhausted by staring out towards the Germans, I got hold of a glass and, abandoning the attempt to understand what was going on, began to drink as well. Behind us, Haig, still absorbed in the map on his knees, allowed his horse to wander over towards the wagons.

"Where's *he* off to?" said Zak.

"He's gone to change his underpants," said Rea.

"Oh, don't start on that again," said Smythe.

"He has," said Rea, giving Zak a meaning glance, "because enemy agents have befouled them beyond all recognition. They have coated them in slime, they have anointed them with treacle, they have injected them with venereal disease, they have – "

Behind us, next to the guns, was a platoon of men. I could not see where they had come from but they looked cleaner and younger and smarter than the group who had just departed. The officer in charge was supervising the loading of one of the guns.

"What's up?" One of our party called to them.

"Barrage, old boy," said the officer, "on cue."

"Yes?" said Rea. His moon face was reddened with the wine. Someone had passed round a hip flask containing neat brandy. Flies buzzed around the remnants of our meal. The officer stood to attention and began reading from a piece of paper: "Commence firing on target west-south-west Ondoise salient."

A man next to him who had a pair of binoculars trained on the horizon said: "Charollais Wood, sir. I see it now."

"Commence to fire – "

I was halfway on my feet when the guns began. Zak was screaming something – I can't remember what it was. But, whether it was the wine or the nonchalance of my companions, I found myself unsure as to what might be the real significance of the distant flashes over in the distance on the hummocky waste before us. That black shape on the horizon probably *was* a wood, wasn't it? When I remember that day now, I sometimes convince myself it was the Germans who opened fire as the ragged line of men staggered out of the trenches towards them, holding Charollais Wood above them in the sunlight. But who or what or why or when the attack began does not really signify, because I was far enough away from it all not to understand it. And I was far enough away from it all to survive.

I myself lost interest in the fate of Charollais Wood, almost immediately, for just as our guns opened fire, there was an evil whistle, a shout of "Look out!" and only a few yards to my left Captain Rea rose up into the air like some medieval vision or a fairground performer. Earth, bread, meat, shattered glass and shreds of cloth materialized in a spray around him, and his peaked cap soared away from his head as if twitched off by elastic held by an unseen giant hand. For a brief second Rea hung above us, pregnant with some divine power, and almost immediately began to fall. When he fell I could see that he was mortal, that his chest was coming into scarlet flower and that his teeth and eyes were being broken out of his head in obscene, fleshly lumps. His head – or what was left of it – at an almost perky angle to the rest of his body, hung for what seemed an age, connected only by shattered rags of skin to the body.

Flung back by the force of the shell's impact, I gazed up at what had been a man, disintegrating violently before my eyes. I had time, such is the leisured pace inflicted on us by tragedy, to notice him fall and bounce, for his head to smack down on the ground and all that wit, disdain and precision to dissolve into so much bloody junk. I did not notice much after that, except that all around me men were falling. At first I thought some were stooping to pick up food from the ground, so easy and natural did their descent appear. Others wore a puzzled look, as if they had just remembered there was something they ought to do but had not done. Quite a few had dazed smiles on their faces.

Over to our right I could see the guns jerking. A cloud of smoke hung over my immediate surroundings, beyond which I could see disordered shapes of men, some shouting, some running, all, after the initial impact, beginning to move oh so slowly into unreal life. The horses were wild with fear. I heard one whinnying in the clouds of smoke behind me, its naked terror oddly offset by the noises of soldiers trying to make sense of all this.

"Over here, sir. . . ."

"Move that detail. . . . Move. . . ."

Smythe passed me. His hair was singed and his eyes distorted. In his right hand he held a chicken leg. He did not seem to have a clear idea of where he might be going. I looked round for Zak and, as I did so, something clouted me from behind and forced me to the ground. I heard another of those evil whistles and another of those terrifying, ragged explosions. It was only then I realized that Zak was on top of me forcing my face into the earth. "Keep down," he was shrieking.

When I finally turned my head and looked up I saw that Zak's mouth was ajar and his eyes were as bright as ever. He appeared to be unharmed. I felt myself carefully and discovered that I, too, had two arms, two legs and, for the moment anyway, my head was still connected to my body.

Away to our left men in blue were scurrying round the remains of the picnic. Like flies, fearful of human intervention, they darted in to the mounds of food, grabbed armfuls of cakes, bread, bottles and cheeses and hared to the waiting wagons. Although some men in peaked hats were shouting and other men in peaked hats were running to and fro with great urgency, there seemed to be no system to the retreat, if this was a retreat.

"Make for the wagons!" Zak was shouting.

I looked around for Haig. I had the idea that if we were near him we might be all right. He was nowhere to be seen. Zak was worming his way on his belly over to where the wagons were. It was now possible to see that the shells had spared the baggage and had inflicted casualties only on people. The place looked now rather like some royal garden party, interrupted by revolution – glasses and cream cakes smeared in the mud next to figures whose temples had been scooped away or who lay, moaning, clutching an arm or a leg, raising their hands to other figures who passed on in the confusion.

I crawled as close to Zak as I could. The shells were now falling short and, behind us, our guns had begun to fire regularly again. I had the absurd idea that if we kept firing, we could silence these terrifying intruders, block out all this unwelcome, shattering metal, and to this end I began to mouth a senseless rhyme – the kind of spell that children cast to help them through a difficult lesson or a lonely patch on a dark road.

> Bang bang
> You're dead
> Knock a German
> On the head
> Bang bang
> You're dead
> Knock a German –

Zak was shouting something at me. To my horror I realized I had been chanting aloud. Did he think I'd lost my nerve? I tried to concentrate on his face, the dark, sharp lines of his profile. That seemed to help. As I watched him he got to his feet and squared up to the distance between us and the wagons. Some of them were already starting to move away, singly, and rattle off towards the dirt-road, while officers on horseback attempted vainly to shepherd them back in the direction of the mêlée. But such attempts were useless. The wagons seemed to have acquired a life of their own and jostled for position like terrified sheep.

"Run!" Zak was calling to me.

I realized I was still lying flat on the ground. Slowly and stupidly I saw that there were now only three or four wagons left, that the officers had given up the attempt to control the flight, and that the whole of Haig's entourage was scrambling over each other in a desperate attempt to reach the comparative safety of the first bend in the road. I looked to my left and saw Smythe, who had recovered his composure, but not his chicken leg.

"Run!" said Zak again.

"GHQ at Montreuil", said Smythe thoughtfully, "is used to every aspect of modern warfare – except of course being fired at. Being killed is not a situation the General Staff contemplates with regard to itself."

"RUN!" screamed Zak.

"You can bet your last bottle of champagne", said Smythe, "that the battle of Charollais Wood will not receive the attention of historians, military or otherwise. I think we may confidently predict, old boy, that – "

He stopped suddenly. I saw that the shells had started to fall on the other side of the wagons and that the column, or what was left of it, had wheeled over to the right in an attempt to avoid the danger. Many of the horses, trapped in the shafts of the wagons, were bucking and kicking uncontrollably, forcing their drivers back into the line. There was now only one wagon within reach. There was a horse attached to it, but no driver. The horse seemed unaware of what was going on around and browsed peaceably at a rough tussock of grass. I looked back at Smythe. To my horror I saw that he was crying.

"RUN!" screamed Zak again.

I got to my feet at last. Smythe, to my surprise, did not follow me. The measured fluency of his speech had given way to stark, dumb terror. I pulled at his sleeve.

"COME ON!" I shouted at him.

"I can't," he whispered. "I can't."

Zak was running back towards us. Pushing me roughly off in the direction of the wagon, he yanked Smythe up and yelled something at him. Then the two of them started after me, Zak pushing and punching the other forward, as if Smythe was a recalcitrant donkey. When I looked back at them I could see that Rea's companion had been hit in the leg.

I got to the wagon first. I pulled myself over the side and sat there, looking back at the panorama behind me. The German guns had realigned themselves on the remains of the lunch party and shell after shell was scoring direct hit after direct hit on mousses, blanc-manges, biscuits and the human debris that had been halfway through digesting it. Zak and Smythe clambered aboard.

"How do you move this thing?" snapped Zak to Smythe.

Smythe goggled at him. When he spoke his voice sounded high-pitched, even ladylike. "For a Jewboy", he said, "you're fearfully brave."

Zak turned away from him and shook the reins. The horse turned its head, looked at the three of us and shook itself.

"It likes it here," said Zak grimly.

"Shot and shell," said Smythe faintly. "Shot and shell."

Zak shook the reins again. After another slow look backwards the horse ambled off. Zak leaned forward holding the reins loosely and the creature followed the last of the column which was now approaching a bend in the road. It seemed to know where it was going for, although we were three or four hundred yards behind the main group, when the horse reached the road, it broke into a feeble imitation of a trot and clipped after the rest of them, without once looking back at its cargo.

Smythe was gripping the high sides of the wagon. His face was a dull, putty colour.

"Look at his wound," said Zak.

I looked down. The lower part of his right leg had been lacerated by a fragment of metal. Although I could see the jagged edges of the shell, jutting out of his skin like a crab buried in the sand, there did not seem to be as much blood as I had expected. "Better leave it. . . ." I said to Smythe. He didn't hear me. He was looking out at the countryside with the weary expression of a very old man. Unbidden, the image of Rea rising from the ground like an angel came back to me. I felt suddenly sick.

After a few miles the countryside shamelessly reasserted itself. There were fields and houses and men with donkeys. There was corn, there were lines of poplars – there were even children. I looked at a group of them by a gate. They were wearing blue denim smocks. They waved at us. Smythe waved back. For some reason this gesture of his irritated me beyond belief. The wagon jolted on, past poppies flowering at the roadside and the fields, loud with insects and baked with sun. I looked ahead but could see no sign of the column.

"Do you think this horse knows the way back?" I said.

"The way back to where?" said Zak.

"To the château."

"Why should we want to go to the château?"

"Because. . . ."

He glared at me. I realized with a shock that I had been happy there. If we weren't going to the château, I wondered, where were we going? As if in answer to my unspoken question, Zak said: "Why don't we go where the horse wants to? The horse has as much idea as anyone else of what is best for us or anyone else for that matter. My God, why don't they put the damned horse in charge of the army? The horse would make as good a job of it as – "

Zak shook his head. He had imitated not only Rea's style of address but also his delivery. It was as if our dead companion had suddenly entered the wagon.

We could not get rid of Rea's ghost throughout that ride. He sat with us as the horse ambled on in the late afternoon sun. I could hear his mocking, delicate voice, as the horse took turn after turn and Smythe, his head lolling over the side of the wagon, grinned foolishly out at the view.

"So you're *lost*. It's no bad thing to be lost. Everyone's bloody well lost, old boy. Don't worry about being lost at all, old man. . . ."

Quite quickly it was quite clear that we were lost. The horse was very good at looking as if it knew where it was going but, in fact, it had even less sense of direction than the Commander-in-Chief of the Armed Forces. When we had been through the same village square three times, the horse finally gave up the pretence and looked back at us through the shafts in a pleading, apologetic sort of way.

"Giddy up. . . ." I said feebly.

The horse looked back at me glumly.

"I want to go wee wee," said Smythe.

"Go then," said Zak flatly.

Zak jumped down from the wagon and looked back down the stretch of road that led out of the village we had just left.

"What do we do now?" I said.

Isaac chewed his lip. "We head back."

"Back where?"

"London, stupid," he said.

When he said the word "London" I saw the city as from my bedroom high above the river. I saw the faces of the crowds on the streets near us, heard the noise of Whitechapel Market and, in the still heat of the afternoon, felt the cool of our kitchen.

"Can we?"

"Of course," said Zak, "you can do anything you want to. If you're alive to do it."

There is an Indian tribe (or if there isn't, there should be) who believe that the spirits of the dead can be appropriated by their friends or enemies.

I don't know which of us took Captain Rea's bravery, indifference, or just contempt. For a long time I thought it was Zak who had learned from him, without seeming to. I think now that Rea was as elusive in death as he had been in life. But I do know that, as we stood together on that empty stretch of road, there seemed to be some ghost to encourage us. Or perhaps it is simply that we were close enough to Rea's generation to be part of it, to know without being able to formulate such an idea for ourselves that those who are not destroyed physically by warfare suffer in other, perhaps crueller ways. "Get out," his ghost said to us. "For God's sake just cut and bloody run, old boy."

When, much later, I read the poets of the First War I wanted to intercede on their behalf, to climb back into history and yell at them to cut and run before it was too late.

It was too late for Smythe, that was for certain.

After Zak and I had finished pacing up and down the road and arguing about which direction to take for the coast, I went back to the wagon in order to tell Smythe that we were not going back to Montreuil. We had some idea of taking him to a farmhouse and telling them that we had to return to our unit, but first, we were agreed we would have to tell him of our decision. It didn't occur to us that he would attempt to oppose it.

"Smythe," I said (back at Montreuil I had sometimes called him "sir" but there didn't seem much point in such titles now), "we're going back."

Suddenly Smythe seemed to be wide awake. "Going back where?" he said.

"Home," I said. "London."

Smythe winced as I said this. I couldn't fathom whether it was what I had said or his wound that was troubling him. "You can't," he said, finally.

Zak had joined us. "Oh yes we can," he said.

"Listen, Jewboy," said Smythe, "you don't just cut and run."

Zak looked at him patiently. "Do you want us to find you a doctor?" he said.

"What do you mean, Jewboy?" said Smythe.

"I mean", said Zak, with even more patience, "that if you want us to get you a doctor we will. But you will have to give us your word as an English gentleman that you won't mention us to anyone."

Smythe shifted in his place in the wagon. He appeared to think he was in control of this situation. I could not help thinking that, to judge from the immense patience and suppressed fury of Zak's manner, he was mistaken.

"What if I won't?" said Smythe.

"Then I give you my word as a Jewboy", said Zak, "that we will take you into a barn down the road and finish you off."

"I don't die easy," said Smythe, who had obviously decided he was in some romantic epic. Perhaps he felt that here, at last, was an enemy worthy of him. I tugged Zak away from him down the battered country road. We sat in the hedgerow, among tall, whitened grasses. Smythe looked down at us from the wagon. He looked, I thought, a bit like a granny who has decided to be awkward.

"We can't kill him," I whispered.

"We'll have to", said Zak, "if he won't shut up, we'll have to."

"But – "

"It's that or go back with him."

I could not imagine how you set about killing someone. The mere mention of London had reduced me to pulp. Would we have to pull at his leg? Hit him on the head with something? It might take hours and even then there was always the possibility that he would recover. Death, which had seemed so easy and graceful an hour ago, now seemed an insurmountable obstacle, a barrier none of us would ever cross.

"What do we do?"

"Suffocate him. Strangle his fat neck. I don't know."

"That's. . . ."

"What?"

I couldn't say it was wrong. Part of me felt it was the only practical thing to do, now that the chance of leaving had been offered to me. Indeed, home, a place I had not considered for months, had now become in the short time since it had been mentioned an almost physical ache. Abandoning the problem of Smythe for a moment, I said: "Which way do we go, though?"

"We ride till we reach a main road," said Zak. "Then we head for the coast."

"Have you done this sort of thing before?"

Zak grinned. "Only in my dreams."

I did feel as if I was in one of Zak's dreams. The lurid colours of the flowers around us, the grotesque figure in the wagon, the sensation that at any minute anything might happen; these were part of his world, not mine. Miserably, I said: "I'll ask him again."

Zak grinned. "He'll do what he's told."

I went over to Smythe. "Look," I said, "I know my friend is a bit awkward sometimes. He's very hot-tempered. He gets excitable. But I think he means it. I mean I think he won't stay. It's nothing to do with us, you see. It's all a grotesque accident."

I started to tell him the story of the laundry basket. Whether it was the stress or the heat or simply the fact that it is impossible to tell the same story twice in exactly the same way, I altered some of the details. Indeed, I became quite carried away with what I called "our adventures". In my version of the story we had stowed away deliberately, been discovered by customs officials, nearly drowned, rescued.... As I tried to explain our presence, I found I was using the first personal pronoun far more than usual. I, it appeared, had views on the war, on the strategy employed by Haig, on any number of questions. I cannot remember what the views were; all I can remember is this gaunt, pallid figure in shabby khaki smiling appeasingly, spreading his arms as he talks to a fat young man with a wounded leg on an empty road in northern France. I think I thought, as I so often do, that I could persuade him. That if I talked for long enough maybe the road, the wagon, the sun and the memory of Rea's neck, ribboned with blood, would disappear.

I realized that he was being more than usually quiet. I found his pose, an affected stare off at the sky, somewhat irritating, but assumed that sooner or later he would turn and look at me. It wasn't until I saw his mouth that I realized I would not be able to persuade Captain Smythe of anything. It had dropped open dramatically, the way my mother's did when she fell asleep in the chair by the fire. As wide and neutral as a fire-grate, Smythe's mouth signalled apathy, nothingness. It drew attention up to the rest of his face – the curiously waxen cheeks and the eyes that looked and looked and looked, but were straining after a light that comes from within. The

111

only thing Captain Smythe lacked was an expression. He was stone dead.

Zak was standing beside me. "What were you on about?" he said.

"I don't know," I said.

"I sometimes think you're hardly here at all," said Zak.

I didn't feel able to disagree with this.

"The first thing to do", said Zak, "is to get rid of the body."

"Yes," I said.

"Get his feet."

Captain Smythe was a stout man. At first he proved almost impossible to shift.

"Stop holding him as if he was a prayer book," snapped Zak.

In the end we poured him over the side of the wagon. He fell on to the road head first and his limbs fell around him, inanimate, careless of their position. We jumped down and began to roll him towards the side of the road. I had some idea that it would be more decent to leave him in the long grass. It seemed wrong to leave those eyes staring up so publicly at the sky. Zak said this was stupid and abandoned the attempt. "You'll want to bury him next," he said.

In the end we didn't even close his eyes, but left him there, somewhere in France, his mouth open like a fish, his fingers strewn in the white dust of the road, lifeless as sausages.

When we got up into the wagon, Zak shook the reins. The horse looked round at us and then lowered its head to the road. It was clearly either a very stupid or a very intelligent animal.

"Giddy up!" I said.

The horse did not move. Zak got to his feet, leaned over the front of the wagon and gave it a shrewd blow to the left buttock. Almost immediately, as if this was some form of courtesy it had been waiting for so that honour might be satisfied and it could get on with the business of pleasing its master, the beast trotted off down the road, its chest high, its hooves neatly and precisely lifted from the track.

"Home, James," said Zak.

The thing I recall most clearly about that journey is not the discomfort, which was considerable, or the scenery, which was unmemorable, or the conversation, which was strained, but the horse. I have never liked animals particularly, although I feel a certain affinity with lizards and fish, and horses in general are too large to take seriously, but this horse, named after the first five hours, Harold, will remain with me longer than many equally casual acquaintances.

The first remarkable thing about it was that it did not seem to eat anything. It showed no inclination to drink, defecate, foam at the mouth, or do anything to interfere with its forward progress between the shafts. It also seemed to have a definite idea of where it was going. It did not respond to pressure from the reins to left or right. When Zak tried to do this, the beast looked back at us reproachfully. At junctions it never wavered, but turned left or right as if it had passed this way before. Once or twice, at crossroads, I saw it lower its head and paw the ground, but otherwise the creature proceeded, without assistance from us, in a direction that we could tell from the sun was roughly north-west. After a while we gave up the pretence of being in control of the vehicle and, slumped against the back wall of the wagon, fell into deep sleep, as the sun rolled away behind the poplars on the skyline and red and grey scraps of cloud draped themselves artistically above the corner of the earth.

* * *

I sometimes think the whole of that ride did not happen to me at all but is part of a film that I saw in 1937. It was a very bad film called *Dick Turpin and Estella* but it made a great impression on me. It introduced to the screen an actor called Kent Weald and the film marked both his screen début and the final, irrevocable end of his career. Weald had acquired, shortly before the film was made, "the most perfect nose in history" from a cosmetic surgeon called Dieter Schalkeeld, still, I have no doubt, practising in the hills of California. There was, at the time, a much publicized controversy as to whether Weald's nose was too short and Schalkeeld lengthened it by two inches, thereby causing his client to resemble, in the words of one cinema critic, "the Wicked Witch of the West on a bad day".

What makes me doubt the authenticity of my memory in this instance is that, although I can remember how the journey began, I cannot for the life of me think how we got off that damned wagon. When I puzzle over it now I sometimes wonder whether the horse did not take us to Boulogne harbour and buy us both tickets on the night ferry. I seem to see it now, rearing up on the harbour waving its hoof at us and saying things like "One day mankind will talk to the animals."

This task I have set myself is hopeless. What I remember always comes in scenes, in fragments of narrative, in the lying habits that guide our thoughts. Someone once said that it was almost impossible to visualize a picture entitled *Goethe Writes a Symphony*, which implies that the pictures we use to help us think must mean something. I am very afraid that they mean nothing, that most of the traffic of our mind, most of the time, is slogans and clichés. They wind themselves about our memories, transforming us into heroes or villains or whatever it is humans are supposed to be.

Alan, for instance, tells me he has a degree from Berlin University. It's possible. It's even likely. But I sometimes feel, as I look at his neat profile, that it's what he thinks he ought to have. It's too neat. We get the past we want, as I keep telling them here at the M.o.I.

I'm staring at the blank sheet of paper I slipped into the typewriter. I still haven't done that press release. At any moment Alan's face will appear halfway up the side of the door and say: "Done that release yet, old boy?"

I'm afraid I haven't even started it, Alan. I'm trying to describe my past. Even though I can't remember what it is, I have the right to sit, vacant-mouthed, at my desk and dream, don't I? Isn't that what we are fighting this war for, Alan? For a free society? For the freedom to be absolutely and totally confused about what we are doing? For the freedom to stare off into space and allow one's mind to empty completely?

One thing about the grey building I inhabit (it is not part of the M.o.I. proper but a commandeered office block to the north of High Holborn) is that, as befits a nation fighting for its life – or rather another nation's – no one in it takes lunch or has any fun. There is the feeling that leisure – especially for those out of uniform – is morally degenerate. The head of our section (a Scot called Dunblane, who regards Alan with the greatest suspicion) takes ten minutes to turn around the square a hundred yards or so to the north of us, on his face an expression that seems to say I AM DOING THIS PURELY AND SIMPLY TO CONSERVE PHYSICAL ENERGY AND STRENGTH FOR THE DURATION OF HOSTILITIES.

On one of my rare trips out of the city last year, I recall looking around the railway carriage, listening to the endless talk about the war, the war, the war, and feeling a deep contempt for those who imagined they were sharing in an adventure. I went to the window of the carriage and looked out as the gritty smoke of the engine swam past and noted how even that simple gesture – in these circumstances – managed to acquire a ludicrous, symbolic dimension. THINKING ABOUT THE WAR A PROPAGANDA WORKER GOES DEEP INTO HIS OWN THOUGHTS. We live in a society where even office files, memoranda and meetings about nothing are considered to have heroic status. We are working for something. We have answered the call. All of us, apart from a few anarchists whose papers are banned and who risk imprisonment for their views, are working for the total defeat and destruction of a once civilized nation.

Sometimes I think I should hand in my notice and return to newspapers. But I am not the sort of journalist to be sent to observe the liberation of Paris. Even on a paper I would end up at a desk very like this, sitting opposite someone very like Alan whose job it would be to advise me whether to print this or that story.

Dates confuse me. I'm almost sure it was 1916 when we left Charollais Wood for the coast. But I'm also fairly positive that it was 1918 when we reached Ombrac. I'm sure about that because when we got back to London the war was over. It is, of course, possible that the Channel crossing took two years. It certainly felt as if it did. But I do have an image of Zak and myself in a farmhouse, lying on separate beds, being tended by a girl called Mimi.

She can't have been called Mimi. I think *that* comes from a film called *The Brave Have Courage* starring a French actor called Hombert Julienne. But I know we were in a farmhouse. I know also that we were fed by the farmer, worked on the land and, late one night, attempted to seduce his daughter. I can see Zak getting larger and browner and more truculent by the day. I can see him lifting hay bales up on his shoulder and hurling them into the barn. I can see him drinking cider in the big, cool kitchen. I can see the two of us manhandling a pig into the yard and the farmer's daughter squealing with delight as we cut the pig's throat. I can see Zak on a tractor in –

Hang on. Did they have tractors in 1915? Weren't they invented by an American serviceman in 1923?

One image that smells to me like the real thing is of Zak and the farmer, by the side of a road in the early morning, arguing about money. Next to them (*that* was it) the horse. Zak bought us into the farm. The two of them haggled for hours over the price. That picture feels right because I know that when we were in France Zak led us, always. And when I think of him spitting on his palm and closing the deal I remember that I was becoming frightened of him and of what he might become.

Gypsies spit on their palms to close deals, don't they? I don't think Zak can have done anything like that.

What is worrying me is that today I am supposed to have lunch with Alan. "Lunch" but not pre-war lunch. Not four bottles and staggering out into Soho in the late glare of the afternoon. Like the coffee and the wine and the cigarettes, it is a ghastly parody of pre-war lunch, a grim mockery of thirties lunch. We go to an Italian place in Charlotte Street and have what Alan calls "automatic" Beaujolais and "ersatz" spaghetti. In return for this favour (he pays), Alan lectures me about my failings.

He is so like Zak. Is that why I argue with him so much? Is that why I am so deliberately awkward? He lives in a world dominated by causes and simplicities. He thinks he knows what he means by the word "morality" and, sometimes, when I catch him wincing at a flippant or cynical remark of mine, I want to say, "Don't think I don't want the certainties of your life, Alan. Don't think I don't want to believe the Germans are three-headed monsters. It would make me feel easier about the millions of tons of high explosives we are dropping on them every night. But I am afraid my life has not been a simple affair. All the great moral gestures I have witnessed have been born of cruelties and weaknesses that seem to negate them."

Auschwitz, he says to me in the pub over the road. He's seen some papers about a place called Auschwitz. I tell him to tell them, not me! The fact is that I do not trust the evidence of my own eyes any more. What other people tell me I more or less assume must be lies, especially if it is concerned with politics.

The night we left the farm Zak and I had a bitter argument. I, as usual, did not want to go. I never want to leave anywhere where I have been for more than two or three weeks. I couldn't, either, get out of Zak what were his reasons for wishing to leave. It was a cold, spring afternoon, though whether it was the spring after we arrived there or the one beyond I could not say. Agricultural time takes little account of such things. Indeed the farmer had been most surprised by our uniforms, and was even more surprised to hear there was a war on. "Where?" he had asked, in dumbshow. And we had gestured vaguely over our shoulders, not entirely sure ourselves from which direction we had come.

"We've got to go," said Zak.

We were sitting in the barn on a pile of straw. Through the open door we could see the farmer's daughter throwing stones. Whether her name was Mimi or not she certainly looked like a Mimi. She had long, yellow plaits and a full skirt that, even when she was in the farmyard, made her look like something from a fashion show. She was throwing the stones at one of the chickens, as it tensed its neck through the puddles, looking for scraps of food. When she made it squawk or flap its wings, she laughed, sweetly. I suppose she was about seven.

"Why?"

"Doesn't it mean anything to you, Amos?"

"What?"

"What we've seen. What's happened to us."

I shrugged. Zak got up and went to the door. When he got there the little girl grinned up at him. He shook his finger at her and she giggled. Zak turned to me. "First we throw stones at things, then at each other, then whole nations go mad. Simply mad."

"Yes," I said flatly.

Zak picked up a stone. He sent it skimming over the trees beyond the yard, high in the air, as if it contained some message to someone out there, beyond the charmed circle of the farm.

"Doesn't it mean anything to you?"

I didn't have to ask what he meant. But Rea was dead. I didn't see how running back to England was going to help him. Since Rea's death, anyway, Zak had become rather proprietorial about his memory. They were the best of friends now the man was no longer there to argue with him.

"We've got to *do* something."

"Like what?"

"I don't know what. But something."

He picked up another stone and sent it off after the first one. It went even higher this time, up and over the thin leafed trees, up into the drab spring world to which Zak was so anxious to return.

"You want to be careful," I said. "You never know where those might land."

I went with him of course. I always did what he said in the end. But when I found he had stolen money from the iron box underneath the farmer's bed, I made *my* moral gesture. We were walking up a narrow lane towards the railway station in the nearby town.

"You shouldn't have done that," I said primly.

"How else are we going to get away?" said Zak.

"I – "

"Do you want to come?"

"Yes, but – "

"Then that's all there is to it, isn't there?"

Simple. I can hear Alan saying it now. You want to stop the Germans, don't you? Then get on with it. Rob, lie, cheat, steal, murder children. What do you think this is, you halfwit? A tea party?

Well, like a halfwit I went with him and stood beside him as he bought the ticket. Needless to say neither of us could speak a word of French. At first we tried telling him we wanted to go to England, but the man behind the counter had never heard of England. Then we tried talking about the Channel but this mystified him even further. Finally I said: "Tell him we want to go to the sea."

Zak mimed swimming enthusiastically. The man behind the counter looked at him. "Ombrac," he said.

For all we knew this could have been the name of a French exponent of the breast stroke. We looked helpful and waited for him to say some more. He did not. In the end we nodded and said, "Ombrac." The man nodded back curtly and gave us two tickets.

When the train finally came, it was full of well-dressed families, little girls in neat white dresses, fathers in stern black suits and little boys in white sailor-jackets, with the ageless impassivity of foreign children everywhere. I suppose it was Sunday. At each station more people boarded the train. Some families seemed to know each other and called across the compartment in greeting.

Others sat, complete and armoured against all intrusion. As the train heaved its way through station after station, leaving each uniquely empty, Zak and I dozed.

And then the sun came out from behind the clouds.

More and more I think it is only physical sensation that we recall. That I remember nothing faithfully between the moment in the barn when the girl was throwing stones at the puddle and the time when, pushing my face up to the window, I felt the spring again, heard in the distance the cry of seagulls.

The train, my tiredness, my unfamiliar clothes, Zak asleep next to me, all form themselves around that impression. And the cry of the gulls calls me on past a row of pastel-coloured villas, a line of sand-dunes scattered with rough bushes and on to a station as pretty as a village in a Grimm fairy tale, with a bright-red booking office, tubs of flowers and the holiday parties spilling out on to the platform, oblivious of time or war or anything except the prodigal light of spring.

OMBRAC, read the sign. OMBRAC.

Almost directly opposite the station, no more than a hundred yards away, was the sea. It had the aimless look I always associate with the English Channel, but the grey waves, curling in under the breeze, were polished to the colour of steel by the light, and the children ran from the toy station with excited cries. I pushed Zak awake. "What now?" I said.

"We get a boat," he said.

His confidence astonished me, who spend my life debating this or that point with myself and can always find a reason for avoiding action. Desperate situations mesmerize me. But Isaac, in those days, had the knack of balancing his energies to the demands of the occasion. I followed him out on to the platform. He stretched luxuriantly in the sea breeze and said: "Follow me."

At the far end of the beach, away from the town, the railway came to an end in a maze of sidings, signal boxes and abandoned wagons. There, too, as far as I could see, the road gave out, blending down into the sand so that it was impossible to tell quite where Man and Nature began their interference with the landscape. There were no houses here, but a line of boats drawn high up on to the beach and two or three figures down by the water's edge, standing, apparently at ease with each other and the grey waste beyond them. "That's the fishermen," said Zak, as if he had expected them to be there.

119

We started off down the rumpled sand and in a few minutes were stepping over rusty cables and picking our way through puddles of tar towards one of the boats. The men down by the waterside, who were wearing thick blue jerseys, had that slightly challenging expression I have often noticed on mariners, especially when they are discovered near the element over which they attempt to assert control. They had faces that were an open book of reference to past storms or long-gone calms and there was a forbidding steadiness about the way they pulled at their cigarettes and looked from us to the sea with equal impartiality.

"You talk to them," I said to Zak.

"Sssh," he said, and pointed ahead of us.

Beyond us the beach ran into the sky and the sea. There was nothing to limit the huge blocks of paleness but, over to the left, a crop of grass on top of the dunes and, near the water nearly half a mile away, a much larger boat than the ones that were near to us. This was nearer to the waterline than the others and I could see no sailors on or near it. Between the ship and the dunes I saw two figures coming towards us. One of them, from this distance, looked like a plump man in late middle age. The other, at first, I took for a soldier but as they drew closer I saw that he was wearing a grey chauffeur's uniform, modified by the addition of epaulettes, ribbons and what looked like medals. This, combined with the fact that he was wearing his peaked hat the wrong way round and that his trousers were so tight as to make the smallest movement indecent, impossible or both at the same time, gave the man the appearance of some roguish Confederate soldier from the civil war in America. He had a large beaky nose, a gaucho moustache and, as he approached us, his index finger went up to the left nostril in an indecently public manner.

The plump man with him had a soft, yearning expression. He carried a black cane, wore a black overcoat and had, to go with these fashion accessories, black hair and a black moustache. His face, however, was the colour of chalk. From time to time he stared away from his companion at the troubled sea, as if he was trying to forget some private sorrow. It was possible, of course, that he simply did not wish to look at his companion, who was, as well as picking his nose, shrugging and gesturing with obvious insincerity.

"Try them," said Zak suddenly.

"You what?"

"Try them. They look like your sort of people."

"What do you mean by that?"

"Oh you know – a couple of long-nosed ponces."

It was said in a jocular fashion. Nevertheless I decided to take it seriously. "That 'my sort of people', is it?"

"That's what they say about you back home, Amos."

This remark annoyed me. It implied that Zak had a whole host of other friends "back home" with whom he discussed my character. But one of the things about friendships like ours, that threaten to exclude the whole world, is that infidelity, unlimited by merely sexual constraints, becomes part of each word, thought or acquaintance made by each partner. Indeed, to talk of "our friendship" seems foolish. Zak and I, by now, were brothers, with all the jealousy, fear and love implied by that description.

"What who say about me?"

"The lads."

"Don't be stupid, Isaac. There aren't any *lads*. Not as far as you're concerned."

One of the things that had irritated me most about his remark was that he was absolutely correct. They did look like "my sort of people". Not the chauffeur, you understand, but his companion. He had seen me and a tiny spasm shook his face. The spasm converted itself into a smile of immense wistfulness. He turned to his companion and said something in French. He had quite a high voice, but the laborious, intricate rhythm in which he spoke gave his words an almost ecclesiastical dignity. I caught only the occasional word "...corrompre...dans la nuit vaste et surprenante...". I can't remember what he said. Only that it did not have the quality of other voices I had heard or of voices I have heard since. Listening to it was like falling asleep and yet knowing oneself awake and, as he spoke, the words seemed to melt into each other, like blancmange in the bath. Not only the words but the things meant by the words, whatever they might be, so that at times, hanging on the different, alien twists of what sounded like one vast sentence, a sentence as large-scale as a cathedral, I had the impression of not being attentive to language at all, but of undergoing some completely different sensual experience, like travelling on some mysterious, scenic railway, through woods, forests, mountains and plains, as strange as that poem I had come across in one of Isaac's father's books: "Caverns measureless to man...and...and...."

The plump man was still talking. I looked round for Zak but saw that he had backed away and was grinning at me satirically. He held out his hand in a mocking invitation towards the two men. For some reason this was my party. I turned back to the white-faced man. I wanted to say something to Zak, but immediately I caught a whiff of the mysterious stranger's voice I was held, bewildered by its complexity and insistence. I was like someone longing for the painful but necessary resolution to a sonata, longing for the thing to explain itself, and yet aware that, when the end came, it would solve nothing, that the only real pleasure was in the waiting, in the twists and turns of these qualified statements and subordinate clauses. In an attempt to break the spell I shut my eyes and said in a loud voice, "English. We are English."

The plump man broke off and looked at me in a distant, grief-stricken way, as if I had just prodded him in the stomach. For a moment I thought he was going to burst into tears but instead he studied the sand in front of him, prodding at it with his stick. Meanwhile the chauffeur brightened up considerably. "English johnny..." he said, rather ingratiatingly, "vair gude fer you know what, OK?"

I didn't like the sound of this man's voice at all. I wouldn't have said his accent was French, more a glottal Mediterranean stew of slippery vowels, missed consonants and sudden wild twangings that could have been American. From time to time, in the middle of all this, came a few bars of pure Cockney. Spittle dribbled down his chin as he talked. Even from ten yards away you could smell wine, garlic and tobacco smoke on his breath, while his body gave off the odour of pepper and scent. As he talked he rolled his eyes in the direction of the plump man and, when he thought he was not being observed, raised his busy eyebrows in a way I had seen my mother do when tiresome neighbours came to call.

"Eeez heez feerst outtin' fer yeers!" said the chauffeur, whose trousers, I now saw, were bottle green, "bu' don' tell nabady 'bout eet, huh?"

I was growing to dislike this person intensely, but the chalk-faced man with the moustache had now fallen silent. I tried to engage his attention but he seemed preoccupied with a few grains of sand that had attached themselves to the toe of his highly polished boot. As my eyes wandered towards the plump man's face, his companion lowered his head and blocked my gaze with a horrifyingly intimate grimace.

"'Ee wanser leef een theesa corka linea rheum, woujer b'leeve?" said the chauffeur, who was in his way as difficult to understand as the plump man. "Wa' a f—in' joke, eh?"

His English was certainly idiomatic.

"We want to get to England", I said reedily, "and were looking for a boat."

Even as I spoke, from the large, isolated boat over to our right an enormous man in yellow leggings emerged. He was wearing not only yellow leggings but a yellow oilskin top and a broad, yellow sou'wester. He had a circular, red, jolly face and in his right hand held a skein of fishing nets which he hurled with some vigour into the back of the boat. The chauffeur looked over his shoulder at the boat and sneered. "I know 'eem vair well," he said. "'e's a gude sailor boy – bend ovair fer 'arf a dollar, know wot I mean, poof johnny Eeengleesh boy, hein?"

The plump man with the chalk face was pacing in a small circle and muttering to himself. His circles drew him farther and farther away from me and the chauffeur, until he was some thirty yards away close to the sea's edge, marking out patterns in the damp sand with his cane and from time to time looking up at the two of us with almost horrified curiosity. At last his eyes met mine. I looked into the black liquidity of that expression and saw, as on a cinema screen, my mother moving about the clean and empty flat, my father sitting in the armchair, his hands crossed above his groin, his eyes on the wall ahead of him. The man's expression trapped me in the way in which his voice had, summoning up all sorts of agonies and pleasures I thought I had long forgotten.

The chauffeur drew a hipflask from his uniform and said: "Cheers. Prost. My name's Albert. OK, Eeengleesh johnny?"

"OK," I said guardedly.

Then the man said, "Yew fin' me repolsive, hein?"

"Not at all," I said.

It had occurred to me that if he did know this man in the yellow oilskins, he might well provide us with an introduction and/or a means of escape from wherever we were on the French coast.

"Naw," said the man, "f—in' Eeengleesh poof johnnies queer couplea bastards, OK?"

"Of course," I said stiffly, not quite sure of what it was he wanted to say, but aware that I had better continue to be polite to him. He gestured contemptuously towards the plump man, who was now gazing out at the Channel as if it concealed the body of a loved one. "'e no gude fer f—in'. 'issa jussa Guermantes thees an' a Guermantes that I dunno why we 'ave ter come of thees place I dunno make you seeck reely no f—in' nightlife at all," he said.

We looked across at the plump man. I smiled helpfully. "How much", I said, "do you think it would cost to get a ride on a fishing boat?"

The chauffeur who had called himself Albert grinned widely and scoured his left nostril with his index finger. I looked back towards Isaac who was standing on the sand behind me. The sea wind stirred his hair and his eyes were shining with amusement. He looked Mephistophelean. I made a questioning gesture at him but he merely smiled and once again indicated the two men, as if to say again: "This is your affair."

"Twenny dollair saz yer right," said Albert. "Yew come be'in' a boat weeth me I see yer right weeth poof johnny sailor boy, OK? I 'ad 'im more times than yew 'ad 'ot dinnair!"

Albert leered across at the man in the yellow oilskins, who gazed back at him impassively. I looked across at the man with the chalk-white face. Albert sniffed.

"Why", I said primly, "do you want to go behind the boat with me?"

Albert leered again and indicated his companion at the sea's edge with a contemptuous gesture of the thumb and forefinger. "You like tha' twenty-four hours a day?" he said. "Tha' yer idea of a good time? Blimey. Eats a biscuit and goes on abaht 'is pajamas. I arst yer."

The man by the sea turned back to us for a moment. He looked like a harlequin in a pantomime. His eyes met mine and I grinned awkwardly. He did not grin back but turned back to the sea, leaving me to the chauffeur. Whatever it was this person wished to do behind the boat (and I was beginning to have a fairly good idea of what it might be), I felt that I would probably be able to talk him out of it. I looked over at Zak again and made the universally accepted gesture for money. Zak grinned. Then I nodded at Albert and we went over to the boat occupied by the man in yellow.

When we got to the boat, its owner greeted us with a wave and a glassy smile. He said something in French and disappeared below deck, giving us as he went the thumbs-up sign. Seen at close hand the man in oilskins was even more unprepossessing than the chauffeur – he had the look of a slightly shifty St Bernard dog. But, as soon as Albert and I were on the far side of the boat and out of view of the rest of the beach, I forgot all about him. For Albert, after a rapid, furtive glance around to confirm that we were unobserved, began to take off his jodhpurs, revealing a pair of long, white underpants and legs as hairy as a South American spider's. He pointed to the crotch and said in a hoarse voice: "Peecneec?"

It was now no longer possible to ignore the implications of his behaviour. "I don't want to go on a picnic," I said.

Albert gestured more violently towards his crotch. "No no no," he said, "peecneec." He made his behaviour even more explicit by taking off his shirt and his vest. "Hew fin' a' me repolsive?" he said, rather plaintively.

"It's not that," I said. "It's just that. . . ."

He flipped out his penis. It was the biggest one I have ever seen in my life. Apart from that I don't think I can bring myself to say anything about it. He started to beat it up and down as if it were a length of garden hose.

"For God's sake. . . ." I said, sounding rather shrill.

"You likea preeka uppa your bum?" he asked artfully.

"No," I said, as conversationally as I could. "No thank you."

"Carm on," he said. "Eeengleesh boy gude fer a f—in' any day, all right? OK? 'ow abert it?"

Big as his penis had seemed at first, it was now even bigger and, having discarded his hat, Albert was rolling it between the flattened palms of both hands, as if he were rolling a cigar. It was getting red and looked as though it might explode at any moment. I averted my eyes. One encouraging thing about all of this was that now he was involved so closely with himself that the man did not appear to mind that my participation in the proceedings was minimal. As I turned my eyes away I heard him grunt, "Eeengleesh boy like ter watch, eh? Good kicks ter see me pull it abaht ver place, eh, johnny?"

I tried to nod. It was obviously important not to disturb his concentration in any way. And then, to my intense relief, I heard a noise somewhere between a yodel and a grunt and, with a thud, Albert hit the ground. When I looked again he was lying in the sand with a beatific expression on his face, his legs up in the air, scratching his exposed behind, wiping semen off his jacket in a calm, reflective manner. "Bluddy gude," he was saying. "I really come a lot. Nexa time you do eet an' I watch, OK, poof Eeengleesh johnny?"

"Of course," I said, "of course."

At this moment the man in oilskins reappeared. His head surfaced above the side of the boat like a puppet in a shooting gallery. He grinned down at us in an encouraging manner. Albert beamed up at him. "Notheer Eeengleesh poof johnny gude time, eh?"

"Oh," said the man in the oilskins, plummily.

He was English.

"Excuse me – " I said, "but. . .I'm English."

"Good," said the man in oilskins.

Albert was pulling on his clothes.

"I want," I said, "to get back to England."

The man in the oilskins winked. "Me too," he said.

"I and. . .my friend," I said.

Albert spread his arms. "Too f—in' right a poof Eeengleesh johnny you gorra frien' I seen 'eem loverly lookin' arse on 'eem any time you ast fer me right we do it all ways nexa time from ver front an evr'yting."

Now fully clothed, the chauffeur slapped me on the back and wandered up along the line of the boat towards the open beach. The man in the oilskins grinned at me confidentially. He seemed, I thought, to be smacking his lips. I tried to make my answering smile full of reserved friendliness, but it came out as a kind of hysterical simper, further confounding the image I felt that I was presenting. "We want", I said, "to get back to England."

"I'm going that way," said the man. "My name's Moncrieff."

"Oh," I said, unsure as what to do with this piece of information. I followed Albert back towards the beach and the man in the oilskins kept pace with me as I went.

"Constantine Moncrieff," he said, as we walked.

When we reached the bow of the boat I saw that Albert and Zak were talking together. They seemed to be getting on quite well. I noticed Zak pass the chauffeur a role of notes and Albert trod back along the sand towards the boat next to which I was standing. From here I could see the other stranger. He was still looking at the sea, his black cane held limply in one hand, his head to one side. He looked more than ever like a sad character from a clown show. As I looked at him I remembered that voice and, on an impulse I didn't fully understand, said to the man standing on the boat above me:

"Who is that?"

"He's a writer, I believe," said the man.

"Oh," I said.

In recounting this experience to others (something I have done only once before now writing it down), I felt that this was the moment when the conviction was born in me that one day I should write books. The man's face promised such mystery and such private pleasure. If I had been told he was an architect or a juggler, I suspect that those would have been the professions to beckon me on, to suggest glamour. Glamour, after all, is not an intrinsic quality. It is bestowed by chance words, suggestions, on the unlikeliest subjects, usually at an age when we are incapable of making a rational decision about anything, let alone something that concerns ourselves.

"I'd like to write," I blurted out to the man. I could not think why I was saying this to him, except that this was not the kind of thing I was able to say to Isaac.

The man, however, looked morose rather than pleased at this piece of news. He swung his large frame over the edge of the boat and glared at me. "Everyone wants to write", he said, "and everyone wants to add to the sum of human happiness. The trouble is that the two are not always compatible ambitions."

Then Isaac and the chauffeur returned. Zak had on his most charming smile and held, in his right hand, a wad of the notes he had taken from the farmer the night before. The man in oilskins waved the bundle of notes away. "Please don't trouble yourself," he said. "I am *en route* for the Sussex coast."

Then he waved across at the man by the sea. "The danger, you see," he said, "is that one seeks for years to express oneself. And finally one does. And one realizes that one is irredeemably mediocre."

I grinned foolishly at him.

"Are you irredeemably mediocre?" he said.

"I don't know, sir," I said.

"You won't know, will you," said the man, "until you *express* yourself."

He switched his attention to Zak. He gave him the sort of smile a gourmet might give a *crème brûlée*. Zak held his eyes steadily into the stranger's.

"Hullo," said the man in the oilskins. "You must be the crew."

I don't think I want to say much more about Constantine Moncrieff, except that, as well as being a clearly successful international pederast, a linguist, *littérateur* and flautist, he was also a highly accomplished sailor. It was far too simple for him to take us straight across the Channel. We tacked round the Scilly Isles and goose-winged our way up the north coast of Cornwall and, by the time we returned to England, had virtually completed a circular tour of these islands. The fact is I resented Moncrieff, not least for the fact that he so clearly found Zak more attractive than me. I don't think I want to mention Moncrieff's diet (raw onions and bread), his small talk (an incomprehensible mixture of scatology and marine commands), or his habit of squeezing his own buttocks appreciatively while muttering things like "*that* needs something up it." It is simply that my enforced sojourn with him seems to sum up the barren hopelessness of my own experience.

For I have, I must admit, had dreams of transmuting the walk-on role I seem to have played in the twentieth century into Art. But there have always been people like Moncrieff there to tell me such a task is beyond me. I, of course, have wanted to say to them that it is precisely because I have spent my time with people like them that the task probably *is* beyond me. Self – that's the only thing glorified by Art. Sometimes its practitioners call it Love or The Spirit; some-times, like Proust, Memory, or like Balzac, Ambition. But they don't mean the real things you and I mean by such words. Real ambition, as you and I are aware, is either so grotesquely silly it isn't worth talking about or else a mere shadow that haunts each hopeless creature in the modern crowd. And as for memory. . .well. . .don't try and tell me that the taste of a madeleine can summon up a whole village, a house, a park, a river. Oh, I am sure such things trail their own connections. But don't expect it to be a *real* park, a *real* village, a *real* river. They will simply be the things you want to remember.

And when we come to what people call the "real world", the world Zak lived in, the world that my friend Alan feels it so necessary to "engage in" (his words), the large words people give their self-interests are even more of a mockery. Alan, for example, who is about to come in and drag me off to that restaurant in Charlotte Street, and who is, I am sure, about to make me "face up" to something or other, has been heard to express the view that we are making history here in the Ministry of Information. I haven't the heart to tell him that time plays cruel tricks on those who seek to be recorded outside time.

"My God," I can hear Zak's father say. "It is time that records us, don't you agree, Amos? Don't seek to be remembered. Especially not for what you were. Do something if you like, and leave it in a bottle and hope that someone will find it. Don't hope to make your mark on the world by engaging with it. If you do that it will make its mark on you, not the other way around."

I can see Zak now, sitting on the bow of that boat, as the spring sunshine turned to rain and the waves reared up about us like animals after our blood. His face was fixed on the horizon, where he thought England lay and, like everyone else after a war, he thought he was going to *do* something. To do something that would make another such war impossible, that would channel the violence of thought and feeling that had allowed him to get involved with the damn thing in the first place away from murder and into self-improvement. I want to pull Zak off that boat and hold him by the collar and scream at him "Murder and self-improvement are often closely related." I want to say to him all the things I dare not say to Alan now, things like "There isn't any war to end wars. There are just wars and wars and wars. And none of it makes sense."

Hell, maybe I do dare say them to Alan. Maybe this lunchtime should be the occasion of our first serious quarrel.

It's time I spoke out. I, too, have a secret to impart.

PART TWO

12.30 p.m.

Alan, of course, has decided to have lunch with somebody else. He's met a man called Harris who, he says, is going to help us "reorganize" the office. We're going to have a new kind of cupboard, thicker carpets and a connecting door between his office and mine. I don't think I like the idea of the connecting door. It means he will be able to come in whenever he wants, often, indeed, surprising me. I won't have time to hide my manuscript.

Alan quite approves of my literary efforts. I think he thinks it adds some sort of distinction to the M.o.I to have what he calls a "scribbler" on the premises. If only I would rectify what he calls my "attitude", all would be thoroughly satisfactory. I often wonder how is it that a German Jew from Stuttgart has managed to transform himself so effectively into a public-school house prefect. I'm allowed to scribble away so long as I show some kind of interest in the completely mechanical task of writing press releases that no one wants to read.

"But", Alan says sometimes, "if you write *good* press releases, isn't that good practice for writing your novel?"

"Oh," I say, "you want my novel to read like an M.o.I. press release, do you?"

Actually I think my "novel" is a bloody sight more convincing than the average M.o.I. press release.

I can hear him now talking with this ridiculous person from House Management. He is planning to have an aspidistra and a special little rack to hold pencils and pens. He thinks this will help him to work better. The trouble with poor Alan is that although he knows I am deceitful and suspects I lie about small things (the way I always used to leave a scrap of food on my plate when I was a kid), he is never quite sure *when* I am being deceitful. Because, unlike Alan, I lie for the hell of it. He would tell an untruth for a good practical reason, but he would never walk around pretending his name was Swansea.

133

Mind you, I'm not sure that his name is Brown. It's probably Braunstein or something like that.

I am fond of Alan partly because I suspect he may have rumbled me. I like people who don't trust me. It was probably the reason I loved Zak so much. I am fond of Alan too, because like Zak he still believes in things. Sometimes, when he talks about Hitler, I am swept away by his words and see myself in a tank regiment, part of our victorious armies *sweeping* (that's the kind of word we use in M.o.I. press releases) across Europe. The fact that I am so tall I wouldn't fit in a tank and so boozed most of the time I wouldn't be able to drive it if I could fit into it is irrelevant. I'm like that boy in the picture, looking up at the sailor pointing out to sea, actually living inside other people's stories.

Perhaps he won't have lunch with this man from House Management. Perhaps he'll have lunch with me after all. The man from House Management sounds dull. Perhaps we will walk across the half-ruined city, bereft of all advertisements, widowed by long conflict, and take Spanish Beaujolais and limp spaghetti – with Mario, who is not a magician.

I'll do this release and take it in to him.

Last night in raids over Germany twenty-two of our aircraft were. . . .

I've got a special form of writer's block. I can't write rubbish any more. I've got hack's block. I can't write anything that I don't believe to be true. Just physically cannot do it. This is a very serious problem for someone in my job. What do I imagine will be achieved by this? Someone else will write the lies instead. Anyway, as Alan keeps reminding me, they are necessary lies. Propaganda is a necessary instrument of war and, as I am too tall and peculiar to do anything but write, I'd better settle down to it.

I wonder wildly to myself whether, in some strange way, my "novel" would be of some use to the war effort. After all, Zak was a Jew. If I could make him more of a hero, bigger, blonder, franker, well, let's face it, a bit less ... Jewish, he would be terrific propaganda for the Allies. I could make him perfect, good at long jumping or whatever it is that Jews are supposed to be good at. The problem is, of course, that he wasn't perfect. And for most of the time, the fact that he was a Jew was completely irrelevant to our friendship.

134

Except of course when he started going to the synagogue. He didn't even call it *the* synagogue – it was just "synagogue". I wondered out loud, in his presence, whether "to synagogue" was a verb, descriptive of some complicated physical action, a sort of soft-shoe shuffle, for which it was necessary to wear a hat. "I want to synagogue," I used to say to him. "Why can't I synagogue?"

"Because", he said, "you're not a Jew."

"I could become one."

"It takes a lot of practice to become a Jew," he said. "You have to pass exams."

All this started to happen after we got back from France.

My Mum and Dad had not expected to see me again. They'd assumed we'd run away to the army, the way three or four boys on our street had done. Zak's father had made the same assumption. I didn't bother to tell any of them about what had happened to us. None of it seemed real. We picked up our lives again as if we had never been away.

Except, as I say, for this business of the synagogue.

I took to hanging around outside it, waiting for Zak to come out.

"Fancy a drink", I'd say, "after synagogue? You must be dying of thirst after all that synagogue."

"Shut up," Zak would say, striding off in the other direction with pale-looking boys with names like Shlomo.

I suspected synagogue wasn't quite as much fun as he made out. Whatever they did in there (and he wouldn't tell me precisely what they *did* do in there), it left them all looking as if they had just drunk a few bottles of used bathwater. And from outside it sounded like a flock of sheep in the throes of an identity crisis. After a while, Isaac became disillusioned with synagogue. "I can't f—in' understand a word of it," he said. "It's all in f—in' Hebrew."

His father – who had offered me my old job back at the bookshop – seemed relieved to discover his son's crisis of faith. Old Mr Rabinowitz's chief concern in life was to make sure that his son believed in absolutely nothing at all. "Don't even believe in bus timetables," he would say to me. "Otherwise you'll turn up and you'll expect the bus to be there. Then what? You've got another disillusioned person on your hands. All this believing in things creates so much disillusion. Why can't he be like you? Why didn't I give birth to a sensible boy?"

After Judaism – which lasted about three weeks – it was Fresh Air.

135

Zak took to slipping out of the shop in the morning and, armed with a rucksack and a huge pair of boots, walking off at great speed in an apparently arbitrary direction.

"Where are you off to?" his dad would say.

"To get some Fresh Air," Zak would reply.

I came to think of Fresh Air as some sacred commodity, some elixir or drug that Zak needed in order to survive. He would return in the evening bent and exhausted, only to announce the next morning that he needed yet more Fresh Air.

"My God," said his father, "haven't you had enough of this Fresh Air? Is there any more of it left out there after the amount you've had?"

"You don't understand", said Zak, looking at the two of us, "about Nature."

I confess I never have understood about Nature. I've nothing against clouds or sunsets or trees or flowers or any of that. They're obviously necessary. But I have no patience with people who go on about them as if they were the first and only people ever to see clouds, sunsets, trees, birds, etc. I measure the seasons by how the crowds on London streets conduct themselves. When they hunch up into their collars, their shoulders as tense as a spy's, I know it is November. I know it is summer when unfamiliar faces swagger by me above open-necked shirts. Spring and autumn I don't see. They always strike me as dress rehearsals for the other two seasons, even though I once saw a twig on the tree planted by some benevolent person at the end of Marchant Row, sticky, tightly furled, enjoying an eerie, private spring all of its own.

But Fresh Air didn't last long either. After Fresh Air came Girls.

"Let's pick up a girl," he said to me one morning in the bookshop.

"Great," I said.

That was as far as we got with girls for a year or so. His father had finally persuaded him to work alongside me and the two of us spent hours playing cards, reading and tormenting customers. When we weren't doing any of these things, we were talking. We talked about the war, about what was going to happen now the war was over, about how everything was going to suddenly change. Surely nothing *could* remain the same after all of that?

And yet, curiously, it did. People came into the shop and asked for books, cars passed you on the street, the winter came and went, twice – and all of it seemed like a shadow play. We could not believe anyone took any of this seriously. And yet they did, and suddenly it was 1920, and both of us felt – surely *now* something will happen, surely . . . now. . . .

When Rajani Palme Dutt walked into the shop, I took him at first for a commercial traveller. We did get the occasional commercial traveller in and Zak and I usually managed to make them last an hour, but on this occasion something about the man's steady, controlled demeanour made us cautious of playing any of our usual tricks. He looked, I remember, like a cross between a civil servant and an Asiatic gent; his thick spectacles and heavy suit made him, at second glance, resemble a retired professor and, as he crabbed his way across the shelves at the back, I was waiting for the kind of inquiry made by retired professors: "Do you have Grant on Ethics?"

In fact he chose quite quickly. It was, as I recall, *Practical Beekeeping*.

"Are you interested in bees?" I said as I took his money.

"Why", said the man, "do you think I'm buying a book called *Practical Beekeeping?*"

Zak and I looked at each other with admiration. Although he did not know it, the stranger was taking part in a game called Ask a Stupid Question and, so far at any rate, he was scoring very high marks.

"In fact," he went on, "I am very interested in bees as bees. The bee itself is of no more interest than the thing in itself, *as* a thing in itself. For the bee to become other than itself it must become part of the social organism. The hive is the contradiction and the supreme expression of the bee as the 'bee in itself'."

As he said this last phrase, he raised the first two fingers of each hand high in the air, to signal the quotation marks. I looked sideways at Zak. This was a more than usually satisfactory lunatic.

"I see," I said keenly.

"Do you?" said the man sharply.

This rather unnerved me. He went on: "Let us postulate", he said, "a hive in which the conflict between worker and hive has become explicit, so that the expression of 'bee-ness' is no longer the fundamental social contradiction of the 'hive' but the negative inversion of the principle, worker bee *as* worker bee."

I decided this man was not to be trifled with. He was quite clearly mad, but something about the controlled passion of his speech suggested that any form of contradiction might very quickly lead to violent conflict. I grinned foolishly. "I see," I said.

"No no," he said, "on the contrary. You do not."

He rounded on Zak, who was seated in a big wooden chair at the back of the shop, cleaning his nails with a penknife.

"The world has changed", he said, "and you must change with it. You must change with it or die."

He turned on his heel and marched out into the alley. I looked across at Zak.

"What was all that about?"

"I don't know," he said.

Looking after the man I saw the face of a girl pressed against the glass. Her nose was squashed white and her eyes, as wide and clear as a doll's, had the frightened, naïve expression of a child. The only strict thing about her face was her hair, but that was strict enough for the pink cheeks and the anxious, bird-like movements of her head to seem not quite sweet. She looked like a milkmaid trying to look like a policeman. I smiled at her encouragingly.

After a pause, the girl pushed open the door of the shop and tiptoed in, as if entering a church. She gazed around her at the wall of books, with a timorous respect. Zak, behind me, uncurled himself from the chair and stood, with elaborate calm, behind me. When I looked round at him I saw his head was rocking backwards and forwards in a kind of sneer. This was, presumably, intended to make him more attractive and mysterious.

"I'm sorry," said the girl.

"What about?" said Isaac.

He sounded, suddenly, like a surgeon talking to a patient before a difficult operation. I looked back at him. Had he done this sort of thing before?

"About ... bursting in ... but...."

"But what?" I said.

I thought I sounded merely rude and inquisitive when I said this.

"I had to follow him."

"Who?"

"Rajani."

"Rajani who?"

138

"Palme Dutt. The man who was in here. I've got a bit of a thing about him."

"Oh."

"I follow him everywhere."

"Lucky old him," said Isaac.

The girl flushed and grinned. She had, I noticed, big hands, like those of a peasant girl. Averting her eyes from us she went over to the shelves and made a great show of inspecting them. Isaac, using his hips rather more than was necessary, strolled out from behind the counter and over in her direction. "What's he got that we haven't?" he said.

Zak's manner, which had started off well, was now rather too close to that of an elderly gigolo unsure of his ground. This last remark was accompanied by a lot of eye-rolling and lip-curling, that made the girl start back from him in something like fright. She was looking, I noticed, at a shelf containing twelve bound volumes of Hansard covering the period of the early 1890s.

"He's a communist," she said.

At this point old Mr Rabinowitz appeared from the back room. He seemed pleased to see the girl. "Hello, Tessa," he said.

"Hullo, Mr Rabinowitz," said the girl, colouring up again as she spoke. The exaggerated demureness of her manner reminded me of some eighteenth-century lady-in-waiting. She had a soft, fluting voice of the kind that goes with needlework and intense discussion about balls and supper parties.

Mr Rabinowitz looked at the three of us with paternal pride.

"Tell you what," he said, "you young people. Go out and enjoy yourselves."

We looked at each other in stark terror. How was this to be accomplished?

"Go on," he said, "go on, then."

"I – " I began, but Mr Rabinowitz shooed us towards the door. Isaac led. I think both of us felt it would be impolite to ask precisely who this girl was. We followed her out into the alley, where a thin rain was beginning to fall. Once outside, the problem of enjoying ourselves did not seem quite so overpowering. We stood a fair distance away from each other. Isaac and I kept our hands in our pockets.

"Are you interested in politics?" said the girl called Tessa.

"*Rather. . . .*" said Zak.

I tried to think of some political topic that might start the conversation going. I was unable to do so. Fortunately the girl supplied the answers as well as the questions.

"I *adore* politics," she said. "Daddy hates me caring so much about politics, but I just tell him, well sorry, Daddy, but I do, I do. It was those pictures I saw, you know the ones?"

Zak and I looked at each other blankly.

"How can they do that to people? How can they let that happen and nobody cares? Nobody gives a damn about what happens."

She smiled at us. I noticed that one of her front teeth was missing.

"I swear too," she said.

I was about to ask her how she knew Isaac's father. But as we moved off down the alley and towards the main road, she supplied an answer to this question as well. "Daddy is Norman Oldroyd", she said, "and does Teeth. He does Mr Rabinowitz's teeth which is super."

I tried to conjure up a mental picture of Mr Rabinowitz's teeth and relate them to the concept "super" but was unable to do either of these things. Tessa was talking as we went. I noticed that, as well as a slightly breathy quality, she lisped. The lisp gave her a charm that she might not otherwise have possessed, lending her childlike enthusiasm a vulnerable edge.

"Daddy says everyone is a communist at twenty and a conservative at forty. If they're sensible. I say he's never been either. He's just been a dentist. He just is totally wrapped up in Teeth."

Here she giggled, a high silvery noise, ringing like a coin in the chill, soured air of the alley. "I'm a communist," she said. "I'm a tremendous communist and I don't care who knows. I think Lenin and all of that lot are just first rate. I think our Government is a frightful lot of frumps, don't you?"

"Yes," I said.

The three of us came up into the Whitechapel Road and, having no particular place to go, walked down towards the Aldgate. When we had gone about a hundred yards, Tessa ran out in front of us and from inside her brown overcoat uncoiled an enormous scarf. She held this aloft as she ran, so that it trailed out behind her, like a streamer. "Let's go to the river," she said. "Let's walk by the dear, dear Thames, all brown and sticky and sort of *there*. . . ."

140

It was probably the way her hair had slipped out from its braids as she ran and bounced on her neck in waves that prevented either Zak or myself from bursting into scornful laugher. But perhaps it wasn't just that. There was something about her enthusiasm that seemed to guy itself. The gap-toothed smile promises some secret world beyond the visible *naïveté*. She seemed to be playing the part of a little girl as part of some conscious plan to satirize women who behaved like that.

We went to the Thames anyway. We looked out at the barges, moored together in mid stream, at the grim buildings on the south bank, and across to the east and the docks that still took my father away from me every day, that, I suddenly saw, separated me from everything round me and drew me towards a world where people talked in high, shrill, posh voices and mentioned the titles of books like a badge of worth. Tessa stared at the grimy water bedecked with floating wood, straw, tyres and all the other cargo of an urban river, as if it were something of astonishing beauty. At one point, as she leaned over the river wall, I thought she was going to applaud what she saw, as an audience at the opera might applaud the settings revealed by a lifted curtain.

"You must come to a meeting," she said. "We're having a meeting about the Pratt case. Rajani is talking. You must come."

"Yes," I said, "we must."

Zak was nodding sagely as if he had been thinking about nothing else but the Pratt case for the last three years. Tessa spread her arms and turned back to us. "Come then," she said. "Oh, it's so nice. To know such dear, dear, dear boys. You must come. How marvellous to know you. Really. How marvellous!"

And turning away from us, her scarf held out behind her, she began tripping away down the Embankment, like a fairy in a panto-mime. Zak and I watched her as she went, too confused to think of following, although now I have no doubt that that is what she intended us to do. There would have been nothing Tessa would have enjoyed more than to have the three of us tripping up and down the Embankment on a cold November afternoon, preferably with no clothes on whatsoever.

But if she was disturbed by our not following her, Tessa gave no clue as to the fact. That was part of her style. She tripped on through the rain, scarf flowing behind her, naiad-like, on her way towards

Charing Cross. For all I know that is where she went that day, for she did not turn back once, but floated off into the grey afternoon until Isaac and I were alone again with the cold, slow river.

"Are you interested in politics?" I said to him on the way back to the shop.

"*Rather.....*" he said.

"Me too," I replied.

He sneaked a glance at me.

"In fact," I said, "I'm a bit of a communist on the quiet."

* * *

We both went to the dentist that week. We were going to go on different days, but in the end we decided to chaperon each other. Zak's father seemed pleased to hear that we were safeguarding our teeth.

Norman Oldroyd turned out to be a small, weasely man, operating out of a front room off Wapping High Street. His waiting room was crowded with apprehensive-looking people. He was known locally, someone had told us, as "Butcher" Oldroyd. The customers were all obviously in the last stages of terminal dental caries. Some clutched their jaws, others massaged their lips. One man was wearing a bandage that went over the top of his head and under his chin – the kind of thing you see now only in the pages of children's comics.

Zak went in first.

He said, much later, that when he had gone to see "Butcher" Oldroyd his teeth had felt fine. When he came out that afternoon, he did not speak, but moaned at me and sprinted for the street. The original plan had been to wait for each other after our appointments in the hope that Tessa might emerge into the waiting room, dressed in white, at which point we might both persuade her to accompany us ... well ... anywhere. But it was quite clear from Zak's face that all he really needed was a blood transfusion and some form of painkiller. I got up and pushed open the shabby white door of the surgery.

There, in the corner, in a white mask, was a man about five feet six in height. In his right hand he held what looked like a chisel and in his left a clutch of sinister steel objects decorated with eyes and prongs. I stepped cautiously towards the chair and smiled appeasingly at Mr Oldroyd, whose eyes were the only visible thing about him. I noticed to my horror that the backs of his hands were covered in thick, grey hairs and that the fingers were thick, like a carpenter's or a plumber's. They seemed to suggest a man used to grappling with huge, solid objects ... like ... teeth. I gulped.

"I haven't really come about my teeth, Mr Oldroyd," I said.

The eyes, stony blue, the colour of a bleak northern sky, shifted quizzically above the mask. "Then what have you come for?" he said. He had a strong Belfast accent.

"A check-up," I said.

"I don't do check-ups," said Mr Oldroyd, "I do teeth."

"Yes," I said, "of course."

"Rinse out," he said.

On the shelf next to the chair was a cracked glass. I went over to it, poured its contents – a greenish liquid – into my mouth and allowed the stuff to shoot backwards and forwards through my teeth. Tessa's father watched me stonily. To my horror I realized I had nowhere to spit. I pointed at my cheeks, now bulging like a hamster's, and then questioningly around the room. Mr Oldroyd jerked one huge thumb over at the corner, where I saw a cracked tin bath, three-quarters full of green water. The water wasn't entirely green – there was quite a lot of blood in it as well. I tried to smile encouragingly at him and walked over to the bath. I didn't feel easy having my back to him. I felt at any moment he might run at me screaming, with those sinister burglar's tools of his.

When I had rinsed out, I went to the chair and Mr Oldroyd came over to me. It was very difficult to hear what he was saying through his mask, which appeared to be made of quite a thick material. Perhaps, I thought madly, it was protective clothing, to stop his victims trying to punch him in the face during, or just after, the administration of treatment.

"What seems to be the trouble?" he seemed to be saying.

His breath smelt quite strongly of alcohol. As he parted my jaw and jabbed at my exposed teeth with the crochet hooks, I tried to tell him, as perhaps many of his patients had done before, that I had changed my mind. I had lost all interest in improving my teeth. I wished simply to leave. But in Mr Oldroyd's iron grip, the most my open mouth could manage was a kind of "Ooh...wah... wah...." Mr Oldroyd had heard this noise before from many of

143

his customers. They all, I thought, protested just before the end, before he caught sight of a speck of black in the ivory and threw himself upon it like a dervish.

"Oooh...." I said more urgently. "Oooh... wah... wah...."

It was then that I heard Tessa's voice. I don't think any sound has seemed sweeter.

"Daddy," she said in that breathy, expectant voice of hers, "what have you done to poor Mr Rabinowitz?"

Mr Oldroyd whipped round like a strangler interrupted at his task. Even though the only thing I could see was his eyes, it was clear from them that his daughter inspired in *him* the same feelings he had managed to create in me and the twenty or so people waiting outside. Sheer, blind terror.

"What have I done to him?" he said. Except that it sounded like "Nwhat have I ndone to him?"

Tessa came towards us. I could not believe she had anything to do with that room. She was wearing a blue coat, studded with buttons and pockets, and her hair was loose again down her back. She still had the look of a milkmaid, but now there was something slightly aristocratic about her as well. A fine lady slumming it perhaps, dressed *à la Petit Trianon*. How, I wondered, had the creature in the mask managed to raise *that*.

It was clearly a question that exercised him as well for, tearing off the mask in a somewhat histrionic way, he said, "Oh Tessa. Tessa."

I thought at first this was the kind of remark intended to convey a deeper meaning, rather the sort of thing that dying drunkard fathers said to faithful daughters, but it clearly had a more mundane application. Tessa smiled at me winningly, showing that gap tooth of hers. "Daddy hates me to come in when there are patients", she said, "because sometimes the patients are in pain. And he hates me to see pain. Don't you, Daddy?"

Mr Oldroyd gave a kind of strangled grunt.

"But I must see pain, Daddy," went on Tessa. "I must see the real world and what is happening in it, the cruel things as well as the beautiful things. I must struggle against them and try to make the world beautiful, Daddy. If I don't do that, I'm nobody really, am I? Nobody at all." She laughed lightly, that high, silver note again. Mr Oldroyd started to put down his tools. Quietly, inconspicuously, I began to rise from the chair.

"But I mustn't keep you," she said, "I'm delaying you."

I was now halfway towards the door. "Not at all," I said. "I've got to meet a – "

And I was back in the waiting room. Faces looked up at me in questioning misery as I appeared. I looked down at them. Suddenly the world was a beautiful and simple place. "Leave," I said. "You don't have to stay here. Leave."

Tessa followed me out into the street, where I came across Zak. Zak was hopping around in circles on one leg, holding his left cheek. I could not understand why this form of motion should help alleviate any pain he might be feeling in the dental area. I said this to him and he uttered a low cry and hopped off up the road. Tessa put her hand on my arm. She was smiling sweetly. "Daddy", she was saying, "is just a very bad dentist really."

"You can say that again," I said.

"Shall we go to Isaac?" she said.

"Yes," I said.

It was raining harder now. We walked up the street after Zak, who was walking north away from the river, up towards Royal Mint Street. He did not turn to greet us. He did not seem capable of speech. Tessa, boyishly impulsive, linked her hand in his and swung it in a motherly way. Her manner suggested that she was about to propose some jolly, outdoor activity to Isaac, in order to take his mind off the pain. "Let's have tea," she said, "and then we must all go to the meeting about the Pratt case."

I opined that Zak was not capable of *either* tea *or* attending a political meeting, let alone the two together. Tessa, as if the reality of his predicament had only just been borne in on her, flung her arms round him and kissed him violently on the left cheek. This set Zak off hopping again. This time, instead of the low moan, he did a long, desperate wail, of the kind I imagined hearing at some aboriginal funeral. Tessa, blushing with shame and confusion, fluttered after him along the drab street. I heard her voice, soft, agitated, attentive. . . . "Oh, Isaac . . . so *clumsy* . . . listen . . . Pratt case . . . Daddy . . . sort of dentistry . . . qualifications . . . loving *me* . . . *do*. . . ."

I saw Isaac nodding rapidly, his hand still up to his cheek. He looked as if he were working his head manually. Then Tessa floated back to me. "There's a meeting next week," she said. "Rajani is speaking at it. You can come to that and meet Rajani. And you'll find out how adorable Rajani is and I hope you'll be members of the Communist Party and everything because it's such fun and so useful really I'll just go back now and help Daddy with the teeth I am sorry he doesn't mean to you're both perfectly sweet and especially you Amos you're like a funny little professor with your face all screwed up you're lovely you really are."

With this remark she lifted herself up on her points and kissed me as far up as my chin – which was as high as she reached. Then, with a wave of those fluttering fingers she was off back down the street. At the first bend in the road she lifted her right arm in a salute and, from this position, gave us a last, fetching little wave. I found I was blushing furiously.

"Do you think I look like a professor, Zak?" I said.

"My teeth. My teeth," was all Isaac could reply.

When I got home that evening, I asked my Dad about the Pratt case.

"Pratt?" he said. "Some geezer 'oo got the bullet."

He wasn't very political, my Dad.

The meeting was held in a church hall up near the Bow Road. Isaac and I got there about six, straight from the shop. I had somehow expected it to be a grander affair. There were only about fifteen people there, huddled together in the middle of a waste of chairs. Most of them were still wearing mackintoshes or coats, and the fog that sat out in the street in yellow circles had drifted in through the open door and hung above the proceedings like a pall, dousing the fervour on the faces of speaker and listeners. Zak and I were to meet Tessa there and, when we arrived, saw her in the front row of chairs, gazing up at her hero, still dressed in the same thick suit, still wearing those formidable glasses, still, for the layman, almost impossible to comprehend.

"The issue confronting us with regard to Comrade Pratt", said Palme Dutt, his eyes searching the faces in the hall, "is not simply the contradiction *in* the contradiction, the abstract principle, *nota bene*, of concrete analysis into foreground/background dichotomy, but the far simpler question subsumed by the Kautskyist/social-democratic-style treatment of the issue as an 'issue', that is to say – how will this affect the British working class?"

I learned from Tessa later that Rajani did not always talk like this. He was, at the time, translating the theses of Lenin into Ancient

Greek, by way of evening relaxation, and the hobby had had unfortunate effects on his prose style. The audience – most of whom appeared to be middle-aged women in hats, with faces reddened from the cold – gazed up at him in silent wonder.

"How will this affect", went on Rajani, "the building of our Communist Party? How will it affect the need to build up strength within our labour organizations in the months and weeks that lie ahead. Scientifically speaking, Comrade Pratt. . . .'

He spoke for nearly an hour. I must confess I was immensely disappointed. If the word "communism" meant anything to me, it was people making and planting bombs, speakers on street corners in violent conflict with the established order. Instead, here was this shady-looking professorial type, delivering a lecture. I looked across at Tessa. It was certainly going down very well with her. She was certainly going down very well with Zak, who was devoting most of his attention to her profile.

". . . the formation of a defence committee for Comrade Pratt, a fighting fund to campaign for Comrade Pratt's reinstatement, and of course a committee to manage the fighting fund. In addition, I think it may be necessary to vote at this meeting for the creation of an overall co-ordinating committee to co-ordinate the defence committee, the fighting fund itself and, of course, the management committee for the fighting fund."

At this point in Palme Dutt's speech the old ladies perked up. This was what they had come out to accomplish. One of them raised an arthritic hand.

"Yes, Daisy?" said Palme Dutt.

"Might we not", said Daisy, "think towards the formation of a committee to liaise with the co-ordinating committee, and to establish strong links between it and the on-the-ground committees, in case there is a danger of the co-ordinating committee getting out of touch with the committees it is supposed to be co-ordinating?"

There was a ripple of laughter at this sally. Rajani seemed to take it in good part. "Indeed," he said, "that has been known to happen."

More laughter. There was then a show of hands on whether the meeting was going to elect committees. The hands said the meeting should elect committees. Then the meeting elected committees. Committees for the defence of Pratt, the safeguarding of the future of Pratt, committees that covered almost every aspect of Pratt's existence. The remarkable thing about these committees, as far as I could see, was that they consisted of the same bunch of old ladies, arranged in different combinations. One committee was an old lady in a hat and an old lady in galoshes and an even older lady in a beret. Another committee (that had not even been thought of at the beginning and seemed designed to control the money allocated to all the other committees, except the overall co-ordinating committee) consisted of the old lady in the beret, an old man in a trilby and a very, very old lady who was seated next to Tessa wrapped up in a rug, who appeared to come from the north, be named Pamela and have no teeth at all. After the election of each committee, the chairman of the committee thanked the comrades and the committees for having the goodness to elect it, the comrades applauded and, when every possible combination of old lady had been tried, Palme Dutt announced that we would sing the Internationale.

"The what?" hissed Zak.

Whatever it was they sang it. They did not appear to know it too well either. Tessa did a kind of soprano descant in the last verse, which earned some critical looks from the old ladies, and then Pamela – who produced some teeth from a handbag and jammed them in her mouth for this purpose – took a collection.

It was proposed that we meet Rajani for a "quiet chat" in a pub some streets away. I could not, somehow, visualize the form this chat might take, but the sight of Tessa swirling through the confused forest of chairs with a radiant smile on her face made it more appealing than it might otherwise have been.

"Wasn't he *marvellous!*" she said.

Zak and I nodded sheepishly as we went towards the fog-laden street.

"How did you become involved in communism?" I said, in a keen voice that I hoped did not sound too much like a professor's.

"Daddy did Rajani's teeth!" said Tessa.

I thought this explained a great deal about Palme Dutt's thought processes. The three of us linked arms, as we had outside her father's surgery, and hurried over the damp cobbles to a huge shabby inn sign in a lighted door, through which Rajani, accompanied by two old ladies who formed a sort of praetorian guard around him, was hurrying. Pamela, who, the formal note of the collection having been dispensed with, had taken her teeth out again, was saying to the very old man in a strong Yorkshire accent: "In the Soviet Republic there is no such thing as unemployment."

"I know!" the old man was saying with quiet pride.

The Communist Party contingent was gathered in a small room at the back of the pub. I attached myself to Pamela and a group of old ladies in woolly hats, in the hopes of finding out who precisely Pratt was. It was, however, extremely difficult to interrupt the flow of conversation, mainly from Pamela who, now she had removed her teeth once more, seemed full of high spirits.

"In Roosha", she was saying, "the workers eat in communal canteens. For them a waiter as such would be completely unknown, apparently."

"I know," said the old man rapidly.

"In the Soviet Republic", went on Pamela, "trains run on time and harvests are harvested on scientific Marxist principles which means that harvests are also on time. Apparently on the communal farms everything is done collectively, so that it is done far more quickly than would be possible under capitalism."

"I know," said the old man.

Pamela looked a little peeved. "How do you know?" she said. "You 'aven't bin there, Albert."

The old man sucked his teeth. "Neither 'ave you," he said.

I thought this would be a good moment to ask who Pratt was and what he had or had not done. I did not, however, like to ask a direct question. In common with most of the political meetings I have ever been to, this gathering was clearly designed for people who *knew*, and if they didn't know they had better damn well pretend they knew.

"What", I said, keeping a careful eye on Zak and Tessa, who were talking earnestly to Palme Dutt and the old lady in galoshes, "do you think are Pratt's chances?"

"Pratt's chances", said Pamela, "are minimal."

I tried to look concerned about this. But fortunately Pamela's concern was enough for both of us. Indeed to have expressed concern in this woman's presence would have been almost obscene;

there was so much concern beaming its way out of her every pore, so much intense and thoroughly muddled feeling for everyone and everything, that the safest policy seemed to be to lower one's head and hope that not too much of this concern came in one's own direction. For there was something terrifying about this concern, something tidal and monstrous about it. It seemed at times more like a shapeless, formless lust for something, a perverted mothering instinct that, if faced directly, would seize one and roll one away in its endless flow.

"Pratt's chances oonder capitalism", Pamela was saying, "are not t'be compared with the situation of, say, a Rooshan Pratt, a Soviet Pratt. A Rooshan Pratt would be in a completely different situation. He would eat in communal canteens, he would get the harvest in on time, he would drive a tractor communally, he would have a share of the means of prodooction, he would not face the 'aunting prospect of oonemployment and starvation which he doos oonder capitalism."

"I know," said the old man.

I decided I had had enough of this conversation and, smiling weakly, made my way to another group. It was curious. As I went round the assembled comrades (they used this word to describe themselves with a tinge of self-consciousness) I was unable to find enlightenment as to who Pratt was, what he had done or had not done and what was going to happen to him now. The comrades did not seem nearly as certain of what had happened to Pratt as my father had been. Some of them said he had been dismissed because of his connection with the Party. Some said he had met with an industrial accident. Some maintained that he had been arrested by the police on a charge of spying for Russia. One old lady appeared to think that Pratt was dead, had been dead for years. When I finally got to Tessa and Palme Dutt I found, to my chargin, that they were also unable, or rather unwilling, to inform me as to who or what Pratt might be.

"Pratt-in-himself", said Palme Dutt in a monotonous voice, "is not the issue. The issue is really how Pratt-in-himself, as a thing in the abstract, may be subsumed under the world-historical Pratt or, to speak more precisely, Pratt in the world-historical sense. The dialect does not allow a choice in this matter, for Pratt or for those who fulfil the historical function of synthesizing the thesis and antithesis with which Pratt confronted them by dropping the bale on that man's head."

The truly tantalizing thing about Rajani Palme Dutt was his occasional habit of making brief, factual references to the world of sensation. Usually he lived at such an intense theoretical level that it was more or less impossible to relate what he said to the everyday world in which lesser mortals caught trams, married, or went for bicycle rides. But every now and then he would tease one with a detail such as the one to which I have just alluded, and those remarks of his still haunt me. He had the rare talent of being able to convince his listeners that he was in possession of certain information that for most of the time he did not feel it was necessary to use. "Facts", his expression seemed to say, "are for children." And yet, if one were to stoop to the factual approach, Palme Dutt managed to suggest that that, too, would be useless against his dialectical mind, since he knew all the facts in the world, had indeed been the first one to make them public, despite the efforts of bourgeois scientists to conceal everything from the details of the Jurassic Age to the sex life of newts from the hungry proletariat.

Eventually the meeting broke up. I gave a small amount of money to help Pratt. Indeed, later, outside the docks, I sold a pamphlet about Pratt, which was so boring I did not read it beyond the first page. I hope Pratt, whoever he was, got off, or came back to life, or escaped, or came back, or did whatever it was we all wanted him to do so badly, for in my own small way I think I helped Pratt.

"Will you walk with me?" said Palme Dutt to the three of us. "In the direction of Leytonstone?"

This seemed a bizarre request. I wondered whether it might not be some kind of secret code meaning, "Will you help me to make contact with a Russian agent?" But, whatever its meaning, I and Zak complied with the request, for Tessa was nodding at the great man eagerly, like a dog that is to be taken for a walk.

The old ladies took their hats and galoshes and went off into the fog. Pamela put back her teeth and announced she had to get back to Kentish Town and that if she lived in Roosha there would be a communal bus and a communal train to take her there but as she lived under capitalism she had best get moving, because her grandmother worried. I estimated her grandmother's probable age at something like three hundred and twenty. Zak, Tessa and I followed Rajani out into the night.

The fog had thickened. It rose up in our faces, all but swamping the lights of the gas lamp opposite. High up against the lighted windows of the building that faced us, it swirled and paraded itself like the vaulted roof of some cathedral. Our footsteps sounded oddly quiet in the empty street and, at each narrow alleyway, I stopped and found myself looking quickly, nervously, around me at the invading shapes of the night. We were taking a circuitous route, crossing roads I did not know, coming out into deserted high streets and taking narrow passages with high walls. Rajani seemed to know the area well.

And then, down one empty alley, I saw he was quickening his step. Every few yards he would stop and glance over his left shoulder at the fog behind us. Tessa, who was holding on to his arm as a little girl might do, stopped when he stopped and joined in his fearful glances behind. From time to time I too looked back and occasionally thought I saw something or someone in the damp, shrouded spaces that surrounded us.

Palme Dutt's nervousness communicated itself to Isaac and myself, until all four of us were scurrying along, breaking here and there into a half-hearted run. We were, I suspect, on the point of abandoning all pretence and hurling ourselves forward into the fog, when I heard a devastating wail from somewhere above us. I looked up and, next to a lamp on a wall about six feet above the ground, I found myself looking at a man, poised like a tiger for a leap. His teeth were bared, his arms outstretched and his shabby grey suit smeared with what looked like blood. But that was not the strangest thing about him. The strangest thing about him was that, in every respect – even down to his glasses – he was the mirror image of the man who walked beside me, Rajani Palme Dutt. Even the suit, battered as it was, recalled Rajani's. The total resemblance was so complete and perfect that I looked from one to the other, unable at first to believe that I was not watching some ingenious optical effect. And then the man on the wall jumped.

He landed on Rajani's shoulders with a howl of rage and fastened his two huge hands round his double's throat. Tottering, Rajani put up his hands and scratched at his attacker's wrists, while Tessa, Zak and I gazed, stupefied with surprise.

"Get him off," choked out Palme Dutt. "He'll kill me."

"Who . . . who . . . is he?" I heard myself say.

"He's my damn brother," said Palme Dutt, as the two of them swayed and fell with a crack to the ground. Rajani's attacker was dribbling freely and, although he had hit the ground with considerable force, went straight back to the attack. The two men were now on the ground – the one who had been on the wall now trying to fasten his teeth into his brother's neck.

"For God's sake, Parminder. . ." I heard Palme Dutt say.

Isaac dashed forward and grabbed the attacker's arm. "Come *on*, Amos," he was shouting. The two of us managed to drag the creature clear. Even with Tessa's help, it was not easy (she was aiming loosely co-ordinated kicks at the man and shrieking things like "Please" and "I beg you no!"). The man was quite clearly in the grip of some manic frenzy.

"Why does he do this?" Isaac said, as the two of us got him into an arm lock.

"We have completely opposing views on the question of co-operation with the Labour Party," said Rajani.

In the distance I heard the sounds of footsteps and a northern voice calling something.

"Parminder is mentally ill", went on Palme Dutt, "and has, for some years, been confined to a private nursing home near Leeds. From time to time he escapes and attempts to hamper my political work. I need hardly say that his existence has been, up to this moment, a closely guarded secret. I don't have to tell any of you what the capitalist press would do with such information. Parminder is an Anarcho-Syndicalist."

"Has he got any other symptoms?" I said.

Palme Dutt gave me a level stare. Parminder was now sobbing loudly and was no longer resisting our grip.

"I mean – does he think he's Napoleon", I went on, "or try and eat grass or anything like that?"

Parminder broke free of our grip and ran rather theatrically to the centre of the passage. "You and Lenin", he said, pointing a finger at his twin, "have betrayed. You have betrayed and betrayed and betrayed. All that interests you is Power. Power is all that concerns you. Where is the communism of Love?"

This struck me as being an unoriginal rather than a certifiably insane statement. But Parminder, whose eyes were red and whose bony hand shook as he pointed it, gave the impression of someone about to break into one of the more conventionally accepted forms of lunatic behaviour. Rajani turned away from him and peered into the fog. "Ah," he said, "here they are."

From out of the darkness came two huge men in blue suits of the type worn by commissionaires or any semi-military civilian occupation. They wore peaked hats on which, in red letters, were the words GLENGARRY PRIVATE NURSING HOME. One of them carried a large white object which, I realized with a shock, must be a straitjacket.

"Come along, Parminder," one of them said, "your budgie misses you."

Parminder started to laugh in what was, I thought, rather a deranged way. The two men slowly moved towards him. One feinted at him violently with the jacket while the other talked in a soft cajoling voice. There was something indescribably sinister about this scene – the gas lamp above us, the swirling fog, and this neutral northern voice, that seemed to be able to hypnotize Palme Dutt's twin. "Easy does it, Parmy," the man was saying, "*easy* does it. . . ." And his friend, as we watched, was helping the creature into the jacket slowly, gently, as one might put an old person to bed. Parminder was sobbing helplessly now. "Revolutions", he was saying, "should be beautiful. They should transform society beautifully and heal the scars of war with that stuff you get in chemists. But you and him make them ugly – you distort them and you lie and lie and lie you say it's for the working class but all you mean is you want Power. How can you have a just and equal society by your methods? The great commitment is so much easier than the little one, isn't it? The care, the attention you give to a child or a bird with its wing broken or a huge SPIDER!"

Parminder shouted this last word and giggled with delight at the shock on our faces. He was now trussed up in the jacket – he looked like a baby lodged in a nappy for the night. As the two men approached him, he went stiff, as a small animal might do, and when they tipped him over and carried him off into the fog, he remained as rigid as a length of steel piping. They could have been carting a carpet, as they marched off into the lurid imprecision of the alley.

"He can be much worse than this," said Rajani.

Tessa was goggling after the shape of Palme Dutt's twin. "Poor man," she was saying, "poor poor poor man."

Rajani gave her a slightly critical look. "He has", he said, "a fairly pleasant life at Glengarry. The food is excellent."

As we resumed our journey, Rajani gave us a detailed account of the ways in which Parminder's political position differed from his. I confess to not understanding most of this. One phrase I recall from the conversation was the suggestion that "the Communist Party should support the Labour Party as a rope supports the hanged man". But most of what Rajani said to us that night struck me as frankly incomprehensible.

"Parminder-in-himself," he kept saying, "phenomenologically speaking, is not a Marxist thing-in-itself insofar as 'Parminder' is a factor *vis-à-vis* the so-called 'Parminderists'."

I told Palme Dutt that I had not realized that his brother had a following within the Party.

"It is not a question", said Rajani, "of whether he has a 'following'. It is a question of whether, historically speaking, it is possible for the so-called 'Parminderists' to arise as a function of 'Parminder', even supposing the man has no existence in the real sense of the word. It is possible, for example, for a concrete historical situation to arise that creates the need for these 'Parminderists', who may be comrades who have never heard or even dreamed of the existence of Parminder."

I thought I was beginning to understand this conversation and said, as we turned out of the alley and into a broad, deserted street that led back down towards Whitechapel, "If Parminder did not exist, it might be necessary to invent him."

Palme Dutt gave me a look of infinite contempt. "No," he said, "that is not what I meant at all."

When we reached the Whitechapel Road, the fog had begun to lift. Palme Dutt the First – as I was beginning to describe him to myself – bade us goodnight and announced his intention of taking a tram to another meeting. As he turned to go, Tessa lifted herself up on her toes and gave him a peck on his cheek, while he inclined down towards her in a fatherly fashion. "Give my regards to your father," said Palme Dutt. "I will endeavour to come to his surgery as soon as possible. I enjoy our little chats."

I watched him stride off into the fog with a new respect.

"When shall we see you again?" said Isaac to Tessa.

"Whenever you like," said Tessa. She flung her arms wide in a gesture poised neatly between the ridiculous and the touching. "We're all communists!" she said brightly and ran off ahead of us. She continued like that all the way down to her father's place, marking out the way in front of Isaac and me as if she were a puppy. When we reached the door of her father's surgery, she ran to us both and kissed each of us in turn. "Goodnight, Amos," she said. Then she turned to Zak. "Goodnight, dark brooding one," she said. "I think you're going to be rather special!" And then she tripped into the house.

As Zak and I walked away, I said: "You're all right then."

"Don't be too sure," said Isaac. "Don't be too sure."

*   *   *

Isaac and I never actually joined the Communist Party. I wasn't entirely sure that anyone wanted us to. Or rather – they would have been happy for Zak to join, but as that might have involved me in becoming part of the membership, they felt it safer not to risk it.

Zak, rather like Alan, had a talent for becoming involved with causes and with people. My memories of him in those years summon up images of an enthusiast, leafleting, arguing, urging me to accompany him and Tessa to meetings, jolted out of the apathy that had been on him since the war, luxuriating in the possibility of new belief.

I can remember after one meeting Zak, Tessa and I sitting at a table apart from the others of one local Party.

"Well," said Tessa, "at least we tried."

"Yes," said Zak.

He leaned forward across the table, his forehead creased with worry. I saw things in his face Tessa could not have seen. I saw him by the side of that road in France, I saw him with his father that afternoon all those years ago.... He suddenly seemed much younger. The fierce eagerness of his expression, those eyes, as big and girlish as ever, touched me in a way for which I was not prepared.

"We've got to fight them," he said. "We've got to fight for a better world."

I can see now, of course, that the phrase, as well as the thought, came from Tessa, and that the pathetic eagerness that lighted up his face was not simply political passion. What I remember feeling that day was sudden regret at the fact that I should be so old and tired already, that I should be such a tall, odd-looking person who could not say a thing like "We've got to fight for a better world" without snickering behind my hand. I got up and bought them both a drink. Pamela was at the bar. She had removed her teeth and placed them in a half-full glass of Guinness. From time to time she swilled the dentures around and white shapes glistened out at me from the peat-black liquid.

"They are in loove," she said.

"Oh," I said.

"They are good comrades and they are in loove."

"Nice for them," I said.

"You", she said, "are not in loove."

"No," I said. "Neither am I a particularly good comrade."

"I know," she said. She sank her head on her hands and looked glumly at her teeth. "If I were in Roosha," she said, "I would have a communal man and I would go with 'im to the communal canteen and we would eat in the communal canteen and then we would go to the communal bedroom and 'e would give me a really good communal f—."

"Very probably," I said.

When I went back to the table, Zak started guiltily and gave me one of his most charming smiles. "Tessa and I might go to Wilton's on Friday," he said. "Do you want to come?"

I looked at each face in turn. They looked as if they wanted me to come.

"No," I said, "it's OK."

Tessa leaned across the table and touched me lightly on the arm. She smiled and I noticed once again that gap in her teeth, sorting oddly with the innocence of her manner. She shook her hair out and smiled again.

"All right," I said.

For some extraordinary reason, Wilton's Music-hall survived the Blitz. Now we are blitzing them – which, as I keep telling Alan, is as morally indefensible as them blitzing us – I suppose it's perfect pocket stage will remain intact for the rest of the time. I can't imagine anyone but an enemy aircraft wanting to destroy it. It always reminded me of a miniature stately home, given over to the people by a grateful owner. It was – and I suppose still is – in the wilderness of streets to the east of Leman Street, and when you went up towards it on a Friday night you could hear the music and the shouts and the singing halfway across the East End. It wasn't – I should say – the golden days of music-hall. The place was somewhere between a pub and a dance hall, with occasional bizarre moments of theatre thrown in, and at that time, in the early twenties, was run by an Irishman called Martyr Molloy.

They called him Martyr because almost his every statement ended with the words "I'm a martyr to it." He was a martyr to drink, to women, to art (as he often reminded those of his customers unfortunate enough to get into conversation with him) and, ultimately, he was a martyr to Wilton's. If one day the history of that particular place comes to be written, there should be a chapter given over to the story of Martyr Molloy and the Fat Woman.

The Fat Woman – if she had a name, she never used it – was, at the time of which I am speaking, the star attraction of Wilton's. Her act, if it can be dignified with that name, was one of the most strikingly anal pieces of entertainment I have ever seen. The Fat Woman sang a song, the words of which I mercifully cannot remember – but it had a chorus that went:

> Boomps a daisy
> Boomps a daisy
> Why don't we all go
> Boomps a daisy
> Boomps. Boomps. Boomps.

During the "boomps" part of this ditty, the Fat Woman (whose breasts, buttocks and thighs were of such gigantic proportions that they had lost all individual character and seemed capable of doubling for each other) would stick out her behind at the audience and strain violently in the manner of one passing a difficult motion. After she had strained, she wiggled. After she had wiggled, she strained again, while the big trombone in the pit orchestra let out an immense farting noise. This drew such howls of laughter from the audience that she would often be asked to "fart" in this manner for minutes at a time, leading the audience on in crescendos of mirth.

Ladies could be seen sobbing into their handkerchiefs, strong men weeping with mirth and elderly couples falling into each other in strong hysterics.

Martyr Molloy did not like the Fat Woman but, due to her immense popularity, was unable to have her dismissed. In order to spite her, he would use her act to leap on to the stage to make what he called his "announcements". Molloy's announcements were a sort of living classified advertisement column, an early and extremely primitive form of advertising. Often while the Fat Woman was in the throes of some excruciating anal mime, Molloy could be seen hurling himself in front of her shouting things like: "Harris's corsets. Number twenty-nine, Parade Street. You'll find they are the best in town!" Molloy made this sort of intrusion even worse by affecting a ludicrous, rather camp, manner when on stage with her, as if somehow he was sharing in the jollity of the occasion. He justified it to customers in the bar on the grounds that as the Fat Woman was his main attraction, he had a duty to his advertisers to interrupt her in this fashion. Most regulars, however, were convinced this was merely an excuse on his part, since many of the announcements he made were on the level of: "Mrs Jackson – your husband wants you home immediate!"

On Friday nights there was no show as such – merely endless routines from the Fat Woman, who emerged through a moulded sculpture strongly reminiscent of a giant pair of buttocks, followed this with a lengthy routine along the lines of "It feels good to be out of there" (this accompanied by many suggestive gestures towards the giant crack whence she had come) and then went into some twenty or thirty renditions of "Boomps a daisy".

That Friday we got there early. Tessa had her arms through ours and was swinging herself along between the two of us as if she were a child being taken for a walk. The foul weather of late November had given way to a succession of clear, cold evenings and, as we threaded our way up from Wapping, Tessa's boots rang a tattoo on the frosty pavement. She looked to each of us, animated, birdlike, but I fancied her gaze stayed longer on Zak's face and, as we neared Wilton's, I let my arm slip out of hers. She let it go with a grateful smile.

We had seats in the gallery. The chandeliers, the moulded boxes and the thick plush of the seats were all, if one examined them closely, tattered and faded, but as the smoke swirled up from the pit and the band played out, Tessa looked down at the scene, an odd mixture of eighteenth-century idyll and Gin Lane roughness, and exclaimed, with the same breathlessness with which she greeted one of Palme Dutt's less comprehensible "mots": "Marvellous. It's all marvellous."

From behind one of the painted flats came the Fat Woman, dressed in what looked like a huge nappy. She paraded round the stage three or four times, to tumultuous applause from the audience, and then began a variation on her bump and grind routine, followed by her troupe, a rather dispirited bunch of early middle-aged women in smocks whose function was to gambol listlessly behind the Fat woman while she thrust out her enormous behind to the rhythm of the trombone.

I looked sideways at Zak. He and Tessa were lost in the spectacle, both their faces shining with pleasure. I decided I was in danger of becoming a miserable bastard and turned my face downward to the bright lights of the stage and the little sea of faces below us, laughing as if there were no such thing as tomorrow or ugliness or being lonely. I forced my face into a smile, and from a smile I forced it into a grin and from a grin I managed a laugh and then – because we proceed by imitation and nothing is quite real anyway – I was laughing as helplessly and pleasurably as they were.

> *Boomps a daisy*
> *Boomps a daisy*
> *Why don't we all go*
> *Boomps a daisy –*

When Martyr Molloy sprang on to the stage that night I knew at once that something serious had happened. He wore his usual fixed-bayonet smile and as he pranced round the Fat Woman he snapped his fingers like some demented gaucho calling for more drinks. But there was an uncertainty about his eyes I recall, a look that suggested that this was not quite *right* – any of it.

> *Boomps a daisy*
> *Boomps a daisy*
> *Why don't we all go*
> *Boomps a daisy.*

Molloy was a tall, thin man with a black moustache and, as he danced around in the spotlight in front of the Fat Woman, he brought up each lanky knee, like a horse, his rectangular head jerking up in rhythm with his feet. His smile widened and widened and disappeared round behind his ears and his brilliantined hair, caught in the cheap light of the stage, glittered like some exotic mineral.

"He's stronging it tonight," said Zak.

At the moment at which the Fat Woman had begun to strain her buttocks to the trombone, Molloy leaped in front of her, and in a high, jolly voice said: "Announcement for Rabinowitz."

The Fat Woman continued to bump and grind.

"Announcement", went on Molloy, whose smile now seemed to be stitched into his face, "for Rabinowitz!" As he said the word "Rabinowitz", he tossed off a showy gesture with his left hand, rather as a highwayman might throw a handkerchief to a crowd at his execution.

The Fat Woman, who had screwed her face down to knee level and was purple in the face with the mock exertions of her anal regions, suddenly turned on him. She had a nasal, rather unpleasant voice. "Gercha," she said, "you an' yore Rabinwotz. Gercha!"

"Announcement", went on Molloy, sounding like a machine that has broken down, "for Rabinwitz!"

"Gercha!" continued the Fat Woman, "geddoff the f—in' stage!"

Molloy's "showman" voice – a rather unconvincing blend of imitation Home Counties and Mexican – slipped into what must have been his natural manner. It rose several octaves too, climbing in queenly fashion that upstaged Molloy's imitation soldier look and transformed him into a wrathful, extravagantly homosexual poseur. "Gercha yer f—in' self, you stupid old queen," shrieked Molloy. "This boy's father's dead."

I saw Isaac slump forward. Then he was up on his feet, struggling along the line of knees and coats that lay between us and the elaborately decorated door at the end of the gallery. Tessa was following him. She seemed to be limping. I remember feeling that this was not quite possible. I had no expression or words or attitude to manage this experience. As a form of escape I felt the welcoming presence of laughter. Perhaps this was funny? Perhaps when people you loved very much died you were supposed to laugh?

But, as fast as the offer of laughter had been made it was withdrawn. It was the people around me – who all, I felt, had fathers, fathers who lived and talked and walked – these were the ones who could laugh, as they were doing at this old, ugly, obscene, fat woman on the stage (she had now resumed her dance. . . . Boomps a daisy. . .boomps a daisy. . .). All that was left to me was tears. When people die you give them tears.

I think, in fact, I am confusing all of this with the death of my own father four years later, on the third day of the General Strike (the only occasion in his life, may I say, that Stanley Barking withdrew his labour at the same time as more progressively minded members of the working class) but, if I am, I make no apologies for the confusion. Old Mr Rabinowitz is as welcome to my grief. They can all have my tears – for all the good they will do with them – both fathers, that boy I saw in Berlin, Tessa, Zak – I offer them all my big, fat, round, cynical, crocodile tears.

Our fathers managed remarkably similar deaths, as it happened. They both contrived to suffer massive cerebral strokes. They both fell, spectacularly, across the scenery of their domestic lives. In both cases the subjects opened their bowels involuntarily. In both cases, when I first saw them, their mouths were open as Smythe's had opened that day in France, and in both cases their hands were curled up in a tight claw, like the talons of some desperate bird of prey. What struck me first, on seeing them, was the ease with which death manages this transition. The black shadow that has tormented us for so long, has teased us with its unknowability, its obstinate determination, acts as casually as the opening of a door.

Zak cried. Great shuddering sobs that shook his shoulders. He felt his way towards his mother and Tessa and faded to the back of the house; the house, too, looked different, as if it, too, had been interrupted in the middle of some everyday action. The table, at which I had so often seen Isaac and his mother sit when we were children, had a sinister, accusing air. The big clock looked as if it were waiting for someone. Someone it didn't like. In all the house was this silence, that seemed to promise to go on for ever and ever and ever. The silence choked even the noise of crying, printing the image of old Mr Rabinowitz, sprawled across the complete works of Carlyle, his thin, jagged face still wincing with the pain of whatever it was that had taken him from us.

"You love him a lot, don't you?" I said to Tessa.

"I think I rather do," she said.

"Well, that's good," I said. "So do I. I love him a lot."

"Yes," she. "Funny old Amos." She looked across at me. "I expect you don't like being called 'funny old Amos'," she said.

"I don't mind," I said. "If people don't hit me, I don't mind."

I found I was crying. She came across to me and put her arms around me. She smelled of dried herbs and expensive soap.

They were married three weeks later. I can't remember where it happened, but I know it wasn't at a synagogue.

I was beginning to think I wouldn't get lunch of any kind. I was beginning to think that Alan proposed to leave me in here until I had written this damned release. In fact, about an hour ago (I think it was an hour ago), he put his head round the door and, waving a piece of cheese at me, said, "We must talk."

I hastily put away my papers and went over to him, expecting to get another demand for the release. But he seemed to have lost interest in that. "I want you to meet somebody", he said, "who may be very helpful to you in your career."

"What career?" I said.

Alan – I nearly wrote Isaac then – laughed. "Writing," he said. "Making things up that aren't true." And he waved me out into the corridor.

When I got out into the corridor, I saw that in his left hand, the one not holding the cheese, was a giant pickle.

"Is this lunch?" I said.

"It is," said Alan. "Don't you know, there's a war on."

"Of course," I said.

Alan's office is, naturally, larger than mine. In it he has not only a desk, a typewriter and a filing cabinet, but a secretary called Eric. For some reason I have never been able to understand, she wears uniform. Her real name is Erica but everyone calls her Eric. She is a huge woman in glasses, who never speaks, but sits, shoulders hunched, squinting round her fearfully, as if at any moment she may be asked by Alan to perform some unspeakable sexual favour. Alan completely ignores her for most of the time.

Also in Alan's office, when I went in there, was a big-boned man in a shabby tweed jacket and grey flannels, whom Alan introduced as Mactavish.

"Hullo, Mactavish!" I said guardedly.

"Are you", said Mactavish, in a not wholly convincing accent, "fra Glasgae?"

"No," I said, "I'm not."

"This", said Alan, "is Henry Swansea."

"Are ye not fra Glasgae?" said the big-boned man again.

"No," I said a second time, "I'm afraid I'm not."

Alan beamed at us both. He seemed to think the meeting was going very well. He went round behind his desk and took out a piece of paper. Alan always likes to have a piece of paper by him during meetings. I think it gives him a spurious sense of being in control of other people's destinies. I saw him write, in bold capitals, at the head of the blank sheet, as I settled uneasily into the hard chair directly opposite Eric, GLASGOW.

"Henry's a writer," said Alan.

"Gude," said the big-boned man. He got up and stretched out his hand to me. I took it. He crushed my knuckles between his giant fist.

Before he could ask me whether I was from Aberdeen or Perth, I said in my primmest possible voice, "What do you do, Mactavish?"

Alan answered my question. This is another habit of Alan's when in meetings. He quite often answers questions addressed to other people, as well as asking other people questions that have just been addressed to him. Often when in these "meetings" of Alan's, I feel I am in some surrealist drama and become seized with a desire to kneel, prostrate myself on the carpet, or stand on one foot in his metallic grey waste-paper basket. "Mactavish is with the Crown Film Unit," he said.

I tried to look interested.

"He made *Tommy Atkins has VD*," said Alan.

Mactavish grunted. "I don't think that is my best film," he said.

"And *I Am a Rear Gunner*," said Alan hastily.

I smiled politely.

"We're looking for a writer", said Mactavish, "who can work with Humphrey."

Alan got up from his desk and started to pace. "It would get you involved, Henry," he said. "I think you should be involved. I think you should do the things you're good at, you know? Because I think you are good. I think you're good."

Mactavish was looking at me appraisingly. He made a great show of being appraising. I felt as if I was being selected for some dangerous and unpleasant mission and started to attempt to suggest that maybe I wasn't quite the sort of person who. . . . This seemed to decide Mactavish that I was exactly the sort of person who. . .and, getting to his feet, he extended that huge hand once more. "This afternoon at four," he said. "Alan knows where you're to come." And delivering another crushing blow to my hand, he strode from the room.

Alan watched him go and then turned to me. "You'll like Mactavish," said Alan. "He's a bit of a bastard, but you'll like him."

Eric drew back the drawer of her filing cabinet with a funereal clank and from it took a large piece of Cheddar cheese. She held this out to me mournfully, watching me through her glasses in dumb misery. I smiled at her. Eventually I took the cheese from her and bit into it. It tasted of soap. I began to chew it thoughtfully.

"We could loan you to them," said Alan keenly.

"Oh," I said.

"Don't you like the idea?"

"I just. . . ."

I could not say what I really felt. I was thinking about Zak's face the day Labour lost the 1924 election. I was thinking about Zak and Tessa and me at meetings, outside factory gates. And I was thinking about Isaac and Tessa looking up at Rajani Palme Dutt as if he were some idol. I saw the three of us, in those years of the early twenties, arm in arm. I saw me almost, but not quite, believing. And then I thought of those cities in Germany (they can't *all* be bloody Nazis) and a sick feeling of waste and hopelessness came over me.

"Do you remember the Zinoviev letter?" I said to Alan.

Of course he did not. He was in Germany at the time.

"It was a letter", I said, "printed the day Labour lost the election in 1924. The *Daily Mail* put it on the front page. It more or less said that Zinoviev and the Communist International ordered the British Communist Party to start an immediate revolution."

"So?"

"So it lost Labour the election. Some say. I had a friend who swore it was a forgery. He said only a *Daily Mail* journalist could have written such a thing."

"What has this got to do with the Crown Film Unit?"

"Well," I said, "I said to him at the time that it didn't matter whether it was forged. In fact the policy of the International was so half baked that I thought it was exactly the kind of thing they would have come up with. The Left said it was forged – and the revolutionary Left said it loudest of all – because it wasn't tactically appropriate at the time. They wanted to disown their opinions, you see, in case they scared the electorate."

"I still don't see – "

I got to my feet. "Don't you, Alan? Don't you see that politics destroys truth? You are forced to say things, not because you believe them, but because they sound right. When I heard my friend denounce that letter, really passionately, as if his life depended on it, I knew I'd lost him in a way. He and I had started to see the world in a completely different way. He thought it could be changed. I *knew* it couldn't."

"This is your – "

I didn't want to talk about Zak with Alan. I wanted to keep them separate. I felt angry that the two images kept coinciding. I went towards the door. "It's all a bloody cesspool, Alan. What's your war *for?* You give up everything for it – the respect for truth, the respect for human life, the – "

He was, almost immediately, very angry. "So you want the Germans here, do you?"

"I didn't say that. I'm saying you should face up to what you're doing. Every night we're bombing thousands of innocent civilians. For what? I'll tell you for what – for reasons of hatred, that's for what. Hatred and revenge. And I don't want to spend the rest of the war telling people out there that it's all wonderful and Tommy Atkins is doing his bit and we only lost three aircraft last night, when it's lies. It's lies, lies, lies – the whole thing is built on lies."

"Sometimes", said Alan quietly, "it's necessary to tell lies. You live in the real world. Face it. Large sections of the so-called civilized West are trying to kill each other. The kind of scrupulousness you are invoking has nothing to do with war. Lies are necessary."

I felt suddenly cold. They were exactly the words Zak had used to me that night of the election, in the middle of an argument almost as fierce as this. And, as I recalled Isaac's words and his face, passionate across the table of that pub in Covent Garden, Tessa gazing between the two of us, distraught that her boys should be quarrelling, I had the sensation of falling through time. I didn't, I saw, quite believe what I was saying, now or then, and yet I was saying it now with twice the conviction I had had earlier, because the war I was fighting was not Alan's war. It was a battle with myself and Isaac, part of some private grief that led me to distrust enthusiasm so. Those who do not understand history are forced to repeat it. I don't understand my history or the history of my times. It is some kind of nightmare for me, from which I am unable to awake. I hear myself revoice old opinions in a stale, old-maidish voice and even their cynicism does not convince me. I do not have enough faith in anything to be disillusioned.

I went to the prison-like window at the end of the corridor, from where one can look down on Holborn. A smart-looking man in American uniform was talking to a girl. Her hair, bobbed above her shoulders, danced with delight when she laughed. The Americans are now our occupying army, bringing with them a normality, a largesse, that shames our tired city. In the paling sunshine the couple talked on, eyes locked, and I thought about my empty room to which I must return.

Unreal city, unreal war, unreal future. . .later there will be real ministry tea.

I went back to my office, took out the manuscript and wrote furiously. That made me feel better. Next door I could hear Alan dictating letters in a loud, purposeful voice. Maybe that made him feel better. I hadn't mentioned my "secret" – but then it isn't much of a secret, only a rumour. I don't actually believe that quite as many were killed in one raid as that man from the Air Ministry said. The fact of the matter is – I no longer believe atrocity stories, or rather I believe them all, both ours and theirs, which comes, of course, to the same thing.

If I can only make sense of Isaac. If I can only make sense of all that, perhaps meaning, like some unstoppable virus, will begin to invade the rest of my life. Perhaps I will know *why* I am rejecting Alan and the war, or else discover that in fact I do not oppose it. The fact of the matter is that, like most of us, I am frightened of discovering my true self.

It was, I think, about six months after the 1924 election – perhaps longer – that Rajani Palme Dutt asked Tessa, Zak and myself to accompany him on a boating trip.

"I never knew Rajani went in for boating," I said to Tessa.

"He loves punts and things", said Tessa, "and gliding along the water like a sort of leaf. It takes his mind off the Comintern and things."

"How is the Comintern?" I said.

"Awful," said Tessa. "They're always drunk apparently. There's a man called Slobedev running it now who Rajani can't stand. He keeps trying to borrow money off Rajani and he's got this ludicrous scheme about the bowler hats. I expect you've heard of that."

I never did find out what the scheme was, or whether it was the same Slobedev who had stood on the pavement near the river all those years ago when Zak fought the O'Malley twins, for at that moment Rajani himself entered the bookshop, where this conversation was taking place. It was, I recall, a bright day in late autumn, and Rajani was wearing a white suit and a straw boater. This was surprising enough in itself, but next to him, also in a white suit and boater and swinging a light cane, was none other than Parminder. Parminder was whistling a popular tune of the moment and when he saw us bowed low. "Honourable lady and gentleman," he said.

Zak came through from the back of the shop. Since his father's death he had taken the business more seriously and was often to be seen cruising the nearby markets in search of first editions, or late at night bent over the accounts making little clicking noises with his teeth. For this reason, and as Tessa and I were never as keen on politics as he, none of us had seen Rajani for some time and, as a consequence, when we set off for the station, I found it necessary to demonstrate my keenness on questions of the moment.

"How is Parminder?" I said.

"Parminder in himself", said Palme Dutt, "qua Parminder is unchanged in relation to the contradictory historical forces he re-presents. He objectively represents the same undercurrents in the society which messieurs the bourgeoisie have cooked up for us as, say, Schnoebbel."

I looked back. Parminder seemed in great form, chatting away to Zak and Tessa in the afternoon sunshine. "Yes," I said, "but is he better?" I did not dare ask who Schnoebbel was.

"He is better", said Palme Dutt, "in the sense in which he may be said to represent currents which, as far as the concrete demonstration of forces within the aforementioned 'society' are, abstractly and concretely speaking, impelled by the same subjectively fascist tendencies, related to – " Palme Dutt passed his hand over his brow and decided to abandon this sentence to its fate. He leaned over to me and in a confidential voice whispered: "He has clear periods."

In the train on the way to Twickenham Parminder told us about his new hobby. He had discovered the joy of cooking and, when he was "better" – he put heavy verbal quotation marks around the word – he wished to train as a chef.

Rajani listened to this with paternal attention. "I don't think you're quite well yet," he said.

Tessa pulled at Rajani's sleeve. "Oh, Rajani," she said, "I think he's fearfully much better. He's like a sylph. He's a new man really, don't you think? Doesn't he make you want to stretch up on your toes and shout and sing and say all sorts of beautiful things?"

Rajani smiled at her. "I'm sure he will be all right," he said. "I am sure he will." Here he gave Parminder a narrow look. "Eventually," he added.

Parminder gave out a brief, nervous giggle. I looked out of the window at the rows of back gardens, all those half-finished lives. A fat man stood by a washing line and looked up disconsolately as the train left him to get on with his life. A child played with a dog in a pile of dark red leaves. I thought about Zak and Tessa's new room above the shop, with its neatly made double bed. I thought about the looks they exchanged sometimes, when the three of us were in the shop together, and reflected that my life, like the season, seemed to be fading and closing.

Rajani Palme Dutt was, indeed, an expert on boating. He asked the waterman below Twickenham Bridge for a double-headed, crown-rowlocked ready-caulked skiff. "With transverse oars," he added. The waterman had never heard of "transverse oars" and told him that, as far as he knew, there was no such thing as a double-headed, crown-rowlocked, ready-caulked skiff. If we wanted a boat, he said, we could have a boat. But we would "have to cut the rest of the bollocks *right out*". After half an hour of Rajani's dialectical brain, however, the waterman had admitted that there was such a thing as a doubleheadedcrownrowlockedreadycaulked skiff, and that it was only his general failure as a human being that had prevented him from getting hold of one. He had, he admitted, pretended to superior knowledge in order to impress us, but now that he had understood the error of his ways in respect of the question of the so-called "boat", he realized that the disgusting lies he had told earlier stank out his mouth and brought shame on the whole profession of watermen.

"The boat in itself", said Rajani, "is, objectively speaking. . . ."

"Have any boat you like", said the waterman, "for free."

"Objectively – " began Palme Dutt again.

"Or pay money," said the boatman. "Whatever you like. Do whatever you like."

In the end Palme Dutt insisted on paying him fourpence-halfpenny which, he informed us, was the social wage appropriate to the labour objectified in the so-called "boat" in so far as its use value could be discovered by those actually using it. He was still explaining this tricky theoretical point to the boatman as we were pushed out into the stream. The man watched us go with a high, manic laugh and Zak and I, who were rowing, pulled strongly out into the stream.

Over to our left a row of chestnut trees like ruined, golden castles stood with almost suspect neatness in the meadow that separated the road from the river. On the other bank was a park and, shrouded in trees that had kept their colour, the shape of a white house, windows winking in the sun. I looked down at the stream. It was difficult to believe it was the same river that flowed to the south of the bookshop, studded with barges and the shabby cargo of the city. A yellow-backed leaf floated past me, on towards Sunbury.

"If", Parminder was saying, "I can't get into catering, I should like to go into politics."

Rajani bristled. "I think", he said, "that wouldn't be a good – "

Parminder laughed, a little wildly I thought, and glared round the boat at the company. "Rajani and I", he said, "have completely different views on the question of co-operation with the Labour Party. He thinks we should support them as a rope supports a hanged man. I think we should support them with bits of bacon and cheese."

Rajani flushed darkly. "Stop this foolish talk, Parminder," he said. "You only do this to annoy me. I have told you before that politics is a serious business and that you do not understand it. I do not wish to have to call for O'Reilly and Schleswig, but if you continue in this manner I shall – "

Zak, Tessa and I developed an interest in the scenery.

"I think we should also support them", went on Parminder, "with surgical stockings and egg sandwiches. I think we should support them with toast and marmalade and watercress soup, and I think we should also support them with fried onions in batter lovely." He giggled, rather self-indulgently, at his own joke.

Rajani, however, was rapidly losing control. "Listen," he said, "I am warning you. We will secure you and take you back to Glengarry if – "

I had never seen Palme Dutt angry before. It was a frightening spectacle. That calm, academic face became distorted with a fury that was even more terrible because it was so slow to arrive. He began to edge towards Parminder in the boat. Parminder, meanwhile, was sticking out his tongue and babbling something about the Comintern. I looked at Zak.

"Rajani – "

"Rajani pajani," cackled Parminder, "stick it up your mummy!"

"STOP THIS PARMINDER!"

Parminder was now rocking around, in an ecstasy of dislike. "Communish bommunism," he was saying. "All you want is to boss people around, you do, just like when you took my frog. You're just the same. Democratic centralism hemocratic fentralism. Pooey. Working class. It's just an excuse. No one can understand a word you say anyway, just like when you ate that semolina that Mummy left to spite me."

Rajani got to his feet. His face was crimson. "IT WAS NOT YOUR FROG!" he screamed. "IT WAS MY FROG!"

The boat was now rocking dangerously. I heard Tessa call to Rajani, but it was too late. The Communist leader had flung himself on his twin and the two were struggling desperately in the bow of the boat. I lowered my oars and threw myself forward after them, but it was too late. With a splash Parminder hit the surface of the water and his twin, leaning over the side of the boat, seized his greying hair and thrust his head below the level of the waterline. "Now listen," said Rajani. "Do you understand the need for the Communist Party to work with the existing Labour organizations in this country as Comrade Lenin has advised us? Do you understand the need for a tightly disciplined party that – "

I managed to seize his elbow, aided by Tessa, and Palme Dutt the Second's head re-emerged, like something from a fairy story. There was water on his hair and weed on his glasses (which were, miraculously, still in the same place) but he seemed unimpressed by his dilemma.

"Bollocks," he said, clearly and distinctly.

Rajani tore himself free of the two of us, grabbed his twin's hair and thrust him down into the river once again. After what seemed like a full minute, he raised Parminder up again and screwed his face down into his. "It was my frog!" he said.

As he said it Rajani overbalanced and the two of them were in the water. The boat was now out in the middle of the stream and, although Zak and I rowed hard against the current, we seemed to be constantly slightly ahead of them. I heard Rajani scream: "Do you accept the need for Leninist discipline?" At least I *think* that was what he screamed. But, before I had the time even to attempt to decipher their argument, the two of them had disappeared below the level of the stream. We tried to row back to them but we could not reach them. All I could see was two identical heads thrashing about in the current and two identical arms closing around two identical throats. Tessa got hold of a boat hook and attempted to prise them apart, but only succeeded in braining one of them (it was, by now, totally impossible to tell which was which). Eventually, in the mass of troubled, white water, there was only one head and one pair of glasses and, as we finally managed to pull ourselves alongside the victorious twin, the single head said: "Objectively speaking, the so-called 'death' of my brother has no existence in terms of its concrete social existence, would you not agree?"

I looked down at the greying hair and the weed-covered glasses and was about to ask Rajani what he thought he was doing, but I stopped the question on my lips. I never did manage to penetrate the mysteries of Palme Dutt One's feelings for Palme Dutt Two, for from the water came a high-pitched giggle and I saw that the jacket collar of the survivor was of white linen. It was Parminder.

"You have just murdered", said Zak tightly, "the leader of the British Communist Party."

"Objectively speaking," said Parminder, "the so-called 'death' of my brother is something which in Marxist terms cannot be admitted in the context of social theory, in so far as the social factor chosen to embody the victorious progress of the proletariat in this, the last stage of messieurs the bourgeoisie's determined attempt to protect their capital, ought not, perhaps, be seen to be a 'non-swimmer'." And he cackled again, swimming off strongly in the opposite direction. Somewhere or other – perhaps at the Glengarry Nursing Home – Parminder had mastered a leisured, powerful breaststroke.

"Oh, gosh," said Tessa, almost dreamily, "he does sound awfully like him!"

We never found Rajani Palme Dutt's body. Perhaps his pockets were so weighted by pamphlets or papers that it never surfaced. Or perhaps there was a sound Marxist reason why a dead dialectician does not, as ordinary mortals do, bloat with water and rise like a sponge to face the cruel day. Maybe Rajani lodged against some rock or crevice in the Thames and, even now, his skeleton knocks and plucks against the weeds of a bank somewhere south of Twickenham. Effectively speaking, Rajani Palme Dutt never disappeared and sometimes I think it is his crazy brother who occupies his place somewhere in the digestive tract of that most English, most persuasive of rivers, that even as I write winds its cold way through wartime London.

When we got the boat back to the bank, we found Parminder waiting for us. He was standing beneath a willow tree, water running out of his jacket pockets, a beatific smile on his face. "Greetings, comrades," he said. "I have a meeting in Fulham on Thursday."

Zak looked grim. "You go for the police, Amos," he said.

"Listen," said Parminder, "Rajani pajani told no one about me. No one. My existence was a very closely guarded secret. You are the only people in the world to know about it. The Glengarry Nursing Home was a front organization of the British Communist Party."

We gaped at him.

"Look," he went on, "do you really think anyone will believe your story? I will deny it. And if they do trust you enough to drag the river for him, I'll tell them you helped me do it. You must know enough about the police to know they're completely stupid."

Zak looked at me. None of us moved. With each minute that passed Parminder was sounding more and more plausible. Perhaps, I thought to myself, his mental condition was caused by nothing more than terminal sibling rivalry. With the termination of his twin, all traces of it seemed to have disappeared.

"We will return to London", he said, "and I will attend the meeting of the Foreign Policy Co-ordination Committee this afternoon. I will then go on to address a study group of the National Union of Mineworkers on the subject of 'Monopoly Capitalism and Protective Clothing: A Study of Asbestos Mining in the Southern American States'."

We did not bother to ask him how he knew the details of Rajani's schedule so intimately. It seemed, I think, to all of us, as we listened to the dripping figure in the white suit, that we were looking at a ghost – only the faint tremor at the edge of his mouth suggested the Parminder with whom I was familiar. I suppressed a vision of him leaping on to the table in the middle of a Communist Party Executive Meeting in order to discourse on frogs or the Power of Love. Parminder must have caught my expression, for he looked at me with the insistent, plausible insight of the insane and said: "I'll never crack. They'll never know. I'll never give them cause. I knew him down to the last full stop. But inside I'll be laughing. Laughing, laughing, laughing at the stupid, po-faced things he will say, at the ludicrous attempt to control something so beautiful and mysterious as the rise of the oppressed peoples, the ascent of the workers and the deprived, the death of the huge, bloated men in hats who swagger around like great fat SPIDERS!"

Here he burst into hysterical laughter. But when the laughter had finished, he allowed his face to settle with a curious, a deadly, calm, and when his features were still, he held up one bony hand and said, in an uncanny imitation of Rajani, "Do not attempt to 'follow' me, comrades. We will say no more of this affair. Look for me only upon the foolish stage of the world. Whence I am bound."

And he turned and limped off through the meadow towards the road. Tessa sighed softly. "Rajani was quite Shakespearean sometimes," she said. "It's funny. I can't feel sad. It's so like him, I can't feel sad at all."

Zak looked back at the river. "Did we. . .?"

"I think so," I said. "I *think* so."

Without speaking the three of us rejoined the boat. We did not speak as Zak and I rowed us back up to the boat house. The water, the still, autumn trees and the washed-out blue of the sky that seemed to belong to another season made it difficult to believe that any of this had happened. Once or twice on the way back home, Tessa tried to talk about it, but was unable to finish what she had to say. By the time the three of us were back in the shop, the whole affair had receded into some sphere untouchable by conversation. It was as if it had occurred, but on another occasion, in a different place, and perhaps a long, long time ago. Later I felt as if we had not seen what we had seen but that it had been described to us by a particularly unreliable witness. I did mention it some weeks later to Zak, when we were in the shop alone one morning, but all he said was: "That's past history. Isn't it?"

* * *

I don't think it was the fact that the General Secretary of the Communist Party of Great Britain was being impersonated by his homicidal twin brother that disillusioned Zak about the nature and process of politics. I think it was that nobody noticed.

To all intents and purposes, as far as I could tell from the newspapers, the policy of the Party remained much the same and, if Parminder did behave oddly at some trade union rally or other, everybody kept very quiet about it. Zak no longer went to Party meetings. He immersed himself in the book trade. When Pamela called one afternoon he hid in the back room and got me to tell her he was away on business.

But he suffered from the lack of an enthusiasm. And his marriage suffered as well.

I had gone to night school to get some qualifications, and worked in the shop only four, instead of six, days a week. But when I was there, I tended to be alone with Tessa, since Isaac was now almost exclusively occupied with buying first editions and gossiping with other booksellers in a pub called the Swan over towards the City. His principal obsession was devising ingenious ways of getting rid of unsaleable works. He piled, I recall, the twenty volumes of a work called *Medieval Tombs in the Isle of Thanet* out on the pavement in the alley and placed a notice on them reading RESERVED FOR BRITISH MUSEUM. He sold them in three days. But he did not discuss books or ideas as he once had and, if Tessa brought up the subject of politics, she told me, he would look away.

"I'm worried about him," she said to me one afternoon.

"I know," I said.

"He used to be so full of...you know...and sort of...I don't know, but big...you know...and now...."

"Yes," I said.

She looked at me wonderingly.

"What do you want to do, Amos?" she said.

"Oh, me? I want to write, of course. I want to describe things. I want to change the way people feel about what they see. I don't want to *do* anything."

She looked at me shrewdly. "You're funny," she said. "You pretend to be all sort of dried up like a stick or something but really you're terrifically passionate, aren't you?"

I made a lecherous face at her.

"I don't mean that way," she said, "although I expect you really are marvellously sort of hot stuff if you wanted to be with girls. I mean about things generally."

"What things?"

"Oh, you know," said Tessa, "justice and injustice and cruelty. And the dreadful class system that keeps us all enslaved and unemployment and the waste of the war and Truth. You know."

"Yes," I said, "I know."

I felt, as I often did when with Tessa, that to become the person she imagined I was would be a fine thing. It would involve an almost complete personality change, a couple of years in a monastery and the removal of some if not all of my brain, but it would be worth it. She clearly felt she still had not done me justice and went on: "And fighting for your rights and love and caring for those nearest to you and sort of concern for Wisdom."

"Ah, yes," I said, "Wisdom. As in teeth."

Here she ran at me and leaped up into my arms. "Funny, satirical, naughty, passionate Amos!" she said.

"Yes," I said.

"You'll find a nice girl soon", she went on, "or perhaps you'll find a horrid one. A real slut." And she kissed me quite hard, on the cheek. Then she allowed herself to fall back heavily. She looked suddenly old and tired. "I don't think he loves me any more," she said. "In the evening, when you're gone, he just sits and stares at the wall. It's been like that since his father died. He just isn't

176

interested. I try to talk to him about things. About me and him and you and all the things we're going to do and about Truth and Unemployment and Revolution and Love. But he just sits there."

I smiled paternally at her, reflecting that life with Tessa, on a hand-to-hand basis, might well become somewhat tiring. But for all her absurdities, I still found her touching. As she wandered away through the piles of books, trailing one hand artfully across the dusty colonnades of literature, philosophy and art, I followed her through the shop. "Look," I said, "he'll be all right. He just doesn't know what he wants to do yet. That's all."

She turned to me. In spite of her background, Tessa smelt not at all surgical. I put a very fatherly arm around her. To my surprise, she began to quiver in what I can only describe as a significant way.

"Don't," she said, "don't touch me, Amos. I'm frightened of what we might do."

"What might we do?"

"We might kiss or something."

The thought of kissing her had not entered my head until that moment. But not only did she mention the possibility, she was making pullulating movements with her lips and allowing her shoulders to heave up and down, as if she was about to sing. Once the idea of kissing her had entered my mind, it became very difficult to get rid of it, especially as, in addition to the pullulating movement of the lips and the heaving of the shoulders, she had allowed her arms to fall to her sides in sudden abandon. I craned my head towards her, forming my lips into the appropriate shape for kissing. We were just about to make contact when she broke away and, with that high, silvered laugh of hers, said: "No. No. No."

I stood there like a goldfish who has just made an unsuccessful bid for a breadcrumb. Tessa flung her head back and, very slowly, grew older again before my eyes. In a still, quiet voice, she said: "He doesn't touch me any more. He's lost interest in everything. In everything."

"I'm sorry," I said.

Three weeks later I got a job on the *Poplar Star and Advertiser* as a trainee general reporter.

The *Poplar Star and Advertiser* was a local paper run by a man called Wearing. Wearing was a short, bald man who had worked in Fleet

Street for some years. I can't remember when I went to see Wearing. Sometime in 1924, but it can't have been then. Zak was still involved with the Party at that stage. Merely thinking about Wearing has the effect of confusing my memory, since he was a man so confused about dates that it was often his habit to place the wrong one on the masthead of his newspaper. I know when I went to see him (on the recommendation of Norman Oldroyd, who knew almost everyone in the area, perhaps because his list of patients was such a volatile one) I was struck by the total absence of staff of any kind. He greeted me in a sort of cubby-hole, off a larger cubby-hole, which he described as the "conference room". In an effort to impress him, I said, before I had sat down: "What do you think of the new government?"

"Is there a new government?"

Let us say this conversation took place about a year after Labour's defeat in the '24 election. I gulped. He was smiling at me benignly.

"There's been one for ages," I said.

"Yes," said Wearing, "and then there'll be another one I expect. That's the way it goes usually, isn't it? Government and then another one, and then on like that."

"Well," I said, "this new government – "

My tone, I noticed, was suddenly that of an elementary school-teacher. To my relief, Wearing held up a plump hand to interrupt my remarks. "Don't bother," he said. "I'm not really interested in current affairs. I get a bit out of touch here."

I swallowed. "Doesn't the newspaper keep you in touch a bit?" I said.

Wearing smiled. "Not really," he said. "I see this as a paper rather than a *news*paper." He sniffed at the sound of the word "news". "We try to keep that sort of stuff to a minimum," he said.

I looked out of the window. There was a small cobbled yard outside and a brick wall. Halfway up the brick wall was a printed notice that said GET TO GRIPS WITH THE POPLAR STAR. I looked back at Wearing and saw he was scrabbling in the drawer of the desk in front of him. Eventually he took out a battered sheet of newsprint and passed it across the desk to me. It was a front page of the *Poplar Star*, clearly some weeks old, and at the top was a gigantic headline. So large was the headline that there was little room beneath it for print of any kind. The headline read: SLOW WEEK ON EAST LONDON ROADS.

Wearing smiled. "We were particularly proud of that one," he said.

"Oh," I said.

Wearing, I learned subsequently, was a man who wanted to make as few compromises as possible with the world of politics. The *Poplar Star* was a *mélange* of recipes, horoscopes, quizzes, puzzles and odd religious maunderings written by Wearing himself, which occupied most of the editorial pages.

"Why", a typical editorial would begin, "does Man labour? For his satisfaction? Or for the satisfaction of others? For Duty? Or for Pleasure? Does Man need to labour at all? Why do some labour at menial tasks while others control the destinies of great nations or mighty armies? Or ships?" He would go on in this vein for pages, often piling up as many as twenty quite unanswerable rhetorical questions. My job initially was to sub-edit this copy, a delicate task, as to Wearing it was all prose that would not have disgraced the King James Bible.

"You want to lose that. . .?" he would say to me wonderingly.

"I see what you mean, Mr Wearing," I would reply, "but. . . ."

I developed a sort of parallel universe, rather like that of a medieval theologian, where I was able to attack and defend portions of Wearing's ludicrous paragraphs, by a form of reference to the "system" whence the said paragraphs emerged. "Do we need", I would say, "to mention the people who control ships? Wouldn't it be better just to mention those who control armies?"

Wearing would look at me doubtfully.

"I mean," I would go on, "we haven't mentioned the people who control horses, say, or those who control motor vehicles."

Wearing would bite his lip. "Maybe we should," he would be liable to reply. "Maybe we should mention those people. I just don't know any more."

Strange to say, Wearing's paper sold amazingly well and, as it was all written by Wearing and myself, it was not expensive to produce. Our technique was to place one "news" story on the front page and leave the rest of the paper free for columns such as "Old Herb's Weather Forecast for 1926" or "This Week's Walk in Poplar". This was our only area of disagreement. Occasionally I would attempt to smuggle in some reference to the real world at this stage of the proceedings and my attempts would always be resisted. Even if it was the story of some local warehouse that had burned down, it was always "too much" for Wearing – and as for the news of a more national character, it set his plump frame shaking with fear.

"Do you think people want to hear about things like that?" he would say. "Terrible things like that?"

"They may not want to", I said, "but they need to."

"Why do they need to? They can't do anything about any of it. So why do they need to, please? And as for the ones who *can* do something about it – well, they know anyway, don't they?"

This point was rather difficult to answer. But I kept on trying.

I saw little of Zak and Tessa after that conversation with Tessa on the subject of my friend. I think I felt that we all knew too much about each other for comfort and that whatever I said to either of them, however innocently intended, would now be made to mean something quite different. I wasn't lonely. I don't get lonely. Wearing employed a man called Arthur to print the paper and, in the evenings, Arthur and I would spend our time in the pub across the road from the *Star*, drinking and discussing Wearing, with the detailed fanaticism colleagues reserve for each other. Now I was out of active politics, I found the subject more and more fascinating.

"I think Wearing should be told about the collapse of the Labour government," I would say. "I think someone should tell him."

"You know that sort of thing upsets him," Arthur would reply. "What's the point?"

I pulled at my pint. "The awful thing is", I said, "I don't know where he stops, as it were. I mean, does he know the war's over, for example? Is he aware there's a war going on in Ireland?"

Arthur looked at me suspiciously. "Is there?" he said.

My final row with Wearing came over the question of the General Strike. There was obviously no question of there being a union for the *Poplar Star*, as I did not know how to set about forming myself into one, but I thought it necessary to inform Wearing that the strike was in progress. As it happened, he arrived late for work that morning (he was married and lived somewhere out near Leyton and quite frequently spent large portions of the day performing complex and mundane transactions for his wife in the market near our offices). I was in the "conference room" looking for a pencil and a rubber. "Did you know", I said, with a touch of malice, as soon as I saw his plump, cheerful face round the door, "that there's a General Strike on?"

He rubbed his cheek and looked at me fearfully. He was carrying a long string of foreign-looking sausages, which gave him the appearance of an extra in a pantomime or puppet show.

"How do you mean," he said, "a General Strike?"

"Everybody has gone on strike", I said (did Wearing know about strikes?) "to support the miners. The whole country."

Wearing put a plump finger in his mouth and sucked at it like a child. "Surely not the whole country," he said, "not *everyone*?"

"Everyone," I said, with a grim satisfaction.

"Banks", said Wearing, "and shops? And hotels? And farms? And women? Have all the women gone on strike? And schools? Are schools on strike?"

I began to suspect Wearing's *naïveté*. Guardedly, I said, "Well, *almost* everyone."

Wearing put his sausages on a broken desk and crossed to the grimy window. It was raining, as it always seemed to be for me in the twenties. When I read about cloche hats and flappers and jazz parties, I don't recognize the decade. For me it was the grimmest period of my growing up. I don't remember the season either. All I can recollect is that this conversation took place at a time when thousands of dockers, miners, drivers and factory workers had refused, for a short period, to fetch and carry any more. And I do recall that it irritated me beyond belief, shocked me into something like horror that I should be in this dark room with a foolish, middle-aged man and his string of sausages.

"How long has this been going on?" said Wearing.

"A few days," I said.

"When will it stop?" said Wearing.

I went through into our office without answering him. On his desk was the layout for that week's front page. It read SHARP DECLINE IN PET SALES IN EAST LONDON. I went back into the "conference room" and saw Wearing stooped over a desk. He appeared to be counting the sausages.

"I wish to give in my notice," I said.

"Notice of what?" said Wearing.

"I'm leaving, you stupid, obstinate, old bastard," I said.

Wearing turned on me. "Snotty little communist," he said. And his face erupted into a half smile, a look of such private cunning that I did not like to remain in the room with it. As I went out into the corridor he seemed to be rubbing his hands and whispering to himself and, looking back at him from the rain-sodden courtyard, I saw he was still smiling myopically in my direction. His newspaper is still published and perhaps he has found someone else to sit with him in that drab little room. I was positive I saw him once, years later, in the back of a car in Bow. But it was an expensive car and it was hard to make out Wearing's face in the gloom. I thought of him, for some reason, just before the war, at the time of Munich, and I imagined him at home in Leyton with his wife, practising that imitation courtliness upon her: "Hitler? I didn't catch that quite. Did you say Hitler?"

Maybe Alan has a point. Maybe I should try and do something. There is a time and place for world-weariness and maybe this is not it. If I am honest I would have to admit that the times in my life when I have been happiest have been those when I have been able to cast off the attitudes I rehearse so carefully – cynicism, detachment, other-worldliness – and act simply and clearly in the light of principles and beliefs that seem, if only for a short while, to make the world a clear and simple place. Well, of course, those were the times, in the main, when I was with Isaac. And it was to Isaac's I went that afternoon – on foot, through the dirty, rainy streets.

He has just come in here (Alan, I mean) to ask if I am "still all right" for four o'clock. He has a touching lack of faith in his subordinates' obedience. Like all naturally anarchic people, he makes a good leader, hovering in your mind, like an extension of the conscience. I will go with him. And perhaps. . . .

Perhaps this sudden certainty has been conjured up by the memory of that walk back through East London on the afternoon I gave in notice at the *Star*. It was like a city at war. At one street corner I saw a group of men and women surrounding a flour lorry. They were screaming at the driver and he was glaring down at them. On every other street were policemen, patrolling the citizens with glances that seemed to say, "If we need to make this one vast gaol we will. You won't win. I'll tell you *that*." But it was over near the Stokely tram depot that I saw the real action.

The rain had stopped as I came into Stokely Street, a short wide thoroughfare at one end of which was a giant hangar in which the London Omnibus Company stabled their vehicles. About twenty yards from the open mouth of the garage I saw, to my surprise, a tram marooned on the rails in the middle of the road. It was, at this stage of the strike, a little like seeing a tiger in Hyde Park. There was something flagrantly unfamiliar about it.

At the wheel was a very attractive woman indeed.

She had one of those necks that sweep up from breasts to chin like a waterfall, huge dreamy eyes which, to continue the water analogy, brought to mind inaccessible lakes or tarns, and an expression which, to completely finish off the water imagery for good and all, was, I feel compelled to say, a little wet. My encounter with Wearing had had a curious effect on me for, instead of hurrying away as I would normally have done, I went over to the group and found as I was doing so that I had developed a somewhat truculent, proletarian swagger.

There was a small crowd gathered round her and, when I pushed my way to the front of it, I saw that she was gazing about her like a monarch on a visit to subjects too long deprived of her company. "The gear," she was saying, "one looks. . .late at night for the cunning of an engine, displaying its ferocity through an assortment of handles, falling on the neck of itself like an exhausted swimmer and one – "

"Excuse me, lady," I said, "you wouldn't be thinking of driving that tram, would you?"

She threw back her head and laughed madly. "To take a tram," she said, "to gallop a tram across open country in search of an ideal! To take such a beast and show it the – "

Her face closed up suddenly and her eyes grew suspicious. "Is this a tram?" she said narrowly.

"It f—in' is, lady," I said, "and what is more, may I ask you once again whether you were thinking of driving it anywhere?"

"I", she said, "am a special constable. . . ."

"You're off your head, you are," said a lady near me.

Suddenly she seemed to see the crowd for the first time. Or rather, to realize that they weren't there to be cured of the scrofula. She stared round her and ended up glaring at me. "You," she said, "you. Is your lust for beauty? Or are you one of the herd of bootblacks who count things of the spirit as base? Are you going to be fine and brave, or are you going to retreat from the beautiful, terrible business of being alive?"

I thought this a somewhat unfair question.

If I'd known at the time that this old bat was Virginia Woolf, I could have asked her a few unfair questions. Questions like – why do you write such bloody awful books? Why are you such an appalling snob? Why doesn't anything you say make sense? But I only found out to whom it was that I was speaking many years later when I happened to see her picture on the cover of one of her books. I couldn't to this day swear that it *was* the author of *The Waves* and *To the Lighthouse*. All I can say is that if you thought she had some problems with those two books, then you should have seen her trying to drive a tram.

Zak always maintained that the whole of the Bloomsbury group was involved in strike breaking and that he personally had seen Clive Bell and Duncan Grant trying to take the 12.14 from King's Cross to Newcastle up a particularly tricky stretch of track to the east of Mornington Crescent. You would have thought that the Organisation for the Movement of Supplies would put Virginia on to something a bit simpler, like relief knitting or mobile washing up.

Eventually she climbed down from the tram and left it behind as if it were a crashed aircraft. When she'd gone, a line of us got up against one side of it and leaned into it. It wobbled away from us and then back into us. A few more joined us and we pushed again. Up the street I saw Mrs Woolf turn and stare back at us.

We all pushed again. This time the tram fell out further away from us and when it returned it nearly blew us over. But some more had joined and, amid a number of shouts and cheers, we pushed the thing back into another rock away from the rails. It was right up to the edge of its own centre of gravity, and it came back at us like an unbroken horse, but yet more of the onlookers had joined the line and this time, with a godalmighty heave, we sent the thing racketing off balance. It hung for a moment above the street like a wounded elephant and then pitched forward on to the far kerb with a crash that recalled the guns in France all those years ago.

"Murderers!" screamed Mrs Woolf at us from up the street. "Murderers!"

But no one paid any attention to this remark.

I didn't notice the crowds scatter, so taken was I by this thing's corpse, laid unceremoniously out in the street. There were flats on either side of the road and all the way up I could see faces appearing. I went over to the tram and kicked its side, hard. "Stay, boy!" I yelled at it.

When the hand came on to my shoulder, there were only five or six others left. I was the one shouting something which was, I suppose, why they tried to clobber me. It's the nearest in my life I've yet got to being a ringleader. "Come on," said this copper's voice, "let's 'ave yer. . . ."

I didn't wait around. Two men from our flats had been up before the magistrate, Terence Shrike, later for some extraordinary reason *Sir* Terence Shrike (knighting a magistrate is in my view the contemporary equivalent of making your horse a senator), and it was fairly well known that Terry handed out two years for looking at a policeman in anything other than a loving and respectful manner. What you got for pushing a tram was anybody's guess. I booted the policeman in the pit of the stomach and legged it up the road.

The only thing in my way was Virginia Woolf.

She was standing at the crossroads at the top of the street screaming in an artistic manner.

Now it is probably not generally known that Virginia Woolf was an expert at hand-to-hand combat, but this lady was no slouch at the direct attack. The copper was way behind but, as I panted past her on the inside, she came at me, all nails and boots and teeth, screaming: "Gone! Gone and lost and betrayed and stolen and utterly destroyed!"

She nutted me into the wall. I came back from that and stuck one on her.

"betrayed!" she yelled, "all is lorst and gorn and utterly swept away and betrayed!"

"Oh, f— off, you old bat," I said and stuck one on her. Hard.

I don't usually hit women, well not hard anyway, but I did make an exception in her case. She swayed back like a drunk into the middle of the road and removed her hat. It was quite an elaborate affair with fruit and veils on it. She flung it at me, spun round twice and then fell forward into the gutter. "You c—!" I heard her mutter. And then she was out cold.

I ran on out into Alma Gardens and down towards the White-chapel Road. That curious exhilaration that follows a violent physical encounter was on me and, as I ran off down the street that led to the alley where Isaac's shop was, I found myself chanting something to myself, some half-remembered slogan from all those meetings Tessa and Zak had forced me to attend.... "The people's flag is something red...stained with the something of our some-thing dead.... The people's flag is...."

I knew by the look of the shopfront that something was wrong. Or perhaps, looking back I can see myself outside that familiar façade and I see at the same time what came afterwards. I think I stepped in slowly and cautiously, but perhaps that was because I hadn't seen Zak or Tessa for some time and for different reasons I was nervous about seeing both of them.

There was no one in the shop. The door to the back room was open and from it I could hear the sound of crying, the sort of dry, compulsive, physical tearfulness that resembles nausea or some other uncontrollable spasm. I was still exulting from my curious en-counter. I had stored it up like a gift for my old friends, "You thought old Amos was this but wait until I...." The story died on my lips as I heard that crying. It made what had just happened seem like a childish adventure.

I went through into the back room and saw Zak and Tessa. He was lying on the sofa, staring ahead of him, and she was a few yards behind him, crying into a handkerchief. I noticed that her dress was torn at the shoulder and, across the base of her neck, was a huge red weal. Zak didn't seem to be aware of any of this. He lay there in a dream, not turning his head as I entered, quite still.

"Zak...."

He didn't answer. Tessa looked up at me. She didn't seem to know who I was.

"Zakky, it's me. Amos. Guess what. I was in a fight."

Still no answer.

"We were turning over this tram and...."

He turned his face to mine at last. "What's happening?" he said. "What's happening out there? Who's doing what to who? Can you tell me? I can't understand any of it. I just can't understand it." Then he started to giggle, a high-pitched giggle. I didn't like the sound of

it at all. "There's a strike," he said, "a sort of . . . ." Then he started
to laugh again.

"What's the matter, Tess?" I said.

At that point Mrs Rabinowitz walked into the room. She was
wearing a black dress and she looked tall and terrible. She looked at
me and said, flatly, "You better take your friend home."

"I'm sorry . . . ."

Mrs Rabinowitz was one of those graceful, supple old women.
She had a pale, oval face and straight black hair. Looking at her that
afternoon it occurred to me that she had not aged since Zak and I
used to come to the shop all those years ago when we were children.
She terrified me, too, as a parent terrifies a child, with righteous,
inexplicable moral outrage. I shifted uneasily from foot to foot and
waited for Tessa to say something. She did not. She looked at her
husband, then at her mother-in-law, but, although she had stopped
crying, she did not speak.

"What's happened?"

Mrs Rabinowitz looked down at her son. "He is not welcome in
this house."

"Syndicalism . . ." began Zak. Then he started to giggle again.

"Zak – "

He turned to me and shouted. When he shouted the two women
jumped back as if physically afraid, but he paid them no attention.
He stared at a point on the wall over to my left and spoke very
rapidly, his words slurring into each other, as if he had no control
over the order of his thoughts.

"Everyone thinks or says they think or thinks they say that we are
engaged in some kind of heroic struggle I keep telling them to
regard this as a heroic struggle is a hopeless mistake Christ people
think of struggles like this as heroic I tell you this isn't even a
struggle what's the point I can't make it fit any more I can't make
it – "

He stopped suddenly, as if he was seeing me for the first time,
and he said: "I was always saying that you were the hopeless one.
That you would never be there when you were needed. I think it
was me I was talking about. What are we doing even? What are we
doing?"

"What happened, Mrs Rabinowitz?" I said.

Tessa started to cry. "It doesn't matter, darling Amos. It really isn't sort of important. It doesn't affect what I sort of ... you know ... what I...."

Zak's mother looked at me with a curious coldness that I could not comprehend. "He hit her, that's all," she said, "and a few other things."

Zak had got to his feet, stiffly, like an old man. "I don't think", he said, in a voice he had not used since we were children, "that I am welcome in pater's house any more. I think I am in fact *de trop*, Barking."

His mother looked at the two of us, unmoved. Then he said: "Oh, she was bloody glad to see him go actually. Weren't you, old girl? Weren't you?" His mother did not speak. To say her face was frozen would not begin to describe its ageless, motionless impassivity. She was more Egyptian than Hebrew as she stood there in the back room, and Tessa's cries started up again, little wounded noises that seemed to have nothing to do with any of this.

"Can I", began Zak, "put up with your people for a few days?"

"Of course," I said, "Tessa – do you – "

"GET OUT!" shrieked his mother suddenly, "GET OUT GET OUT GET OUT!"

If Tessa had planned to say anything, she did not manage to say it. Instead she started to cry again and, before I was able to go to her, Zak's mother had swept across the room and put her arms round the sobbing girl. Zak came towards me. "Shall we go, Barking?" he said.

"I – "

"Shall we?"

So we went out into the alley, past the weeds on the broken pavement, the serrated roofs of the building opposite and all the bleak and crowded landscape that had not changed since I was a child.

"Zak – " I said, when we were outside.

He turned to me and gripped my arm hard. "Amos," he said, "I don't think I'm very well."

I am afraid that Zak's illness and my experiences of the General Strike will have to wait for another chapter. It is now roughly six o'clock, perhaps seven, and for the moment I cannot write about anything other than what has just occurred to me.

At about a quarter to four, Alan put his head round the door and

188

grinning excitedly said: "Ready for the off?" He has a store of these prefabricated "British" phrases, including such gems as "Toodle-oo, old thing" and odd, quite invented pieces of slang such as "Must go for a big one" when leaving the office for a lunchtime drink. I smiled up at him, having stowed the manuscript beneath the desk, and said I was ready.

Alan has an official car and, when we came out of the front of the building, it was waiting for us, purring in the November dark. The door was opened by a soldier in uniform and when I stepped into the back I was lost in a deep swirl of leather. I was reminded, for an instant, of "Margot" Perrindale's car and then, before I had time to think about "Margot" or her friends, we were off into the late afternoon.

"Isn't it just a beautiful city?" said Alan. Sometimes he adopts a vaguely American accent. I decided he was trying to impress our driver and nodded curtly. Looking out at the shadowy squares and remote, shuttered office blocks, I thought London seemed a dead city, a place that had waited years to rediscover its true nature and was in the middle of a spiritual, rather than a physical blackout. It was in mourning for something – maybe for those who climbed into those planes that droned off high above us for Germany night after night. I thought about the men who flew those things – the ones at the back, dropped under the tail in a tiny wire cage, and then I thought about the phrases one heard on the wireless, night and day, the ease with which "heroism" and "sacrifice" were exchanged as a kind of payment for the real death of so many young men.

"Why", I said slowly, in a kind of drawl, because I knew that that would annoy him, "doesn't someone or other negotiate a peace? They're finished, aren't they? Even if Adolf doesn't know it – some of them do."

Alan took his hand carefully away from my arm. "There are some people you can't negotiate with," he said.

I looked out of the window again. We appeared to be heading back down towards the river, in the direction of my old home. I had a sudden vision of my mother, seated at our kitchen table scraping together a meal. From time to time she would lift her head and listen for something, the sound of approaching planes perhaps, and then address herself to her work again. She was wearing a headscarf. It was not until I saw the headscarf that I realized that I was recalling not my mother, but a still from a film called *Make the Dinner Go Round*. God knows what my mother is doing. I haven't been back since –

I looked sideways at Alan. He seemed unusually nervous. "Why is it so important to you, Alan, that I *join in*?"

He smiled to himself, distantly. "Look," he said, "let's not talk about it, OK? Just come along and have a look. That's all."

"Who", I said, "is this Humphrey?"

Alan looked a little sheepish. "I don't actually know," he said. "Everyone over at Crown just calls him Humphrey. And they say it in the sort of way that implies that there should be no need to ask Humphrey *Who*. So one just goes – "

"Humphrey."

"Quite. And nods."

I grinned. "What did your parents do, Alan?"

"They got killed."

"Oh," I said.

He had made this remark in the kind of way that suggests further inquiries would not be welcome. I decided, therefore, not to make any.

We were coming down towards Tower Bridge now. Nervously I looked out at the river. I hadn't been anywhere near home for at least four years. Alan was watching me. "Do you know this part of the world, Henry?"

"Christ, no."

I sat back with great casualness as we turned up into Leman Street. Alan yawned.

"Why do you think we are fighting this war then?"

"Because . . . look . . . ."

I did not wish to begin this argument of ours again. Fortunately, at that moment, the car swerved into the side of the road and Alan scrambled for the door. It was not until we were out on the pavement that I saw, several hundred yards down the road, a group of men in Nazi uniforms, holding sub-machine-guns. Beyond them were a line of men with their hands above their heads and, beyond them, a cumbersome-looking film camera, set on what looked like a wooden trolley. One of the Nazi officers waved to us.

"That's Josh Piggot-Smith," said Alan. "I very much want you to meet him."

Josh Piggot-Smith clicked his heels and flashed a quick Nazi salute in our direction, then returned to the group of Nazis. They did, I had to admit, look very like Nazis. Alan led me up towards the group. The tenseness I had noticed in him in the car had returned. He kept peering about him as if, at any moment, the Germans might turn their guns on him and march him away.

"They look quite frightening," I said.

"Yes," said Alan.

The bizarre thought occurred to me that, if we *were* in Nazi Germany, it would be Alan that these officer-class types would arrest. I was all right, wasn't I? Nothing Jewish about me. As this thought came to me, an image of Isaac returned, on the bed in my parents' flat, in the middle of his "illness". Scraps of an argument we had had came back as well, some discussion about being English and how the English were traitors, double-dealers. I remembered the discussion because it had stirred something strange in me, forced me out of my usual pose. "Listen," I heard myself saying, "I don't know about the other bastards, but I care. I do care about wrong things being done to people. I mean, I want to fight against it. But so often the people who shout loudest about injustice are the ones who perpetrate it themselves . . . ."

With a shock I realized I had been speaking aloud. I turned to Alan and he said: "Sure. It's only in England a Jew gets to assess a Nazi's performance."

I gulped. I could not recall the conversation that had given rise to this somewhat oblique remark. To my relief I discovered we were now in among the film crew, talking to a tall man in a jersey with long lanks of whitish hair falling across his temples into his eyes.

"This is Henry Swansea," Alan was saying, "the writer."

I could not quite credit this description of myself, but the stranger seemed to accept it. He was talking now, gesturing towards the crew as he talked, while a young man of about seventeen or eighteen with a megaphone in his right hand bustled towards the German officers. "I want the German High Command to get into the lorry and have their lunch, please!"

The tall man in the jersey was talking. His right hand rose and fell to emphasize his already over-positive phrasing. *"Swastika Dreams"*, he was saying, "is quite unlike any other film I have made, which is why I was very excited about involving more people than would be usual from the M.o.I. It is a narrative film, but one that returns, insistently, to the Blakean Armageddon, in this case an invasion by the Germans. Against this image I set parallel visions of Englishness, our heritage, the acme of the liberal tradition, represented by the Cluggs."

As he spoke, from behind a lorry farther up the street, came a man of about fifty, wearing a smock and a battered hat. In his right hand he carried a pitchfork. Behind him was a girl of about seventeen, with pink cheeks and a straw bonnet. Before I had had time to get over this apparition, they were followed by a man in a cloth cap and a white muffler who, on catching sight of Alan, raised a thumb in salute and shouted in a distinctly unconvincing Cockney accent: "Gercha, mates!"

"That's Paul Lancing-Green," said Alan. "I want you to meet him later."

The tall man in the jersey continued to talk. His hands whizzed through the air like the sails of a windmill. A small crowd of technicians had gathered beside him, like men anxious for an audience with some royal figure, but oblivious of them the man continued to talk. Curiously enough, the technicians showed no sign of impatience. They seemed to like being kept waiting.

"The Cluggs are a family, as England is a family. From Somerset to London they wind like a rose around a pillar, symbolizing the resistance to the alien presence. Meanwhile, London which I evoke in the film by using, simply London *itself*, is – "

From the other side of the camera came Mactavish. He slapped one of the technicians on the back and raised his eyebrows to the sky, as if to signal disenchantment with the man in the jersey's monologue. "Where are the bloody German planes?" he said.

What I found most bizarre about all of this was not the behaviour of the film unit but the way in which I noticed Alan watching them and me. He had a curiously jumpy, official manner that made me feel as if I was part of some experiment, some test. Mactavish and the tall man in the jersey began to have an argument and Alan pulled me away up the road towards the man in the cloth cap and the white muffler. "Paul is dying to meet you," he said.

Lancing-Green was jumping up and down on the pavement, slapping his hands together in order to try and keep them warm. Alan slapped him on the back and said, in what I thought was an oddly artificial voice: "How goes it, old bean?"

"It's a reg'ler cold day, guv, I'll grant yer," said Lancing-Green, "but we'll 'ave a go at them Nazis. Cor lumme, we will, I'll be bound."

"Good, isn't he?" said Alan.

Lancing-Green stretched and yawned. "So this is our new writer, is it?" he said.

"I – "

Alan looked between the two of us. "I just wanted you to meet. He's down here to take a shufti."

Almost immediately, as is Alan's way in large gatherings of people, he left us, and began an intense discussion with somebody else. I could see his head wagging up and down as he talked and caught the occasional word. . . . "We said we'd give them twenty-five thousand and they would come in for twelve but frankly . . . ." I smiled awkwardly at Lancing-Green. "Don't know where he gets the energy," I said.

"The chosen ones are full of drive," said Lancing-Green.

I was beginning to dislike this man.

"Were you at the House?" he said.

"I – "

"I'm sure I've seen you at one of Toby's things."

"Very probably."

Lancing-Green came up close to me. "I'm glad you could come," he said. "It's tonight."

"Oh, really?"

"I've got a note."

So saying, with a circumspect glance around him, he passed me a grubby sheet of paper. I crammed it instantly into my pocket and, following his lead, looked around to see if anyone had seen me. Alan seemed to be still deep in conversation, but over on the other side of the road a tall man in Nazi officer's uniform gave me a broad wink.

"It's OK," said Lancing-Green. "Welch-Carpenter is with us."

"Oh, good," I said, completely lost.

The tall man in the jersey had now come over to us and apologized for keeping me. I said that was fine. He handed me a huge file of papers. "The schedule," he said. "I think we'll have to talk later."

From the huge lorries men were carrying enormous circular

lamps, which they positioned on steel supports. They looked a little like the searchlights that were used by anti-aircraft gunners at the beginning of the war. As far as I could see, they were being trained on an enormous warehouse on the other side of the street. Alan had moved off into the crowd of extras and abandoned me to Lancing-Green.

"Isn't it a bit late for lunch?" I said.

"Humphrey doesn't really worry about things like lunch," he said.

A man in a fireman's costume rushed up to us. "Paul – ", he said, "is it 'Schrike a light, guv' or 'Giss a 'and, chief'?"

"I don't know," said Lancing-Green. "I'm not in this."

Over on the other side of the street, crowds of men were approaching the warehouse in a loose but determined line, rather like a group of beaters on a grouse moor. I saw the tall man in the jersey – who must, I had now decided, be the elusive Humphrey – running towards one of the lorries. He was shouting something. And from behind another vehicle came an even more bizarre line of people – beefeaters, old ladies with white hair pushing bicycles (who on closer inspection turned out not to be old ladies with white hair but girls of twenty in wigs), a fat man got up to look like Henry the Eighth, an old man in a smock pushing a wheelbarrow, a cart-horse, a boy in the costume of an Eton schoolboy (who wasn't a boy but a girl) and a whole troupe of dogs, nearly all of them pedigrees of one kind or another.

I looked down and saw that Alan was standing between us. He had that subdued air of meek naughtiness that usually meant he was planning some administrative coup or other. He held his light-weight jacket into his body with his right hand. He looked, as Alan so often does, like a refugee, like someone on the road out of Warsaw or Berlin with a sack on his back and the helpless, naked look of the twentieth-century city-dweller on the move.

"Shall we go now?" he said.

I was mystified. Was I not going to see this elusive gentleman in the jersey? There was something about Alan's behaviour, too, that I did not like, a contained air of pert triumph, as he looked between me and Lancing-Green.

"What happens now?"

"Oh," said Lancing-Green with a yawn, "they're just going to set fire to that warehouse."

Which, as we were standing there, they did. The whole of the front of the building went up in a sheet of flame, triggered by the line of men opposite, who immediately backed into the middle of the road and began lining up hoses on the blaze, without actually using them.

"We ought to go," said Alan, and pushed me back through the crowd.

"What's – "

"Oh, Humphrey's always setting light to things."

I saw that the camera crew was focused on the blazing building (it was impossible to tell whether the place was really alight, or whether it was an illusion created by jets of gas shot out from holes concealed at the base of the wall) and that, from inside the warehouse, a group of men in helmets was coming towards the wall of flame. To my horror and amazement, I saw that they were singing – a sort of anthem, of the kind sung by Welsh choirs. "TURN OVER!" the man in the jersey was screaming, "TURN THE RUDDY THING OVER!"

A huge wild-eyed man rushed past me. I saw it was none other than Mactavish. His rough tweed jacket was grimy and torn and he was yelling at some distant group of men: "ARE WE BLOODY RUNNING SOUND?"

"Alan, what *is* this?"

"It's only a film, old thing," he said. "Only a film."

Our staff car was now about fifty yards away. As we came up towards it, a hand grabbed me and pushed me forward into the road. Instead of going to my assistance, Alan started to laugh.

"Shout!" hissed a voice in my left ear.

"Shout what?"

"Shout 'BRITAIN!'" said the voice.

I looked to my left and saw that the camera was being pushed towards me on a low, four-wheeled trolley and that I was surrounded by people in civilian clothes. A young man with a megaphone was herding us towards the camera, which moved, like some monstrous, impartial eye, with relentless, predetermined gravity, across the line of faces and then back towards the blazing building again.

"BRITAIN!" the man next to me was shouting. "BRITAIN!"

All of my life I have felt like an extra. I am the kind of person who is never given any good lines. But the indignity of actually *being* an extra, especially in a film as confused, bizarre and pretentious as *Swastika Dreams* appeared to be, was something I was not prepared to tolerate. I fought my way back through the crowd towards Alan. He was standing on the pavement. I saw that he was laughing. It was difficult going as, from almost every direction, more extras were being pushed out into the road, but I fought and clawed my way through them like a swimmer struggling against a tricky current. I saw one of the men who had pushed me out in the first place look across to Humphrey, but Humphrey, on catching sight of me, waved his arms enthusiastically. "No, it's good," he said. "It's good, it's good." He was waving to the camera crew as they swung past the suddenly created crowd and, as the trolley was pushed off towards the blazing warehouse, he followed it at a brisk run. I was back on the pavement.

Alan was still laughing. "I don't understand your attitude, Henry," he said. "I don't understand it at all."

"I don't understand yours, for that matter," I said. "Will you please tell me what this is all about?"

His mouth closed. "We must go," he said. "We must go. Come on."

The flames were still high as we climbed back into the car and drove back towards Westminster. Alan didn't talk at all in the car. Just sat in the deep shadows of the back seat and occasionally studied me, calmly and slowly, as if I was the subject of some experiment. When we came back to the office he went straight into his own room, since when I have not heard from him. I hear his voice occasionally and the sound of Eric's typewriter, but he has given me no clue as to what that weird interlude was intended to mean.

As soon as I got back I pulled out the sheet of paper Lancing-Green had given me and smoothed it out on my desk. The message – which was scrawled in rough capitals – read: SEE YOU TONIGHT FOR THE BIG SHOW.

It's funny. I can't rid myself of the uncomfortable feeling that someone is testing me. But who is it? And what is the test supposed to show?

Isaac. 1926 . . . .

Simply writing those words makes me feel easier. Fiction writers, I suppose, the kind that old Mr Rabinowitz and I enjoyed, are people who gain harmless pleasure out of correcting history, and, for a moment anyway, I am determined to enjoy the illusion of control. There are things out there that are determined to control *me*.

Soon – the noise of doors slamming all along the corridor – the clatter of official feet on the stairs, and the called farewells in every office. Like the sound of the charwomen singing in the early morning, it is a noise that, in spite of its brave attempts at humanity, serves only to confirm the awful, pervasive power of this building. I sit in my empty office, my head full of slogans and austerity.

PUT OUT THAT LIGHT! IS YOUR JOURNEY REALLY NECESSARY?

My journey is back, back in time, to explain how I came to be here, staring at a blank sheet of paper. If I can't explain that, I shall be one of the undead of the war, like those people sleeping in the Tube, long after the Blitz.

There he is anyway. Isaac, back at my parents' flat, a blanket round his shoulders, shivering like someone with the flu. My mum didn't ask any questions. She brought him in, gave him a meal and put him to bed. I think she had always been grateful to anyone who felt able to befriend her peculiar, solitary son and, at last, for reasons she would never understand, she had been given the chance to repay his kindness to me.

Not that I understood what was wrong with Isaac or what had happened at the bookshop. Tessa never called or left a note, neither did his mother. I never dared to go round there and, after that first evening, I did not attempt to ask Zak what had happened. I had tried as we climbed up the steps of the Peabody, and his lips had shut tightly, like an old woman's or a young child's. "I can't," was all he said. "I just can't." And that was all.

The General Strike was when I started my wanderings up to the West End. Night after night I would leave our district and head down the Embankment towards Charing Cross. I had no work, although I eventually found some on another local paper, writing lead articles on "non-political" subjects, but I found I was curiously happy. I don't think I was relishing the collapse of Zak's and Tessa's relationship (although I often worried that that might be the case); I think it was simply that at last I had someone to look after, a simple, easily defined need that had to be met. Sooner or later, I told myself, things would be mended between them. In the meantime – it was like the old days, like when we were kids, running home from school from the O'Malleys, or hanging round the bookshop with his father.

He seemed worse after the strike folded. I never brought a newspaper home – I knew any mention of the real world would upset him – but somehow or other he found out. The day Citrine and the rest of them sold out, he sat on the bed in the living room, shivering helplessly.

"Shall I get a doctor?" I said.

"It's nerves," my mum said. "It's nerves."

I simply couldn't understand what had turned my once so decisive friend into this shivering, fearful wreck. More than once I started down the alley that led to the bookshop, but I never summoned up the courage to go in. More than once I wondered what had happened to the small girl with the slight lisp and the gap in her front teeth, but I never found out. It was as if the marriage between her and Isaac had never been.

* * *

It cost a lot of money to take Zak to Vienna. It cost even more to obtain a course of treatment from a doctor who had been recommended to me by none other than Ramsay MacDonald. But it was worth it. It was worth it not only because Zak seemed better afterwards (which was more than you could say for Ramsay MacDonald), but just to have *known* Sigmund Freud I count among the great privileges of my life.

Mind you, he wasn't cheap, Freud.

For about a year after the General Strike, Isaac simply refused to speak. He just sat on his bed, the blanket round his shoulders, and when anyone from the branch or from head office came to see him, which they did quite a lot at first, he just sat looking at them, his head on one side. He wouldn't see doctors. He wouldn't go out. It wasn't until the spring of 1927 that I got him down the stairs and into Marchant Row with my mum watching from the window.

Zak was leaning on my arm when we turned down towards Wapping and the river. It was on the corner of Royal Mint Street, I seem to remember, that we walked slap bang into this little old lady with a crinkly black dress on. She fell back on to the pavement. I picked her up, dusted her down and asked her, with some concern, whether she was all right.

'As well as can be expected!' she simpered. She had a huge black fan which she kept fluttering in front of her eyes and it was only when she dropped it that I noticed – poor woman – she had a moustache. Quite a thick, bushy one. She widened the simper into a grin, revealing a row of teeth, yellow and stained, and said in a bass, girlish voice: "Dinna fash yersen!" I didn't understand this at all. She went on, rather flirtatiously: "Two wee boys oot for a bit o' skirt?"

I looked as blank as I could. Then the little old lady shot out her hand and gripped me hard on the wrist. I looked down at her hand. The knuckles were white with strain but that wasn't the most interesting thing about it. It was a man's hand.

"Listen," said a low and urgent voice from behind the now upraised fan, "my name is Ramsay MacDonald and I am the leader of the Labour Party. If you are, as you seem, a decent working man, I beg you to help me. Please do not ring the *Daily Mail* or any other national newspaper, but get me somewhere until the attack passes."

I made as if to speak but the voice went on, cultured, Scottish. But there was real pain in it. "As you can see," he said, "my need to dress as a woman is sometimes impossible to suppress, even when Parliament is in session. I assure you, though, that in no way is my costume intended to benefit the enemies of this great country of ours. It is a product of an environment which, as far as I can make out, is – "

Ramsay MacDonald was about the most boring man I have ever met in my life. I think the real reason he dressed as a woman was not related to sexual gratification of any kind. It was most probably a last, desperate bid to make himself interesting. But he wasn't any more charismatic in a silk dress and matching taffeta undies than he was in a pin-striped suit.

He was sobbing as we got him into the flat.

My mum looked on aghast as we got him on to the bed and stripped him down to his pants. It took forever. He had about eight pairs of knickers and corsets on as well as a barrage of buttons and straps on each stocking and bloomer. Whatever his motives for getting into drag, it was pretty clear that he put a lot more effort into it than he did into the poor old Labour Party.

"'oo's this?" said my mum.

"I am the leader of the Labour Party", said MacDonald, "and I hope that you will think of me as a friend. It is my firm belief that the decent working men and women of this country do not – "

Et cetera, et cetera.

He was still sobbing as we got him a pair of baggy trousers that had once belonged to my old man. In fact, he got rather stroppy about the trousers and tossed his head rather a lot at the thought of wearing them. Then he got rather boastful. "I have been", he said, "to every ladies' lavatory in Westminster. I just walk in in my silks and undies and *no one* knows. I go into the cubicles and pee sitting down and then – " His voice dropped to a hushed whisper. "I write about it on the walls."

When he'd finished telling us what fun he'd had in public conveniences, he got on to the joy and satisfaction he experienced when dressed as a woman.

"People open doors for me," he said, in the refined accents of an Edinburgh tea-room. "They pull out chairs. I think, if I may be so bold here among ordinary decent working men, British labourers, horny-handed sons of toil, great big, hulking he-man dockers, huge, thuggish bruisers of – " Here he burst into violent tears. Sitting on the bed, he put his head between his knees and wept. "I'm disgusting," he said. "I'm repulsive and ugly and horrible and vile and I wish I was dead. What I do is sickening."

"You're no worse than anyone else in the Labour Party," I said. I looked across at Zak. No reaction. He was looking at MacDonald as if the man were some abstract problem he failed to understand.

"Are they all at it?" said MacDonald with something like relief.

"There are worse things than dressing up as women," I said. "Things like crawling to the rich and powerful when you should be standing up for ordinary people and – "

"Oh, *politics*," said MacDonald, "*politics* . . . ." He tossed his head again. "I try not to bother my pretty little bonce about that!"

He pursed his lips and put one hand upon his knee. Beribboned, lipsticked, marooned in crackling silk, his wig at an angle, his hairy legs splayed out in front of him, he looked like a parody of a Degas drawing – *"The Ballet Dancer with the Moustache.*

Study in Pencil." But I wasn't looking at him. I was looking at Zak.

Zak was backing away across the room, like Macbeth being haunted by one of his victims. He stayed glued to the far wall while my mum and I got the Labour politician into my Dad's old gear – an old ragged jersey and wellington boots several sizes too large for him. As we scoured his face with soap, set aside the wig, undid the nails and pulled the heavy ear-rings off him, he said: "I've been for treatment. I've been all over the world."

Zak started to edge towards the door.

"It's awful," went on MacDonald. "I feel I've betrayed the whole Labour movement."

Zak stopped. I could see he was mouthing something but could not hear what it might be. MacDonald's voice sank to a whisper. "Jimmy Thomas does it too", he said, "and Walter Citrine borrows my – "

Finally we jammed a flat hat and muffler on his head.

"Thanks, laddie," he said, with ghastly cheerfulness, "thanks a lot!"

He got to his feet. Even in the complete male outfit he still didn't quite convince as a man. It wasn't that there was anything effeminate about his appearance, rather that a strong odour of implausibility seeped from every pore in his body as, dressed in the old clothes of the late Stanley Barking, he tried out a few remarks that he obviously thought of as typical of the London working class. "Garn, mate," he said, "becha life you don't 'ave a tanner!"

We all laughed politely.

"Coo, guv," went on MacDonald, obviously emboldened by our tolerance of his performance, "schrike me pink wiv' a load of fevvers!"

Zak started to giggle uncontrollably. I didn't like the sound of this laugh – even though it was noise and noise of any kind was welcome from someone I'd come to think of as being mute. It fluttered up to the edge of hysteria. I noticed, too, that Zak still had his eyes fixed on the eminent Labour politician.

I put my arm round MacDonald and steered him towards the door, keeping him as far away from Zak as was possible.

At the door he started once again to weep uncontrollably. His large hands were cupped round his face, but through the tears you could see the piggy little politician's eyes watching us all and, as I heard my mum behind us whisper, "Poor *love*...", Zak's laugh sharpened into a self-mocking wail. There was no doubt about it. Behind his hands Ramsay MacDonald's eyes were gleaming in some private triumph.

I kept on going. When we got down to the street he slapped me on the back a few times, swore me to secrecy and, for some reason, reverted to broad music-hall Scots. "I'll be OK, laddie!" he said. "I'll be areet the noo!" He tapped the side of his nose with his finger. "I'm cured."

This was about the most obviously crazy thing he had yet said in my view and evoked some response from me. "Oh," I said, 'that's good."

"Aye," he said, "just need to sort oot the rough edges. But I'm on the road tae recovery a' right. I'm in gude hands ye ken."

I wondered what charismatic quack it might be who had persuaded a man so obviously on the edge of a major breakdown that he was "on the road to recovery". He answered my unspoken question for me. "There's a wee doctor", he said, "oot in Vienna. He's the heed man oot there for all a' this. In strict confidence, laddie, strict confidence."

"Oh," I said.

"Aye," he went on, "Sigmund Freud a' Vienna is your only man for the head cases. Christ our Blessed Saviour he will set you right, I declare by the body of Christ – "

He stopped suddenly, his brain clearly overloaded by recent events. Then, without another word, he turned and walked off down the street. He walked in a slow, bandy-legged kind of way, like a Glasgow docker who has just consumed twenty pints of lager. He was singing some music-hall song under his breath. When he got to the end of the street, he turned to me and put both thumbs up. He winked broadly. It was quite clear that Ramsay MacDonald thought everything was fine.

But I like to think that, in the dark days of the National Government, at least once he (and maybe Snowden too) got behind closed doors, slipped into mounds of crackling calico and simpered and moued and pirouetted before one of those huge old mirrors of the chambers of Westminster. And though some people still talk of Ramsay Mac as a traitor to the working class or a decent man trying to do his best, to me he'll always be a rather fey, middle-aged lady.

One thing she had done, anyway, was give me a lead on how to get Zak well again (after that brief outburst of hysteria he had gone back to his place on the bed, blanket round him, staring soundless at the wall). Until that moment I had been unaware of the existence of psychoanalysis. Difficult though it may seem to you, dear reader, there are probably still people out there in the East End of London quite unaware that, when worn down by the problems of the world, a quick and simple solution is often to lie on a couch and talk about one's mother to a highly qualified stranger. In 1927 in the Whitechapel area, if you allowed the world to get you down, you tended to go and jump under a bus – still a popular option for members of the working class foolish enough to opt for neurosis. But I, through sheer chance, had a name and, in my leisure hours (there were still plenty of them), I attacked every public library I could find for information about this mysterious Sigmund Freud.

I wasn't particularly interested in his theories. What I wanted was his address.

I found it in the end – although by that time I had waded through enough of his work to wonder whether going to see him was a good idea at all. My letter was, I thought, a rather brilliant parody of one of his papers, mentioning a few key facts about Zak and Tessa (whom I referred to as Tessa O——), and was gladdened to receive the following answer (flattery is the sincerest form of parody, is it not?).

Dear Herr B——

Excuse the impersonal nature of this greeting. I take care to preserve the anonymity of my patients even when addressing them directly. I am worthily esteemed to have received your letter of last month in which you have most cogently set out the most interesting aetiology of symptoms in the patient Herr Isaac R——. I trust you will pardon my English. In writing to you I am, quite literally, *tongue tied*. (I am sure your studies of analytic literature have made you aware of the significance of this expression in the German language!)

I am at present engaged in the analysis of Fraulein Oota L——, a young girl of seventeen troubled with persistent hyspnoetosis and vomiting ever since she was approached by a certain Frau Olga M—— in their lakeside cottage near B——

B——. If you had seen Frau Olga M—— I think you would understand!

In all seriousness, dear friend, I must confide in you that I have had serious doubts about the relationship between masturbation and gastric disorder whose consistency I first adumbrated in 1919. I would be glad of your comments dear colleague.

Ever,

SIGMUND FREUD

I assumed Freud had confused me with someone else. He was in touch with so many analysts – and patients – all over the world and was so passionately aware of the risks involved in naming patients, that he tended to get very confused about who he was actually talking to. When we were in Vienna he frequently referred to me as Fraulein K——, which I found embarrassed me.

· In spite of what I took to be the man's massive eccentricity, I wrote back to him and, almost by return of post, received a second letter that I conjure up out of the darkness.

Dear Herr B——

I would of course be delighted to see your friend Herr R——. I am grateful for your lucid account of the onset of the condition and apologize most heartily for the "cock-up" in the question of your identity. When I tell you that I confused an eminent Viennese neurologist only the other day with the notorious Baron N—— of Salzburg, an enuretic with a clear aetiology of symptoms including persistent masturbation, mutism, castration complex, aphonia and hysterical vomiting – as well as severe financial difficulties caused by the collapse of his merchant bank – I am sure you will agree with the Latin poet who wrote "virtus nascitur in stupra".

How pleasant it would be for our Swiss analytic "friends" if they could ignore the faecal ceremonies of defilement in which so many of their high-minded thoughts have their certain origins!

I await your arrival with keen interest and enclose a list of my scale of charges.

SIGMUND FREUD

Well, as I said, it wasn't like going down the shops for a few slices of salami. It was pricey medicine. This was one of the things that made me feel it must be OK. I've always worked on the assumption that the more you pay for something the better it is likely to be.

Somehow we raised the money for the trip and the fees. It wasn't easy. Isaac's pals up at head office didn't help much. They all seemed to be of the opinion that psychiatry was a bourgeois deviation. In the end it was the neighbours who put up the money – neighbours and people from the paper where I was working (I think this was called the *Clarion*). It took me damn near a year to collect it but people gave. They didn't ask about the *kind* of doctor. All they wanted to know was that the money was to make someone well. It's been my lifelong experience that the less money people have the more generous they are with it. That isn't sentimental generalization – it is simply what I have found to be the case.

I remember the train journey to Vienna. Isaac crouched in the corner of the compartment with a plaid rug over his knees, the European landscape unreeling at the window as we raced and clacked over bright knots of rail. The faces and streets of London seem to melt into white as I attempt to recall precise movements from the journey, and now it is as if the giant apartment blocks of Vienna, the Hofstruder or the Kaltenbrammerdamm, hovered above the ever receding horizon, while a deep, calming voice, that I felt I knew from my reading, echoed in my head beckoning the two of us onward.

Dear Herr Amos B——

Yes, yes, let us proceed, as the Romans say "quam celerrime". Your friend sounds to me not at all, as you suggest in your last letter, "unvermogend" as we Germans say, although I would like to know more of the circumstances surrounding the assault of Fraulein Tessa O——. I received the impression that this incident had taken place *at the top of a flight of stairs*. Is this correct?

If indeed such should prove to be the case, I am irresistibly reminded of the case of another patient of mine who was also prominent in public life and whom I shall call Count K——. As you seem acquainted with my published work I need not remind you that Count K——, a man suffering from intense fabulative mania, a condition associated with aphonia, congenital boastfulness, cramps, diarrhoea and incurable rectal itching, was discovered to have assaulted a party of nuns *by a lake near some mountains*.

As the poet says – the sexual and the social are connected in ways that, as yet, we can only guess at. Nations too have a conscience and hidden dreams and those who, like your friend, seek to rearrange them, must suffer doubly in their encounter with the world. I need hardly add, as I am sure it has occurred to you, dearest colleague, that the "General Strike" of which you have spoken was nothing more nor less than a *withdrawal of labour*, lasting nine days!

Cheques should be made payable to me at the above address. I would be grateful if you could postdate them. This is for tax purposes and I hope you will forgive my desire for you to be here after your friend's treatment has been completed.

SIGMUND FREUD

I looked across at Zak. He too was watching the landscape. As we thundered through the frightening complexity of yet another city, I saw him bite his lip. One fat tear squeezed from his right eye and trickled helplessly down his cheek. I looked away.

"Excuse me," said a voice at the door of the compartment, "is this seat taken?"

* * *

What I should have said was "Yes it is and clear off before I throw you off the train." But I didn't. Well, how was I to know who it was standing in the corridor of that travel-dirtied carriage? Even when I try to remember his face I can't. It's a blur. It has become hopelessly confused with the photographs I have seen in the ministry, so that instead of the original impression of an immense, clerkly drabness, I am left with a glaring tyrant with huge yellow teeth and a mocking, satanic voice.

Of course, to us now he is a sound – a disembodied voice that mocks and apes our own attempts to describe and explain the world. Well, that's what the war has done for him – in the same way that it has created heroes, or reduced me to the lowest pitch of anonymity. I want to take the sheaf of memoranda off the desk and write, like Auden's unimportant clerk, I DO NOT LIKE MY WORK:

But I won't. I'll write this instead.

One thing I am quite certain of and that was his manner. He had the cut-price formality of an undertaker. The slight inclination of his head and the commercial priestliness of his hands, folded high up on his chest, suggested the sort of floorwalker in a large store who refuses to sell you carpets or furniture until you have assured him that you are the sort of person he ought to talk to.

He had a prominent nose, too, and eyes that seemed pressed out from behind. But, you see, he didn't introduce himself on that occasion and, even if he had, his name would have meant nothing to me.

"It is not," I said, "and very nice to hear an English voice."

"Yes," said the stranger, with curious insistence, "isn't it?"

Ever since he had come into the compartment Zak had been looking at him. He'd given up looking at people so I took this to be an encouraging sign. He seemed to remember the man from somewhere. The man smiled rather awkwardly at him and Zak simply carried on staring, blank, hopeless, the look of someone who has suffered a stroke.

"My friend's not very well," I said.

"I'm sorry to hear it," said the stranger. He winced slightly as he said this. He was obviously the sort of person who finds disease of any kind an embarrassment and, just as he was wincing, Zak's head fell forward and his tongue lolled over his lower lip. I rushed to straighten him and the stranger studied the evening landscape.

"And where are you bound?" I said.

"All sorts of places," said the stranger.

I rattled on, talking as usual to cover the awkwardness. "We're going to Vienna," I said.

"Ah," said the stranger.

And after a pause, rather like a man studying pornographic pictures who allows his eye to fall on the dirty bit when he feels suspicion has been allayed (he's *really* studying the sky or the book with the innocuous images in it), the stranger looked full at Zak. His eyes had a hypnotic concentration about them as they retraced the outlines of his profile. I couldn't read the meaning of his gaze at first and then, with a jolt, I understood it.

My friend disgusted him.

We didn't speak after that and when we reached the station I let him go without a word, but that stare stayed with me for days and, much later, when I had come to think of him and people like him as Zak's evil genii, I wished I'd taken him to the door of the carriage and pushed him out into the Austrian night. But there it is. We like to be brave and wise after the event, don't we? Even if I had been given a secret preview of the history of the next fifteen years, I expect I would have let him go, as I did, without a word.

I couldn't get him out of my mind though.

It rained as the cab took us across the town. Isaac stared out at the rain and then back at me. He didn't seem to understand why he was here. I looked out at the boulevards, the soulless parks and the blocks of flats, like abandoned wedding cakes, and felt I didn't understand either.

Freud's house was a tall, prim, elegant affair, part of a terrace, and we were welcomed at the door by a housekeeper who told us we were expected but that we would have to wait. As the door closed behind us, shutting out the rain and the unfamiliar streets, I felt for the first time a great sense of peace. Something about the way the heavy clock in the hall ticked suggested another kind of time – while the darkness of the stairs and the heavy furniture seemed designed to insulate sensitive visitors from the pain of too much daylight. Zak looked around him. He seemed to me like a child, waking to a new day. "Hey," he said, "I like this."

From upstairs a door opened and a plump woman came out, her hands folded over her stomach. She looked down at us and said something in German. To my astonishment, Zak replied. To my even greater astonishment, his reply seemed to cause her some amusement.

"What does she say?" I said.

"She says", said Isaac, "that I look as if I need feeding up."

"Who is she?"

"The lady of the house."

The plump woman lifted a plump finger in my direction. She waggled it. "Ve haf cakes!" she said.

As she said this, to her left a door opened and into the gloom of the landing came a grizzled, white-bearded man in a dark suit. He paid no attention to the plump woman but came to the balcony and leaned over it. He did not speak but, from his pocket, produced a heavy fob watch, at which he stared for some moments. His glare suggested that he was engaged in something far more important than merely telling the time. When he had finished looking at the watch he put it back in the pocket on the other side of his waistcoat and patted it in a ritual, formalistic manner. Then he said something in German.

Isaac, to my consternation, laughed.

"What is he saying?" I said, by now slightly irritated by the reversal of our roles.

"He says, Amos," said Zak, "that he is pleased to meet you."

"I thought", I said, "that you were the patient."

Freud – I had recognized him by now – was still talking. Zak listened.

"He says", went on Isaac, "that what amused him about your letter was its satiric quality."

"Oh," I said.

"He says", went on Isaac (Freud was talking animatedly, laughing and gesturing as he spoke), "that he is so often attacked but so rarely parodied. He takes it as a compliment, but thinks one can always parody oneself more amusingly than others. He hopes you enjoyed his parody of you in his letters."

"I –"

I was beginning to feel distinctly threatened by this conversation and by Zak's sudden and unfamiliar liveliness (not to mention his nearly flawless German), but the white-haired man was talking again –

"He says", said Zak, "that you interest him because, while appearing to not mean what you say, you do actually...actually...can't quite get the German here...hold on to the truth of your absurdity. He says he is always fascinated by people who don't believe in anything, or rather by people who say they don't believe in anything, because he says their unconscious passions must be so strong."

I turned my face up to the landing and spoke to the doctor myself.

"I think", I said, "you have made a mistake. I'm not the one who is crazy. He is. I'm just paying the bill."

Freud shrugged and grinned. Then Isaac turned away from me and trudged up the heavy stairs. He looked like a man coming home after a hard day's work. When he reached the landing he stood looking at Freud and, after an impressive, theatrical pause, the doctor went across to the door from whence he had just emerged. He opened it, turned back to Isaac and gave a shrewd, courtly gesture of welcome towards the room beyond.

"Starting right away then?" I almost shouted.

Freud spoke again.

"He says", said Isaac, "that the housekeeper speaks excellent English."

And went into the room after his new doctor.

I turned and saw behind me a small fat woman who could well have been the woman I had seen earlier on the balcony. Or not, as the case may be. She certainly looked very like her. Hadn't Zak said this was the lady of the house? Didn't that mean Mrs Freud? Or perhaps the words for "wife" and "housekeeper" in German were the same? Or perhaps Freud and/or Isaac had made a Freudian slip. I knew all about Freudian slips, having spent three weeks studying them in Westminster Public Library. Whoever she was, she was wearing a pinafore, and I noticed, had a large boil in the middle of her forehead.

"Zer Doctor can English also," she said.

"Oh," I said.

Her smile widened. "Ve haf for you lodginks found."

Well, they had for me lodgings found, in a shabby street half a mile away, in the basement of a large house. And I spent the first week in Vienna cowering in there waiting for Zak, who was either in the consulting room, or else taking endless walks in the streets near us.

I don't know what Freud and Zak talked about in that dark, forbidding consulting room (I had not, at that stage, seen the inside of it, but I thought of it as dark and forbidding and so, indeed, it proved to be). It is possible indeed that he had studied Freud, in the period just before his breakdown when I had hardly seen him. But whatever it was they discussed, while I sat in my shabby room staring out at the feet of Viennese pedestrians, the change in his manner, the sudden thaw, which had been perceptible from the moment we had got inside Freud's house, became a spring, and at the end of each day I saw a new aspect of a new personality. It was like watching something ripen, or seeing the green swathes of a valley spread out under the light after snow. In many ways this

Isaac was like the boy I had known before the war, but it was as if he had shed all the manners he had needed to ape then, and kept only the lightness of touch, the courage in the face of any possibility, that had been the thing I had most loved about him.

Fun, that was what Zak got from Freud. Which may seem a strange reward for a course of psychoanalytic therapy. But one of the things I most enjoyed about Sigmund was his sense of humour. On form, he was one of the funniest men I have ever met.

From time to time the two of us would walk the streets, losing ourselves in the back alleys or among the crowds on the broad thoroughfares, crazy with trams and signs. It always, for the first three or four weeks of Zak's analysis, seemed to be raining. It was on one of these walks that Zak told me the analysis might have to last a whole year.

"A year?" I said. "I haven't got that kind of money. And anyway what am I going to do in bleeding Vienna for a year?"

I was starting to become disillusioned with Freud.

"His housekeeper's fixed you up with something," said Zak. And winked suggestively. "She likes you," he added.

The next day I came to the house and was met by the woman with the boil in the middle of her forehead. While Isaac trudged off upstairs, I was taken into the kitchen and sat at a huge wooden table. So imperfect was my command of German language and etiquette, that I was still unsure as to whether this was Freud's wife or some senior domestic. I accordingly pitched my manner somewhere between the respectful and the dismayed as I said: "I didn't realize it took as long as this to be cured of mental illness."

She wagged her finger at me. "Vy you always takink the Michael?" she said, "zer Doctor iss a good voman."

On the table was a gigantic chocolate cake.

"You a gut boy," she said. "You can eat him."

"Was that addressed to me or the cake?" I said.

The fat woman laughed and wagged her finger again. "Vot ve vont", she said, "iss some dirt on Jung."

"I'm sorry?" I said.

"You know," she said, "Jung. Ve vant dirt on him. Ve vant know if he iss involve in courtcase, or hed up for exposing himself. Sings of ziss nacher. Yes?"

" You mean Freud wants – "

The woman laughed even louder. "Freud don't know his anus from his elpow, mein Herr. He could not find his way up zer Kurfürstendamm viz a vite stick in broat daylight. But ve, *ve* vont ziss dirt on ziss Jung cherecter, ve vont – "

"Who", I said, "is *we*?"

"Ve", said the woman, "are zer pipple who cares for zer Herr Professor. Who do not vish to see him make of himself a monkey. Mein Gott! Freud cout not get up in zer mornink if it vos left to him. Ve who luff him, who care for him, who believe in his scientific vurk, vatch offair him as iff he vos a rare species of antelope in zer zoologische Garten, yes?"

I was puzzled as to how I was going to get this "dirt" on Jung, especially since as far as I knew he was resident in Switzerland. When I put this to the woman with the boil on her head she laughed wildly. "Svitzerlent?" she said. "Svitzerlent? Zat's vot he tells all zer girls. Zat he is gone to Svitzerlent. Don't believe it. He iss round here somevere. Anyvere he can get vot you English call a piece of crumpet. He hes got the hots for anything viz two legs zat can move. Mein Gott. Look at me, hein? An ugly old brute like me from Berlin. He has up my draws talked himself. Oh ja. Natürlich."

I tried to remember the name of Freud's wife and whether she was from Berlin. Surely this ghastly creature could not be married to the dignified old man upstairs.

My task, anyway, was simple enough. I was simply to watch all the daily papers and study court reports, especially those dealing with offences of a sexual nature, and bring them to this woman in Freud's kitchen. There was, she said, no need for me to have a command of German. All I had to do was to look out for the name JUNG and I was on the right lines. My other duties were to watch the front of the house in case Jung should try "to sneak his dirty self up against us some night or other". For this I was to be paid what appeared to me to be an extremely substantial sum. I pointed out to the woman that it more than covered the cost of the analysis and asked, politely, where it was coming from. I was still not entirely sure that she wasn't some ex-patient of the good doctor who hung around his house making lunatic offers to those enjoying the great man's attentions.

"Zer money gum from Freud himself", she said, "to ensure his peace of mind from ziss man, ve consider any expense worthwhile. Mein Gott, don't zink ziss peculiar. Zere are a lot more peculiar zings happen here every day of zer veek."

As she spoke a fat girl came from the scullery door with a frying pan in her left hand and a tomato in her right. She had long, unkempt hair and a dreamy expression. She did not stop but walked straight into the opposite wall. This seemed to amuse her. For a while she continued to forward march into the obstacle. Then she stopped and began to wash herself systematically, laughing softly as she did so.

"ARBEIT!" shouted the woman with the boil on her head.

"ICH KOMM, KAPITÄN!" shrieked the girl and, picking up the frying pan and the tomato, she scurried back to the kitchen like an animal startled by a gunshot.

I watched her go and raised one eyebrow. "Is it like not being able to pay the bill in a restaurant?" I said. "I mean – do you have to wash up in order to finish the analysis?"

"She iss crazy," said the woman with the boil on her head. "You don't heff to be crazy to vurk here but it helps. Because zer Herr Professor deals viss zer cranks and lunatics, zer cranks and zer lunatics vont all to vork here. Zer pastry-cook sinks she is a wampire bat. Zer unter scullery maid iss masterbatink in broat daylight und – "

The door from the other side of the kitchen, the one that led through to the hall, opened and a small, neat woman in a black dress came in. She had a mild, sorrowful face and a sweet, impartial smile. Immediately she was in the room I knew that this must be Freud's wife, and at the same moment remembered her name. Martha. That was it. Martha. Like the good sister in the Bible. The woman with the boil on her forehead was getting to her feet and the two of them had a brief, and apparently sensible, conversation in German. It sounded as if it was about domestic matters. I rose to my feet too, feeling rather like a footman who has been caught kissing below stairs. Freud's wife smiled at me sweetly. The conversation finished and she went out into the hall. The woman with the boil on her head snarled after her. "Meatballs," she hissed, 'alvays vonting meatballs. Vot is so vunderful about meatballs, please?"

"I quite like meatballs," I said.

She started to scream something at me in German and I, who had decided that this woman was quite as crazy as she claimed the rest of the domestic staff to be, got up and edged towards the door. But before I had a chance to reach it, from the heavy table in the middle of the kitchen (which had two huge drawers at each end) she had taken a rough linen bag, which contained about twenty gold coins.

"Listen," she said, "I am not quite so crazy yet. Do vot is asked and you vill be paid. Here is twenty." She flung me a coin. I picked it up and goggled at it, lying fatly in my palm. She started to laugh. "Yes yes yes," she said, "upstairs zey're all nice and normal. Upstairs zay are zer picture of mental health. But down here, vere ve do zer cooking, vee are all as crazy as bats." She marched across the stone-flagged floor towards me. "But vee luff him," she said. "Vee care for him."

It is possible, I suppose, that these were the only class of servants that the Freuds could afford, and there was, Martha Freud informed me later, a servant problem in Vienna at the time, but it is certainly true that their cook (as I found out the woman with the boil to be) was able to support her eccentric campaign against Jung extremely generously. She was, I subsequently learned, paying three other men to *keep an eye* on a man who, as I kept telling her, was the other side of the Swiss border.

I felt very grateful to Fräulein Glauber though. For it was she who enabled me to stay in Vienna for a year, even if most of it was spent cutting out court reports from local newspapers. There were a surprising number of people called Jung had up for sexual offences in Vienna between 1927 and 1929 and, although none of them had anything whatsoever to do with the great Swiss analyst, they all brought Fräulein Glauber great personal satisfaction.

"Zere he goes, zer dirty bastard," she would say, "ett it again. My God vy doesn't he put zer sing in splints . . . ." Et cetera, et cetera.

At the end of each month she would pass me a sum of money, which would then go towards paying my landlord and Dr Freud's bill.

And all the time Zak grew chattier, easier. If he talked about Tessa and whatever it was that had passed between them, it was to Freud he talked not me. Once, in a beerhouse, when Freud was away for a week at a conference, he said to me: "Freud's obsessed with lakes. Everything has to happen near a lake. Or in the mountains. He's obsessed with lakes and mountains."

"Yes?"

"And if you dream," he said, "you can't dream about doing it with a woman. Oh, no. That would be far too obvious, wouldn't it? You have to dream about lakes and fountains and handbags catching fire and God knows what else, don't you? I'm going to dream about penises", he said, "and see what he makes of that." He looked at me sideways. "Amos – " he said.

"Yes?"

"Has it ever occurred to you that we might be a couple of poofs?" I thought about this for some moments. Then I said: "No. I don't really think so."

We went out into the street then and began another of our long displaced walks about that still puzzling city.

"What do you think of him?"

"Who?"

"Freud."

"Oh," I said, "I think as a *theory*, as a theory it's fine."

Zak was looking at me oddly. I wondered whether we should be talking about such things. Wasn't it all these abstractions that had sent him crazy in the first place? What was different about this conversation, though, I realized, was that we were able, for the first time, to discuss the differences between us. Was this, I wondered, because of his treatment? Or because I was becoming more confident? There was no doubt about our roles now. We each allowed the other his title.

"Don't you think", said Zak, "that you need theories? Visions of how the world should be. In order to change it. To make it better?"

"No," I said.

"No," he said, "maybe not."

We were in an empty park. It was late autumn and they hadn't yet swept away the huge piles of leaves that lay around us. We were somewhere near the back of one of the palaces (I think it was the Schönbrunn) and in the October sun the imperial roofs glistened in the distance, as securely anchored in the past as the calm of Freud's consulting room. Why, I thought but did not say, do we derive our scale of grandeur, our absolute standards, from another century and not from this? Why is it that everything in the twentieth century seems used up and shoddy?

"The only thing", said Zak, kicking at the leaves, "that you might need – is a guide. If there was something monstrous being done. As monstrous as the things we saw on the Somme. You might need a guide. To tell you they were true. Otherwise you wouldn't know."

"Don't you just use your eyes?" I said.

"That's not always enough," said Zak. "Sometimes an inspired guess is the only way at the truth. Because the truth is weirder and more complex and more shameful than ever we could imagine."

"You're saying", I said, "you should follow your instinct sometimes. I agree with that. Don't shackle your instinct to a system. Follow your instinct right through to the end."

Zak sighed. "Maybe that's what I'm saying," he said, "but suppose it's the wrong instinct?"

I laughed. "Suppose."

We went back towards the flat then. On the way he started to ask about me. What was I going to do with my life? I was cut out for more than hack journalism, wasn't I? Didn't I want to write? The way he wanted to do things? Couldn't we both make a niche for ourselves somewhere? "Society", he said, "is just an adventure."

"It may be for you, Zak," I said. "For me it's just trouble."

I didn't tell him then (as I don't tell Alan today) about the twenty-four novels, the epic poem set in Japan, the doggerel verse satire on the Establishment or the seven hundred and twenty rejection slips ("Dear Mr Barking, We have read *The Docks* with some interest but feel that at the present time . . ." it is a load of old rubbish).

The only thing that frightened me about that conversation was the thought that, if Zak were to become a pragmatist, pragmatism would be, for him, another kind of passion. If he was to see himself as the kind of politician whose task was to do well out of doing good, to achieve the heights of power as quickly as possible and not shackle himself to any elaborate political code, there was literally no knowing to which party he might tie himself. Like Disraeli at his first election – he would cheerfully stand on his head if standing on that would get him influence. My own experiments with ambition were quieter, safer affairs.

I was afraid for him, I suppose. As I had always been.

"People like you", I said, when we got back, "live at a different speed from people like me."

"And what speed do you live at?" he said.

I didn't try to answer that.

In fact, as his analysis continued through into the winter of '28, I began to wonder whether it was me and not Zak who needed treatment. My dreams had become inexplicably violent. Many of them involved Tessa. Once I dreamed that I was trying to strangle her, only to realize halfway through that I was in fact squeezing out a cloth for my mother. Once Tessa appeared to me naked, carrying a white coat I recognized from her father's surgery, and on another occasion I dreamed Palme Dutt and Haig were undergoing treatment in Mr Oldroyd's surgery. "Teeth in themselves", Palme Dutt was saying, "are not, collectively speaking, 'bourgeois' – since they act, in concert. . . ."

Things up at Freud's house didn't help. Fräulein Glauber had hired an under parlour maid who thought she was Rameses III and who attempted to wall herself into one of the coal bunkers with some of Freud's wife's jewellery. She had also an unhealthy obsession with what she called "number twos" and would crouch outside the WC when Freud was in it, straining her ear against the door for any unusual sounds. ("But", said Fräulein Glauber, "she iss a gut vorker. She cleans like a vistle.")

My worst dream, though, was a waking one. It was of that stranger that we had met on the train. I couldn't, for some reason, rid myself of him. When I was in the local library, when I was off on one of my solitary walks, when I was locked in the steaming, stone-flagged kitchen with Fräulein Glauber and the under parlour maid, the image kept returning to me of that face and that awful, hate-filled glance he had given my friend. Once or twice – although I dismissed this as hysterical fantasy – I was sure I caught sight of him on street corners, and on one occasion I could have sworn I heard his voice behind me in a restaurant.

It was the Christmas of 1928 when I started to "see" him most of all. As I wrote long, laborious letters to my mother, finished off a play called *Barking Mad* ("The title", one agent wrote to me, "seems effortful." What did they want – *lazy* titles? Titles that didn't try?), the man's features and presence were at every turn of my day. And as Zak and I, between bouts of analysis for him and writing for me, walked and talked (by now our discussions were almost a formally rehearsed debate on the relative merits of politics or the arts as a career), I stopped at street corners and sniffed the air like a dog after rabbits. "He's here. He's been here."

"He being who?"

"Nobody. Sorry. Nothing. Nobody."

It wasn't until the spring – or maybe later – of '29 that I actually saw him. I do remember that it was the last day of Zak's course of analysis, which had cost him, or rather Freud, about as much money as my father earned in his life. He was, the good doctor had told him, completely cured. His case was of such great interest that Freud was planning a paper about it. Fräulein Glauber had told me, in strictest confidence ("Your frient meks zer Volf Man look like zer Archduke Franz Ferdinand") that Zak was the most "amazink pervert ever that vos in Austria". We had the money for the return fare and were about to return home.

The night before the last session, Zak had gone to sleep early. I, as so often, could not sleep. I paced the room a while, tried to write, couldn't, and then, from the street above, heard a low cough. I recognized that cough. I had heard it before.

From our front window you could look up through a gap about six feet wide to the street. There, squatting against the railings, still wearing, incongruously, a bowler hat and carrying on this occasion what looked like a fishing-rod case, was the man I had seen on the train.

"What do you want?" I said.

"Just remember," he said, "not the one who wrote *Ulysses*."

Behind me I could hear Zak's snores, like those of a child. I looked back at him and the stranger grinned. "Tell the Jewboy I haven't got it in for him," he said, "it's the good professor *we're* after."

"Look. What – "

He waddled up close to the railings. "We've got *all* their names", he said, "and there won't be a single one of them left by the time we're through."

I didn't understand a single word of this. The man turned to go and I shouted after him: "What? Who? When?"

He turned back and gave me the big yellow grin again. "Tell him not to go tomorrow," he said. "OK?"

Then I started to shout at the geezer. Don't know why. Something about him had frightened me. That was all. I cursed his tall, black-coated back as he waddled off up the street into the Austrian moonlight. Behind me I heard Zak stir.

"What's up, Amos?" he said.

"Nothing," I said. "Just a bad dream, that's all. Just a bad dream."

Next day I tried to persuade him not to go. But this was out of the question. You couldn't miss a day, he said. This, it appears, would quite destroy the purpose of the exercise. I gave up trying to persuade him, helped him to get dressed (he still found that a problem) and saw him off as usual. When he was round the corner I locked up the door and, taking another route, made my way up towards Freud's gaff.

I saw the stranger immediately I turned into the street. He was walking very fast on the opposite side of the road, still carrying the fishing-rod case. I followed him. He struck off into an apartment block at the end of the street and across a wide, forbidding court-yard ringed by windowed cliffs of brick. He was scurrying, like a man late for an appointment, and never once looked behind him. I can't have been more than twenty yards away when he darted in through a gap in the line of windows and doors and rattled up a stone staircase. I followed him.

He ran up the stairs with the deadpan skill of a commuter. The staircase was an open one and outside, in the courtyard, I could see that it had begun to rain. Eventually he reached a landing in which there were three or four doors, all painted the same, grim, battle-ship grey. Groping in his right-hand pocket for a bunch of keys, he made for the one in the centre. I waited at the top step of the flight leading to his landing. Only when the door was open did I run up after him.

Then he heard me. He whipped round and tried to bar the door, but I forced my way through and the two of us fell into the hall beyond, the fishing-rod case falling away to my right. I was so dis-orientated by the twists and the turns of the staircases and courtyards that I had not realized where we were. From the far window – a wide expanse of dirty glass at the end of a filthy sitting room, on the walls of which were countless pictures and photographs all scribbled and scrawled upon in black or blue crayon – I could see that we were almost opposite Freud's apartment. And that, down to the left, framed neatly against the window, was the stern profile of the great analyst. From this height we could see down into the room – whose heavy black door was normally closed to me – and, prostrate on a couch facing up at the ceiling, I saw

219

Zak. He was talking. About what, though? Childhood? Lakes? Me?

All this I saw in a moment. Then I realized that the stranger was grappling with a series of locks on the case and that it contained, not a fishing rod, but a highly polished rifle in three sections. The stranger was fitting the thing together rather clumsily, as if I had been made to disappear. Perhaps he was so confident of his ability to defend himself that I might as well have been absent from the scene.

Right, I thought, *right*.

As I got up to go towards him, I saw that almost every one of the pictures and photographs were of eminent scientific figures. The only ones I could recognize were Freud and Einstein, but all of the others either had white coats on and were holding test tubes or Bunsen burners, or else had the anonymous, scrawny passion I have since come to associate with leaders of the scientific community. The other thing was – they were all, quite recognizably, Jewish. The graffiti – moustaches, blacked-out teeth, false glasses – had an obscene neatness about them so that, at first, they seemed to be part of the pictures.

"Who the hell *are* you?" I said to the man.

He cackled. "Told you," he said. "Not the one who wrote *Ulysses*."

By way of reply to this I hit him on the back of the neck and he fell forward across his case. I tumbled on to him, but he had, it seemed, been prepared for this. He thrust up at me with his elbows, winding me, and then kicked backwards with the undirected passion of a boxed horse that has just been jabbed in the fetlocks with a drawing pin. I fell to the floor and he fell back on top of me.

We began to writhe and struggle. Inch by inch (he was much stronger than I was) I realized he was pushing me towards the large, grey, front door of the apartment. I kicked back and screamed, but it was useless. Eventually the stranger rolled me on to the landing with one giant heave and I heard the door slam behind me. Behind it he was cackling again. I didn't wait to hear what he was saying.

I cleared the staircase two steps at a time, landed in the courtyard and raced for the exit by which we had entered. I was halfway across when I saw that there was a narrow alley that led straight back to the street where Freud had his apartment. I went for that. As I came out into the light of the open road I could have sworn that, high above me, I heard the sound of glass splintering. Well, he would need to do that to take aim.

Once I was inside Freud's house, I ran straight past the astonished Fräulein Glauber and headed for the stairs and the sacred door. As soon as she saw what I was doing she started up the stairs after me. Even to think of approaching the consulting room when it was occupied in that house was a bit like running naked into Westminster Abbey during a service.

"Vot you tryink to do, English?" she yelled. "You bin runnink after that Jung I told about and – "

But without even bothering to knock I had yanked back the door and was yelling into it: "He's going to shoot you. He's got a gun and he's going to shoot you!"

As my eyes accustomed themselves to the darkness of the consulting room I saw Freud, sitting in a high-backed chair, his white-bearded, square face immobile, untroubled. Zak was lying on a couch on the other side of the room. He, too, looked as if no news could possibly destroy his peace of mind. "*He* being – " said Freud.

Already, the massive calm of that room, the heavy furniture, the curtains, the pervasive atmosphere of pure reason were beginning to make me think I had dreamed the whole thing. I stood foolishly by the open door, my arms hanging by my sides. "We met him on the train, Zak," I shouted, "on the train."

Fräulein Glauber was by now on the landing. She did not share Professor Freud's calm at my intrusion.

"Train?" she was yelling. "Train? Don't you sink PENIS iss a bedder vurd than TRAIN. SAY YOU MET HIM ON A PENIS, MY FINE FAT FRIEND!"

Freud was looking at his housekeeper-cook with slightly more concern than he had afforded me. She did not, at that moment, one had to admit, look like a woman capable of cooking his or anyone else's dinner.

"Fräulein Glauber," he began "ich *glaube* – "

This seemed to amuse him for some reason and he went off into a long, wry-sounding monologue in German, which reminded me of the evening I had spent at dinner with him (not that you would be interested to hear about that), while Fräulein Glauber continued to scream, "MET HIM ON A PENIS WITH ZER REST OF ZER – "

Then the first bullet smashed through the window and into the far wall. Zak rolled neatly off the couch and on to the floor. Freud, too, with surprising speed, dropped to the ground: Only Fräulein Glauber and I, in the safety of the landing, remained on our feet. Freud had quite a funny impression of a joke psychiatrist, which he went into as a second bullet sang past the place where he had been sitting. "Mein Gott," he said, "zis man has killink feelinks towards me."

"GET DOWN!" I yelled. "AND KEEP DOWN!"

To my shock he was giggling, like a man who plays with children, as yet more shots banged into the wall above him. Then he and Zak began to crawl on their bellies towards the safety of the landing. When he reached the doorway, Freud pulled himself through it, turned over on his back and yawned. He showed no signs of getting up. Neither did Isaac.

"Have you any idea who – "

Freud grinned. "Who hates me? What a question. Don't ask such questions." He rolled back on to his front and muttered into the carpet, "Ci–vi–li–zati–on and its dis–con–ten–ts." Then he looked across at Zak, who was lying close beside him. He shifted his tongue about his mouth and there was something cadaverous about the grizzled line of his face. Zak looked back at him. He spoke in English, clearly and simply. "Like you," he said, "our friend out there is disenchanted with the world. For such people the best cure is to change it."

The wild thought occurred to me that Freud might charge for this conversation. Fräulein Glauber, who had remained silent for longer than I had ever known her to, began to shake convulsively. The stranger must have been firing randomly by now. I could hear bullets hitting the wall of the block. Below us I could hear screams and shouts.

"IT ISS ALL YOUR DOINK!" screamed Fräulein Glauber suddenly at me, "IT IS ALL YOUR FAULT! YOU ARE COMINK INTO MY KITCHEN AND VOLFINK CHOCOLATE CAKE UND YOU ARE ALL ZER TIME IN LEAGUE WITH – "

Freud looked up at her and said something rapidly, and quite harshly, in German. As soon as he had finished she bowed her head and with a sort of half bow scurried off down the stairs. Freud shrugged, quite a difficult thing to do when you are lying on your back. "We are surrounded by illness and disease", he said, "and hunger and misery. And for those who seek to remedy this.... If only the follies and crimes of great nations were susceptible to the analytic method."

They were quite obviously continuing a conversation to which I had not been invited. Now that Isaac's analysis had, in its very closing stages, been forced at gunpoint into the public arena, I felt myself entitled to watch. I leaned on the balustrade listening to the cries and screams from the street.

"As long as I can remember," Zak was saying to Freud, "as long as I can remember, I have fought to stop the hateful stupid way people are governed and the way people from my class have been twisted and beaten, denied their birthright and – "

I hadn't heard Zak talk like this since the days of Pratt. From what I could remember, it could go on for some time. Freud let him talk though and when he had finished he gave him a long, fatherly smile. "I am afraid", he said, "I am only a doctor. And need disease to live. When people talk to me about 'stamping out' this or that disease or crime, I shudder at the word. Yes, I need disease to live. Perhaps that is why I cannot bear the idea of it disappearing all together."

Outside the shooting had stopped. From far away, as if he was trapped in a bottle, I could hear the strange man screaming. He was screaming in English. There was no mistaking what he said. "QUACK! COME OUT YOU JEW DOCTOR QUACK! COME OUT OR WE'LL COME AND GET YOU! HEAR ME? HEAR ME YOU JEW DOCTOR QUACK?"

Then I rose to their level. "I think", I said, "you'll have a problem getting *him* into the consulting room."

Zak had already started down the stairs. It was clear from the behaviour of both doctor and patient that the session, and indeed the analysis, was at an end. But, as I think I've already said, I'm not so good at ending relationships. "My God," I thought as I stared at those firm glasses and that mocking, grizzled grin, "I've even got Zak's f—in' transference." I wanted the good professor to say something to *me*, you see. But he didn't. He turned and went back into his consulting room without a backward glance.

Isaac walked ahead of me, taking long, assured strides. He went straight on down to the street. He didn't look up at the windows of the opposite flats. If the stranger with the full eyes, the prominent nose and the shopwalker's manner was still there, he gave no sign of it. Neither were there anything like police or interested spectators. There was just me and Zak and, when we reached the corner and came into a narrow, cobbled alley, Isaac started to run. Not the way you run for a bus or to escape pursuit, but the way you run when you're a child and for some reason you feel happy and want the world to move even faster than it's already doing. He stretched out his hands like a child doing an impression of an aeroplane and made buzzing noises with his tongue.

And I? Well, as we sped out into a wide boulevard, across a square empty of traffic and under the leafless trees of early spring (I couldn't swear that was the season), I whirled my arms like a windmill. From now on, I thought, we'll do a lot of running. From now on, whatever it is we're doing, we'll give up the pretence of being nearly thirty or whatever we're supposed to be and we'll be eight, like when Zak fought the O'Malley twins in that field just up from the river. We'll be eight. All the time.

"I'm cured!" called Zak. "Zer Doktor Freud hass cured me!"

"Ja, ja!" I called back, flailing the air, "I am feelink so incredibly *vell*. . .you know?"

"Ye–eah!" said Zak, "Ye–e–eaahh!"

And then, at one of those Viennese café tables out on the pavement, I saw her. She was sitting on her own, a coffee in front of her, reading a newspaper. She wore an elegant black hat on the side of her head, a green blouse and a tastefully slim skirt. She was smoking a cigarette and reading a newspaper. Her hair, once so artless, had been cut, dyed blonde and bobbed in the manner of the twenties. It peeked out from her hat artfully. Fashionable. She looked fashionable. The gap in her teeth was about the only thing I recognized.

Isaac saw her at the same moment. He advanced on her as if in time to dreamy ballet music. I followed him at the same pace. My legs felt heavy. When she saw us she folded her newspaper, very slowly and carefully, as if she had a lot of time to do things like that and wanted to do them really well.

"Tessa," said Zak, "what are you doing here?"

She put the newspaper in her lap. When she was certain it was there and wasn't going to fall off or fly up into the air, she smiled. The smile took almost as long as folding the newspaper. "Wall Street's gone for a burton," she said.

I didn't know what she was talking about. She kept the smile going, as if it were the last note of a piece of romantic music and she wanted us all to enjoy it. "I can't care somehow," she said. "I can't care about any of the rotten system any more. I really couldn't give a damn about it."

On the front of her newspaper was a picture of a man who looked as if he had just jumped out of a window. It was difficult to decide, when you looked at the picture closely, whether he really *was* jumping out of the window or whether some clever photographic trick had been played. Was it that the building was sliding past him in a blur, yanked out of its roots by some unseen, giant hand? His expression suggested anything was possible.

I looked at the picture and I looked at Tessa, still unable to believe either of them.

"Tessa," said Isaac again, in a wondering tone, "Tessa."

She grinned again. And, for a moment, I caught something of that old, breathless, schoolgirl charm. "Say you like my stockings," she said. "Go on." Then, and only then, did she turn towards me. "You too, Amos," she went on, "you admire them. Go on."

But I didn't say anything at all.

* * *

I want to write about Tessa. I want to conjure up again that extraordinary change in her. I think that day, the day Zak finally discovered himself again, all that purpose and drive that seemed to have been blocked and baffled by the events of the First War, was also the day when I finally took on my Jacques mask.

Now, as I write, alone in the near-deserted building, such thoughts bring me face to face with myself again. I look at the angular, whitened face in the glass panel of the door and am suddenly sick to the heart of wise, old before his time, professionally bitter Amos. Since this is only a mask, why lay such claims for it? Why boast so pathetically – as I seem to do in these pages – of how no creed, no party, no person apart from one, could ever get past me? I don't have the courage of my own disillusion any more.

What if Alan is right about that place (I can't bring myself to write the name)? Suppose I am actually in the middle of that monstrous moral spoonerism, a Just War? And Churchill is right to bomb them flat night after night, because they are, as we have been taught to believe, a nation so universally guilty and corrupted by Nazism that –

That what? That they must be destroyed as we say they have destroyed others?

I am an unimportant clerk in a large department in the capital city of an old and corrupt imperial power. I don't believe my country *can* be right any more. If I started believing that, I should have to believe in –

That was partly why I stopped there in Vienna in '29. I was sure I heard Tessa's voice. I couldn't believe, at first, that it was only in my head, since it seemed to be coming, loud and clear, from Alan's office. Alan, I am almost sure, has gone home. I got up, opened the door to my office and tiptoed along the darkened corridor. There is something terrifyingly untenanted about empty office buildings at night, full of impersonal shadows. I kept close to the side of one wall. As I came close to Alan's door I thought I heard voices, but when I stopped the voices seemed to stop also. I inched forward. I was not mistaken about something being out of place. I could see, without going any further, that the light in Alan's office was still on.

But who could it be? At nine o'clock?

I went back, wrote this, couldn't settle to it, and now . . . . Well, here goes . . . .

This time I marched straight up to the door and saw that it was open. Sitting at Alan's desk, or rather on Alan's desk, in a blue skirt, peaked hat and rather natty-looking pair of stockings, her hair bunched out under the cap, in her right hand a flat notebook, in her left a sharpened pencil, was none other than Tessa Rabinowitz, née Oldroyd. That oval face was now decorated to look like an image from a film or poster. There was nothing of the milkmaid or the housewife or the would be "fast" girl about Tessa. She was one hundred per cent wholesome war department propaganda. She could have been raking in plastic battleships in the ops room at the end of a croupier's cue, or comforting the "boys" in some bar near a distant aerodrome. What also struck me about her was the intense bloom hostilities seemed to have brought to her cheeks – the sparkle dancing in her eyes, provoked, presumably, by so much death and destruction. She smiled when she saw me – a wide, confident grin. I noticed the cinematic gloss of her lips, the new, eager thrust of her chin and, most of all, I noticed that gap in her front teeth. It was gone for ever. Healed.

"Tessa – " I said.

"Come in, old sport," said Alan, "I think you two chaps know each other."

"Er – "

Tessa stood up. She was all elbows and knees suddenly. Bashful is the only word to describe her. "Amos – " she said.

"Sergeant Oldroyd", said Alan, "is on the press side in the ministry. We wanted to give her the rank of captain but she wouldn't hear of it."

"Oh," I said, "I see."

Tessa grinned sheepishly. "I've been all over the shop," she said. "It's sort of rather marvellous. I'm like those girls who used to run away to sea and become cabin boys and then they shook out their hair under the cap and chaps kissed them. Except nobody has."

"Have you heard", said Alan, "of the name of Dai Cellan Jones? You probably read his stuff on the Normandy landings. He was the only newsman there, I can tell you. He was dropped on to Crete too. And into Occupied France in – "

"Oh, shove it, Brown," said Tessa. She smiled again, gawkily. I went into the office and closed the door quietly behind me. I had indeed read Dai Cellan Jones's copy and had always assumed it had been composed in some pub in Fleet Street, so highly coloured and heroical was it. His dispatches usually began "I am standing under a wall of flame forty feet thick and bullets are flying past my ear...." I could not, somehow, connect the creature in front of me, either with the woman I had known eight or nine years ago, or with the author of all that front-line blood and thunder. My God, I thought, the war has transformed us all, taken us up and turned us into the opposite of ourselves. What has it done to me? I put my hand up to my face. Well, it has turned me into nothing. Into someone who no longer even has the courage to dissent. For most of Zak's life I trailed along behind him, a spectator, and now, alone, I avoid even the hint of the presence of great events. What was all this about Dai Cellan Jones?

"I've heard of him," I said cautiously. "Why?"

"Because you're going to meet him", said Alan, "tonight."

He got up and went over to the door. "Anyway," he said, "I

expect you two have a lot to talk about. I have to get some papers. Back in a moment."

He went out swiftly into the corridor. After he had gone there was silence between the two of us. Eventually I said: "Dai Cellan Jones – "

"No such person," said Tessa crisply. "I mean he's a sort of committee. Which is how he manages to get about so much. One minute up with Bomber Command, the next in the blazing deserts, the next with a commando unit up a fjord or something. There's a bloke called Hughes who does the voice for the radio bits, but there isn't any such actual person. I would have thought you would have seen all that, you funny old cynical person."

I breathed deeply. "What is all this?"

"Did he take you down to the Crown do?" said Tessa.

"Yes. How did – "

"It's a big show," she said, "really big stuff."

"And what are you – "

"I'm just a WAAF really", she said, "up at 'Butcher' Harris's hole in High Wycombe. I was in Ops and then Training, but I couldn't stand it."

"Did someone you know get – "

"Old thing *everyone* I knew got the chop. Night after night after night. You'd be kissing the chap one thing, the next he was in bits all over the Ruhr. It's the most God-awful slaughter. Not that 'Butcher' Harris gives a monkey's. So long as he's pounding Dutch refugees he's happy. I was fearfully LMF I'm afraid. Are you LMF? You look as if you're LMF."

"What's LMF?"

"Low Moral Fibre. Chicken, as the Americans say. I'm fearfully chicken. I think chicken is the only thing to be."

I went to the door and looked along the corridor. I could see no sign of Alan. Then I went back in to Tessa. "What's all this got to do with me, Tess?"

"Bomber Command has been getting an awful lot of flak, if you'll excuse the expression. And from what I hear they have something rather big on tonight. And they want a big show press-wise. That's the griff at the moment. But it may all change. I mean they may decide they don't want a big show press-wise. We may pull out all the stops and the old man will say, 'Hold your horses.' But isn't that this war, don't you think? Or anything else for that matter."

"What have you been doing since – "

She smiled and, for a moment, below the professional services manner, I caught a glimpse of the Tessa I had known before the war. The smile said, "It would take too long to explain" and "Please don't let's talk about that" and –

The fact of the matter was, suddenly, I didn't want to know particularly. I wanted to know precisely what the "show" was and why I, Amos Barking, unimportant clerk, should be anything whatsoever to do with it. Before I had the chance to talk any more to her, Alan was back in the office. He had a curious, rather stilted, official manner. "First," he said, "there's something I have to ask you."

I coughed.

"I'm going to ask you man to man," said Alan, sitting awkwardly on the edge of his desk, "OK?"

I felt suddenly, horribly embarrassed. Was he going to want to talk about sex? It's a subject I don't like discussing. I have been to bed with several women, but have never felt the remotest urge to discuss any of them – as you will probably have noticed.

"Are you", said Alan, sounding like a vicar, "actively pro-Nazi?"

"No, I'm not," I said swiftly and a little crossly. After I had said this I wondered whether I had used the right tone. After all, it isn't every day that one is accused of such things. Should I not have sounded more horrified? The fact of the matter was that it struck me as such an absurd allegation that, at first, I assumed he was joking, but when he folded his arms, nodded and looked even more like a vicar who had just been assured by an adolescent parishioner that he (the parishioner) had never masturbated in his life, I realized this was a serious inquiry. I was rather offended.

"Is this your idea, Al?" I said (he doesn't like having his name shortened):

"Partly."

"You mean – "

"I mean the security people have been taking an interest in you."

"Since?"

"Well, since they discovered your name isn't Swansea for a start. Or Henry for that matter."

I got up, mainly to give myself time to think.

When I joined the ministry in 1938 security was extremely lax. I joined largely because of a man I met at a party in Knightsbridge. His name – I think – was Prackling and, for some reason, he seemed to think I knew his father. In fact I had never met his father and indeed, if his father should have proved to be anything like him, I would probably have crossed the road to avoid him, but Prackling was not to be dissuaded. "'course, yes," he said. "If you were at Stowe in '29 and at Christchurch in '33, you...."

At the kind of party this was, everybody had been to school with everybody else. As far as I could remember, I had said I was at Haileybury in '26 (or maybe Westminster in '31) but little details like that don't matter to the average public schoolboy. The idea that it is *difficult* to pose as an old Etonian or an ex-Guardsman is a myth put about by these institutions in order to justify the ridiculous fees they charge. They were all so drunk and stupid that I could have said I was at Neptune in '76 and up Uranus in '98 and got away with it.

"Come over heah," said Prackling. "Bongo's here. And Duffy. And Brangbourne-Welch. And Steamer."

I smiled weakly.

"And Winston Churchill as well," said Prackling.

I assumed at first that this was some sort of code name for some previous lion of the lower fourth, but when I reached the group in the corner of the room I was amazed to find the well-known politician, complete with cigar and (in spite of the lateness of the hour and the interior nature of the location) a large, trilby hat. I ignored him, as he seemed drunk.

"You remember Swansea, don't you?" said Prackling. There were shouts of "Yah" and "Of course" and "Frahfly well". Apparently I had once shoved one of them down a lavatory bowl. This, I felt, looking at them, was a pretty sensible thing to have done.

"What are you doing?" said one of them. "Are you still in the City?"

"Yah," I said.

It turned out all these berks were working for the Ministry of Information on plans for what they described as the "coming war in Yorp". I could not believe this – the thought that anything of real importance was being entrusted to such idiots!

"We're getting the average dimbo ready for the big shoot," said a man called Temple-Crutchley-Jones with huge, horn-rimmed glasses. "It's fearfully interesting."

Then, for the first time, Churchill spoke. "There will be war", he said, in a deep and sonorous voice, "on the beaches and on the hills and in the lowlands and in the highlands and in the plains and on the surface of rivers and in the dry deserts of the east and the oceans of the cool west also there will be war."

No one paid any attention to this remark. Someone said that he was only at the party because he was Steamer's third cousin. I, however, found it fascinating. Not because of what he said – everyone in 1938 knew there was going to be a war – but because of the relentless, hypnotic quality of the delivery. He was the first person I had ever met who, partly because of the vulgarity of the way he spoke (a sort of ersatz "great prose" style) and partly because of the fact that his remarks were ignored so completely by those around him, had what I would describe as a genuinely prophetic quality. It is, after all, the very nature of prophets to be ignored. If they weren't ignored, they wouldn't be prophets but rulers or teachers, or some other class of person who is always wrong.

"There will also be war", droned Churchill, swaying slightly in the smoky haze of that drawing room, his hand steadying himself on an elegant carved table, "in the rocky places and the smooth places. In the wet and in the dry places. In the steamy and the humid and also in the temperate places. In the parks and gardens and also on the thoroughfares. On the railways and aerodromes and the amusement parks. In the museums and art galleries there will be war. In the theatres and cinemas and dance halls and grocers' shops and lingerie departments there will be war."

"Shut up, Churchill," said somebody, "shut up."

I edged closer to him. I was drunk as well. I was rarely sober between 1936 and the outbreak of war. A lad called Pongo started to hit the side of the wall with the flat of his palm. Prackling began to ask how my mater was.

"What, sir," I said (I was rather proud of that "sir" – perfect imitation Maugham, I thought), "what, sir, will be the effect of all this. . .war?"

Churchill turned his huge, bleary eyes upon me. "The war", he said, "will have an enormous effect. It will have an effect on reservoirs and fishtanks. It will have, without doubt, an effect on zoos and petshops. It will have an effect upon schools of music and dancing and, also, in due season, it will modify ineluctably the way in which secretarial colleges develop and prosper. It will strike at the very foundations of our democracy. It will have an effect on beaches and hills. On lowlands and – "

Very slowly Churchill started to slide towards the floor. There was something astoundingly dignified about this. I have never seen anyone pass out with such style. As he hit the floor he seemed to fold into himself like a concertina, until all that was left of him was a battered pile of clothes, a hat and a cigar. I saw Churchill many times after that – often at the Ministry, in the early days, with Brendan Bracken, but he never made such an impression on me as at that first meeting. It wasn't what he said, you understand. It was what he didn't say. And, of course, the way he said it.

For certain the company that night in Knightsbridge did not appreciate the man. They left him there in the corner and continued to talk about what Corker had told Porker. At the end of the evening, leaving with my arms around Prackling, I was told it would be grand to have me "on board" and I woke next morning to discover I had made an appointment with a man called Hodge, who was the immediate superior of these idiots. I often wondered, afterwards, whether Hodge was related to the man I was with at the battle of Charollais Wood, since he had the same high-pitched voice and the same talent for being difficult to remember. He probably was.

I made a good impression on Hodge. Principally, I think, because of Churchill. I could not get the empty, evocative rhythms of his talk out of my head. It was as if, for the first time, I had begun to understand the war that seemed destined to come. It was going to be nothing less than a giant, monstrous cliché. And I, of course, wanted to be part of it.

I wasn't asked about my origins or asked to produce any papers or proofs of intelligence, birthplace, age, sex or talent for administrative work. If you are introduced by the right people in this country, you have no need of documentation. That, as Alan would say, is what makes Britain such a truly free, open and democratic society. Provided, of course, you can get someone to introduce you.

Only someone like me, I thought bitterly, as I sat there facing Alan across my empty metal desk, would dare to question my credentials. Only an immigrant or a Jew or some other kind of outsider would have spotted that commodity I had learned to conceal so well – that secret intelligence that spells treachery. I should never have talked to him, never have confided in him. Christ, I thought, most probably he isn't a German Jew from Stuttgart. He's been lying to me. He went to Eton and Christchurch and his name really is Brown.

The silence between us had now become something worth discussing on its own. It was a silence that enabled one to hear the clock in the corridor outside, hear the distant rumble of a lorry in the street below and once or twice – or so I thought – hear in the night sky the drone of aircraft.

What was Tessa doing here? And, more importantly, what was he doing with her?

"Well," said Alan eventually.

"As you know," I said, "I came in with Steamer and Brangbourne-Welch and Prackling and – "

Alan was looking at me quizzically. Every single one of those public-school idiots who had amused me so much had joined up as soon as war broke out. Most of them, although they were nearly forty, my age, were killed in the first year of the war, because most of them, through the same bizarre English intrigue and accident that got me into this place, managed to join the RAF as pilots. Temple-Crutchley-Jones, who was unable to see farther than the end of his own bed, had managed to train as a fighter pilot and was killed on the first day at Biggin Hill by driving his Spitfire straight at a milk-churn under the impression that he was at forty thousand feet and the churn was a German bomber.

As I thought about those young men (they thought of themselves as young anyway) whom I had found it so easy to despise, I felt a hot flush of guilt. Maybe I was a bloody spy. I didn't believe in any of this. Maybe there was such a thing as mental treachery. Maybe I was committing it even now by thinking of the past, of things that didn't or couldn't matter, things that happened ten or twenty years ago. Alan was looking at me. "Look," he said, "we're both the same, you and I. We're both people without papers. You know? People who don't quite fit."

"Is it because of my view of the war?" I said.

"No," said Alan, "though that started it."

There was a pause.

"It's because of something that happened this afternoon, isn't it?" I said.

Alan shook his head.

"That stuff down by Tower Bridge. It was – "

"What?"

"Some kind of test?"

Alan shrugged.

"Was it?"

"Not so much," he said.

"What then?" I said. "What is this about?"

He ignored my question. "We went to your mother's flat", he said, "and built up a picture. It was pure chance I happened to mention your name to Oldroyd. Some opinion was that you were still rather dodgy, rather a not-quite-cricket type. But I said give him another chance. Which is why I took you down to Crown. To see the lie of the land."

"Alan, what *is* all this?"

"Have you heard", he said slowly, "of Operation Thunderclap?"

"No," I said, "it sounds completely and utterly improbable."

"Yes," he said, "it is really." Then he smiled. "But you, me, Oldroyd and dear old Cellan Jones", he said, "are going to sell it to the Great British Public. It's your chance to get clear, old thing."

"But what", I said, "*is* it?"

Alan tapped the side of his cheek with a pencil. He looked at Tessa and then he looked at me. "It's bombs," he said, "rather a lot of bombs."

"Oh," I said.

Well, bombs were what we had been writing about for the last three years. Our job is bombs. Our *raison d'être* is to let the gentlemen of the press know what Harris and his team are doing. There was nothing new about bombs. Only Alan's serious expression and Tessa's world-weary smile suggested that on this occasion we might be talking about something rather different.

"Bigger than Hamburg?" I said.

"In a way," said Alan.

"Berlin?"

He leaned forward across the desk. "Dresden, old bean," he said, "and you're coming with us."

PART THREE

It is morning. I am writing this in the office. I have been here since seven or eight. Tessa and Alan have gone out to look for coffee and left me to scribble. "Is this a time to write things down?" said Tessa.

"Yes," I said, "it's always a time to write things down." Even if they are recorded by an untrustworthy, hopeless, confused creature such as myself, events must be recorded. They are, as I told them both, too important to leave to the historians. Just as no one else will ever write the true history of Charollais Wood, so no one will ever dare reveal, unless it be in fictional form, the reality of Operation Beefeater. My God, when I said this war was going to be a cliché, I didn't realize quite how much of a cliché. Any story conference in Hollywood would have rejected what has gone on tonight as totally implausible.

Anyway, I have to write. I have to write quickly, because they will be back soon and after they return I don't want to write any more. I will be finished with writing.

I am so *stiff*.

And you see, because what has happened is so extraordinary, it seems in some strange way to justify what happened to Isaac. So I want to set down that part of the story too, to bring the two of them to some kind of conclusion. My only problem is knowing which story to tell first. Knowing where to start. . . .

Well, it starts, all of it, I can see now, with Tessa. And I might as well start with Tessa outside that café in Vienna in '29, with her fashionable hairstyle and curious, fashionable manners. That was the same Tessa who was next door with Alan in her neat, blue, WAAF's uniform. That was the Tessa who, all those years ago, had skipped off down the Embankment, suddenly unbraiding that beautiful hair. That hair . . . I notice that when we met her in Vienna I have described it as blonde. When we first met her in the bookshop,

237

I see, I haven't described the colour, but in thinking of it now I see it as deep, rich red. And now? Now, the Tessa next door, Sergeant Oldroyd, the attractive personable woman who has gone out to get the coffee – well, she has hair something between blonde and red, a sort of chestnut mouse colour. So perhaps all my memories are correct.

It is Tessa whose presence seems determined to link the *now* with the *then* and so I must be very careful as I describe her outside that café. It will be, I suspect, impossible to prevent the hurt I felt then from colouring it. Although it was fifteen years ago, I remember it as precisely as the smile she gave me just now in Alan's office, and to write about it is just as painful.

"Well," said Zak, when she'd bought us a coffee, "what are you up to?"

She smiled. "Journalism," she said.

"Pays well, does it?"

She looked at me and breathed out carefully. I'd got the impression that she had been mathematically precise about the amount she had parted her lips. "Not so bad."

"And what are *you* doing in Vienna?"

Zak and I exchanged glances.

"Come on. . . ."

Her voice was quite different now. That hardness had gone. It seemed supple, caressing. "What are the Terrible Twins up to?"

"I came for a rest," said Zak.

"Ah."

After she'd bought us a coffee, she bought us lunch, and after she'd bought us lunch, she bought us dinner. And then, at ten o'clock at night, quite drunk, we boarded a sleeper for Paris. At least I thought it was going to Paris at the time.

I couldn't sleep and stood in the corridor watching the night. Tessa came out after a while, in a garment that could have been a dress designed to go to bed in or a set of night garments designed to be worn in public. She was smoking again with the languid precision that seemed to characterize all her movements now.

"How's he been?"

"Not very well."

"I thought not."

The train shook on past high, anonymous buildings, the endless, vacant possibilities of highways and the touching completeness of domestic interiors.

"He could have done. . . ."

"Oh, sure," I said, "and he still might."

She turned to me. As well as the cigarettes and the hair and the clothes, she'd got this little smile. The smile was a sort of fashion accessory too. She left it on her lips for just the right amount of time and then she said: "You'll enjoy Berlin."

"Oh," I said, "is that where we're going?"

She put her hands up to my cheek. "Still the same cynical little eyes," she said. And went back to her compartment.

When I got back to our sleeper Zak was sitting up in bed, his arms folded. He was smoking one of her cigarettes. They were fat, sweet-smelling things.

"What's the matter?" I said.

"I'm in love," he said. "I'm still in love with her."

I climbed into my bunk. I always got the bottom bunk when travelling with Zak and he always got the seat by the window.

"At least", I said, "she dresses a bit better."

"I'm not in love," said Isaac.

"I didn't attempt to fathom any of this. I lay on my side, rolling and swaying in the snake-like womb of the train.

"Our generation", said Zak, "missed it. Missed it completely."

"Don't all generations do that?"

"I don't know. Ours did anyway."

The train howled dismally, dragging its powerful skirts through yet another lightened, empty station. Zak stirred on his bunk and yawned. Once again, as he made the last remark before we both drifted off to sleep, I caught that world-weary tone to his voice, a sudden sensuality, a languor that the old Zak would never have allowed. Freud had had the effect on my friend that Swiss finishing schools are popularly supposed to have on nice young ladies. He had given him poise.

"This time", he said, "I don't intend to make a mess of it."

I didn't ask what he meant by "it". I heard his breathing become steadier and then, when he was deep asleep, I lit a borrowed cigarette and stared out at the darkness. We were in open country now and no houses, farms or lights broke the endless wall of the night. My lips were dry with a kind of fear as I stared at my reflection in the window of the compartment. Over my shoulder I seemed to see the face of the stranger from Vienna, his bulbous eyes and hands upraised in what could have been compassion. The train wheels joined in the upper-class snarl of the stranger's voice and both seemed to be talking about killing things.

The next morning at breakfast, Tessa said: 'If you two boys wanted, we could put you up in Berlin for a few days. Then take you back.''

"Sounds OK to me," said Zak.

"Fine," I said.

We were all very polite to each other. And did not discuss the past. All Tessa would say was that she was working for the *Daily Express*. Once that would have provoked a shriek of rage from Isaac. Now all he said was: "Oh. Is that interesting?"

"All right," she said. "All right."

She was much less attentive to Isaac than to me. She was intense and sisterly to yours truly. Which worried me a lot. I've always been a shabby dresser and from time to time she would straighten my collar above my ragged jersey or scold me for the state of my shoes (I've never been one for polishing shoes – I tend to let them grow mould as I wear them). Once she even rumpled my hair, which irritated me.

From time to time I'd catch them both looking at me as if I was a shared secret between them. I'd find myself in the middle of a sentence or an anecdote ("Good old Amos always got a joke, right?") and suddenly unable to complete it. It was all very difficult.

When we got to the hotel, an extremely expensive place just off the Unter den Linden, I said to Zak, "Look – if you two boys wanted – "

"*Please*, Amos," he said, "*please* – "

I didn't make any more jokes like that. Zak and I shared a room anyway.

She wouldn't tell us who she was going to interview.

"Can we come?" I asked.

"No," she said.

She went out during breakfast and did so for the next two days, while Zak and I hung around the hotel. When I asked her where she was going she said: "Difficult. Negotiations. . . ." And gave me some more of her smile.

In the evenings she told us how she'd got the job. It turned out it was something of an accident. She'd met a man in a pub.... She looked, actually, as if she'd met quite a lot of men in quite a lot of pubs since we had last seen her.

After she'd gone out on the third morning, I went into her room. Her notes were lying across her pillow like an abandoned card game. On one of them I read the following:

> Imagine a stern-faced man with a level eye and a commanding military step.
> This is Herr Hitler, the man who is revitalizing Germany.
> He has no hobbies, no wife, no children – all he thinks of is the new nation that he is forging out of the old!

This was crossed out and underneath it was written:

> The monster who is preparing to slaughter millions – Adolf Hitler promised today that the German jackboot would spare no one!
> Evil, 34-year-old Hitler spoke to me today in his secret hideout in –

This, in its turn, was crossed out and underneath it, in uncertain, schoolgirl handwriting, was written:

> How poss describe Hitler?
> Phenomenon. YES. But....

I crossed this out and wrote underneath it:

> Impss describe Hitler. Or anything come to that.

As I was wondering what to write next I heard the door open behind me and a voice said: "Spying?"

"That's right," I said.

Another voice said: "Let us see what you have written!"

In through the door after Tessa came a little man with a club foot. His elaborate, not quite placeable uniform only made the deformity more obvious. He dragged himself into the middle of the room and glowered up at me. Close to, the uniform was even more improbable. There were whorls and crosses and half-moons and tassels where I had never previously seen tassels on a uniform. He looked like a senior Sea Scout undergoing a severe crisis of identity. I gave

241

him what Tessa had written and my scrawled addition as well. On a separate sheet of paper he wrote:

It is not propaganda's task to be intelligent. Its task is to lead to success. Therefore no one can say your propaganda is too rough, too mean – these are not criteria by which it may be characterized.

He licked the top of the pencil and underneath *that* he wrote:

The Führer is a God. He is a King.

Then he said: "That's what I call propaganda. Your English idea of propaganda is to say a guy is good instead of lousy. Right?" His accent shifted into a curious blend of Berlin and Chicago. It sounded like something assumed as a joke that had become a habit. He started to do a kind of Groucho Marx lope around the room. "Hitler is a schmuck", he said, "but a clever schmuck." To complete the image he drew out a cigar from his top pocket and lit it. "Way way back," he said, "I was a little bit Bolshie. You know? Yes? Yes? Yes. This is the Red City, you guys. Red Berlin. Gauleiter of Berlin, that's me. But people don't want Bolshie. They don't think Bolshie. They don't talk Bolshie. They're way up to here with Bolshie this and Bolshie that. Bolshie is like too much hard work. Right?"

"Right!" I said.

"Right!" said the little man. Suddenly his act stopped, or rather, changed its character. He leaned across an elegant hotel chair, thrust his bottom out and said, in a voice whose sincerity seemed closer to parody than his earlier manner: 'I love my Führer.'

"Good," I said.

Then he went back to the Groucho Marx act again. He loped about the room in concentric circles then shot off towards the shelves by the window. He whipped two or three books off, examined them closely and threw them over his left shoulder, then he did a bent-knee plus bottom-waggling stroll over to the bed. When he got there he stubbed his club foot on the wooden legs. Undeterred by this he winched the other leg up so that it lay full length in front of him.

"How she gonner describe der Foihrer?" he said, now almost impossibly East Side, "how she gonner get der guy acrawss? No hope!"

"Not in the *Express* anyway," I said.

"*Right!*" said the little man, vaulting up on to the bed and raising his legs rather artfully into the air as he placed his hands behind his head. "Maybe in the *Mail* more. Maybe in the *Mail* she could the Foihrer describe already I don't know. They got the right approach to English prose for dat to happen maybe I don't know. But de *Express*? It's for dead men. Right? Jeez I love your English papers."

I was, I admit, a little nervous of this man. Berlin was a nervous city. On my way from the station I had seen squads of men in brown uniforms and, even opening the long windows of the room and looking down into the street you were aware that people were fighting for control of those gigantic avenues and squares. I've seen many pictures of Berlin since, but never was it as complete and mal-evolent as then. I went to the windows. There didn't seem to be anybody on the street. "Who – " I began, but behind his back Tessa signalled me into silence.

"I starts," went on the little man, whose Bronx accent was now of rib-tickling proportions, "wid a good idea. Right? Josef Goibbles is a *good* idea. You check?"

"You are – ?"

"Am I, though? Am I Josef Goibbles? Or am I someone else, yes? Am I dat creep Roehm? Ad I dat Jew Heydrich? Or am I – " He sprang off the bed and hurtled across the room, moving with the grace of a demented crab. I smelt his breath – brackish, like dead leaves. "Abe Solomons. A Noo York taxi driver. Huh?"

"Well," I said carefully, "you certainly don't dress like a taxi driver."

"Dat's good," said the little man. "Dat is very good." He was chuckling now – his chin popping up and down and into his throat and his shoulders being raised and lowered as if on a wire. He looked, it had to be admitted, very like a New York taxi driver. I began to wonder if he was a New York taxi driver – and, if he was, what possible reason he might have for wanting to impersonate a leading member of the Nazi Party. He stopped suddenly and looked over his shoulder. "But I am, though," he whispered urgently, "only don't tell those murdering bastards."

Tessa spoke. Very carefully and slowly. She sounded as if she was trying to pass me a message which she did not wish this man to decode. "Herr Goebbels", she said, "has been a little – "

"Dat creep Goibbles," said the little man, "dat shyster Goibbles –

sell his own grandmudder for two pfennigs. Jeez, what an asshole!"

I saw that Tessa was mouthing something at me. It took me some time to work out what she was saying. I tried "It's a failure", "Bits of eel here" and even "Get us a creel, dear" until I realized she was trying to say, "Schizophrenia". I looked down at the little man in the uniform. It made a lot more sense if you proceeded on the assumption that he was suffering from schizophrenia. He was kneeling down now. He shuffled, still on his knees, to the window and the balcony and crooned out at the street: "Berlin! Jeez, I love dis town!"

I was still unsure, however, whether this was a New York taxi driver who thought he was Joseph Goebbels or whether Joseph Goebbels was walking around under the impression that he was a New York taxi driver. I was debating this question with myself when he leaped up and raised his hands to the ceiling in his most spectacular demonstration yet.

"The past", he screamed, "is nothing. The present must be ignored. Only the future!" He began to pace up and down. He paced very well for a disabled person. "We invent. All it is. We invent. We call for a leader. Who? From where? Who shall he lead, this man? A new German? Yes? Yes. And we invent him. As tough as Krupp steel. Yes?" He was quivering with excitement. "The Führer himself. Tough. Why? Because we say so. Yes? And as the Führer says so it is destined to become. What a man! A God! A King! So we have said. Where? We can answer this. Oh, yes. In our propaganda. And who then is the mouth that must create and speak this our propaganda? Is he too, you ask, a creature *of* that propaganda?"

He wheeled on to me and answered his own question with a passionate, brutal roar. His mouth writhed into the space between his cheeks until it seemed that all his body was being dragged along by those lips, soaked in saliva, red, enticing.... He seemed beside himself with rage. "NO! HE IS NOT! THE MOUTH INVENTED ITSELF! HERR JOSEPH GOEBBELS IS NOT A FIGMENT OF ANYBODY'S IMAGIN-ATION! HERR JOSEPH GOEBBELS IS THE ONLY ONE OF THE HALF-BAKED NAZI BASTARDS WHO *is* HIMSELF! WHO IS THE NATURAL CREATIVE INSTRUMENT OF FATE! YOU HEAR? YOU'RE TALKING TO THE MOUTH NOW AND YOU READ YOUR JEW BIBLE, DIDN'T YOU? IN THE BEGINNING WAS THE WORD AND THE WORD WAS GOD AND DON'T YOU F—ING FORGET IT!

ок?'' Then he fell on to his knees and whispered: "Führer, leader, I'm sorry. Führer I'm so sorry. Nothing. Nothing. Nothing."

Nobody in the room moved. Until the man in the uniform got up and said: "Lady. Der Foihrer don't see youse today. Itsa too busy for him, OK?"

"Fine," said Tessa.

Through the open door came Isaac. He studied the man in the uniform very carefully. He looked, for a moment, like a great doctor about to make a diagnosis. Then he smiled in a knowing way and I saw the shadows of his heroes flit across his face. He folded his arms and leaned against the doorjamb. He looked like the sort of person who could handle Goebbels – should this prove to be the man himself.

"Is Heydrich a Jew?" said Zak.

"From way way back," said the man, "on his mother's side. An' what does der guy do? He sez you wanner be a Nazi you gotter have a fam'ly tree dat dates back to 1250 or som'ting. Would you believe? Dese guys are crazy. Dey wanner be found out, I tell you sincerely. Dey'll never make it. And dat creep Goibbles. He's a split poissonality too. You know? He is. He t'inks he's a Noo York taxi driver. You know how he woiked this one out? He t'inks his costoom makes him look like one, right? You believe this."

"Yes," said Zak, smiling sarcastically. He seemed to be enjoying this. He came into the room and studied the little man. He looked at me. "You know what I left out?" he said.

"Out of what?" I said. But I knew what he meant all right. Out of the magic formula that was going to make him rich and powerful and remembered. Out of the magic words that were going to make him somebody instead of a peculiar creature like Amos Barking.

"Force and fraud," said Zak. "I left those out."

As he said this I stared at the little man in the uniform and it seemed to me then almost certain that I was looking at the Nazi propaganda chief. I couldn't, off the top of my head, think of anybody else in the Western world with the necessary acting skill to persuade me that this was he. Anyway, I wanted him to be Josef Goebbels and, as I advanced on him, I found my skin was prickling with excitement. "He's a Jew," I said, indicating Zak. Zak coughed self-deprecatingly. When I got level with Goebbels I prodded him, just to make sure he wasn't a waxwork. I noticed he was trembling.

Once again I smelt that brackish, dead leaves smell on him. "He's a Jew," I said again.

"Jeez," said Goebbels thinly, "woujer b'leeve it? I got nut'n against der Jews. Jews is good people. Good people. Some of my best friends is Jewish as it happens. But – "

"Policy is policy."

"Business is business."

I hit the little man hard in the pit of the stomach. He doubled up, coughing with pain. I hit him quite hard. I punched him in the face and Goebbels howled. I kicked him in the crotch and Goebbels wept. I broke Goebbels's glasses and Goebbels crawled across the floor, retching in pain. I ground my heels into Goebbels's bleeding chin and saw the blood flow on to his absurd uniform. I really gave Goebbels a hard time. I did not spare him at all. I jumped up and down on his chest and I said things like "This one's for Zak" and I dragged him across the white hotel carpet and banged his head against the wall until he begged for mercy. I was a real hero as far as Goebbels was concerned, while Isaac watched from the door, that distant, sophisticated smile on his lips.

Honesty about the past is an impossible dream. All we have to go on is memory that lies and cajoles us. That and the memories of others whose tricks are worse. If I am honest about it, I think I began to doubt even then, as I shook Goebbels by the shoulders, that it really *was* Goebbels I was shaking. But, oh God, how I wanted it to be Goebbels. How, even now after all these years, I want to believe that it was him. When he was unconscious I picked him up and threw him on the bed.

"My information", said Tessa, "is that that is Herr Joseph Goebbels."

"Journalists usually provide you with inaccurate information," said Zak thoughtfully. "Anyway, even if this is Herr Joseph Goebbels, I don't think the Nazi Party will want to make an issue of it."

I spat on Goebbels's upturned face. He grunted beatifically in his coma.

"It wouldn't make good propaganda, would it?" said Zak.

"No," I said, "we'd have to kill him. And then make up a song about him."

Then both of us started to sing:

Raise the banners in strict formation
The SA march in close formation.
Clear the streets for the brown battalions
Clear the streets for the storm troopers
Millions look with hope to the swastika
Soon Hitler's flag will fly over the streets.

The "Horst Wessel Lied" loses a lot of its impact in translation. But we gave it a lot of energy. Goebbels stirred. "Dat's good," he said, in the Bronx. "Dat is a good toon."

"You wrote it," I said. "You ought to know."

Tessa's face was flushed. "I came here", she said reedily, "for a serious newspaper."

Zak walked across to the bed. With a sort of terrible, abstract passion, he said: "Listen. Do you think even a serious newspaper can cope with all of this? Do you think it could describe anything more complicated than a walk in the park? We're living through crazy times, Tessa. Interesting times. That's an old Chinese curse, didn't you know? 'May you live in interesting times.' It's all gone mad, didn't you know? It's all gone crazy. And nice little moral gestures like this" (here he indicated me) "won't get us out of the mess any more than trying to describe it all for some chimerical quantity known as a 'serious newspaper'. Jesus, what a contradiction in terms."

I flushed with anger. "Oh," I said, "and you're all for ducking a few of the bad guys in the river instead, are you? In the correct manner, whatever that is. Just because I try to act simply, straightforwardly, whenever I see this poverty or injustice of whatever you're on about, I – "

Zak smiled again. The smile was beginning to irritate me. It was just a little superior. "You, Amos," he said, "being an ordinary nice chap, go looking for precisely the sort of moral trouble where you know you'll shine. But don't kid yourself that behaving decently in the privacy of your own back yard or a hotel room is going to stop the rape, murder, cruelty and the rest of it for one second. It won't. You'll just have been – *good*, won't you? And your kind of morality is supposed to be its own reward."

"And what's your solution to this, then?" I said, indicating the sleeping figure of the Gauleiter of Berlin.

"You must embrace the stupidity of the times," said Isaac. "When they are hysterical you must sob and laugh with them, when the time comes to be serious – put on your solemn face. Act it out. Act it out. This history of yours is nothing but a performance."

Tessa started to try to say something, but he rounded on her, his finger jabbing downwards at Goebbels. "He wrote a song about some drunken bastard who was killed in a bar-room brawl," he said, "but the song was *believed*. That's what history does to liars and cheats and rogues and criminals. And if you're to beat them at their game you must be as clever as they are, as quick as they are, you've got to be there before them. That's your responsibility. The history of the good little men, the history written by the Amoses of this world, won't forgive if you do not. If you sit on your arse and wait for nice, neat, moral issues to come to you there won't be any history at all, there'll be a disgusting, animal wail from people like that."

"He's going back to the Party," I said flatly.

Zak looked at me oddly. "You must be joking," he said. "I haven't got time for all of that. Sorry, son. Haven't got the patience for Marxism. I've sat it out for as long as most and it's started to *bore* me. From now on – I'm going to enjoy myself."

Goebbels muttered something in his sleep. "This fine young Jewish thug. . . . This magnificent specimen of Aryan Jew-baiting . . . the collective security of proletarian Führers. . . ." He jerked his head back and his cap rolled off the bed and on to the floor.

Zak flipped him over on to his face. "Let's get this creep's clothes off," he said.

Then Tessa started on him. She was a journalist. There was such a thing as professional ethics. Herr Goebbels, if he *was* Herr Goebbels and what kind of journalist did we think she was if she couldn't check on the identity of the person she was talking to, Herr Goebbels was her contact and she was his guest. He was, she said to us, going to arrange a world exclusive with Adolf Hitler who, whatever else you might think about him, was a man with strong views, with newsworthy views (where, I wondered, had she learned all these words) and the Sunday papers were after him as well, it was disgusting the rivalry why couldn't journalists work together?

"How", I said, "do you know he's Goebbels?"

"I met him in a lift in Vienna," said Tessa. "He seems a bit odd because he's suffering from a slight attack of schizophrenia brought on by overwork. Anyway – " At this point she started to break down. "I can't possibly file a story saying that Joseph Goebbels thinks he's a New York taxi driver called Abe Solomons. The news editor would laugh in my face. Nothing short of Goebbels telling Sefton Delmer that this was the case – preferably on the radio – would satisfy that bastard." She was crying quite hard now. Her make-up was starting to smudge. It improved her appearance I thought.

"He might tell the world soon," I said.

"He only told me because I don't matter," sobbed Tessa.

"It's unimportant people who are trusted with secrets. And . . . lunatics are very cunning."

Here she started to giggle as well as cry. Then I started to giggle. Then, at last, Isaac joined in. We were all shrieking with mirth as Zak began to pull off the Gauleiter of Berlin's trousers. We shrieked even harder when he took off his tunic and underpants.

"You can't make sense of any of this," said Zak. "It's all a stupid, cruel, practical joke. All of it. You just have to climb on and hold your breath."

"I thought", I said, shaking with uncontrollable laughter as Tessa peeled off Goebbels's vest and held it aloft, "the Communist Party was going to do that for you."

At the mention of the words "Communist Party" Zak knelt on the ground and sobbed with hysterical glee. He pounded the carpet with the Nazi leader's underpants in a desperate attempt to get himself under control. But it was hopeless.

"The Communist Party," he said, and broke off again into wild giggles, "the Communist – " But now even half the word was enough to set us off. We rolled on the floor kicking up our legs. "The Communist Party", he got out finally, "is ridiculous. But not ridiculous enough as far as I'm concerned. I need something *really* bizarre. Don't you think?"

"What are you going to do?" I said, waving around one of Goebbels's boots. "Get into the uniform?"

This set us off laughing again. When we'd finished, Zak wiped his eyes and went up to the naked body on the bed. He took Tessa's pen and squirted ink on to his fingers. On the little man's chest he wrote: I AM JOSEPH GOEBBELS. I AM ALSO A NEW YORK TAXI DRIVER. And then we got out of the room. Fast.

All that remained of the encounter – as Tessa reminded us many times in later years – was that the first in-depth interview with the Führer was in the *Sunday* not the *Daily Express* – in spite of "Herr Goebbels's" expressed preference for the *Daily Mail*.

> Herr Hitler is a tall, English-looking man with fanatical blue eyes and clipped moustache under an energetic nose.
>
> He served as a private in the German army and rose to the rank of sergeant, rejecting all offers of a commission.
>
> His strength, and that of his 100,000 armed followers of the Fascist "Storm Division", has been their obvious sincerity and the easy comprehensibility of the Fascists' political demands.

I told Tessa she was lucky to have ended her career on a newspaper so quickly. How can you have the nerve to work for an organization that has the effrontery to claim to print the truth about the events of the previous day? The events of any day once gone are a secret as impenetrable as the real identity of that man with a club foot I assaulted in the bedroom of the Hotel Steinplatz or the need of a leader writer on the *Sunday Express* in the September of 1930 to use the word "energetic" to describe Adolf Hitler's nose.

* * *

Tessa cried rather a lot on the train back through Aachen. She cried almost all the way through Belgium. I don't think it was just Belgium. I think the strain of pretending to be a hardened professional journalist was telling on her. When she wasn't crying she was giggling. She was, she said, the first journalist to have secured an unreportable scoop: NAZI PROPAGANDA CHIEF "THOUGHT HE WAS TAXI DRIVER" SAYS HOTELIER IN NUDE ASSAULT DRAMA.

I think that was my title.

It wasn't just that she wasn't *hardened*, it transpired. She wasn't a journalist. She'd been out with a journalist. He was so professional and so hard that he had left her in Vienna for some German girl twenty years his junior (he, as it turned out, was fifty, which made Tessa twenty years his junior as well, but she didn't seem to see anything remarkable in that). He'd gone on about his news editor.

She didn't even know what a news editor was. She used the word the way she'd always used words in conversation. She hadn't a clue what any of them meant she told us. Instead of saying "proletariat" every second word she might just as well have been mouthing "cucumber" or "terrapin", all through the last decade. She was Tessa Oldroyd, an ignorant dentist's daughter from Wapping.

It was raining when we got to the boat. We struggled up the gang-plank surrounded by the unique sadness of English faces, English families. Then we leaned on the rail in the drizzle, looking back at the pale shapes of customs house and station, our last hold on Europe. Tessa sobbed into a handkerchief too small to be of any practical use. As she sobbed her face softened and there was nothing but pity between her and me and her and Zak. "Thing is", she said through her tears, "I'm not even a dentist's daughter any more. Zak's mother had died when we were in Vienna. They had written, they had left messages, but none had been received. Tessa had gone home to Daddy, but the long-suffering Norman Oldroyd, who had borne everything from her whimsy to her Marxist critique of his teeth-filling activities for many years, had ordered her out of the house on learning of her relationship with the journalist – who had, as I recall, a name something like Paraquat. She was, he had said, no better than a prostitute. Since the man had abandoned her in Vienna, she told us, that was what she felt like.

The boat's whistle wailed. I patted her on the shoulders. I patted her as if I was testing a bed or a sponge cake – slowly, deliberately, to see how much she sprang back. She hardly sprang back at all. She was totally and utterly defeated.

We went below to the bar. Zak took her arm and led her to a side table while I got the drinks. I looked back at them when I was up at the bar and I saw she had leaned her head on his shoulder and he was patting her absently. He caught my glance and shrugged elegantly, as if to say, "What can you do?" All through the sea passage, as we looked out at the yeasty Channel, he squired her – that's the only word to describe the gentle pressures on her arm, the occasional straightening of those damp locks of hers and the soft, humorous voice he used to describe what he called his "illness".

What did I do? I sat and watched and drank and smiled.

"My money's almost run out," she said, as we looked out at the miles of grey water.

"So's ours," said Zak.

I said it. They were thinking it, but I said it: "You can stay with us," I said. "Of course you can. Unless – "

"We won't go back to the shop", said Zak, "just yet."

I've always thought of the boat train as a sort of outdoor therapy for English men and women who need to recover from the shock of realizing that there are other nationalities in the world. There was, I remember, an elderly couple sitting opposite us. I had spotted them in the crowd on the boat, still too cautious to have a public conversation that might be overheard by their own kind. Now – halfway through Kent – they were relearning the ways of private, public speech, the subdued sideways snarl that will be familiar to all users of the English public transport system. WE'RE HOME, said the man's sagging shoulders. THIS IS GOOD. I KNOW, said his wife's curls as she inclined her head towards him, BUT NOW THE BASTARDS CAN UNDER-STAND WHAT WE'RE SAYING.

I looked away from them out at the overfinished English countryside. Zak had his arm round Tessa. She was asleep. She looked younger than when I had first met her ten years ago.

"Well, it's back on the paper for me," I said, "if they'll have me."

Isaac grinned. "I'm going to have another shot," he said.

"At what?" I said.

Isaac waved his hand regally at the countryside; his gesture included the couple opposite us, the lumpy vowels heard from the corridor as worried English faces pounded past with luggage, everything, his finely made fingers seemed to say, everything. . . .

"I'm going to look this time," said Zak. "I'm going to look very hard and see what's going on."

At this point the man opposite leaned forward and tapped Zak on the knee. "I'll tell you what's going on," he said. "Communism. That's what's going on."

"Get away," I said.

"It is," said the man's wife. "It's just around the corner. In waiting."

Zak started to laugh. "Well," he said, "that's a consolation."

And out of the window I could see the first garage, pub, arterial road that suggested the huge, sprawling city waiting for us to the north-east.

I've been trying to think whether Tessa talked about how Zak's mother had died. Was I even there when she told him? I certainly have no clear recollection of how he took the news. I am doubtless confusing this moment with something that happened last night, in the middle of the first, wild, babbling conversation between Tessa and myself.

"But *no*, Amos, *no*.... Oh, can't you see, darling friendly sort of Amos Thingy, that was all because of old Mrs Thing that he couldn't do sperms."

Tessa's manner of the moment, by the way, is a sort of Grand Guignol version of the act she had that first day in the bookshop, just after the Great War. It is something of the débutante, something of the lass from the services and just a touch of the demented shop assistant. It nevertheless manages a degree of charm, perhaps because it is now performed as if Tessa (and the person to whom she happens to be speaking) is perfectly well aware that this is simply an act, that no one in their right mind speaks like this and that at any moment she is about to revert to a normal voice.

"Do *what*?"

"He was absolutely impo, old thing. Impo as a newt. It wouldn't go up. Or even sideways. Or in any direction at all. I tried everything. I even sort of tried talking to its little self as if it were a sort of plant, you know? But it stayed in its little shell and looked all sort of fearfully shy and not on and wouldn't do sperms if the colonel himself told it to. Gosh, it was fearful. That's when he started to hit me."

"Hit you?"

"You remember the day you came round? The day of the General Don't Let's Work to Spite Them Thingy. Well. He'd been hitting me fearfully and it was awfully strange because Mrs R. very much took my part which I thought was good of her, me being a frightful old Yok, you know? It was because he was worrying about the S. of the W."

"The what?"

Tessa grinned.

"State of the World."

"Oh."

Blue rather suits Tessa. She was, and presumably still is unless someone out there has persuaded her to remove it, wearing a straight skirt, a battledress and a peaked hat. She has made her mouth up in a full bow and her eyes sparkle and glow like those of a cinema heroine. She carries a neat little pair of leather gloves and on her shoulder is a sergeant's stripe. I simply don't believe it.

I suppose that when she took up again with Zak she was at her lowest. Is that why, when I look back at what I have written about her then, she seems drab, distant? I think it is probably that Tessa is simply one of those people who can never be quite "hit off"' or described, even by someone as desperate to do so as I am. She has a charm that supersedes description. In fact, if any of the three of us managed to stay in tune with the times, I can see now that it was Tessa. Tessa, unlike me, has graduated into the forties, learned the language perfectly. Her resignation in the face of awfulness, the weird understated bravery in which she specializes (she told me that she had actually – unofficially of course – been all the way and back on a Lancaster raid with someone called "Tommy" Macfarlane), all of it is so perfectly in harmony with the moment that I simply want to stand before it and marvel as if I were in front of some acknowledged masterpiece that I was seeing for the first time.

When I got back this morning I looked back through these pages and saw that I had given no indication at all, really, of what it is that Alan and I do here. Perhaps the habits of secrecy are ingrained in me so strongly that I have – as so many do – censored myself. But now it seems necessary to do so, for unless I do so, I cannot make the enormity of the task facing me clear, even to myself.

Our job, essentially, is to sell Bomber Command. Or rather, as I think I said, to look at ways in which its work might be "explained" (Alan's word) to the great public. The cruel fact is, so far as I can see, that nobody likes bombers. Since '42, the strategy of hitting more and more civilian targets has, as well as provoking disagreement from some in the ministry, allowed the odd vicar to write to the *Evening Standard* protesting against the lowering of our moral tone. "Are we," one of them asked the other week, "who fight for the names of justice and decency, etc., descending to the level of the inhuman butchers of etc. etc. . . ?" It's a position with which I have some sympathy. And now I am being asked to. . . .

Anyway, I will try to tell this story in sequence, as it happened.

"Why", I said to Alan, "Dresden?"

"Because", said Tessa, "'Butcher' thinks it would be fun to hit

Dresden. Anyway it's full of refugees. Butcher hates refugees. Bloody South African monster."

Alan paid no attention to this remark. "As I keep telling you," he said, "the war isn't over yet. And from what we know the quickest way of demoralizing them is to hit them way behind the lines. And, as you may have noticed, the Russians are rather walking away with the idea that we're finished in that quarter. I think the old man wouldn't be averse to showing them what we can do. Portal has more or less given him full reign."

"So what – "

"We go in in two waves," said Alan. "First 244 motor bombers, all Lancasters. Three hours later, 529 four-motor bombers, again all Lancasters. Then in daylight, on two days running, the Yanks'll put in 527 B17s. All together 2,431 tons of HE bombs and 1,476 tons of incendiaries over three days."

There was an odd silence in the room.

"Alan," I said, "is there something I don't know about? I mean, have they got something top bloody secret out there or – "

Tessa yawned. "It's just a town, old thing," she said. "It's rather an old town. So it'll burn well. And there's absolutely bugger-all anti-aircraft stuff out there. It's undefended."

Alan was talking again in a low monotone. "Harris's mob have got the notion that there may be something of a stink about this. He knows all about the risks. And he knows quite well what Churchill will do if there is a row. He'll dump him. Churchill's just another politician, that's all. Which is where we come in."

Tessa gave another of those yawns. They were, I realized, an expression of nerves rather than tiredness. "Operation Beefeater. That's us."

"Are we – "

"The theory is that we get in first. Before anyone asks us to apologize. We hit them with everything *we*'ve got."

I gaped at him. "Hit who?"

"The Great British Public. As I am sure you are aware, the GBP will do almost anything if it's told to and what we intend to do is whip up enough support to cancel out any countermove from the Weeping Jesus mob. Along with the second wave of Lancasters will be a specially equipped plane containing twenty-four pressmen – "

"Dai Cellan Jones," said Tessa.

255

"A hand-picked team from the Crown Film Unit, a bloke called Sorrel from the BBC, the works. And – " He paused menacingly. "You."

I coughed.

I had never been in an aircraft before. I do not, as it happens, like the idea of flying. The idea of flying in aircraft at which people are liable to be shooting was not at all appealing. Suddenly the debate about the moral implications of area bombing acquired a new sharpness. From what Alan had said I knew at once that fire-raising, as at Hamburg, was the intention, a fire that sucks in oxygen and builds a greater and greater concentration of heat as the barrage continues. An image from that time came back to me – of someone coming to the door of a house and being pulled across the street, cindered by the force of the heat storm.

"And what do I do?" I said.

"You and I", said Alan, "co-ordinate the way we handle the press afterwards. Which won't be the hole-and-corner affair in which we usually indulge. At eight tomorrow we cook up something that matches what we give them tonight. We do *not*, as Bomber Command has done in the past, sound as if we are apologizing. Because, if I may make so bold, the whole bloody population of Dresden, in my opinion, is not worth the bones of one British Grenadier."

"I say," said Tessa, "put that in a memo to 'Butcher'. He'll probably use it in a speech."

Curiously enough, the terror I felt at the prospect of climbing into an aeroplane was nothing to the anger that had overcome me. What angered me was not simply the enormity of what was proposed, but the idea that they (whoever "they" were) thought that they would get away with it.

"Listen, Alan," I said, "you're always telling me this is a democracy and how great that is. Do you imagine for one moment that this sort of trick will stem the row over something like this? Because it won't. We'll be called to account. We'll be having to explain and justify. Everyone will be running for cover."

"Oh, no, we won't," said Alan. "We'll explain it to them. Very slowly and clearly. And they'll understand."

"Like Adolf," I said, "you reckon to keep it simple, do you?"

He lowered his face into mine. For a second I caught a whiff of hatred, something like the violence I had caught off Zak that night before the Olympia affair (I must write about that too, I must write it *all* down) as he said: "Listen. You're a nice little Anglo-Saxon, aren't you? You're as full of scruple as an egg is of meat. Let me remind you that out there in Europe millions are being killed. Millions. So awful, so unimaginable is what is happening that your nice little English soul can't comprehend it. The world is a darker, nastier, crazier place than you would imagine and you had better learn to face up to that, even if it is a little Jewboy who has to rub your nose in it."

Tessa voiced what I was thinking. "Don't you think", she said, "he sounds just like Zak?"

"But if you don't get away with it," I began slowly, "then you really will have – "

"I want to try," said Alan. "I want you to try. I want your nice little English conscience to grapple with this one, you see. I've sat next to it for three years and seen it sniff at my nasty Jewish directness and I'm sick to the stomach of it. It smells in my nostrils. It smells of the official hypocrisy that is real hypocrisy, that turned back ten or fifteen of my friends in 1940, all of whom are now, I am sure, in camps. The English 'let's keep it clean' approach. It isn't clean. The monstrous things you see aren't a dream, they are actually happening, and I want to see you see them. I want to see your face when stick after stick of bomb goes down into that town. Because then, maybe, you'll start to understand."

"He's fearfully intense, isn't he?" said Tessa.

I yawned. "What you're really on about", I said, "is my attitude. Like an English public schoolboy you want to see my attitude change. That's the most important thing to you, isn't it? I don't think how the raid goes down matters a damn."

The plan was very carefully arranged. The press and M.o.I–Crown contingent were to go with the second wave in three converted Lancasters. We were to be part of the second wave of the British attack, starting at about half-past one in the morning. Lancing-Green was to accompany us.

"Naturally," said Alan, "this is between us and Harris's mob at the Air Ministry, which is why Lancing-Green was so cagey with you. We don't want to get back tomorrow and find someone up there's got wind of it, because otherwise we'll all start boxing nicely and apologizing and before you know where you are we'll have an atrocity on our hands."

"Isn't that what it is?" I said. "Bombing an undefended town with no military importance. Isn't that an atrocity?"

"An atrocity", said Alan, pushing his face into mine, "in wartime is something you apologize for. The truth, as Metternich once remarked, is whatever is confidently asserted and plausibly maintained."

"History will – "

"History will what?"

I had meant to say that history would judge us but the remark stuck in my throat. I had no such confidence in history. History is nothing but a ghastly chapter of accidents. I know. I had a ringside seat for so bloody much of it.

There was, Alan said, a car calling for us in fifteen minutes. I asked if I could go home and was told I could not. I asked why the announcement had been made so late and Alan said: "I didn't tell you earlier because this is extremely secret."

"And you didn't trust me."

"Quite."

After he had finished describing our duties (which, in essence, seemed to be merely to act as witnesses) he went out once again, leaving Tessa and me alone.

"Why do you suppose they do want us there?" I said.

She shrugged. "Someone to blame, I expect," she said.

"And you're – "

"Oh, I'm coming," she said. "I know the poor bastard who's going to fly us."

I didn't ask her to amplify this.

"He's doing it as a favour", she said, "and he wouldn't go without me. He thinks I'm lucky."

"Oh," I said.

She yawned again. "Don't let's talk about this," she said. "Let's talk about the old days. When you and me and Isaac used to sort of do things and the world hadn't gone completely crazy."

"I think it had gone crazy then," I said, "except that we couldn't see it."

Tessa grinned. "Everything's crazy. Do you know 'Butcher' Harris wanted to bomb Cheltenham last year?"

"He what?"

"It was a sort of controlled experiment. That was the rumour. Just to see what would happen. Apparently it is laid out just like Darmstadt. He wanted to plan the raid to perfection, and asked to have a dry run on Cheltenham."

"You're joking."

"Maybe."

There was another awkward pause.

"Why don't you want to talk about him?" she said.

I knew who she meant. "Because. . . ."

We could hear Alan scrabbling around in the next office.

"Because I'd started to hate him," I said.

I think it started with the ease of his seduction of her. The way in which that squiring manner gave way to a protective embrace, the way I always seemed to be interrupting some private joke, the way, suddenly, I was eighteen or nineteen again, permanently shut out of female company, always the odd one, the peculiar one. And, too, is it not usual to dislike people to whom you have been too kind? I had spent months collecting for Zak to go to Vienna. When I returned my job on the paper had gone and I had had to scratch a living offering freelance articles to newspapers.

Zak would not, at first, go back to the bookshop, which was shuttered up, the curtains drawn across the windows and the bleak little alley silent once again. I went there one spring day, just after we got back, and saw the grass in the muddy area, heard a lone bird trilling at the back where old Mr Rabinowitz's garden had been in the old days. I tried to peer through a gap in the curtains, but it was no good. The sign was still there – RABINOWITZ AND TURNER. Maybe Turner would come and collect his inheritance, I thought, as I turned back up to the Whitechapel Road in the thin, spring sunlight.

At home Zak and Tessa were given the best bedroom by my mother. Every night I heard them making love. If what Tessa told me just now is correct, then Freud had certainly earned his money. For in those first months back in England they always seemed to be making love. And I always seemed to be listening. She'd give a startled little squawk at the appropriate moment, rather as if she had sat on a patch of wet in a new dress. In the morning we were all very polite with each other. If they had made love in the afternoon, which they did quite a lot, there was an awkward half an hour during which I contrived to go for a short walk.

Eventually Zak announced they would be moving back to the shop.

"Oh," I said, "you're going back to selling books?"

"I'm going to use it as a springboard," he said.

"To do what?" I said nastily. "Stand for Parliament?"

"You'll see," he said.

At this time, I remember, he looked vaguely Indian. Like one of those public-school Indians you see about the place. He had bought himself a black suit and he wore it with an open white shirt, accentuating his air of an off-duty clerk. He had, almost all the time, an abstracted manner, as if he was a scholar taking a break from a library. But his smile, which he had started to use professionally, was anything but academic. When he smiled those big brown eyes shone, as girlishly inviting as ever. He groped for his hair too, in the way he had when we were children, tugging at it as he spoke. But there was nothing awkward in the gesture – he had grown into all his gestures, the way I seemed to have outgrown mine without their ever fitting me.

Eventually, it doesn't matter how, except to say that it was even more ludicrous than the way in which I got a job at the M.o.I., I got a job on a national newspaper. Never mind which one. My mum, who had not altered her cuisine or her conversation in nearly forty years of my acquaintance, opined that I would be leaving soon "to get yerself a girl".

"No girl'll have me, Mum," I said.

Tessa bought a lot of the sort of clothes she thought a bookseller's wife ought to wear and helped him paint the shop. They had political meetings, or rather discussion groups, there, but I don't know what was said at them, for I never went. At the end of 1930 she became pregnant, but she lost the baby at four months. I don't think I ever spoke about it to her until last night, in Alan's office, when suddenly the grief she must have felt invaded me like an alien thing. It's curious. We never understand our friends or lovers until long after the event. I suppose that is a good reason for trying to hang on to them.

Then, one afternoon in 1931 approximately, Zak and Tessa called round to the flat. They both looked dressed for an outing.

If it was always raining in the twenties, in the thirties it was that everyone always seemed to be talking. Everyone, as far as I could see – with the possible exception of myself – had Views. I could hear Tessa and Zak as they came up the stairs that Saturday: "But if we hadn't gone off the gold standard....", "Unemployment is...." Unemployment was the thing about which most people had Views. People like us who had jobs used it as a kind of litmus test of others' sincerity when arguing about politics. To say, as I sometimes felt like doing, that I could not give a stuff about unemployment as long as I personally had a job, since although I felt sorry for the poor devils who had no jobs I could not for the life of me see how to set about getting them work, would have been close to blasphemy. Where once Concern had been crankish, peculiar, now everyone showed Concern, the way they wore a new hat or wide lapels to their jackets. But for most people, I felt, Concern was no more real than cloche hats or long strings of pearls. It was another way of passing the time.

When they came in the door I saw that Isaac was wearing a trilby hat, its brim well down over his forehead, and Tessa was wearing a black dress I had last seen in a very early talkie called *Hang Me High*. They looked a little like gangsters, I thought. I was eating a large piece of toast. Although it was three in the afternoon, I had only just got out of bed.

"We're going to a new meeting," said Isaac.

"What meeting?" I said.

"It's the New Party," said Tessa. "It's a sort of wonderful new . . . well . . . party, really."

She was recovering some of her old verve.

"Not like any of the silly old parties," I said, allowing butter to trickle down my chin.

"Oh, absolutely not," said Tessa. "Daddy's joined it. He says it's doing an awful lot for dentists."

"The small man," said Zak, with heavy irony.

Tessa and her father (who had retired after drilling his way through an elderly lady's jawbone) were now on the best of terms. He spent his time – she told me – doing something called Animal Dentistry. I was constantly on the look-out for budgies hopping along the Whitechapel Road clutching their beaks, or dogs, their paws over their eyes, being dragged backwards into that room in Wapping.

"Oswald Mosley", said Tessa, "is sort of in it. And he does wonderful radiant things in speeches and looks fearfully handsome and brave and has a profile and is frightfully bright and has left the Labour Party because it isn't New."

Isaac sat on the sofa and cradled his hat in his hands, transforming the front parlour into a villain's state room by his presence. I started to butter myself another piece of toast.

"The Labour Party", he said, "is finished. It has been consigned to the dustbin of history."

I've always disliked people who use that phrase. You may have noticed that when they use it, it is always someone else or something else that is in the said dustbin. They are always putting down the lid or calling Fortnum's to have it taken away. Isaac used the phrase now with a knowing little sneer at me as if to say, "And that is where you are too, old chum." I continued to butter my toast with more than usual concentration. Tessa started to pace about the room. I noticed she was wearing a scarf, which she fingered as she walked in a somewhat extravagant fashion. Only her clothes still suggested the lost girl we had met in Vienna. Unable to find her way back to the milkmaid persona of the early twenties and having discarded her attempt at hardline fashion, she had ended up looking like a glamorous jumble sale; she had, too, a quality of grating helplessness, an ability alternately to move and irritate, that stirred my feelings for her in a new and not totally pleasant way.

"Oswald M.", she said, "was fearfully brave up at Ashton and all sorts of thugs are after him but he is going to sort of break the mould and create a whole new thing and it's all going to be brand new, Amos, you must come, you funny old thing, because it is New, really."

I rose wearily. "There's no such thing", I said, "as a New Party."

"There are old ways of thinking," said Isaac.

"Please don't argue," said Tessa. "Please don't argue, you two. I love you both so fearfully much I can't bear for you to argue, so just come, Amos, please, won't you? I promise you. It is completely *New*."

The meeting was at Battersea, in a shabby church hall. We went over in a cab for which I paid. I sat for most of the time looking out at the warehouses and the river and the barges moored together at the edge of the current and thought about the past. It was November, I think, or February maybe. A dead season anyway. And I remember that ride as dead. The three of us hardly talked as Zak sat forward in his seat turning his hat backwards and forwards in his hands. As we pulled away from the river and went south, I said: "Are you actually a member of the New Party, Zakky?"

He didn't answer.

"Or is it so new it doesn't have members?"

He yawned.

"I mean, just so as I know, old friend. Just so as I know what I have to do. Are we hecklers? Are we for it? Are we socialists these days? Or are we tories? Or are we just after climbing on any wagon that looks good?"

Still no answer.

"Your Dad – "

"Shut up about my Dad, Amos," he said. "My Dad was mine. Not yours, OK?"

It had been dusk when we started out from Whitechapel. Now it was fully dark, with a thin rain beginning. I paid off the cab at the top of the street and the three of us walked down, past a line of terraced houses, to a yellow brick building, put some way back from the road. Outside it said, ST SAVIOUR'S CHURCH HALL.

"Remember?" I said to Zak.

But he didn't appear to. As we went in I reflected that when a relationship is in decline, one or other party always tried to capitalize on the past. I might have guessed it would have been me.

There were about two or three hundred people in the hall and, instead of Mosley, we got his wife. Which I thought was a fair bargain. She didn't seem to have an idea in her head, but her hat was the most effective I have ever seen on a public speaker. Most of the audience were the same fifty or sixty grey-faced people who seem to spend their lives going to such meetings, but as we struggled along the row at the back, I caught sight of a face that promised there might be more interest than I had expected in the evening.

"Look, Tess," I said, "it's Pamela...."

Pamela, who must by now be at least a hundred, was wearing a huge black overcoat and a giant black hat with flowers and fruit on it. On her knee was a large carrier bag and as we approached her she produced a pair of false teeth from her coat pocket and started to try to jam them into her mouth. The woman next to her prodded her. "F— off, you stupid 'aporth," I heard her say, "you've already got your teeth in."

Which indeed she had. A brand new pair of gnashers, which gave her open mouth a terrifying, military appearance. They were stained with lipstick. As we sat down in the seats next to her and her companion, she said: "In Roosha the likes of Mosley would be sent for corrective therapy at a camp in the far north where, although conditions would be far above what you would find in the average British penal institution, they would soon learn the error of their ways."

"They would, Pamela," said the little woman next to her.

"F— off, Nettleton," said Pamela.

Lady Mosley had begun her speech – which was a sort of "Come on, team" appeal to all of us to pull together and get Britain out of the mess she was in. There was a great deal made of the plight of the unemployed which rang curiously true (enforced idleness being something of which she obviously had a deep understanding). Pamela paid no attention to it whatsoever, but rummaged in her bag muttering to herself.

"Pamela," I said, "remember me?"

She turned red-rimmed eyes upon me. "In Roosha", she said, "the likes of Lady Mosley would be made to dig communal 'oles with communal agricultural implements very mooch in the way my own father was forced down the pit to implement the capitalist mode of production. The likes of Lady Mosley would be taken to communal centres in places sooch as Novosibirsk, a spa in the north of Siberia, and given large 'ats with flaps to go over 'er ear' oles."

It was clear that Pamela had lost whatever marbles she once may have possessed. Her little red eyes gave no sign of recognition, even when I babbled something about Isaac and Palme Dutt and the party meetings we had attended together in the early twenties. About the only faculty she had not lost was the power of speech. Everything else seemed to have gone, but the ability to talk in long, monotonous sentences about the class struggle seemed unimpaired. Her friend, who had introduced herself as Myra Nettleton, beamed up at her as she spoke. "The problems that confroont

Britain now are exactly the same as the problems that confroonted Britain in the 1920s and, for that matter, in the nineteenth and eighteenth centuries and for that matter the Stone Age if you ask me, young man. If Stone Age man had bin able to eat in communal canteens and attack dinosaurs with communally made implements and share the prodoocts of 'is labour on an equal basis with oother Stone Age men – "

"And women, Pamela – "

"F— off, Nettleton. If this 'ad bin possible it would not now be possible for Lady Mosley to come down 'ere from the Ritz Carlton and lecture workin' people sooch as myself on the future of this country when if we lived in Roosha there would probably not 'ave bin a Stone Age as far as I can see, oh good there they are – "

She broke off her ramblings to produce, from the depth of her bag, a group of soggy-looking rock cakes which she weighed experimentally in each hand. At first I thought this must be her dinner and was unable to suppress a feeling of pity for the poor deluded old woman, and then I noticed that she was measuring with a somewhat expert eye the distance between her and the speaker on the platform. Lady Mosley was explaining that in the country she always took a personal interest in all of her workers. An old man called Gaffer Gargery, for instance, who was a champion rickmaker, had once told her that she –

Pamela lobbed the first of the rock cakes up at the platform. It landed just short of Lady Mosley, who shied like a horse that has seen some obstacle in the road ahead. A second followed. All around us, I noticed, people were getting to their feet and other missiles were joining Pamela's contributions, one of which had hit a fat man on the nose. "IN ROOSHA," Pamela was screaming, "IN ROOSHA YOU WOULD BE FORCED TO ATTEND COMMUNAL – "

Meanwhile, a fat man on the other side of Pamela was introducing Lady Mosley to the cut and thrust of proletarian polemic by shouting, "Bollocks, you old c—!" in a pause between sentences. Other geezers on the platform started to mutter and look mean but the fat bloke just kept on shouting, "Bollocks. Bollocks. Bollocks, you old c—!" When she got on to the future of Britain half our row rose as a man and began to shout and slow handclap. I noticed that Lady Mosley and the other future protectors and guardians of the working class were looking a little nervous and, when half the hall were on their feet and shouting, one of them started to slide towards the edge of the platform.

It was then that I saw him.

He was still wearing those drab, clerical clothes and his eyes still had that phoney orator's look about them. He looked as if he hadn't changed since Vienna. I looked down for signs of the fishing-rod case but saw nothing. As the body of platform speakers and hangers-on abandoned their positions, he strutted to the front of the stage and shouted something at the audience. I couldn't hear it for the racket in the hall but I nudged Zak.

"He was in Vienna," I said. "Let's take a look."

Zak didn't stop for me to explain this remark but followed me as I dodged out along the line. They were clapping in rhythm now and singing, "Bollocks, you old c—" to the tune of "John Brown's Body" – quite a difficult thing to do.

In the street outside it was raining. The New Party mob were scurrying towards two large, black cars, shielded by a phalanx of umbrellas. I saw the stranger from Vienna make for the second of the vehicles and, followed by Zak and Tessa, ran for him. I grabbed his coat just as he was climbing in and was dragged in after him. Behind us I could see the crowd from the hall had spilled out on to the pavement. The car started. Zak and Tessa fell in beside me and someone slammed the door. The crowd from the hall were halfway to the back bumper when the chauffeur, without asking too many questions about his passengers, drove off at speed. As the car roared to the end of the street, a woman in the far corner of the car looked down at us through invisible lorgnettes and said: "William – who are these?"

The stranger shook himself free of my arm. "Hecklers," he said. "They're hecklers."

The woman crossed her arms and looked out at Battersea sliding by. "How amusing," she said.

"We're hysterical," said Zak, "laugh a line."

The woman looked at the stranger called William who was about to say something else about us but stopped himself in time. I got the impression he was scared of this woman. I was scared of her. We crossed the river and she looked down at it sternly. Then she patted the seat next to her and beckoned Zak to join her. There was quite a way to walk from the floor to the seat – it was that kind of car – and

266

Zak approached her without much of his usual style. Come to think of it – that characterized all of his relationship with the Honourable Lady "Margot" Perrindale, daughter of the Third Earl of Debenham, heiress to the Glintochet Estate in Argyll, socialite, wit, memoir writer and complete and utter pain in the arsehole.

"Margot" Perrindale was called "Margot" to distinguish herself from her cousin Margot. At one time Margot had decided to become "Margot", but for some reason had ended up calling herself Norma instead.

"Margot" told us as we stopped at a stall for some frightfully amusing sandwiches that she had given an enormous amount of money to the New Party under the impression that it was actually a party, and had been going to leave the meeting in some bad humour anyway on account of the lack of champagne, Evelyn Waugh, et cetera. The events of the evening had, however, appeared to politicize her to some degree. She had not, she told the stranger called William, who spent most of the time sulking in the corner of the car, come "ite" to be "tiled" she was an "iled" cunt by a load of "illitrite lites". "Cimmie", she said to Tessa, whom she addressed as Viscountess Marchbanks, "is ite of her tiny mind!"

The man from Vienna abandoned his earlier hostility and adopted a tone of helpful solicitude to us that was even more sinister than his moody glances of a moment ago. "Margot" treated him as I imagine she would a servant, ignoring him as she grew more confidential to us. I noted she was patting Zak's hand a lot when we were back in the car. "Tom", she said, "is very bad." I wondered who "Tom" was. It turned out they called Mosley "Tom", although his name was Oswald.

"What's the matter with him?" said Tessa in a scared little voice.

"Tom", said "Margot", "wants to give it all up and become a swimming-pool attendant."

"It's all been too much for him," said the stranger from Vienna.

There was then a lot of stuff about overwork and how he never let up on himself, during which another young woman whose name I did not catch emerged from somewhere further up the seat and said, nodding at Zak: "Don't you think he looks like Tom, 'Margot'?"

"Margot" looked at Zak. Her very glance, slow, confident, from head to toe in her own time, seemed to turn Zak into something that existed only to be looked at. Her family had been looking people up and down like that for some seven hundred years. The aggressive, sexual nature of the stare brought something out in Zak too. He sat there like a bull brought out for exhibition, his forehead flushed and puzzled.

"Yah," said "Margot", "he does."

"Yah," said the stranger called William in an unsuccessful parody of her manner, "yah he does."

The rest of the journey was mainly taken up with being introduced to the other occupants of the car. There seemed to be about twenty of them, tucked away in the suede recesses of the interior, and most if not all of the male ones were called Roderick.

But there were problems more serious than a superfluity of Rodericks facing the New Party. As we pulled up in front of a Georgian terraced house in Chelsea, I saw on the pavement outside a tall man with a drab hank of dark hair, a nose like a fashionable anteater and underneath it a thin strip of a moustache. He did – I had to admit – look incredibly like Zak, but that was not the most striking thing about him. The most striking thing about him was that he was wearing a one-piece bathing costume and doing the knees-bend in the road at nine thirty at night in the pouring rain in the middle of Bryanston Square.

"Evenin', Torm!" said "Margot".

"Evenin'!" said Mosley affably.

From out of all three cars a whole host of people with names like Porker and Scratcher and Jojums and Slinker disembarked and flowed on into the lighted house. They greeted Mosley warmly and gave no indication that it was unusual to find him in a bathing costume at this hour of the night. He, too, nodded at us, his wife and friends with cool charm, then flexed his legs and sprang to an "on guard" fencing position.

"Is he OK?" I heard Zak whisker to "Margot".

"Oh, sound as a bell mentally", she said, "but he spends far more time doing press-ups and so on than looking after political things. He's in training, you see. For the great moment of destiny."

"He'll be finished by the time it comes," I muttered, as Mosley began to wave an imaginary sword in front of him and thrust his right leg out in a fencing lunge.

Zak, Tessa and I followed the crowd into the house, through a hall and into the tall, elegant front room. Then from outside we heard a "Ha!" followed by a kind of slashing run outside in the corridor. "Ha!" came that voice again. The room fell silent. After all, it was his house.

* * *

First of all Mosley wanted us all to do press-ups. There was considerable disagreement about this. One of the Rodericks, who was smoking a cigar, maintained that one press-up would be enough to kill him. A bloke who looked rather like a wallaby, who was addressed by the others as Joad (I couldn't work out whether this was his name or some vogue, upper-class insult) diverted the conversation into an amazingly low-level philosophical analysis of what we *meant* by the word *press-up*. What were "press-ups"? Should we not rather say "press-down"? Et cetera, et cetera.

In short, the New Party was a fairly typical example of any political party designed around the proposition that government is an art or a science rather than a criminal conspiracy. Everything about the discussion reeked of that fateful word "blueprint". The word itself was used several times by Mosley while several of the Rodericks chucked around phrases such as "the people" and "the good of the nation" as if we all understood, or agreed, what was meant by them. After about half an hour Mosley went out into the hall, from where we heard a series of short runs followed by a brief, banshee-like wail.

"He's doing the 'attaque cours de saltimbaque'," drawled "Margot".

"Tray diffiseel!" said one of the Rodericks.

All this time Zak had sat immobile on the arm of one of the chairs, Tessa next to him. She hung on to his arm in those days and looked at him looking at things. He, in his turn, looked at things more intently than he had been used to, as if she was supplying him with extra voltage of some sort. I tried looking at the chandeliers, the trolley laden with drinks in the far corner of the huge, circular, walnut table by the window, but I ended up looking at them. They made a nice couple.

To take my mind off the way Tessa's nails were making tiny

circles on Zak's wrist, I concentrated on his resemblance to the fascist leader.

It was, the more you looked at it, a remarkable one.

It was as if Zak actually had the same face transplanted on to his shoulders. He had no moustache of course and his skin was darker than Mosley's, but apart from that you could have been forgiven for thinking they were the same person. The only real point of difference was the extraordinary lack of repose in Mosley's face and the wealth of it around my friend's eyes and the sudden half smiles at the edge of his lips. Tessa flattened her right palm and began to try and push it through his spine. Zak breathed out slowly and looked at the carpet. "Margot" fished for his gaze. "What does our heckler think?" she said. All eyes joined mine in looking at Zak.

"Is this a heckler?" said a tall bloke over by the window.

"Yah," said "Margot". She seemed, suddenly, quite ferocious. I noticed how blunt her nails were, how, under the pearls, the set of her neck and shoulders had the squat power of a working woman. She looked, quite suddenly, violently horsey.

"But", she went on, "he's an *attractive* heckler...."

There was general laughter. In this well-lit, beautifully proportioned drawing room, the notion of heckling seemed vaguely amusing. I looked away from all the faces creased with food and good humour and looked out at the square, black with rain.

For a long time Zak did not make the answer expected of him. He stayed looking at the carpet. Then Tessa's arm slowed to a stop and he looked up. His eyes travelled over the pyramid of faces in the room and came to rest on a vacant space, uninhabited by any of his audience.

"Listen," said Zak eventually, "you talk about 'breaking' with the past. All of you want above all else to make history. I can see it in your faces. Everyone wants to step on to the stage of history. Of course. Oh, I tried. For years I tried."

They were all listening to him from the moment he started to speak. Tessa moved one manicured hand to the back of his neck and started to squeeze it as he spoke. He showed no sign of being aware of her.

"But John Bull doesn't want to make history, does he? John Bull doesn't want big ideas. John Bull wants to grumble on his way and

270

be left alone. John Bull wants the past you're so anxious to break with. I found that out myself years ago."

One of the Rodericks uncoiled himself from the mantelpiece and peered down at Zak.

"And what", he said, "does John Bull want?"

Zak put his hand up to Tessa's and drew it down into his lap. "Well," he said, "John Bull doesn't want to *think*, that's for sure. He wants to think he thinks but he doesn't want to grapple with anything funny and foreign like – an idea. John Bull wants – "

He paused. The noise from the corridor outside had ceased and through the open door came Mosley. He was sweating freely and as he stood just inside the room he pushed that long shank of hair back across his forehead. He put his hands on his hips and splayed up his elbows as if about to perform some rustic version of a Cossack dance. As if prompted by his entry, Zak rose to his feet and flung both arms wide in an orator's gesture. As he did so I caught a glimpse of the public speaker he might have become. Other shadows, possible Isaacs, flitted across the dark, handsome screen of his face – Isaac the lawyer, Isaac the artist, Isaac the showman . . . but they were all vanquished by a sudden violent smile that seemed to exult in nothing but the transparent stupidity of smiling.

What's the word to describe my friend? Self-destructive – that's it.

"John Bull wants a *show*, that's all," said Zak. "He just wants something to look at. Doesn't matter what it is. Unimportant. In politics all that is required is a large and colourful lie. That's all you need to get your party going."

So turned in on itself was the conscious irony of this remark that it was difficult to tell how serious he was. He was like a man parading a private joke in order to discomfort strangers, but as I watched him his mocking glare seemed almost one of command. Tessa was sitting back against her chair. Her face was white.

There was a long pause. "Margot" straightened her dress. "And what do you suggest by way of a show, *heckler*?" she said.

Zak's arms dropped to his side. He shrugged. In the end it was I who spoke.

"Why not pick on the Jews," I said. "It seems to be the fashionable thing at the moment."

Then I headed for the door in long strides, threatening the coffee tables.

271

Tessa followed me and, eventually, he followed her.

When he got to the door Mosley put a hand on his shoulder. "My word," he said to Zak, "we need people like you."

"Like a hole in the head," I said.

Mosley slapped him on the back. "That's what I mean," he said. "Guts. Drive. Ambition."

"Jewish," I said.

Mosley shrugged. "So?" he said. "I should worry?"

Maybe my grandfather was Jewish. Maybe that's where the name "Amos" comes from. Of course, as Zak said, only a lousy Jew would have accused Sir Oswald Mosley of being anti-Semitic at this point in his career. He hadn't made any public statement of hostility to the Jews (but they can *sense* it, right?). Only a lousy, too clever for his own good Jew would dream up the idea that patriotism and love of empire lead logically to anti-Semitism. Race is just another stupid badge like communism or patriotism. Another pair of distorting glasses fogging one's view of the world. As we walked back down the square, Zak's angry, flushed face and new impeccable manners really did make me feel as if I had behaved like the outsider, the immigrant. He walked several paces ahead of me, while Tessa fluttered anxiously between the two of us. "Oh, don't be silly, Amos darling, it was all sort of rather splendid and I wasn't sure quite what. . . ."

I wanted to go to a club but Zak and Tessa wanted to go back to the shop. Typically, Zak chose this as the original ground of the argument he wished to have with me.

"You don't belong in your old home any more," he said. "You've lost contact with real people, with our kind of people. You go up to that newspaper and make smart remarks and pretend to be something you're not. You're trying to escape from our background. I tell you this. You can't."

"And what are you trying to do, Isaac? Sucking up to that appalling woman? Christ, what were those people? You don't imagine they speak for people like us, do you?"

"You're beginning to sound like Pamela," he said. "You're beginning to sound like a phoney."

"Please don't, boys," said Tessa. "Please don't make it all awful and everything, I don't think I can bear it if you do that, I really can't, I – "

We walked on down through deserted Chelsea. I ran to catch up with him.

"Well," I said, "just explain to me what the idea is."

"Of what?" said Isaac.

"I mean this tonight. We weren't going for the good of our health, were we? What was the purpose of it all?"

A crowd of elegant young women teetered across the darkened square in front of us. Further up the street I heard a car door slam. The rain had stopped. Somebody wanted to know if Peter was coming too. Somebody else laughed. Zak was holding out one hand, crooked at the wrist, the fingers trailing down. He gave the arm belonging to the hand a convulsive twist.

"What's that, then?"

"The combined totalitarian salute," he said. "Gets you in with Social Credit, YCLILP Communist Party, New Party – "

"Zak," I said, shaking him urgently, "can you tell me what we were doing there? Can you tell me what you believe in now? Please. For as long as I've known you you've always – "

"I've always what?" he said harshly.

We were somewhere at the back of Sloane Square now. Tessa had fallen silent. She stood back and watched our argument with big, scared eyes. Zak turned to me and I saw, for the first time in his eyes, a look of pure dislike. So it is that time and ridiculous creeds separate us from our friends.

"That", he said, "coming from you, is rich. Is *rich*."

And grabbing Tessa by the hand, he turned and walked off down the road. I let them go. But I wailed after them before they turned the corner: "BUT YOU'RE SUPPOSED TO KNOW, ZAK! SOMEONE'S SUPPOSED TO KNOW!"

I went into a bar behind Victoria Station and got drunk. When I was good and drunk I tried to start a conversation with the other people in the bar, but no one seemed very interested.

"My principles", I kept saying, "aren't allowed to be real."

"You've had enough," said the barman. "Out."

"When I kick Goebbels," I said, "I really kick Goebbels. I don't mess about. I let him have it."

"Of course you do," said the barman.

"But not in his book," I said.

"Which book is this?" said the barman.

"The Book of Isaac," I said.

"Oh," said the barman, "is that in the Bible then?"

I got up and swayed. Swaying felt quite good so I swayed a little more, for display purposes. Then I said: "It might as well be in the f—ing Bible. Because although it looked good at first, although it started off nicely, although it was once one of the most important things in my life, it is now quite simply a load of old f—ing rubbish."

After that they threw me out.

Towards the end, you see, I didn't spend enough time with Zak to know what he was thinking or what game he was playing. He had become as foreign to me as those figures one reads about in the newspapers, who plan invasions and treaties, parades and days of mourning, none of which make any kind of sense. I used to see Tessa sometimes, in the neighbourhood. She had become a slightly over-dressy housewife. Every time I saw her she couldn't stop. She was buying something "for the house". There was no hint of another baby.

It was pure accident that I learned that not only had Zak kept up his interest in Mosley's activities, he was actually a member of the party. And by this time it was no longer the New Party but the British Union of Fascists, with a uniform, a salute and, according to one of the papers, a Fascist Air Corps somewhere out in Beaconsfield, consisting of three or four blokes and a glider. At the time this did not seem as surprising as it does now. Mosley had a Jewish bodyguard (Ted "Kid" Lewis) and he himself at that stage was always careful to keep anti-Semitic propaganda out of his own speeches.

In the absence of more stimulating company, I had taken to drink. My mother and I hardly spoke now. Our relationship was rather that of an elderly lord of the manor and his butler. In the evenings I would start with a beer in one of the pubs near where I worked, then, when the first editions came out, graduate to Scotch. First of all I drank with a man called Forrester who was, like me, a subeditor. Then with a girl called Parker, who affected a beret and said things like "It's all going to go bang anyway", and in the end I drank by myself.

That particular evening I wanted to get drunk where there was no chance of being recognized. Which was why I took a cab across to Chelsea. I was sitting in a pub off the King's Road, in the farthest and deepest corner of the place, watching the faces at the bar, when at a table over to the left just inside the door of the saloon I saw Isaac and "Margot". They hadn't seen me. Indeed it was surprising they were managing to get their glasses up to their lips without spilling the contents. They were indulging in the kind of hand and eye contact that, when observed in a public place, always makes me think one or other party is married to someone else. I pushed myself back into my chair. Now that I could see them, I could hear every word they were saying and yet I dared not rise or make a sound in case they should see me.

"Torm", "Margot" was saying, "is exhausted."

"Yah," said Zak flatly.

"Worn ite," said "Margot"

"Yah," said Zak.

Had he been taking elocution lessons? His manner was that of a playful public schoolboy. I noticed that he had acquired a new suit.

"We all went dine", continued "Margot", "to the Black Hice. And saw a frightfully funny man called Jenkins who wants to find the Fascist Catering Corps, which we all thought a frightful laugh. And then we had a sort of bugle call which was wonderful and then I decided that Torm was looking frightfully peaky. So we packed him orff to Deauville for a rest."

"Yah," said Zak.

Then he put his hand up to her cheek and stroked it. He let his hand stay there for some time and then, like a musician leaning on a chord, allowed the fingers to fall slowly around her face. He looked as if he had been doing this sort of thing all his life.

"Mussolini", said "Margot", "is most frightful fun. He's simply marvellous with young children which I think Italians are in the main, don't you? We had him down to Sunningdean and he did this most marvellous impression of a frog which had us in stitches. Apparently he's going to invade Abyssinia which I think is a frightfully good idea. For him."

"Yah," said Zak.

When I think, as I sometimes do now, that Zak was playing some complex double game (what I saw last night has convinced me more than ever that nothing in politics is quite what it appears to be) I seem to think he had a satiric snarl to his voice as he broached the next remark. But I couldn't be sure. My wish, for him as for myself, is that his life wasn't altogether without point, but perhaps it is that wish that is corrupting my oh so corruptible memory on this question.

"What Torm needs", said Zak, after a bit more of the "I could eat you" stuff from her rather protuberant blue eyes, "is a double."

"You what?"

"Like in the films, darling," he said, "you know. A double. Someone to be him."

"Darling – "

"So he can be in two places at once."

"Margot" giggled. A long drawn-out sound that had all the charm of a piece of chalk being dragged backwards across a blackboard. "Are you poking fun?" she said.

"No," said Zak, "not at all."

"You're not a spy in our camp, darling?"

"Not at all," said Zak.

He leaned towards her and grinned. Once again I was struck by his extraordinary resemblance to the fascist leader. "Margot" grinned, wolfishly amused. "Torm might think it amusing," she said.

"I think", said Isaac, moving his right hand to her plump white knee exposed through the gap in her fur coat, "that politics should be amusing. Don't you?"

Was it when Hitler moved into the Rhineland that I bought myself the flat in Charlotte Street? I know something important was happening. Maybe it was the night of the Reichstag fire. Or the night they shot Schleicher. Or the day after Kristallnacht. Whatever it was, I didn't think much about it. I was mainly worried about the way my mother had cried when I told her I wouldn't be living with her any more. I couldn't explain to her why I had done it. There was no girl involved. I didn't want a girl. I just wanted to be alone and to get drunk. I wanted a table of my own to fall under, that was all.

Let's say it was 1934.

I was thinking too about Isaac and that woman. And about Tessa. I thought about Tessa a lot. One evening I got a cab and drove down to the bookshop. The front window was crowded with books, but not of the sort of which the old man would have approved. They were cheap thrillers, mainly in paperback, piled in no sort of order, on the top of each pile a sheet of paper stating the price. To my surprise the door was open.

I pushed it open and went in. I walked slowly, fearfully, back through the place into the back kitchen where once Zak and his mother had sat in the evenings, sorrowful in the lamplight. To my horror it was filthy. There were cups and plates on the floor, coated with grease. A cold pot of tea stood at a crazy angle by the sink and on the sideboard (new since Mrs Rabinowitz's day) was a pile of yellow newspapers.

Then, from the front door, I heard a sound. Immediately, instinctively, I ducked down below the level of the sideboard and waited for the sound of voices. There were none.

After what seemed like ten minutes but was more probably two or three, I peered round the side of the door. There in front of me, his back facing the shabby shopfront and the darkened alley, was Isaac. At first I didn't realize it was him. He was wearing a pair of jodhpurs, a black silk shirt and high leather boots. He looked, in fact, right down to the moustache that now adorned his upper lip, the exact image of Sir Oswald Mosley. As I watched I saw his hand go up to the moustache and tug at it. It came off like the skin of a rotten orange. He replaced it at a slightly saucier angle and grinned fiercely to himself. Then he crossed over to his right, up to what I saw was a full-length mirror that had not been there in the days when I knew the place.

As I watched he began to pace in front of the mirror. First he paced three paces to the right and then he paced three paces to the left. He suddenly rounded on the mirror as if it was lying in wait for him and waggled his finger at it. "Moreover," he said, "moreover – " He stopped. The face in the mirror grinned back at him, obviously pleased with what it saw. Then suddenly his arm shot out to full length and his voice rose a full octave, a terrifying scream in the deserted place. "THE SPIRIT OF THIS GREAT NATION", he yelled, "IS ONCE AGAIN ON THE MOVE!" His voice dropped to nothing again, like a storm suddenly abandoning its attack. I saw him look down at his feet and mutter, in an irritable voice, "*Four* paces to the left and then *five* to the right, and then – " He went back to it like a ballet dancer doing exercises up at the bar, pacing to the left, flinging his arms up in the air wildly, running back, shouting with frustration if he made a mistake. Then he began to slap himself about the face. "ONLY ONE PART OF THE BODY MUST MOVE AT ANY ONE TIME!" I heard him shout. Then he turned and bowed to an imaginary guest. After he had bowed, he fixed his eyes on some distant, quite arbitrarily chosen spot on the floor and gazed at it in a Rasputin-like manner. His gaze now was almost tangible. Breaking off concentration suddenly, he wiped his brow, as if the effort of will had exhausted him. Back to the mirror for more of the pacing. Then from the street outside I heard a car horn and Zak turned to the door. "Coming darling!" he shouted.

This was, somehow, even more frightening than the Mosley impression. It was a sort of half-and-half Isaac – someone who had actually been taken over by another world, aping its upwards inflexions, its careful casualness. . . . I very nearly got up then to call to him. But before I had the chance to do anything as foolish as that, he was gone.

I went across to the window and looked out at the street. There, bright and incongruous in the alley, was the huge black car I remembered from the Battersea meeting. Next to it I saw the stubby figure of "Margot" and the man from Vienna. As I watched Zak dashed out and vaulted into the back of the car, as if about to dodge an invisible reporter's questions.

I lay on the settee. Later on Tessa came in, loaded with shopping. She had given up looking like a smart housewife and now she just looked like a housewife. As soon as she saw me, however, she recovered some of her usual manner and began to flutter her eyes a little. But it was a tired affair, like watching a horse out to grass try a gallop. Almost immediately she was a housewife again, a woman in her thirties with tired eyes.

"What are you doing here?" she said.

"I came to see you," I said.

She put down the shopping.

"Where have you been?"

"I went to see Daddy," she said. "He's moved to Woodford you see which is super for him. And so I went to see him."

"How was he?"

"He was out," she said. And burst into tears.

"What goes on these days?" I said.

"I don't know," she said. "I just don't know any more. I never see him. He's never with me. He's always somewhere else, I don't know where. I don't know what he's doing or who he's with."

"You never do know other people," I said. "You think you do but you don't. They are an unknown quantity. When they leave you they disappear."

She raised a tear-stained face to me. "You're so good and kind and sensible," she said, "funny old sensible, kind Amos."

I didn't much like any of these adjectives. If they were accurate I was even more sure I didn't like them. She started to cry again. "I just don't understand what goes on out there," she said. "I just can't understand any of it."

"Why should you?" I said. "It's all completely, utterly cruel and stupid."

"When he comes in at night," she said, "it's always at night, he won't let me see him. He runs through to an empty room and then. . . . It's as if he's turning into a vampire or something."

"Maybe," I said.

"Will you have some supper, dear old funny old Amos? And we can have a glass of wine and sort of talk about all the things you're doing because you're doing marvellous things aren't you I bet you are really come on."

"OK," I said.

We had supper together in the small room they used for eating, beyond the kitchen. We didn't talk about Isaac. We talked about the old days and about people we had known then who had got married or moved away. I wanted to talk about Isaac, but I couldn't think of a way of starting the conversation that would not finish it in three sentences. "Isaac is Oswald Mosley's double." Or: "Zak thinks he's Oswald Mosley." Or what about: "I think Isaac may be turning into Oswald Mosley."

She was never much of a cook, but I found a bottle of wine in one of the cupboards and, deciding to abandon all discussion of Isaac, I found I was enjoying myself. I didn't notice the noise of the car in the alley, I didn't hear the slam of the door or the rapid steps through the shop, and it wasn't until I heard his tread on the first stair and Tessa laid a hand on my arm, that I realized Isaac had returned.

"That's how he comes back," she said, "always like that. Like a thief in his own house."

I let him get halfway up the stairs and then I went out after him. He ran as soon as he heard me and, by the time he had got to the bedroom, he had the door half closed, but I jammed my foot into it.

"No," he said thickly. "No."

"Yes," I said, and started to push.

Behind me on the stairs Tessa was shouting something, but I couldn't hear what it was. I pushed harder and harder. Eventually there was a low moan from inside the room. I pushed back the door to see Isaac staggering back into the bedroom. Tessa was behind me on the landing now.

The overcoat was sprawled on the shabby brass bed they shared. Zak was halfway out of the breeches, doubled up like a man surprised halfway through some dubious sexual encounter. He shuffled back to the bed and sat on it heavily. "Get out," he said.

"No," I said.

Tessa was now trying to push past me. I wouldn't let her. She wasn't trying very hard. She uttered little animal cries of distress as she struggled against me.

"Look," I said, "what is it you're doing? Is this some kind of joke? A charade? Are you – "

"Oh, it's all a big joke," he said. "Wasn't that always your line? None of it means anything. We don't take anything seriously, do we? Nothing is real for you, you – " He stopped and followed the direction of my gaze. I was staring at a deep cut just above his left eye. He put his hand up to it and looked at the blood on his hand with the curious, distant expression our own wounds so often inspire in us.

"Who was it?" I said. "Communists, was it?"

"Hecklers," said Zak. He lay back on the bed. "They disrupt our meetings, they break up our rallies and marches. I tell you they are looking for trouble. And we will give it to them if necessary."

Something in my expression – pity, horror, disbelief – irritated him and awkwardly he started to pull up the breeches. I noticed that the moustache was slightly lopsided, although the coiffure now matched Mosley's perfectly.

"What do they shout?" I said. "'Hail, Rabinowitz'?"

"Such a wise little boy you were", he said, "and so nice to a poor Jew like me."

He began to beat his breast in a comic expression of the old men I remembered from his father's funeral, battered lumpy faces, all wearing the history of Europe, all telling of cruelties as yet unpractised here.

"Really appreciated it, Amos. A good little Anglo-Saxon kid. My God, my father loved every minute of it. What a favour you were doing him. Christ, he couldn't believe it. Get out of your own class, my son, get on with the nobs, be one of the f—ing gentry – "

"Zak – "

"SHUT UP! YOU THINK THAT YOU KNOW WHAT IT IS LIKE TO BE SOMEONE ELSE, WELL, YOU DON'T. YOU DON'T KNOW ANYTHING ABOUT ME AND YOU NEVER WILL, JUST REMEMBER THAT! WITH ALL YOUR HUMAN SYMPATHY SCHLOCK! I DON'T WANT IT, THANKS!" Then, very quietly, "People are what they are born into. White, black, the religion, the family. These things mark them, Amos. They separate us like huge, steel fences in one of those compounds you see. You'll never understand me. I'm carrying around a different set of luggage. Look, I'm a stranger here, OK? So you had better give up trying. You're just like my dad was. You want to say a few magic words – not even words with any guts to them, but hopeless, wet words like 'love' or 'art' or I don't know what and you think all this will go away. Well, look. This is one Jew you haven't convinced, OK?"

"What are you doing Zak? What's the game? Do you – "

"YOU DON'T UNDERSTAND IT, OK?"

"We live on the same planet, don't we?"

"Don't heckle!"

With his trousers on he was suddenly rather impressive. He snatched up the coat and flung it around him like a cape. His eyes ranged about the room with insane concentration. He's not well, I thought, and checked the idea instantly. He's crazy. But . . . it was impossible to tell, as he paced the narrow room imperiously, whether he was in earnest or whether the performance was simply designed to discomfort me. All the gestures, all the language of fascism were there, as he turned over bowls, ripped books off the shelves and kicked aside ornaments, and yet I could not stifle the impression that this was aimed at my appreciation of the act, a way of saying, "Come on, Amos. This is the kind of thing *you* like. If they ever come here, *you'll* be OK. Won't you?"

"OUT GO ZER HALF MEASURES!" he was screaming. "OUT GO ZER SHILLY-SHALLYING TALK! LET'S CALL A SPADE A SPADE, SHALL WE, GENTLEMEN? YOU DON'T LIKE ZER JEWS. I DON'T LIKE ZER JEWS. NOBODY LIKES ZER JEWS. NOT EVEN, AS FAR AS I CAN TELL FROM MY

RESEARCHES, ZER JEWS ARE LIKINK ZER JEWS. SO LET'S GIVE ZEM ZER OLD HEAVE-HO, SHALL WE, GENTLEMEN? LET'S GET ZEM OFF DOUBLE QVICK, EH?"

"ZAK, STOP IT!"

Tessa was sobbing. He rounded on her at the door. "No," he said, "you stop it. You stop it. It's your f—ing country and I haven't noticed either of you doing anything to stop it as far as I can see. I'll see you maybe." Out in the alley I heard the horn go. One long wail. Zak pushed past us. "Sorry," he said, "busy."

"Darling – " began Tessa.

"Sorry," he said, "sorry, both of you." And he was gone.

We went to the window. You could see down into the alley. In the light from the shopfront we saw "Margot" and the man from Vienna. Zak, as he had done before, vaulted into the back of the vehicle and they followed him, in a grotesque parody of military-style despatch. The car reversed up the alley, turned at the head of the cul-de-sac and roared up towards the Whitechapel Road. Tessa was still crying, long, helpless sobs. The tears of a woman abandoned. I looked at the bed they had shared. It seemed to me that the past tense was the appropriate one to use. On the sheet was a copy of the *Daily Mail*. The front page read: HURRAH FOR THE BLACKSHIRTS!

Tessa continued to cry. I went across to her and put my arm round her. "What's happening?" she said. "Will someone explain it to me?"

But I didn't say anything at all.

Did I say I was a sub-editor on the *Daily Mail*? Did I mention that? No? Well, it wouldn't have looked good, would it? After all this is supposed to be a searingly truthful account of my experience of the twentieth century, and a lot of people are going to feel that my professional career is –

I was, anyway. That day Zak came home I was on the *Mail*. I didn't mention it because I was ashamed of it. A lot of the things Isaac said to me that day were true, I suppose. There is a lot else I have not been honest about. Tessa for a start.

I suppose it is fairly obvious from reading these pages that I was desperately, hopelessly in love with Tessa from the first day I saw her in Zak's father's bookshop. Is it? I don't know. It is to me. From that first day she was the kind of ludicrous English rose I had been taught to expect would one day be mine. I loved everything about her. I loved her lisp, I loved her hair, red, mouse or blonde, I loved her body. I lay awake at night and thought about her body. The small, firm breasts, the straight shoulders, the white legs that –

Oh God, oh God, oh God.

She'll be back soon. She's probably met a member of the armed services and is kneeling before him, fumbling with his fly buttons, her glossy cinematic lips reaching for his thickening –

Actually, I'd better face the fact. Tessa is now somewhat "fast". She is now, although she carries with her the clouds of glory of her other personae, a Services Gal. She could have walked straight off a recruiting poster. And when I think of her behaviour last night she seems almost a creation of the British War Propaganda Effort. I think now of the girl who sat with me that night in the bookshop, wringing her hands like someone in an engraving. "Can't we do something?" she kept saying.

"Maybe he is going through an identity crisis," I said. "Maybe we should force feed him lockshen soup and have five compulsory readings of the Talmud every day. Maybe we should – "

"Please, Amos – "

1944 Tessa wouldn't say, "Please, Amos." She'd say, "Permission to debrief, sir" or "Turn it up, Admiral" or else give me a few more verses of "Bless 'em All", complete with obscene gestures.

Where did I leave us all last night? I forget.

I think Alan had just gone off to collect *the plans*. I must admit that I felt "the plans" sounded a little improbable. But when he returned with a roll of white paper tied up with a rubber band with TOP SECRET written across them, I really felt that we were in the middle of some not very convincing drama concocted by the Radio Features Department. And when Alan spread them out along the table, and Tessa and I crowded behind him, I found I was looking modestly down at the floor, in the manner of "Algy" White in *No Frontiers are There*. When we went out to yet another black, official car and started off through London, I found I was looking out at the dark city with my lower lip thrust out before me. I couldn't understand why I was doing this until I remembered I had seen a film called *Heroes Are Not Here* in which somebody (possibly Trevor Howard) spent much of his time doing just that in the cockpit of a bomber. It is fantasy that sustains us for most of our lives. No wonder they want people like me on this damn raid, I thought, they want me to explain it to them, to make it real.

In the darkness of the back of the car, I slipped my arm through Tessa's and she responded by squeezing my hand.

"I've been fearfully loose since he. . . ."

"I'm sure," I said.

"They're up there for simply hours", she said, "and once one of those things goes into a dive. . . ."

"Yes?"

"Eighty per cent certain they'll be for the chop," she said. "I was at Witchleigh in the Ruhr business. Awful. Night after night. And sometimes you know one of the boys would say to me, 'Tess – would you post a letter for me? I've got a funny feeling I won't come back.' Because of the censorship, you see. They wanted to write to their mum or something. And on a rainy Sunday I'd slip into the village and post these letters. And, you know, it's funny, they never *did* come back."

I wanted to ask her about what had happened to her before she joined the Air Force, but I did not. I found myself rising to her manner, learning that peculiar understatement I had noticed in some of the flying crews on my few visits up to one of the bases in Cambridgeshire. Although I do not, as a rule, smoke, I accepted the cigarette she gave me and found I was inhaling deeply. Alan was in the front next to the driver. He had not spoken since we had got into the car.

"Later," said Tessa, "I'll give you all the gen on ME NOW. Later."

I never saw the rest of the press contingent. I never even found out the name of the airfield from which we left. All I remember is the huge, bulbous shape of the Lancaster and the sight of someone I recognized running towards us across the grass, carrying what looked like a metal box. It was Lancing-Green. "I've got ten mags," he said. "Come on."

The cockpit of a Lancaster is more than nineteen feet above the tarmac and, as we approached the aircraft across the wet grass, the Perspex hood and blisters shone in the lights of the car. I'd been inside these planes once before, on some official Ministry occasion, but was unprepared for the interior of this one. The centre of the plane – a fairly large area behind the navigator and the wireless operator – was usually stuffed with electronic equipment, but in this ship it had been removed and four bench seats placed up against the walls of the fuselage. In the base of the aeroplane was a gigantic square pane of what looked like the Perspex of the cockpit. It was through this, Alan explained, that our friend Lancing-Green would be taking pictures of the raid.

"I'm going up the front to talk to Guppy," said Tessa, whose manner since boarding the aircraft had become casual to the point of self-extinction. Alan, Lancing-Green and I, who had been kitted out on the airfield itself (I was still unsure as to quite how official this trip was), looked at each other self-consciously. Alan was wearing a leather jacket and a huge pair of goggles that made him look like a First World War flying ace. Tessa giggled: "Don't use the Elsan," she said. "It freezes your bum off at twenty thousand feet." So saying she crawled off forwards. All I had seen of the crew was two shapes in the cockpit as we drove up. The first encounter I had with the mysterious "Guppy" was a voice over the intercom. He asked a number of unseen people whether they were OK and their replies, which I did not hear, were presumably satisfactory, for he went on to welcome us aboard and to tell us that someone or something called "Met" had predicted there would be break in the cloud cover for almost five hours and that during this period, at approximately one in the morning, we would be able to proceed "as per our briefing". Whether he had any idea of the bizarre mission on which we were engaged I do not know.

"If", I said to Alan, "all you want is a *Boy's Own* description of whatever it is that is happening over there tonight, why didn't we do what we usually do? Write it in the bloody office? Is it necessary to go through all this?"

As I asked this question a face came through a hatch to the rear of the area in which we were sitting. It had a moustache and wore a peaked hat and belonged to a man of about fifty. Its eyes were shining madly. "Bomb the bastards," it said. "Bomb them flat."

I looked at the face. It was vaguely familiar.

"Bomb every single f—ing one of them," it went on. "Bomb them until they squeak."

Then the face popped back out of sight. I have been wondering since whether this was the face of Sir Arthur Harris, the man in charge of Bomber Command, but as no one in the aircraft paid it any attention or referred to its presence, I had no way of knowing whether this was the case. Whoever it was, anyway, was irrelevant. Our presence made about as much sense, as far as I could see, as the raid itself. Why ask for reasons any more? Wasn't I simply part of an experiment designed to demonstrate the absurdity of the task I had been performing for the last three years? Alan gave me my answer, as Tessa returned to the main body of the plane.

"Because", he said, "I want us to know for once. I want us to know what we're talking about." He breathed deeply. "And", he said, "I want to see it."

Tessa grinned. "His brother came from Dresden," she said. She seemed to know more about Alan than I did.

"Oh," I said, "and what happened to him?"

"It would take too long to explain," he said. He sighed a long, drawn-out breath. The pilot was telling us where to strap ourselves and the huge Merlin engines were roaring into life. It appeared as if we were about to depart.

"There's a man in underpants out there," said Tessa. "He's got a top on and a peaked hat and from the waist up he looks quite normal. But he isn't wearing any trousers. He's running around the runway waving a banana and shouting 'Bomb the bastards.' He *looks* rather like 'Butcher' Harris."

Alan gave a thin smile. "Aircrews are known", he said, "for their black sense of humour."

"How do we defend ourselves?" I said to Tessa as the noise of the engines screamed higher and higher and I heard the pilot's voice calling out a series of incomprehensible checks.

"There's a rear gunner", she said, "in a kind of glass bowl at the back with four useless 303s. That is, unless he has fallen out already."

I felt myself driven back into the seat. There was a sudden terrifying thrust forward and a moment of release and weightlessness. When I looked down I saw for what felt like the first time the lights of the airfield. I saw the shapes of the ground crew scurrying away across the grass and, through the huge Perspex shield, I was sure I saw, for a moment, the man in the peaked cap I had seen earlier. He was, I noticed, wearing no trousers and his lips were distorted with rage. What he was shouting I do not know, but it could well have been "Bomb the bastards!"

It was something like an eight-hour round trip. But I don't

remember the journey out or the journey back. I remember Tessa talking a great deal, about the danger from fighters, about the lack of manœuvrability of any heavy aircraft, about how there would be markers to tell the bombers where to unload, of how "Butcher" was very concerned his men shouldn't "creep back".

"What does that mean?"

"That means dropping the bastards early," said Alan.

What I do remember, though, what I will never forget, is the vision through that Perspex shield as we came in over the city. I had expected things to be flying through the air past us, but there was no opposition that I can recall, of any kind. There was an eerie silence – only the noise of our own engines and suddenly a giant, artificial dawn. Looking down I could see the insect shapes of bombers below us, hovering like moths over the map of the landscape. And below them I could see at first streets, houses, fields, all illuminated as if by mistimed morning. At first I could not understand this light. Where was it coming from? It wasn't a glare but a steady glow. And then I saw a massive bank of cloud over to the east. At first I thought this was part of the cloud which I thought I could see below us and then I realized that it was not natural cloud cover at all. It was the smoke of a gigantic fire – a glow that went on and on and on below us, like the heart of a furnace, split open to the sky. The whole city was burning.

At the edges of the glow I could see red, green, white flares, which must have been the markers. I noticed Lancing-Green winching his camera closer to the Perspex and, as he did so, I made as if to pull him back. It was as if I could feel the heat coming up from the blazing town. Absurd of course, we were at twenty thousand feet. But as well as the heat, I thought, through the cramped leather of my oxygen mask, that I could hear the screams of women and children and smell flesh, mile after mile of flesh, burning in some giant sacrifice to the God of War. I can still hear those screams that I could not have heard, now as I write. They will not go away.

In fact, the raid and our passage over it can have lasted no time at all. But it seemed like hours. I do not remember how it was that we turned and found ourselves once more in the blackness over Saxony. The image was still in front of my eyes, even when we dropped to ten thousand feet and somebody pulled out coffee and chewing gum. Even when we had landed on the empty airfield that image was still before me – the awful, unbelievable pointlessness of it.

"Alan," I said, at some point on the journey back, "why did you want me to see that?"

He didn't answer.

"Why?"

I knew now that there wasn't going to be any attempt to tell anyone about this. I knew there was only one reason why he had wanted us to go. He wanted a record of what had happened. I don't know what story he had spun Bomber Command to persuade them to let us go.

"I wanted you to see it," he said. "I wanted you to see what we write about and talk about and try to make sense of. I wanted you to stop sounding as if it was all so bloody easy. I wanted you to see a bit of history."

Tessa stretched. "It's funny," she said. "The boys who fly these things. Some of them think we should be doing it and some of them don't. But it doesn't really make any odds. They just do it anyway, you see. They can't afford to worry about all of that."

There was a conference when we got back, although I don't remember much about it. To my amazement, our pilot (whom I had hardly seen) was about to rest and then go back up in the air for another nine hours over Germany. I felt as if I had been under some drug and that everything since the previous evening had been happening to someone else.

"Were you really going to – "

"Going to what?" said Alan.

This was in the car as we drove back towards London.

"All that stuff you told me last night?"

"Of course not," he said. "This is one we keep bloody silent about. Unless someone hanging around SHAEF or AP starts asking questions. I just wanted you to see it. I knew you wouldn't come if that was the only reason I gave you." I reflected, not for the first time, that it was difficult, in a world clearly run by lunatics, to disentangle truth from fiction. Operation Beefeater had sounded quite as credible, if not more so, than Operation Thunderclap. *Simply so that I could see it.* But I didn't want to see it, Alan. Any more than I wanted to hear your life story afterwards. I don't want to have to understand or come to terms with this cruel and ridiculous world.

I can see why I infuriated him.

It was in the car on the way back to London that Alan told me his story and it is, for me, inextricably bound up with the dirty streaks of dawn in the sky and the hum of the official car on the empty roads. As I listened, I began to understand not only the events of the previous night or the real anger I had inspired in Alan, but things that had happened a long time since – between Isaac and myself. More and more I could see that the real contradiction, hinted at and unexplored in these pages, is in me. I see now that I have assumed that Alan had been relishing the task allotted to him, that I am cast as the only one with a moral sense, and yet, unlike Alan, I have not once thought hard about the complicated questions the war poses. It is so bloody easy to take up moral attitudes when one is not involved – which is presumably why Alan wanted to implicate me more seriously in what the people who rule us judge necessary for the successful prosecution of the war. All my life I have been a spectator, with a spectator's passport. (And now. . . .)

I suppose it was listening to Alan, too, that shook me. His story has captivated me, shaken my confidence in my drab, self-protective vision. I look back through these pages and the personality that emerges is not an attractive one – a liar, a deliberate suppressor and distorter of the truth, someone who uses his eyes but does not see, someone who condemns without due consideration. *All these years I have been seeing shadows. Last night I saw the real thing.*

But I will fight my way back to what I am. Somehow or other. Now, while I wait for the two of them to return, I will explore the task I can see that I set myself at the beginning of this narrative. Myself. What I am. I avoided that question for so long and used Isaac to do so. Why? Perhaps because, as Moncrieff said to me all those years ago in France, I was frightened of what I might see.

The shadows that I saw were real to others. It's only tonight that I have seen history in action. That was what Isaac was suffering.

I was at Olympia on 7 June 1934. There's a precise date for you. I wasn't there the day the Scottish Sea Scouts took over the hall for a display of folk dancing, or for the afternoon an American evangelist called Cannon spoke for three hours to an audience made up almost exclusively of middle-aged women. I was there for the biggest fascist demonstration ever seen in this country, for the moment of triumph and collapse for Mosley and the British Union of Fascists.

I was there, of course, by accident.

I had, in fact, gone to Olympia to see round a furniture exhibition.

Some time during that summer, Tessa and I decided to get married. We knew it would take time. She couldn't even *find* Zak to ask him if he would grant her a divorce. She didn't know how one would set about getting a divorce even supposing one could find the person one wanted to divorce, but both of us agreed that quite soon we would be married. Maybe it was just because we had been to bed together and, although that seemed harmless enough and tender enough, we wanted to make it even safer, even less like a grand passion than it obviously was. Between Tessa and myself everything was calm and friendly. We were both of us in retreat from the world and getting married – even if it wasn't immediately a practical proposition – seemed like the ultimate retreat. We played at it, just as we played house in that half-empty bookshop where once I had sat with Isaac's father, reading as if my life depended upon it.

"We need a wardrobe," she said one afternoon.

"All right, love," I said. I liked using the word "love".

"To keep the sort of jam in, you see," said Tessa, "because this summer I am going to make a lot of jam."

When Tessa and I were together she made a lot of jam. She was making jam the night she left me, the night of the Munich crisis. She was making jam when she lost our first baby at three months. She was making jam all through the siege of Madrid. And it was to get a wardrobe to put the jam in that led us up the Hammersmith Road on the afternoon of 7 June. Straight into nearly five thousand people.

They were swarming up the road towards Olympia – a sea of dark bodies and white faces, here and there a line of policemen visible among the mass. The crowd was extremely various. In some parts it was a fighting crowd, in other parts a puzzled crowd, and in others a determined, serious crowd, looking for other parts of the crowd to confront. As we pushed on through the mass of people, the crowd opened sometimes to reveal patches of calm, as unexpected as the glade of a forest, then closed in on itself, seeming to draw us in, to digest us and then to cast us out again, only to be swallowed – nearer and nearer to the heart of the conflict.

"There are a lot of people going to this furniture exhibition," said Tessa crossly.

"I'm not sure, my love," I said, "whether it *is* a furniture exhibition."

"What is it", she said, "if it isn't a furniture exhibition?"

"It's the Blackshirts," a man to our left was saying. "Hurray for the Blackshirts."

A man next to him punched him in the face, perhaps to express his disagreement with this remark. The first man slid to the flood, blood pouring from his mouth. A third man started to hit the second man. Tessa said: "Let's go back!" But it was too late to go back.

"Don't worry, darling!" I said. I used words like "darling" as well. Quite a lot. After all, we were planning to get married, weren't we? "Darling" was the sort of thing one said to a wife, wasn't it? She was lucky really that I never called her "pet lamb" or "honey child" or –

I can still remember that night she left, her saying to me: "Do you know, darling Amos. I don't think I can stand it any longer. Because it's all like being in a sort of play with you. It's all sort of acted. It's as if nothing is quite real. Do you know what I mean?"

"Yes," I said, "I know just what you mean."

But in those days I used the word "darling" with some confidence. I may even have said it again as we pushed our way forward, with me holding firmly on to her hand. "Don't worry, darling! It'll be all right darling! Darling, it'll *be all right!*"

Some way into the crowd, a man the size of a small car asked us where we were going.

"We were going", I said, "to a furniture exhibition."

He looked narrowly at the two of us. "Where?" he said.

"Olympia," I said.

I think he must have interpreted this as a deliberate slight either on the meeting or on those sworn to oppose it, for he grabbed me by the collar and started to pound my chest with his free hand. Somehow or other – with Tessa pulling me from behind – I worked myself free and started off into the crowd at a run. It was a close afternoon, grey and overcast, and as I ran my lungs seemed to have lost the power to reflate. The big man followed us, screaming something. We dodged around male bodies in clinches, through small swathes of policemen, on and on, faster and faster as the big man pursued us, shouting, waving. . . .

Then, as we approached the unscalable sides of the building, a door miraculously swung open and then clanged shut. Behind us. Suddenly there was no noise, no light, nothing but a sour smell of dust. We were in a dark corridor, lit by one shadeless bulb. Next to us was a small, ferrety man, holding a wad of tickets. "Moscombe?" he said.

"That's right," I said. I judged it wise not to disagree with anything this man might have to say.

"Row E," he said. "Give the bastards hell."

"Absolutely," I said, and started off down the corridor, Tessa behind me clutching the tickets.

The man had given me five of them for some reason. I think there were as many forged as there were real tickets for Mosley's Olympia speech. It was an unreal occasion in more senses than one. I never did discover whether we were supposed to be ILP or Communist Party or perhaps a fifth column of BUF supporters designed to heckle the hecklers. As Tessa and I came up through a doorway into the vast hall, I heard a noise somewhere between a roar and a sigh pass through the body of people in the place. This was, I realized, from the moment I saw the stage hung with flags, the lights and the uniformed stewards, a carefully staged battle. At last, I thought, the words bandied around so freely were about to be made to mean something. "Anti-fascist," I thought to myself, dully, as we slipped into our seats. I suddenly felt a strong urge to go to the lavatory.

What I did not realize at the time was that the meeting was twenty minutes late in starting. Those who wanted to hear and those who wanted to heckle watched each other, trying to gauge motives from faces, and there was, between neighbour and neighbour, a great suppressed tension as we waited for the performance to begin.

"Amos," said Tessa, "can we – "

"No," I said, "we can't. We're stuck."

Suddenly, about ten yards to my left, I became aware of a group of men pouring down the central aisle of the hall. There were seven or eight of them, moving like people with serious, vaguely military business in hand. Their coats, when viewed more closely, were a not quite successful attempt at the soldierly. They gave these characters a somewhat seedy, Chicagoan air.

As they passed on down the hall, the music (of which I had only just become aware) acquired a solemn, menacing air and I saw in the centre the man we had glimpsed over a year ago that rainy night in Bryanston Square. Mosley had a trembling, suppressed violence about his profile that somehow managed to conquer the less successful aspects of his public persona. In spite of the fact that he resembled an anteater, that his glances were too obviously designed to launch a thousand postage stamps, the fear that I had felt when I first came into the hall was still in me. Nostrils aquiver, he sowed the ground of the hall with looks of a thoroughbred haughtiness. The man was assuming a dignity that does not quite exist in England: he looked, I thought, like ersatz royalty as he mounted the platform and yet I found I was gripping Tessa's hand hard as the music rose to a climax and then, abruptly, was silenced.

"Tell you what," I said to her, "they're not fielding the substitute."

She looked at me blankly.

The lights faded and the people ebbed away from the figure of Mosley. Once again, through the stiff wastes of the hall, there was a great sigh, as if the audience had just appreciated that all of this, the flags, the music and the uniforms, was not prepared to melt at the first English snigger. I looked along the row of faces beside me and thought, "Where is it, please? Where is our famous English sense of the ridiculous?"

He was speaking now. Like most orators, Mosley brought to the act of speaking a physical charge that was clearly designed to make his words transcend the traditional tasks of language – the communication of ideas or emotions. The audience was intended to be *at one* with this distant puppet, tacking backwards and forwards across the huge stage as if propelled by a giant piece of elastic. His phrases were not a rational product of his brain, shaped to the conscious attention of those in the hall, they were – or at any rate were intended to be – "torn out" of him by the attention of others. The row after row of faces were intended to rise, one after the other, with the conviction that the leader's voice was nothing more or less than theirs. The crowd was to become the figure on the platform. For a moment it seemed as if the latent narcissism of the English was about to break ranks – that the thousand upon thousand in the place would rise to the mirror image of their basest desires and fears, arms up at the salute – HAIL MOSLEY HAIL MOSLEY HAIL MOSLEY. Germany, it seemed for a moment, was here in spirit.

And yet Mosley could not quite carry it through. Something about his self-consciousness, the school-prefect style of oratory, the weight of history he seemed to carry in his voice and gestures, defeated the simplicity of his aims. "I say, chaps," his voice seemed to say, "you're supposed to follow." The crowd somehow sensed the weakness behind that plea and did not do so. Almost before he had got through the first paragraph, from way behind us over to the left I heard a distant voice, thin as a sparrow's, piping up in opposition. And the hall did not turn round to crush him. It was if the first sinner had risen to confess at a prayer meeting. There was a massive sigh of release in that great, grey place.

The spotlights swung away from the leader and out on to the rows of faces. Mosley, with almost too much eagerness, squared up to the opposition and, in one moment, the meeting had moved from celebration and into struggle.

As heckler after heckler rose up and the spotlights swung back and forth and the stewards fought their way into rows to seize those shouting, Mosley's face hardened into a mask. His violence of thought and feeling was becoming mechanical, losing its appeal, as behind and in front of us scuffles broke out like fires in a dry forest. At the side of the hall I remember hearing the scream and the dreadful clatter of a body on the stairs. There was some flavour of East European cellar violence about the occasion as more and more hecklers rose, more and more noise came from the exits and, up on the platform, the leader poured his emphatic scorn on all who dared to oppose him: "Before the arrival of the Blackshirt movement, free speech did not exist in this country.... Today the power of those who seek to disrupt English audiences has come to an end. The interrupters go out, as you have seen them go out tonight."

"Come on," I said to Tessa. "Let's go."

Our row, for reasons I never understood, seemed peaceful. Our neighbours were seated, arms folded like villagers watching a cricket match. Perhaps they were amazingly well-disciplined communists, waiting for a signal that never came, or maybe a crowd of gnarled fascists (most of them seemed to be over sixty) in full agreement with Mosley's text.

Whatever they were they did not oppose our departure. It was only when we got to the gangway that a huge Blackshirt approached us, arms folded.

"Where do you think you're going?" he said, in a rather nannyish tone.

"Out," I said.

"Why?" said the Blackshirt. "Don't you like the speech?" He sounded hurt rather than cross.

"Oh, the speech is marvellous," I said, "marvellous. It's just that my wife is pregnant and she doesn't feel very well."

"Why did you bring her," said the Blackshirt, "if she's pregnant?"

This seemed to me to be an absurd remark. Behind me the noise of the scuffles continued. I peered past the man on the stairs. "I forgot," I said.

He gave us both a pitying glance. "Out," he said, "out."

And that is how I left Mosley's Olympia address, hand in hand with Tessa, decorously, like someone tiptoeing away from a bad film. On the stairs, as we went down to the street, there were no stewards and no hecklers. It was as quiet as a London club in the afternoon. We walked on down the stairs, pushed open the door and found ourselves in a side street.

It is curious. As I remember that moment, it is early evening. And yet we cannot have been in the hall all that long. I remember saying to Tessa, "Well. That's the end of that." I remember the dusk (and yet if it was June that would make it later, about ten), the lines of surprisingly homey, suburban-looking houses opposite us and the familiar smell of London in the summer, a dusty cocktail of aggressive scents.

Perhaps it is Tessa that is confusing my memory again. I do recall that atmosphere between us, heavy with unshed friendship, and on my side a longing for consummation that was impossible. I suppose I never felt she was mine and I was never real enough to her for her to consider the possibility. "If I am a hopeless, lost, irrelevant dreamer," I said to her once, "who has not yet been able to say or do what he feels, who doesn't yet *know* what he is or wants to be, it is because I have not found anyone to make me so."

"Aaaaah," she said, stroking my hair, "poor funny sad cynical little Amos."

I know I put my arm round her when we reached the daylight. That's all.

About thirty yards up the street a group had gathered round some victim and were, as far as we could see, kicking and shouting abuse. There were about ten or twelve of them and, though I could not see who it was they had managed to get on the floor, it was quite clearly not much of a contest. I could hear screams. Just one, from one human throat, on and on and on. I gripped Tessa hard. "Let's go," I said.

"We can't," she said.

"What do you mean, we can't?"

"Someone's being hurt up there," she said.

"I know," I said, in an exasperated tone. "I am aware of that. All over the world people are being hurt even as we speak. But what makes you think we can do anything about it? We can't help that poor bastard up there."

"We – "

"You're as bad as he was" (we both knew who I meant by "he"). "You always want to be there. To bloody interfere. Face it. This is one occasion when we can do nothing, so please *come on.*"

I tried to tug her away but she pulled against me. I saw in her face that set determination that sat so easily on her little girl's repertoire of expressions. No wonder, I thought, I loved both of the –

"Someone's being hurt, Amos. Really hurt."

"Look – "

"It's real, Amos. It is *real.*"

She broke away from me and ran up the street towards the crowd. I stood where I was for a moment and then, when I realized she was not going to come back, followed her. She was shrieking something at one of the men on the outside of the group. "IT ISN'T HIM!" I heard her yell. "It isn't him!"

I couldn't understand what she meant. I didn't understand until I was level with them and then I found I too was shouting at the top of my voice, pulling at jackets and faces: "IT ISN'T HIM! YOU'VE GOT THE WRONG BLOODY MAN! THIS ISN'T HIM AT ALL! MISTAKEN BLOODY IDENTITY!"

Zak was curled up in a foetal position on the pavement. His hands were clasped over his head and he was making whimpering noises. A big fat man was kicking his neck, quite slowly. Between kicks he withdrew his foot and looked round at the crowd as if for appreciation of his technique. Tessa started to scream. Zak was wearing precisely the same uniform that Mosley had been wearing on the platform – the legs, the belt, all of it. Even though it was ripped and battered and torn and covered in blood it still completed the illusion of resemblance perfectly. The only thing that made me sure it was Zak was the conviction that the real Sir Oswald would be most likely to be in the back of a Rolls-Royce somewhere. Being kicked was clearly a job for a double.

Groaning, Zak turned towards us and, as his eyes lifted up at the sky, Isaac-ness flooded back into his face, the eyes losing that bright Mosley sparkle and thawing into the puzzled abstract gaze of the intellectual. As I watched, one hand went to his lip and tugged at the Moustache. He seemed to expect it to fall from his face, as if it was only secured with spirit gum, and when the short hairs tweaked his flesh, a puzzled, childish hurt crossed his face. The big man started to kick him again. I went into the circle. "YOU'VE GOT THE WRONG BLOKE!" I shouted. The big man stopped and looked at me reflectively. "THIS ISN'T HIM!"

More curious eyes turned towards me. "Who", they seemed to be saying, "the f— is it, then?"

But the pause was all I needed. I went to him and cradled his shoulders in my arms. And in that pause the crowd seemed to recollect itself. They heard too the low moan coming from the man on the floor and saw perhaps (oh God, I hope they did anyway) that trickle of blood coming from his lips, and took compassion on him. The big fat man looked down at me. I started to talk at him wildly. This wasn't Mosley. I was a doctor. I was a policeman. Some fascists were coming this way. We'd better get going. All the time I was easing Zak further into me, until I was an indivisible part of him. If they were going to kick Zak they would have to kick me. I think they would have done that all right, except that, from round the corner of the side street, came, for no immediate visible reason, a line of policemen. They held their truncheons at the ready and, as is the manner of policemen on such occasions, looked as if they were looking for something to hit. Behind them came a random wave of the crowd and our group scattered back into the neighbouring houses. I bent over Zak and covered my head with my hands. There was a succession of thuds above me, shouts, screams, I was kicked once or twice, but when I looked up again the street was miraculously empty. There were no police, no rioters, nothing but me and Tessa and Isaac and the drab fronts of the houses.

Zak was dead white. His eyes were completing some vast internal pilgrimage and attempting to focus on houses, street and the two faces above him.

"Zak."

He didn't answer.

"Zak. You were used as a decoy. Right? While he made his getaway they sent you out of one of the back exits. Yes?"

He didn't seem to have heard me. Then finally, choking on some blood, his head fell forward and I heard him mutter: "Did . . . you . . . hear . . . my . . . speech?"

Tessa started to sob. Zak sniffed and snarled in my lap. "Oiks," he said, "beastly common little oiks." And fainted clean away.

I picked Zak up in my arms and from over to our right came a large black car. At its wheel was a uniformed chauffeur and in the back were "Margot" and our friend from Vienna. I didn't move towards them. "Margot" wound down the window and leaned out. "Horp in!" she said.

"No," I said, "you horp out."

She grinned fiercely. I noticed her teeth were yellow.

"Weren't you – "

"He was rather repetitive," said "Margot", clumsy and repetitive."

"Looks very like him, don't you think?" said our Viennese friend.

I left Zak with Tessa and went over to the car. "A decoy," I said, "right?"

"Oh, absolutely," said "Margot". And grinned again.

I never found out precisely what happened between her and Zak. I suspect she was the kind of woman who gets bored easily. Certainly Zak never had time to speak about the affair. My guesses as to precisely what had transpired were based on that awful, haunted look in his eyes that day at Olympia and the way, as the big car purred on the other side of the street, he looked up at it as if it were some carnivorous animal. It was a fine evening and in the sky, visible between the roofs, were scraps of cloud, tugged along overhead by the sudden light breeze. I looked at the clouds and asked the Almighty an unspoken question along the lines of "Did thou who made the beauties of the heavens, etc., also make

'Margot' Perrindale the Fortieth Baroness of wherever it is?" She was speaking again.

"Joyce thinks", she said, "you should have your Jewboy back again."

"Who the f— is Joyce?" I said.

The shopwalker grinned. He too had big teeth. Maybe it was a condition of membership of "Margot's" set. "Me," he said. "Me. Me. Me."

With that his grin seemed to expand to skeletal proportions, plastered across his grim, unctuous face like a transfer. And remembering him now, that is how I see William Joyce, Lord Haw-Haw (as he later became but seems, now, to have been even then). When I think about Lord Haw-Haw and am once again astonished that I actually knew him, I conjure up not the braying voice from Berlin, not the seedy ex-teacher who will go to the gallows if we ever win this war, but a very pleased senior flunkey to the nobility peering at me from out of a Rolls-Royce with a grin that seemed to beckon to the grave. Time, that has dealt so harshly with my friend by banishing him from the history books, will perhaps one day do the same for Joyce and do him the stupendous favour of allowing him to be once again obscure. Even as I write, he's fading, fading . . . not the one who wrote *Ulysses* . . . the man from Vienna . . . with the clasped hands of a shopwalker.

I thought very hard before I spoke to "Margot". What I came up with wasn't particularly witty or cutting but I think, even at this distance, that it was the right approach. "Why don't you", I said, "'horp' out, 'Margot' or whatever your f—ing stupid upper-class name is, and I'll push those big yellow teeth of yours right back down your horrible aristocratic throat?"

She seriously considered this proposition for some moments. Then said: "No thank you."

The car pulled away. I never saw either of them again.

I went back to Tessa and Zak. She was crying and stroking his hair. I didn't know whether we should move him and spent about ten minutes going to the end of the street to see if by any chance there was any trained medical assistance hanging around with nothing to do. There wasn't. In the end we got him up between us and staggered with him back up the street away from the crowds.

After about fifty yards we couldn't carry him any further. Out of some vague notion that this was the decent thing to do, we dragged him into a shopfront and sat beside him.

"Get a doctor," said Tessa, almost sullenly.

"Of course," I said.

But from the far end of the street we could hear the noise of the crowd. We were bottled in. I got Isaac's head into my lap and tried to get him to talk. I had some idea that if I could get him started, it didn't matter on what, he would be all right.

But he didn't respond to anything. He was a curious putty colour and his eyes wouldn't focus on you.

I left Tessa with him and walked on about a hundred yards to the other end of the street. There was a crowd here, smaller than at the front of the building but equally vociferous. They were punching each other, clawing each other and yelling. One man had a bottle which he was waving impartially at the mass of bodies in front of him. "COME ON, THEN!" he was shouting. "COME ON, THEN! LESS 'AVE YER! COME ON, THEN!" Free speech, I thought bitterly. Suppose somewhere out there there was the theoretical constant of democracy – the impartial, floating voter with an urge to hear and consider for himself Mosley's mishmash of anti-Semitism, Marxism and jingoism – how would he manage to make up his mind? How would he get into the hall for a start?

There was nobody there but the press, the fascists and the antifascists. The people they were allegedly trying to convert were all at home in bed.

The issues that tormented Isaac though will not go away. They have returned to haunt me. After last night they are huge and menacing, like some propaganda poster avoided for so long but none the less an irrevocable part of one's mental landscape. I can't find the answers I found then. I can't withdraw now.

People tell me I should fight for democracy. It's my democratic right not to fight for democracy, I want to say, but the remark sounds as silly and hollow as so much of what I have said to Alan must have sounded in the three years we have worked together. Now as I write it is Alan's face I see before me. He has somehow acquired Isaac's body and is lying with him on that road outside Olympia. You need more than quick wits and a good idea to overcome something like fascism. You need hatred and cruelty, you need vast reserves of sadistic feeling, you need the urge to kill thousands of innocent people. And if you flinch from that you will be avoiding your duty. Nazis aren't troubled by scruples such as yours. Scruples such as yours are for people who never leave their armchairs.

I don't know what complicated game Isaac was playing at the end. It wasn't tough enough for them, that was for sure. To wipe out what is evil, it seems as if we have to become evil ourselves. There is no escape from that. Where I have wronged Alan is in assuming that it was easy for him to harden his heart.

When I got back to Tessa, she said: "He isn't moving."

"No," I said.

She was holding him as a small girl might clutch at a doll. She looked up and down the street. I don't know what she was looking for. Her father maybe. Whatever help she expected, it wasn't there.

"I think he's dead," I said.

"Yes," she said. "I think he is."

I felt that dreadful calm that is the first reaction in the face of death. I stood in the road and looked, first one way and then the other, at the warring crowd that hemmed us in. The evening seemed to have grown hotter and my collar was glued to my neck. In the end I said: "We've got to get him away from here."

"Yes," said Tessa.

And the two of us looked helplessly from one closed exit to the other, avoiding each other's eyes, painfully aware of the pressure of each other's heart.

* * *

It was Isaac who brought Tessa and me together and it was Isaac, or rather his memory, that pushed us apart. Gradually, I think, we realized that all that kept us together was the fact that we had been in love with the same person. After his death, we hardly ever spoke of him and the less we spoke of him the more he was between us. I don't want to go into how or why we parted in the end (seeing Tessa again has wakened all of that and made me realize how much I wanted to be the sort of person she could love). In fact, when Zak died in her arms in that empty street outside Olympia, I started to die, to shrink, until all that was left was the sour, humble clerk that has so angered Alan.

I suppose Alan, like Zak, somehow believes in me. He wants to wake me up. To make me into a person like he is, someone who cares and thinks and feels naturally for others. I wanted to tell him last night that if I ever cracked I wouldn't blossom into that kind of person at all. Out of me would flower some ghastly synthesis of the moment, a sickly sweet odour of pure propaganda, exquisite untruth.

I want to tell Alan, and Zak, that I'm dead. I'm finished.

Oh, things *happened* to me. The day my mother died in 1936 I took a short cut on my way to see her and walked into the Battle of Cable Street. But I don't remember that. I remember my mother's face, yellow on the pillow, and her hand in mine like some alien claw, and me walking down to the street after she'd gone, finding myself unable to cry, the way I had after my father died. To say things happened to me is a mistake. Things happened around me. Deaths, quarrels, wars – none of them affected me. Unlike Alan's story which has so affected me, I –

I will get on to Alan's story. In a minute. In just a minute.

"You always live through people or causes, Amos. You never experience them for yourself."

That was something else Tessa said to me the day she left. I reminded her of it last night. She laughed.

When we got back to the office, Alan said: "Well. Now you've seen. Now you've seen this war. What do you think?"

"I don't know," I said.

"You'd better make up your mind," he said, "don't you think?"

"Yes," I said.

Alan, it seemed, has been "seeing" Tessa. They are talking of getting married. I said I was very happy for both of them. They said they were very happy I was very happy.

"But what about you, old thing?" said Tessa. "Are you going to be Orl Korrect and things? Or are you going to sort of wither away like a leaf or something frightful like that? It's you, Amos. You we're worried about."

Well, it's me I'm worried about too, Tessa. Me is why I am sitting here while you and your forces sweetheart comb the London streets for coffee, arm in arm, sure of your purpose and destiny, knowing you're part of something. And I no longer have the facility to mock that, to sneer as I once did at those with clear simple convictions. Oh, I want that certainty back again! But it won't come back now. I know it won't. I know just what it is that I lack. I've had a glimpse of the love and the purpose from which I have been excluded all of my life.

After we got back up to the office, Alan went out of the room, to allow us time to talk. We talked then a lot. Now that I knew she was with Alan it was easier to discuss Isaac. It was easier to talk about ourselves too. We agreed that it never would have worked, that we had been fooling ourselves.

"It was funny," she said. "From the first day I met you in that bookshop I knew you were the sort of person I liked as a friend. And I knew he was. . . ."

"He was what?"

"You got so involved with him," she said. "You got so caught up in what he was thinking or feeling. And there was always some great issue of the moment, wasn't there? Some *thing* that had to be done. That was exciting too. Even when he was awful he was exciting."

"Yes," I said, "he was."

She lit another cigarette. The office had that stale smell of last night's smoke. The papers on the desk didn't seem real. It was hard to credit that they had anything whatsoever to do with what we had seen.

"Is Alan like that for you?" I said.

"A bit," she said. "Not the same, but a bit. It's funny how you and I make for the same people, isn't it?"

"All history happens twice", I said, "or three times if you let it."

She put her hand on my shoulder. The nails were painted, something she had never done when I had known her before the war, and her luminous, made-up face had almost a carnivorous look as she said: "You're so clever, Amos. And you've read such a lot. And you think about things so much. I do hope it does all come right for you."

"Maybe I've read too much," I said. "I've come to the conclusion that the only way you can understand the world is by living in it. Not by trying to understand it. That way you just go crazy."

I was angry with her. I was jealous of the certainty she had re-acquired so easily. I was jealous of the way she looked at Alan as he came back into the office and suggested that the two of them go out for coffee.

Everywhere I can see this love and this purpose and this affection and this certainty of purpose, and I don't have it. I resent it when I see it.

I don't like it when I see it.

I saw it in Tessa's face as we climbed out of the official car and went in through the side entrance to the ministry building. I had seen it in Alan too, and on the face of the man who flew the plane last night. And it was in every syllable of the extraordinary story Alan told to me in the big, black car as we raced through Cambridgeshire. All these people can be at peace with themselves because they risk themselves, their clear knowledge of what is good comes from their close acquaintance with evil.

Much as I want to retell Alan's story, I can see now that it would be a hopeless task. I would make of it what I see I have made of Isaac's, an approximation, a parody. The habit of lying goes too deep with me. How, I ask myself, can any of us tell another's story? Isn't it precisely my thesis that we each make our own? We invent and destroy our own destinies.

All I will say is this. Alan's story was a long one. It reminded me at times of an unpublished novel by Thomas Mann. I felt his life needed a lot of work from a good sub-editor. He should have cut out the bit about being born in Dresden. I found that an unconvincing coincidence. I didn't believe his brother either. Too good to be true. Neither did the character of Heinz, a local member of the Hitler Youth, ring entirely true. I know Nazis are supposed to be unpleasant, but Heinz I felt was a little too much. I didn't quite credit the stuff about the pets.

Alan's home life (his real name is not Brown or Braunstein, but something that sounds a bit like Leberwurst) I found too good to be true. Do they really eat that much lockshen soup? There was a good middle section about his life in Berlin, where street violence was well evoked, but the latter part of his story about his attempts to gain entry into Britain began to remind me of a Hollywood film written by a committee of radically minded chimpanzees.

"Look," I said. "I know you think Britain stinks. I think it stinks too. I know we turned back thousands of would-be refugees from Hitler. Don't think just because I'm British, Anglo-Saxon and the rest of it that I am party to all of that. I'm not responsible for English history, thank you very much. I don't actually like very much in this rotten little island. Including, as it happens, the present war you want to rub in my face all the time."

"Your problem, Amos," he said, "is that you're what you are and you won't face up to it. You're quick enough to tell me I'm a German Jew. Yes, I am. That's my history and my destiny. I accept. Believe me, there have been plenty of times when I didn't want to accept it."

Then there was a lot of stuff about his brother and concentration camps and hiding in attics and, pretty soon, as I knew we would, we got on to the subject of camps. Camps where women and children were forced to strip and be gassed. Camps where organized slaughter of the innocents took place day after day. The Allies wouldn't act on these camps. Why? They didn't even believe in their existence. They suffered from my problem. They could not conceive of evil on such a scale. That, said Alan, was almost the greatest conceivable evil. I said, once again, that I could not believe the picture he was showing me. He pushed his face into mine and screamed: "WHAT DID YOU SEE TONIGHT? WHY DID I TAKE YOU UP THERE? THAT'S WHAT IT'S LIKE, MY POOR LITTLE ENGLISHMAN! THAT IS WHAT PEOPLE DO TO EACH OTHER OUT THERE WHILE YOU'RE HAVING YOUR BLOODY LITTLE CUP OF TEA AND TELLING YOURSELF YOU HAVE THE FINEST DEMOCRACY IN THE WORLD! SO FINE YOU FEEL FREE TO DECIDE NOT TO DEFEND IT! SO FREE YOU SEEM TO HAVE THE LUXURY OF DECIDING WHAT IS TRUE AND WHAT IS NOT TRUE! WHY? BECAUSE YOUR NOSE HAS NEVER BEEN RUBBED IN THE FACTS! ALL HISTORY EVOKED IN YOU IS A SNIGGER! A DEFEATED GIGGLE! WAKE UP, LITTLE MAN, BECAUSE THIS IS ACTUALLY HAPPENING! YOU UNDERSTAND THAT, LITTLE ENGLISHMAN?"

Tessa did not interfere in this discussion. She watched, white-faced, with that same strained air of casualness I had noticed in her from the first. After a while she lit one cigarette from another and stared out at the developing landscape, a distant expression on her face.

We had a lot more about Alan's life then. The women in his life sounded even more unbelievable than the Nazis, plucky pastors, devoted parents and heroic brothers who cluttered up the rest of it. He had made love passionately in haylofts, meadows, boats, hammocks, trees, glaciers, four-poster beds, gutters, places where I would not have dreamed of sleeping alone let alone with anyone else. He appeared to have made thousands of women tremble and sob with passion and seen an equal number die in agony, be carried away by security police, betray and/or be faithful to him and others. How is it possible, I wondered, for one man to have had quite so much sex and another to have had quite so little? How is it possible for one to have lived so much and another to have lived quite so little?

"You won't accept things," he said. "You won't accept what you are. That's all I want you to do."

"OK," I said, "you tell me, you tell me what I am."

He grinned. "You're a typical Englishman," he said. "You've a marvellous talent for hypocrisy. You have a way with language that spells away your true feelings. You're a clerk in the Ministry of Information. You're a brilliant propagandist. That's the heart of you. A gung-ho little Englishman. I want you to stop pretending you have the cares of the world on your shoulder and I want you to play a brave little English tune. That's all."

As he spoke a tune started somewhere at the back of my mind. I tried to quell it but the tune would not go away. It conjured up afternoons I had spent with Zak on the Whitechapel Road when we were kids, it brought back my father and his big, helpless eyes, it brought back a feeling that I thought I had lost, a sort of ache that had been behind all of my attacks on this city or this country. I tried to shake it off as one might push aside an insect or something unclean, but it would not be denied. COME ON, AMOS, YOU'RE JUST AN ORDINARY LITTLE ENGLISHMAN.

> Bless 'em all bless 'em all bless 'em all
> The long and the short and the tall
> Bless all the sergeants and WOs
> Bless all the –

"Look – " I said.

Alan smiled. "It's not a big thing," he said. "I just want to see you do your job properly. I want to see you be part of something. I happen to think you could do your job very well if you faced up to it. Your talent is for lying, for excuses. You may not like what you have to do for your country, to lie and tart up the truth, but this is one occasion when you have to do it. That is the only truth that matters as far as I am concerned. We can't afford the luxury of scruples any more than that pilot tonight can afford the luxury of being afraid."

"I – "

"And if you have scruples you must have the courage to follow them to their conclusion. Which will be rejection of everything that is happening. You can't hide behind your country and abuse it at the same time, any more than you can dodge history. Although, my God, you try, don't you?"

There was more about Germany then more about what the local Nazis had done to some Jewish kid one night. And how the local police had done nothing and the local population, it appeared, had seen nothing. Like the English, said Alan, the Germans are very good at acquiring glass eyes when it suits them. I half listened to what he said, but all the time this tune was humming at the back of my brain.

> *Bless 'em all bless 'em all bless 'em all*
> *The long and the short and the tall. . . .*

He ended, as he had begun, by talking about his brother. His brother had been taken away one night. He had been there. He remembered the way the officers turned over the house. He remembered his brother screaming. He wanted me to remember too, before I made my choice, before I decided what kind of person I was to be.

"STOP IT!"

But you can't stop it, can you? You can't spell away the world out there, the world of politics where ideas become reality. Looking back at what I have written I can see that that is what I have tried to do with Isaac's life, to cast it in a secret, private form, to confuse lies with truth until there seems no reality, no objective standard of truth, possible. That is, of course, a fashionable line of escape. Things happen. Whether they happened or not can be tested and discovered. To abandon that hope is to abandon hope in any kind of justice or decency. What happened last night happened. About the rest, I can't say. I can plead in my defence that very often what I have written is not half so monstrously absurd as what occurred over Dresden.

Just before they left, Alan went out of the room once more, leaving Tessa and me alone. I couldn't think why at the time. Now I think it may have been tact. I looked at her determined chin, the regular mass of curls and the unusual, square-cut shoulders, and felt as if we had been left alone to say goodbye. When I look back through the pages of this manuscript (which I do about as often as I write additions to it) I think my most honest reference to her is one of the earliest. On page 14 she appears as my wife. I notice that I have given us a kitchen which has the advantage of something called "well-lit spaces". The fact that she isn't my wife and that we haven't got a kitchen makes no difference to the validity of this description of her. That is what I want her to be – practical, amused, helpful and, above all, married to me.

When Alan had gone she came over to me and put her hand on my shoulder.

"It's not simple with him," she said.

"No?"

"No," she said.

There was a pause.

"Could it be simple with me", I said, "again?"

"Darling old Amos thing," she said, "it would have to be more than simple.

It would have to be right."

She lit another of those endless cigarettes. For a while we talked about the war. It sounded, as she talked about it, almost as incredible as Alan's. A man called Porteous Smythe had made love to her one night in the cockpit of a Lancaster, only to be blown to bits over Germany the next night. She had seen a senior officer of Bomber Command reduce a twenty-one-year-old New Zealander to tears by accusing him of cowardice. The senior officer had last been in a plane in about 1930 and the New Zealander had completed twenty-eight missions. Harris, she told me, had at one stage planned to reduce not only Cheltenham to ruins but also Aberdeen, Dublin, Hull and a place called Bourton-on-the-Water.

I believed all of it. In the end we stopped talking about the war, hers and mine. We had begun to take it seriously and I think that depressed the two of us. We came back gradually to the subject of Us. I wondered what Alan was doing in the corridor.

"So what is it?" I said. "You love him or you don't love him?"

"If you want to know," she said, "in the end he's too like Zak was. All of that's over. I can't warm it up again, can I?"

"Maybe not."

"But that's what I mean. If I want something new, it can't be like that with you either, can it?"

"I suppose not."

I felt suddenly weary. I got up from the desk and went to the window. Down there in the street London was waking, the bright winter sun pouring out across office workers, traffic, the whole unreally civilian crowd. We're back to normal, I thought, like some vampire town feeding off the life blood of other cities miles away, where women and children are screaming, dying in charred, unrecognizable shapes. I saw a woman greet someone on the other side of the street, her hand going up in welcome.

"But", I said, "I'd have to change I suppose."

"Yes," she said, "you'd have to be yourself. Do you know what I mean by that?"

"Yes," I said, "owning up. It's what I've never done. I know that. Accept my own life. Bite on the bloody bullet."

She crossed to me at the window and together we looked down at the town, stretching like a cat in the growing sun. She held my arm hard. "You're the only thing that ties me to the past, Amos. And the past is all I've got. But the funny thing is, you see, old dear, that I don't exactly want the past. Well, I mean, I want it. I want to feel there's some connection but I also want to feel it's changing in my hands like sort of sand or something, do you know what I mean?"

"Maybe."

She turned to me. "The thing is that in one way I've always wanted you, even when it was you and me and Zakky. But the thing was I never allowed myself to want you with your cleverness and being outside of things and all sort of wry and frightfully LMF but fun. Such fun really. Because you see I thought I would never get you. I thought nobody would ever get you. I thought that there wasn't a you to get if you know what I mean."

"But now there is?"

"It's funny. Alan and I talked about you a lot. He always said there was someone really special in you, if only it could be conjured up. And I see what he means. He's done it in a way, in a way Zak never could. But isn't that Life, really? This chap in your office or next door that you never think of as anything but the chap next door or in the office or whatever turns out to be the most important friend ever sort of thing. Like falling in love with the dull boy, the boy at the back of the class that you never noticed."

"Oh, that's me, is it?" I said.

"Don't be *stupid*, Amos," said Tessa.

"Sorry," I said.

Down in the street the first workers were coming into the ministry building. Sober, priest-like, with briefcases, hats and umbrellas, they picked their way through the flagrant beauty of the morning, looking neither to left nor right. Business as usual. In spite of sunshine war, famine, rain, London Can Take It. I felt a weird tug of patriotism, a violently sentimental feeling of belonging; like the tears provoked by a bad film, it shamed me and pleased me and would not go away. "You're like everyone I've ever known," I said. "You want me to change my attitude. You want me to be a normal human being. It's too much to ask."

She squeezed my arm. "You see?" she said. "You are better. But look at you. The other half of you. All stiff like a poker. All sort of odd and distant and peculiar. I don't want that Amos."

"No," I said, "neither do I, really. If I could accept all this. What's happened. The war. The *wars* for God's sake. I mean. . . ."

I felt close to tears again. Maybe it was the view down the sunlit street. I went back into the drab office and looked at the files, the steel-grey cabinet, the dull green, official walls. That helped.

"I'll try, Tess," I said.

"Good," she said. "We won't be long. I have to talk to Alan."

"And when you come back?"

"We'll know, won't we, old thing?" she said.

"Know what?" I said.

"Whether we're going to make it", she said, "or whether we 're for the chop."

And with a smile and a gay wave, the kind of brave little gesture one might make to a lover who was taking a more serious risk than mere self-examination, she went out into the corridor. I heard Alan mutter something, heard Tessa laugh. And then they were gone.

Well, I have to change to win her. I always knew that, the way I would have had to change to take part in any of it, in any of what has happened to me. No. Nothing has happened to me, has it? I haven't let it. I have just watched. Without even the dedication of the professional witness. I can see now that the determination I had at the beginning of this manuscript, to be a truth teller, cannot and never will be. I'll never cure myself of lying. I'll never change what I am, lying, cunning, fantasizing Amos. And she wants me to admit that.

> When a man marries a woman he finds out whether
> Her knees and elbows are only glued together.

She'll be able to tell. Because my propaganda for myself, even when I write alone here, even when I talk to the empty page, has broken down. My publicity service for myself is no more. They've opened me up, the bastards, first Zak, then her, then Alan – they've broken my cover, I'm feeling things. Hateful, unstoppable, terrifying feeling. Can't I be like those men out there? With the briefcases and the closed expressions? It's so hard.

But I want you, Tessa. I want you – forties', thirties' and twenties' Tessa, I want you. For the reasons I know you want me. Because it's hard to deny so much mutual history. And yet, by the same token, it is one of the most difficult things of all to accept. The actuality of an individual, a nation. I don't want it. But I can't avoid it any more.

Get on with it, Barking. What's the phrase? "There's a job to do." Do it. Submit your precious self to that. Don't be like you were the first day you met her. Remember? Trying to look as if you weren't interested in girls. It's what holds you back now from going to that typewriter and starting your job which is, I am afraid, to support the country where you were born. Beastly thing, patriotism, much better to pretend you're not British. You're above all of this. Except you're not. You want life to continue as it always has. You are tied by language, by the food you eat, by the music that moves you, by *all of your history*, to this right little tight little island you take such pleasure in abusing. You love her the way you love the girl, go on, Amos. You can win Britannia, old bean. She just needs asking out. Get on with it.

Oh, before they come back I will have done it. I will have acquired a new face. I'll be the person Alan wants me to be. The person Isaac never saw. Well, go on, Amos. Use your talents. Explain last night away to the GBP. Tell them it's all right to murder thousands of civilians. Make it sound good. That's what you're good at. Write a release in a million. Put your lying to good use for once. Explain away Dresden. Go on. Make it good now. We're waiting. Make it really strong.

"Last night over Germany a daring reprisal raid struck deep into the heart of Nazi power by hitting them where it hurts. Say what you like, Mr Hitler, you won't be making any porcelain shepherd-esses tomorrow because the intrepid flyers of the RAF have just roasted the entire contents of that fiendish haven of war activity, Dresden. Goodbye, old china, as we say in the RAF. Braving the night skies and the fiendish possibilities of running out of fuel, a death-or-glory squadron hit these Krauts right where it – "

Bless 'em all bless 'em all bless 'em all
The long and the short and the tall
Bless all the sergeants and WOs
Bless all the –

Go on, then. Justify. Justify or condemn. One or the other. You don't have the courage to carry condemnation to its logical con-clusion, so justify. Go on. Justify.

"This is Amos Barking reporting. I'm just an ordinary Londoner, a kid from Whitechapel who came up the hard way. I took it on the chin when the girl I loved went off with some other feller and believe you me I'm taking it on the chin now she's run off with another feller. I'm British and I don't expect to get the girl. But I'm a damn good loser. And that's what millions of Germans will have to be this morning when they find out that our boys have stopped a daring move by thousands of refugees to *get away* right in the bud. The way we look at it here at the ministry, it's this simple. If your government starts a war, even if you're six years old, IT'S YOUR F— ING FAULT. Did they ask the children of Coventry before they dropped their load of bombs? They did not."

I can do it. I know I can do it. Before they come back I won't be a grovelling half creature, I'll be seven feet tall. I'll be proud to be British once again. I'll know wrong from right and right from wrong and all of that old bollocks. I'll have it off perfect. Just watch my dust.

You'll get no promotion
This side of the ocean
So cheer up my lads bless 'em –

"In order to make peace secure we must have total war. In order to make the world safe for democracy, it will be necessary to raze it to the ground. Only then can free elections be held. Each corpse will be given the right to vote. And a bar of chocolate. Freedom to us in this island, where I was born within the sight of Bow Bells, living in conditions of equality, among people of all races and creeds, even Jews, my God, I'm tolerant really, as I said freedom is so important to us Britishers that nothing must be allowed to stand in the way of our getting it. As my old friend Isaac Rabinowitz, a Jew by the way but that never came in the way of our friendship, used to say, 'I should be so mucky to be an Englishman.'"

That's almost what he said, anyway.

Come on, Amos. Justify. Justify. You know what you have to do. Just bite the f—ing bullet and sing the tune you were always supposed to sing. Admit it. You're no truth teller. You're no writer. You're a propaganda merchant. That's your skill. Go to work, boy. Don't dodge it. This is War Work, old bean.

"Amos Barking here. Last night over Germany we struck an undying blow for freedom. We let the Germans know that we would not tolerate any more of their sickening anti-Semitism. Racialism, we said, has gone far enough, gentlemen. It is an evil perversion and the entire German nation is infected with it. Nasty little bunch of smelly, conceited, violent, anal little squareheads that they are. Tarantara zing boom. We went in over that Nazi strong-hold, the city of *Dresden*, and we really gave it what for. Nazi cats and dogs suffered too as – "

That tune. It won't go away. It sings in my brain. I sit here at the desk as the sun rises higher in the sky and I try and I try but I can't make it fit. I cannot justify what cannot be justified. I cannot believe there is truth or justice of any kind where all is so grotesquely per-verted and wrong. Why wasn't I born in some other place, a long way away? Somewhere light years away from this twisted f—ing century.

Bless 'em all. . . .

"Amos Barking reporting again. There will be those who attempt to make the bombing of Dresden some kind of 'atrocity' comparable in some degree with what has been done in Europe by the Nazis. I want to say that this sort of obscene parlour game, this monkeying with history, is part of the modern disease of lying and distortion undertaken by totalitarian regimes, unlike the government of this great nation of ours which I belong to wholeheartedly, being as I am part of the great cockney pride of ol' London town, schrike a light, guv, knock me dahn wiv a fevver, etc., etc."

They'll be back soon.

Make it all go away, somebody, can't you?